PRAISE FOR
*Mortal Arts*

"Set largely in Scotland in 1830, Huber's well-done sequel to *The Anatomist's Wife* includes all the ingredients of a romantic suspense novel, starting with a proud and independent heroine." —*Publishers Weekly*

*The Anatomist's Wife*

"A riveting debut. Huber deftly weaves together an original premise, an enigmatic heroine, and a compelling Highland setting for a book you won't want to put down."
—Deanna Raybourn, *New York Times* bestselling author of the Lady Julia Grey novels

"Lady Darby is an engaging new sleuth to follow . . . [A] history mystery in fine Victorian style! Anna Lee Huber's spirited debut mixes classic country house mystery with a liberal dash of historical romance. Fans of Tasha Alexander and Agatha Christie, rejoice!"
—Julia Spencer-Fleming, *New York Times* bestselling author of *Through the Evil Days*

"Anna Lee Huber has delivered a fast-paced, atmospheric, and chilling debut featuring a clever heroine with a shocking past and a talent for detection. I'm already anticipating Lady Darby's next adventure."
—Carol K. Carr, national bestselling author of *India Black and the Gentleman Thief*

*continued . . .*

*Berkley Prime Crime titles by Anna Lee Huber*

THE ANATOMIST'S WIFE
MORTAL ARTS
A GRAVE MATTER

# A
# GRAVE MATTER

### ANNA LEE HUBER

BERKLEY PRIME CRIME, NEW YORK

THE BERKLEY PUBLISHING GROUP
Published by the Penguin Group
Penguin Group (USA) LLC
375 Hudson Street, New York, New York 10014

USA • Canada • UK • Ireland • Australia • New Zealand • India • South Africa • China

penguin.com

A Penguin Random House Company

Berkley Prime Crime Books are published by The Berkley Publishing Group.
BERKLEY® PRIME CRIME and the PRIME CRIME
logo are trademarks of Penguin Group (USA) LLC.

Library of Congress Cataloging-in-Publication Data

Huber, Anna Lee.
A grave matter : a Lady Darby mystery / by Anna Lee Huber—Berkley Prime
Crime trade paperback edition.
pages cm
ISBN 978-0-425-25369-4 (paperback)
1. Upper class women—Fiction. 2. Anatomists—Fiction. 3. Grave
robbing—Fiction. 4. Ransom—Fiction. 5. Upper class—Scotland—Social
life and customs—19th century—Fiction. I. Title.
PS3608.U238G73 2014
813'.6—dc23
2014005610

PUBLISHING HISTORY
Berkley Prime Crime trade paperback edition / July 2014

PRINTED IN THE UNITED STATES OF AMERICA

10  9  8  7  6  5  4  3  2  1

Cover illustration by Larry Rostant.
Cover design by Lesley Worrell.
Interior design by Tiffany Estreicher.

*For my mother, whose love and strength is as fierce as a lioness.*
*With affection and gratitude.*

# ACKNOWLEDGMENTS

Every book presents its own challenges, and this one was no exception. My unending gratitude goes to the following people for helping me to not only complete *A Grave Matter*, but craft it into the best book it could be.

My brilliant editor, Michelle Vega, for all of her confidence, understanding, and expertise.

My intrepid agent, Kevan Lyon, for her support and encouragement.

The entire team at The Berkley Publishing Group for their expert contribution to the design and composition.

My writing group partners, Jackie Musser and Stacie Miller, for continuing to make me a better author, and being willing to read a rough draft and provide feedback on such short notice.

My family and friends, for their continued love and support.

My amazing husband, who never ceases to amaze me.

And my greatest blessing—my beautiful daughter, who I was pregnant with through much of the writing process of this book. Your stamp is written all over this book in big and small ways, and makes the story all the better for it.

# CHAPTER ONE

*Remember, friends, as you pass by,*
*As you are now so once was I.*
*As I am now, so you must be.*
*Prepare yourself to follow me.*

—EIGHTEENTH-CENTURY GRAVE EPITAPH

CLINTMAINS HALL
BORDER REGION OF ENGLAND AND SCOTLAND
DECEMBER 31, 1830

The flames leaped high into the starry sky. Revelers clapped and reeled about each other in the golden flickering light, there and then gone, swallowed by the darkness and the whirling mass of their fellow merrymakers. As the orchestra behind me paused between songs, I could just make out the feverish pitches of a fiddle and the low thump of a drum playing a Scottish jig. It floated on the crisp night air through the open French doors. What the players lacked in skill, they certainly made up for in exuberance.

The professional musicians playing in the ballroom behind me had also gotten into the festive spirit. Our hosts, my aunt and uncle, the Lord and Lady Rutherford, never would have stood for anything less. Most of the assemblage of local nobility and gentry were dancing, just like their servants and the villagers outside, and those who were not were either too old or too infirm to join in.

Or perhaps they'd simply wished for a quiet moment to themselves.

Unfortunately my brother, who'd been hovering about me all night, failed to understand this.

"Kiera, stop sulking," Trevor chastised, appearing at my side.

"I'm not," I protested.

He arched an eyebrow in skepticism. "Then why are you off in this corner by yourself?"

I nodded toward the scene outside. "I'm watching the antics of the servants at the bonfire. It's quite diverting." Once or twice I thought I saw the silhouette of one of our servants from Blakelaw House dance across the light, but they were too far away to be certain.

"That may be, but you're supposed to be diverted by our antics in here," he teased. Though his tone was light, I didn't miss the glint of annoyance in his bright blue eyes.

We had argued over my coming to the Hogmanay Ball. I had not wanted to attend, while Trevor had insisted I must. Ultimately he had his way only because he had pointed out that many of our loyal servants would feel they couldn't attend the accompanying bonfire if I remained behind, no matter how strongly I protested otherwise. But even my reluctant attendance still wasn't enough for him. He had to linger about me all evening to ensure I was enjoying myself, which was irritating in the extreme, even as it was also endearing.

"Come."

He gripped my elbow below the fashionably puffed sleeve of my midnight blue gown and tugged me toward the dance floor, where the orchestra played the first strains of a waltz. He pulled me effortlessly into the swirl of couples circling the gleaming wooden floor. The women were dressed in bright full-skirted gowns and the men in austere black coats and colorful tartan kilts.

I considered arguing with Trevor about his high-handedness, but then decided it would be silly. I *did* want to dance, and my brother was as skilled a partner as any. When he swung me into a tight turn, surprising a smile out of me,

I suddenly realized how long it had been since we faced each other so. Certainly, I had danced with Trevor far more than any other gentleman of my acquaintance, for he had been forced to partner me by our childhood dancing master. We had stepped on each other's toes and smacked one another in the face with an errant hand too many times to count. Once I had even bloodied his nose.

But that had been a long time ago. Sometimes it even seemed to me that it had been in another life. One I had lived before my disastrous marriage to Sir Anthony. Before his death and the resulting scandal from the charges brought against me because of my involvement with his gruesome work.

I shook away the troubling memories and tried to concentrate on the room before me. Trevor and I glided expertly across the floor to the Schubert waltz, proving that neither of us had forgotten how, though I suspected it had been far longer since I had done so than my brother. Trevor had always been a popular dance partner, and I doubted that had changed in the years since I had attended a ball in his company. Though even at my most awkward, he always had time for a dance or two with his little sister. That may have only been a small matter to him, but it had meant a great deal to me.

"Where have your thoughts gone?" His voice was flippant, but he couldn't hide the concern I saw reflected in his eyes. "From the way you're frowning, I expect my toes to be strategically crushed at any moment."

I tilted my head. "As if my feet in these dainty slippers could cause you much discomfort."

"You think not, but I seem to remember that the bone in your heel has always been remarkably sharp."

I smiled sweetly. "Only when I'm grinding it into your instep."

On the next dance step, he shifted his foot back as if to avoid my encroaching foot, and I laughed.

He grinned at my amusement and spun me in a faster circle, making the skirts of my gown bell out.

My cheeks flushed as the heat of the ballroom and the exertion of the dance began to warm me. I suspected Trevor and the other gentlemen might be sweating beneath their snowy white cravats, but he gave no indication of unease. Aunt Sarah had confided in me earlier that she worried the large ballroom would not hold the heat generated by the fireplaces on each end on this cold winter's eve, but her concern proved unnecessary. Even though the gathering was not as large as I'd expected, being mostly extended family of my mother's brother, Lord Rutherford, and his wife, and nobles and gentry from the nearby Border villages, the four score of people present still warmed the space quickly.

The Rutherford Hogmanay Ball and the accompanying bonfire and ceilidh dance for their tenants, the local tradesmen, and the servants of all who attended were an annual tradition. It had been many years since I last took part, but I had not forgotten the festive air, or the spirited ratafia punch so heavily brandied it burned the back of your throat. Great bowls of it stood on tables at one end of the ballroom next to bottles of whiskey, brandy, champagne, and a lavish spread of food—all within easy reach so that fewer servants were needed to attend to the guests of the ball, allowing them to enjoy their own gathering.

As a child, I remembered watching my mother ready herself for the Hogmanay Ball. Though I had been less fascinated than my older sister, Alana, who couldn't wait to grow old enough to attend, I was nonetheless still enchanted by the sight of my parents together, descending the curving stair at Blakelaw House, dressed in full evening apparel. My father and mother certainly made a handsome couple, but it was the eager gleam I saw in each of their eyes, the joy and anticipation that arced between them that intrigued me. They kissed each of us children good night at the top of the stairs, and by the time they reached the bottom, it was as if they'd forgotten us entirely, so lost were they in each other and whatever mischief they anticipated that night.

I wished I could say that some of that enchantment

remained. Perhaps had my father chosen differently, selecting a husband more like himself for me, someone steady and honorable, and without nefarious intentions kept hidden from us all until after the vows were spoken. Perhaps then I would feel more excitement at attending the Hogmanay Ball.

An image of Sebastian Gage swam to the forefront of my mind, as it inevitably did whenever I contemplated such matters. It had been almost two months since I had seen the golden-haired gentleman inquiry agent I had partnered with during two previous investigations, and somehow entangled myself with romantically, but the memory of his face, his voice, his lips pressed against mine had not lessened. The manner in which we had left things after I departed Edinburgh had not been satisfactory, but neither of us had been ready to discuss the tangled web of emotions that stretched between us. I had been raw with grief over my friend's death during our most recent investigation, and he still had secrets he hadn't reconciled with sharing.

As Trevor spun me through another set of turns, I couldn't help wondering if Gage was still in Edinburgh. Was he attending another Hogmanay Ball, much like this one? Was he dancing with a lovely young lady?

"Stop."

I glanced up at my brother. "What?"

"Stop contemplating whatever it is you're thinking about," he clarified and then shook his head. "It's not making you happy. And I refuse to allow you to have any more gloomy thoughts. Not this night." He leaned closer toward me, a twinkle in his eyes. "If need be, I shall force you to drink two, no *three* glasses of that vile ratafia punch, and then proceed to push you into every available male's arms one after the other and order them to dance with you."

"You wouldn't," I replied, feeling less confident than I sounded.

He narrowed his eyes. "Try me."

I searched his face for any sign of weakness. "You know

you would be risking your coach's leather seats. I cannot always handle such strong spirits."

"Oh, I know," he chuckled ruefully. "Remember Dottie Pringle's card party? You vomited down the front of my jacket."

Our cousin Jock laughed loudly at Trevor's words, clearly having overheard at least part of our conversation from where he danced with a pretty brunette next to us.

I turned to scowl at him as a blush burned its way up into my cheeks. "I didn't know their wassail was mostly spirits," I replied defensively.

Trevor's stern expression cracked at that. "Well, regardless, I'm willing to risk my coach seats to keep that stark expression from returning to your eyes."

"How do you know the punch won't make me maudlin?"

He arched an eyebrow. "I've seen you foxed, Kiera."

"Wish I had," Jock called out from over my shoulder.

I turned to glare at my annoying cousin, but his wide unrepentant grin had me smiling instead. "Fine," I declared with a melodramatic sigh. "I shall endeavor to be joyful."

"That's my Kiera," Trevor declared, swinging me around so sharply that my legs were lifted momentarily from the ground.

At a normal gathering, such behavior would be highly inappropriate, but at the Rutherford Hogmanay Ball it was a matter of course. I estimated that half the assemblage was already well on its way to being sotted, if the giggles and raucous laughter were anything to go by. Mr. Trumble and his dance partner were barely able to stay on their feet as they twirled drunkenly through the assembly, narrowly missing the other couples. It was impossible not to join in the good cheer.

As the waltz entered its last stanza, a cry went up from across the room. Trevor and I turned toward the sound, but were distracted as Uncle Andrew leaped up in front of the orchestra, where they were positioned on a dais in the corner of the room. The strains of the waltz slowly died away, and a murmur of excitement swept over the crowd.

"It's nearly midnight," he declared, lifting a small glass of whiskey. "Let's toast the Old Year, and welcome the New Year in."

Everyone scrambled to find their own glasses of the preferred Scots toasting beverage. Trevor reached out to grab two glasses from the tray of a passing servant and handed one to me. Jock and his dance partner joined us, along with our cousin Andy—Uncle Andrew's oldest son and heir—and his fiancée, the aptly named Miss Witherington.

"What are you still doing here?" Andy asked our tall, dark-haired cousin. "Aren't you our first-footer?"

"Nay. Not this year. Yer mam asked Rye," Jock informed us in his Scots brogue, naming one of our other cousins, who had recently been widowed. Though educated as a gentleman, Jock refused to soften his accent. A fact that none of the rest of us had ever minded, but that aggravated his mother and older sister. "She thought he could use the good luck it might bring to him."

We all nodded in agreement.

"First-footer?" the very English Miss Witherington asked in confusion.

"Aye. It's an old Scottish tradition," Andy explained. "The first person to cross the threshold of a home after the stroke of midnight on Hogmanay is the first-footer, and they can either bring good or ill fortune to the house. The luckiest are tall, dark-haired men bearing gifts."

Her brow furrowed. "And the unluckiest?"

"Well, women, fair-haired men, and redheads are all regarded to be unlucky in varying degrees." Andy grinned. "So it's best to simply plan who your first-footer will be ahead of time to avoid any unhappy surprises."

Miss Witherington scrunched her nose in a manner which I suspected she thought was endearing. "But isn't that . . . well . . . silly?"

The rest of us shared the look of the long-suffering Scot faced with English ignorance.

"Nay," Jock protested. "Ole Mrs. Heron in the village tells of the year she fell ill with the ague, her home flooded, and she lost two of her sons, all because she had an unlucky first-footer."

Miss Witherington's eyes narrowed skeptically.

"In any case, it's a tradition," Andy told her with a pacifying smile. "Much like your mistletoe and greenery, and the Yule log at Christmas. There's no harm in following it."

"I suppose not," she hedged, returning his smile with one that didn't reach all the way to her eyes. I suspected she was merely placating him. I wondered how much these Hogmanay gatherings would change once she was mistress of Clintmains Hall.

"Ten seconds to midnight," Uncle Andrew announced, and then began to count us down as we all joined in. "Eight, seven . . ."

I couldn't help but smile, feeling an unbidden surge of hope and anticipation in my chest that this new year would be better than the last. After all, last year I had celebrated Hogmanay quietly with my sister and her husband in their Highland castle, afraid to face the world following the scandal. And now I was welcoming in 1831 at a ball of all places, surrounded by family who loved me, despite my quirks, and facing down those acquaintances who still eyed me with suspicion. I found myself wondering where I would be a year from now.

". . . three, two, one!"

A shout went up as everyone raised their glass and wished one another a Good New Year. I downed my tot of whiskey, feeling the warm, smoky liquid burn its way down my throat and into my stomach.

Trevor leaned over to kiss me on both cheeks. "Good New Year, sis." His eyes shone with the force of his affection, and I returned the sentiment, blinking back a sudden wash of tears that stung my eyes.

Jock reached out to wrap an arm around my waist, and I laughed as he pulled me into a hug. Then the whole party broke into song, as was the tradition, singing Robert Burns's folk tune, "Auld Lang Syne." Miss Witherington, of course, did not know the words, and she looked around at us in bewilderment, likely having difficulty understanding as we all sang it in the heavy Scots dialect as it was intended. I smiled at her in commiseration, but she either didn't want my sympathy or, more likely, simply wanted another chance to demonstrate her dislike of me, for she shot me one of her withering glares.

When the song finished, everyone hurried out into the large two-story entry hall, crowding down the steps, and peering over the railing to see below. The front door was opened with great ceremony by the Rutherford butler, letting the old year out, and welcoming in the new. This was swiftly followed by the arrival of our cousin Rye, standing before the door with gifts tucked under his arms. A cheer went up at the sight of him, and he smiled rather shyly, unused to the attention. It was a nice change, as their usual first-footer, Jock, was quite the braggart, playing up the part for all it was worth.

Uncle Andrew and Aunt Sarah stepped forward to invite Rye into their home, but as they did so, another figure appeared beyond Rye's shoulder. A hush fell over the assembly as the figure stepped forward into the light, showing us his bright red hair and coarse clothing splattered in mud and a dark red substance I knew from experience must be blood. It was a young man, and his eyes were wide and very white in his grubby face.

He moved forward, forcing Rye to shift to the side. Several people gasped as the redhead crossed the threshold of Clintmains Hall at the same time or just a little before Rye's foot touched the marble floor of the entry.

The hall began to buzz with murmurs of shock and dismay. A harmless tradition first-footing might be, but most Scots were superstitious enough that they had no wish to test its validity. At least, not if they were given a choice. But it was too late. What was done was done. The suspicion was laid. Perhaps Rye's foot had crossed the threshold first, but perhaps it had not.

"But what if they crossed at the same exact time?" the woman behind me wondered. "What happens then?"

No one seemed to have an answer for her, but from the tense atmosphere that had suddenly spread over the hall, I knew no one believed the outcome could be good.

"I mun' speak wi' Lord Buchan," the young man gasped to Uncle Andrew. His chest rose and fell rapidly as he tried to catch his breath. He was less than twenty years of age, his body still awkward and coltish, and extremely self-conscious. When he glanced up and realized the entrance hall was filled with people staring down at him, he flushed a fiery red that almost matched the hair on his head and the blood splashed across his linen shirt.

Worried the lad needed serious medical attention, I pushed past several of the people standing in front of me on the stairs still flustered by the man's appearance. But as I got closer, I could see that most of the blood was dried, and from the quantity it was clearly not his own, or else he would not still be standing.

Just as I was about to say something, Lord Buchan appeared out of the crowd to the left of the front door. "Willie, what is the meaning of this?" His eyes flicked up and down the young man's form. "What has happened?"

The young manservant's name startled me for a moment, for I couldn't help but think of another Will—a friend who had died so recently, and so horrifically. But this Willie's words swiftly recalled me to the present.

"It's Dodd," he replied with wide haunted eyes. "He's dead."

# CHAPTER TWO

Someone behind us gasped in horror, and the agitated murmuring began again.

The Earl of Buchan's brow furrowed in confusion. "Dead? What do you mean? How?"

"He's been shot. Oot by the ole abbey. But that no' be all." Willie shook his head, still breathing heavily. "The graves. One o' 'em was dug up."

One lady actually shrieked at this pronouncement, and the people in the back of the room and on the balcony above who couldn't hear young Willie demanded to know what he was saying.

"Dodd, the ole caretaker at Dryburgh House, has been shot," one man in the crowd hollered. "And a grave at the abbey's been disturbed."

More voices were raised in dismayed shock, and I turned to look at Trevor, who moved forward to stand beside me, a sick feeling entering my stomach. He met my eyes with the same knowing look of dread.

"Dug up?" Buchan spluttered, clearly having trouble grasping the implication.

"Body snatchers," I murmured softly, not wanting to alarm the entire assembly, though I knew that more than a few of them must have already had similar thoughts.

Lord Buchan, my aunt and uncle, and cousin Rye all

turned to look at me, and I watched as understanding slowly dawned in their eyes, first of the grave robbers' intentions, and then of my unpleasant history with the product of their trade.

"You mean . . ." Buchan began. I didn't know if he was that slow to comprehend or just too stunned to make the connection with the abbey cemetery.

"Have you had trouble with them in the past?" Trevor turned to ask our uncle, as he had only returned to the area himself three months prior.

He frowned. "Unfortunately, yes."

I was surprised to hear this news, as I'd had no idea that the body snatchers were traveling so far afield to find fresh corpses. But then it made sense, as all of the cemeteries nearby the medical schools in Edinburgh and Glasgow had added heavy security measures. They'd had to do something to keep the resurrection men from stealing their recently deceased and selling the bodies to the schools and local anatomists.

"But watchmen have been hired to guard the cemeteries these criminals most often target," Uncle Andrew added. "So I don't quite understand how . . ."

"But the graves at Dryburgh Abbey aren't new," Lord Buchan protested, finally grasping what the rest of us were saying.

I glanced at him in surprise.

"The newest grave there is my uncle's. And he died almost twenty months ago." His already heavy brow lowered farther, and I was surprised when he looked to me for answers. "What could they possibly have wanted from an old grave?"

"I . . . don't know," I admitted.

Aunt Sarah cleared her throat and nodded toward the assemblage still gathered in the entrance hall. They were pressing ever closer, trying to hear what we said. "Perhaps I should escort our guests back to the ballroom." She arched her eyebrows at her husband in silent communication.

"Er, yes," Uncle Andrew replied, looking at the crowd. His butler gestured toward a door behind him, to the left of the entrance. Uncle Andrew nodded at Willie and then at the circle of men closest to him. "Gentlemen, if you will," he murmured, indicating they should follow him. "Ah, you, too, Kiera. If you don't mind?"

I blinked in surprise, not having expected my uncle to include me. He was a good man, but not usually the most tolerant. I had always been aware that he didn't exactly approve of me or my painting, even if he'd never said a word against me. His disapproval was evident in his stilted conversation and stony expression whenever my art became the topic of discussion. I had also overheard him express his condemnation of my father's choice of Sir Anthony as my husband—an objection I had ignored at the time as just another indication of my uncle's stodginess, but later wished I'd listened to more attentively. Though, to be fair, even Uncle Andrew had not predicted the exact cause of my disastrous marriage. I'm not sure anyone could have foreseen that.

In any case, my relationship with my uncle was one of polite distance. We supported each other in that we were family, but beyond that, we were courteous strangers. So to hear him request my presence, especially in regards to a matter that was rather delicate and highly inappropriate for a young lady's ears, at least in society's general opinion, certainly astonished me.

I allowed Trevor to guide me through the crowd as we followed in Uncle Andrew's wake. Aunt Sarah was addressing the gathering behind us, some of whom protested our withdrawal. It appeared everyone wanted to know what the young man had to tell us.

The door through which we disappeared led into a small receiving room lined with slatted walls of gleaming oak. A bench and a few chairs were all the space held, as well as a pair of landscapes depicting the countryside surrounding Clintmains. The fireplace sat dormant, though a log and kindling had been laid, ready to be lit. I shivered, but I couldn't be certain whether it was because of the drafty room or the topic we were about to discuss.

"Now," Uncle Andrew declared, once the door was closed,

sealing us off from prying eyes. "Tell us what happened," he told Willie, not ungently.

The young man shuffled from foot to foot, and his shoulders slumped over. He clearly was unnerved by my uncle's and Trevor's muscular figures and by his employer, Lord Buchan's, scowling visage. I sidled a step closer to the lad, hoping to offer him some sense of solidarity. His troubled gaze flicked to mine and I gave him a reassuring smile. Behind the panic, I could see pain in his eyes, and I realized that in our quest for answers, we had forgotten that this Dodd had likely been his mentor, and possibly his friend.

"It's all right," I said. "We just want to find out what happened to Dodd." When he still didn't answer, I prompted him. "Did the men who were digging in the grave shoot Dodd? Did he catch them in the act?"

"I dinna ken, m'lady," he finally replied, lowering his head in shame. "Dodd said he saw lights o'er at the abbey and wanted to find oot what they were. But I told 'im he was seein' things. Or else a group o' merrymakers were out scarin' themselves on Hogmanay. But he went to look anyway. An' I let 'im go alone." He scuffed his boot against the floor. "I was angry at 'im for makin' me stay behind when everyone else was goin' to the bonfire."

"You heard the gunshot?" I guessed.

He nodded. "I . . . I was puttin' our tools up—we'd been fixin' a bit o' fence doon by the river—when I heard it. 'Tweren't very loud. Mare like a cracker. I went to see what it was, but by the time I found ole Dodd by the west door o' the abbey, they was gone, whoever done it. And . . . and ole Dodd were hardly breathin'." The boy swallowed loudly and swiped a grimy finger across his nose. "He pointed t'ward the graveyard—that's how I ken to look there—and . . . and then he jus' died."

I offered him my handkerchief, but he shook his head, and lifted the hem of his already filthy shirt and wiped his nose.

I glanced at the others, who all listened with silent

frowns. Lord Buchan, in particular, looked distressed, and I wondered how close he had been to his old caretaker.

"Willie," the earl said, his voice rougher than it had been before, "run round to the bonfire and fetch Paxton. Tell him to ready the carriage."

Willie nodded, holding his head a little higher, and bowed swiftly before dashing out the door.

Uncle Andrew moved to the door, catching it before it closed behind Willie, and beckoned his butler into the room. "Send one of the footmen to get Dr. Carputhers from the ceilidh at the bonfire," I heard him murmur, and my heart sank. Evidently Uncle Andrew's sensible nature had returned, and I could not argue. It should be a surgeon who examined Dodd's body, not an anatomist's widow with three years enforced instruction. The possibility should never have even entered my mind. The fact it had, and I hadn't been as horrified by the possibility as I should have been, was somewhat surprising.

"If you don't mind, I'll join you," Uncle Andrew told Lord Buchan as the butler left to do his bidding. "If there's been foul play, as the lad suggested, then I'll need to examine the evidence anyway." As one of the county's magistrates, Uncle Andrew ruled on many of the crimes in the region, though they were usually minor disputes between neighbors or petty thefts—nothing so serious as murder.

I turned to stare unseeing at one of the landscapes. I reached up to finger the amethyst pendant given to me by my mother that I almost always wore around my neck and wondered at my strange eagerness to assist. The past two investigations in which I had helped, I'd been compelled to take part only because my sister's family and an old friend had been involved. They had needed and asked for my aid. Otherwise I never would have presumed, or even wished, to have anything to do with the inquiries. But I had discovered something in myself that apparently I wasn't eager to dismiss, or have others dismiss for me.

I bit my lip, knowing in this instance there was nothing

I could say. With family, I should have felt able to offer my help, but I knew Uncle Andrew. He would only flash me his disapproving frown and ignore my suggestion.

And after all, who was to say he wasn't right? I wasn't an inquiry agent, not like Mr. Gage or his father, Captain Lord Gage. Just because I had aided in two murder investigations didn't mean I was qualified to conduct one alone. In any case, I was supposed to be distancing myself from things like murder and corpses. They would only remind people of my scandalous past and make my return to society more difficult.

It would be best for all if I was not involved.

Which was why I was so surprised when Uncle Andrew did address me. "Kiera," he said, and then hesitated when I turned to look at him. I folded my hands demurely before me and waited, silently hoping he wouldn't think better of whatever he was about to ask me.

And amazingly he didn't.

He cleared his throat, clasping his hands behind his back. "What do you think of all of this?"

"About Dodd and the disturbed grave?" I asked in clarification, lest I had missed something the gentlemen had discussed while my attention was focused elsewhere.

"Er, yes," he replied, and rocked forward on his heels. "I only ask because . . . well . . . you . . ."

"Have some experience with this sort of thing," I finished for him, sparing him the embarrassment of having to say it.

He cleared his throat again. "Quite."

"Well . . ." I glanced at Trevor but, upon seeing his stony expression, decided it would be best to avoid his gaze. "If one of the graves at Dryburgh Abbey has been disturbed, then someone must have been digging there. And doing so at night on the grounds of a deserted abbey, with only the light of a lantern to guide them, certainly suggests a desire for secrecy."

My uncle nodded, following my train of thought.

I turned to pace the small space in front of the door. "If

Dodd surprised them and they wished to remain undiscovered, they might have shot him. That seems a logical enough explanation to me. At least, the most logical we have so far."

I frowned. "But why was someone digging in an old grave to begin with? What were they looking for?"

I glanced at Lord Buchan, but he merely shrugged. "Most of those graves belong to old monks, local commoners, and a few members of my family. But as I said, the most recent burial was almost twenty months ago."

I furrowed my brow and resumed pacing. When several moments passed without anyone offering an explanation, I wondered aloud, "I suppose the body snatchers could have just been incredibly stupid and unaware that a body that long buried would be far too decayed to be of use to a medical college."

Trevor's mouth twisted in skepticism. "I have a hard time believing anyone is that ignorant. Especially if body snatching is your chosen trade, so to speak."

I crossed my arms over my chest and turned to face them. "I agree. It's far more likely they were looking for objects buried with the bodies—clothing, jewelry, what have you." Seeing the distressed expression on Lord Buchan's face, I added, "But there's really no way of knowing until you find out which grave was disturbed and examine it to see if anything was taken."

Uncle Andrew nodded in agreement.

I noticed he didn't correct me. It would be they who examined the grave, not I. But absurdly, I had been hoping against hope that I was wrong. That he would insist I come along.

My uncle leaned in to confer with Lord Buchan, and I stifled a sigh and resumed my perusal of the landscape. It really was an incredibly dull and uninspiring piece.

Trevor shifted closer to me. "Perhaps we should return to the ballroom."

I glanced up at him, wondering if I could, or even should, try to stall him.

He arched an eyebrow in sarcasm. "Don't tell me you're

actually interested in that landscape. I don't have nearly your artist's eye, and I can still see that it's dreadful."

I couldn't stop a smile from quirking my lips. "Hush. I think one of Uncle Andrew's relatives may have painted it." I darted a look over my shoulder to see the other two men still deep in conversation.

"Well, someone should have done us all a favor and kept the paintbrush out of his fingers," he drawled.

"How do you know it wasn't a woman?"

"*Her* fingers, then. Now come," he urged, cupping my elbow.

I knew there was no use arguing, yet still I found it hard to comply.

But before we could move more than two steps toward the door, a footman from Uncle Andrew's staff rapped softly on the door before opening it.

"I'm sorry, m'lord. But Dr. Carputhers appears to be a bit . . . indisposed," he said, choosing his words carefully.

Uncle Andrew frowned. "How indisposed?"

The footman cleared his throat. "Very." And as his employer was waiting for a more specific response, he added, "He's drunk as a wheelbarrow."

Uncle Andrew sighed heavily. "Well, we did invite him to a ceilidh. The man wouldn't expect to be on duty."

He dismissed the footman with a wave of his hand and began to pace, rubbing his pointed chin. Meanwhile, Trevor tugged on my arm, urging me to return to the ball. I hesitated a moment longer, wondering if I should offer to help, but my brother glared down at me, seeming insistent that I not say a word. So I gave in, allowing him to pull me toward the door.

"Just a moment, Trevor," our uncle called out behind us.

My brother glanced at me, and I tried to keep any of the anticipation I felt from showing on my face, but I must have failed, for he lifted his eyebrows in gentle reproach. "Yes, Uncle," he replied, turning us toward him.

Uncle Andrew stood stiffly in his formal coat and blue and

black tartan kilt with his arms behind his back, studying me across the short distance that separated us. I could tell he was wrestling with himself, much as my brother-in-law, Philip, had wrestled with his conscience before he asked me to assist Sebastian Gage during our first investigation together four and a half months prior. Uncle Andrew likely rebelled at the notion of exposing me to such an unsavory thing as murder, and yet he knew I possessed the skills he needed to help him understand the crime. Had I been a man, he would not have hesitated. But I was a female, and what's more, his niece. He was supposed to protect me from such things, not encourage me to speculate on them.

He grimaced and turned away. "I know I shouldn't be asking you such a thing, but . . ." he sighed, almost angrily ". . . it seems I have no choice." Gathering his courage, he looked me squarely in the eye. "Kiera, would you be willing to assist us? Perhaps it's not necessary," he hurried on to say before I could answer. "But I'm not so experienced with murder, or anatomy and those things . . ." He waved his hand vaguely in the air. "And I would rather be sure. I know that once the body has been moved . . ."

"Yes, Uncle," I replied before he stammered on. "I will do what I can."

However, Trevor was not as resigned to the necessity of my lending them assistance. "Isn't there another surgeon you could ask? What of your local physician?"

"I'm afraid not," Uncle Andrew replied. "And Dr. Kennedy is visiting family in Ayrshire."

My brother frowned.

"Believe me, Trevor, if I thought there was any man near enough and capable enough to lend us their assistance in this matter, I would not have asked your sister." His eyes hardened in censure. "I didn't approve when Cromarty asked her to assist in that murder investigation at Gairloch, or when she got dragged into that mess with the Dalmays. But . . ." he turned his head to the side, and I could see the tendons standing out in stark relief ". . . I begin to understand the predicaments those gentlemen were in." The expression he fastened on me was tinged with reluctant admiration. "Kiera is nothing if not discreet. And she did receive instruction from one of the foremost anatomists in England, unwanted as that was."

Trevor turned to study me, his brow heavy and his eyes clouded with uncertainty. I thought I could guess at some of his distress. After all, I was his baby sister, and he had been looking after me all my life. That he believed he had failed me once, in regards to protecting me from Sir Anthony's nefarious intentions, was bad enough. And he had no intention of letting me come to harm again. At least, not while I was living under his roof.

He had heard about my involvement with those previous investigations, and likely felt just as much disapproval as our uncle, though he'd not told me so. The fact that I had come to him angry and broken following my last investigation did not help matters. I had been poor company these past seven weeks, but that had more to do with my grief over the death of my friend Will than the investigation itself, disturbing as that had been. I wondered if he understood that. Or did he blame my melancholy on my continued involvement with corpses and murder?

"Are you sure about this?" he asked, searching my face. "You do not have to help, no matter what he says."

"I know," I replied, holding his gaze steadily with mine. "But this is something I want to do. Something I can do." I moved a step closer and lowered my voice. "I need to feel useful. And I want to help find whoever killed Dodd. For Dodd. For Willie. If I just walk away . . ." I left the sentence unfinished, knowing he recognized the guilt I would feel.

He continued to regard me, and then just when I thought he would argue further, he reluctantly nodded. "All right. But I insist on accompanying you."

I agreed and we turned toward our uncle.

"Of course. If you wish."

Trevor scanned me from head to toe in my evening gown.

"You'll need your cloak, and gloves or a muff. What of your slippers?" he fussed. He suddenly sounded so much like our nursemaid growing up that I couldn't help but smile.

"These shoes will be fine. But I would appreciate a pair of gloves," I told my uncle. "Preferably an old pair. If they should be ruined . . ."

He nodded, understanding the implication. Blood was not easy to wash out. "I shall send a servant to fetch whatever you require."

## CHAPTER THREE

The drive to the abbey took less than ten minutes, down a road bordered by winter fields of trampled hay and barley. For several minutes before the road turned away from it, I could see the Hogmanay bonfire blazing in the distance, a beacon in the darkness with the hazy shadows of the dancing villagers whirling around it. I huddled in my corner of the seat and tried not to shiver. I knew the night breeze would slice even colder once we stepped out of the carriage.

Trevor sat stiffly beside me, staring out the opposite window. I couldn't tell exactly what he was thinking, but I knew he wasn't pleased with this turn of events. Neither was our Uncle Andrew or Lord Buchan, both of whom seemed reluctant to meet my eyes. I did my best to ignore them, but it wasn't easy when my nerves were already stretched taut with a disquieting mixture of dread and anticipation.

I didn't know exactly what to expect. Willie had heard a gunshot, just one, so Dodd had likely died from a wound to his head or torso. From the amount of blood on Willie's clothes, I surmised Dodd had bled out, so the scene could be quite gruesome, or not. It depended on the wound and how much movement Dodd had made while dying.

As far as the disturbed grave, my guess was no better than the next person's. The body would be all or mostly bone and perhaps some hair, which would save us from the uncomfortable sight and smell of decomposition.

If the body was even still there.

Had the body snatchers taken it as planned, or abandoned their work after shooting Dodd, worried about the arrival of reinforcements? I supposed it depended on how close they were to being finished, and how ruthless they were.

If the bones had been left behind, then I presumed there would be two victims for me to examine. Such a thought didn't cause me as much discomfort as I'd expected. But the thought that I might be growing accustomed to all of this did.

After the horrors of my marriage to Sir Anthony and my enforced involvement with his work—observing his dissections and sketching the results for his anatomy textbook—I had been keen to escape anything associated with that world. I had viewed the victims' corpses from the previous two investigations I had been involved with only out of necessity and a desire to see justice done for my friends and family. But this crime had nothing to do with me. I had no relation to Dodd or Lord Buchan. I should have no desire to be near this tragedy, despite my uncle's reluctant request for my assistance. Instead, not only had I allowed myself to be coaxed into lending my aid, but I could also feel an undercurrent of excitement running through me at the prospect.

My late husband's colleagues had called me unnatural when they discovered my contribution to his anatomical work, and not for the first time, I wondered if they might be right. Or else why would I be running toward a dead body and a disturbed grave when by all rights I should be fleeing in fright?

Trevor's shoulder bumped against mine as the carriage made a sharp turn to the left into the grounds of Dryburgh House. Through the dark outline of the trees, I could see the pale stones of the Earl of Buchan's manor gleaming in the moonlight. The coach made another turn onto the gravel of the house's drive and then rolled to a stop.

My heart jumped as I felt the manservant leap down

from his perch on the back of the carriage. A moment later, the door opened and Lord Buchan pulled himself forward to descend. I was the last to disembark, with the assistance of my brother, and was instantly grateful for the kid leather half-boots loaned to me by my cousin. I had changed into them before we left and my feet now sank into the mud at the edge of the drive. I grimaced at the realization of what my gown's hem would look like after this midnight foray, and silently said an apology to my new maid, Bree.

Dryburgh House stood some distance away from us to the right, farther up the gravel drive. Its west front, on the far side of the house, bordered the River Tweed, whose waters rambled southward only to sweep around in a wide curve to flow north again, forming the small peninsula on which the old abbey had been built. The carriage had stopped on the drive just short of a well-trampled trail that led south, paralleling the river, and straight into the trees bordering the manor's lawn.

I had visited the ruins of Dryburgh Abbey with my family several times as a girl, and also once with William Dalmay ten years ago, the summer he acted as my drawing master. I felt a twinge of pain as the memory of Will's earnest joy and excitement also brought to mind his recent death. It sometimes seemed impossible that he had been gone just ten short weeks. And now I had to face this place that, until now, I had forgotten I last visited in his company. It was almost too much to bear.

I closed my eyes and inhaled deeply, trying to push aside the image of Will's haunted gray eyes.

Someone gripped my elbow, and I opened my eyes to find Trevor watching me closely, a look of concern tightening his features. I offered him a smile of reassurance, grateful he couldn't know the real source of my distress. Let him think I was nervous about viewing Dodd's body, for that was where my mind should have been focused.

Young Willie hefted one of the lanterns the men had removed from the coach and set off down the path into the trees with Lord Buchan trailing close behind him. Uncle Andrew followed next, carrying the second lantern, while Trevor and I brought up the rear. The dirt of the trail was soft from the recent rain, but the temperature had also cooled considerably in the past few days, hardening the earth just enough so that it wasn't a muddy mess as the drive had been. Even so, I was forced to take care where I stepped, and to heft the skirts of my gown and chocolate brown cloak to keep them from trailing in the muck.

I was grateful for the fur trim of my hood surrounding my face, for it kept the chill from my head, but unfortunately, it also obstructed my view. I could see little more than straight in front of me, but the sounds of the nighttime were all around. Every pop of a twig or creak of the barren branches made me glance about to locate the source of what I had heard. The low rush in the distance I knew to be the river, but the scratching and clattering and creaking in the gloom of the forest surrounding me I could not always immediately name. I was reminded of a Scottish proverb I'd often heard quoted: *The day has eyes, the night has ears.*

Suddenly, in a break through the trees, I could see the moonlight illuminating the gable of the south transept with its large five-light window, now empty of all glass. Little else remained of the Dryburgh Abbey church, but for a fragment of the choir and the north transept, and the reddish-brown sandstone bases of the pillars that once held aloft the soaring roof of the church.

When the eleventh Earl of Buchan, the current earl's uncle, acquired the monastic ruins forty years earlier, it was little more than an overgrown wreck, true to the name of ruins. The earl set about preserving what was left, adding a large formal garden within and around the stones. The effect was charming and romantic, but my father had noted that Buchan, who had been an eccentric antiquarian, also couldn't resist adding a few "improvements," namely an inscription and an obelisk south of the abbey. His nephew, the current earl, seemed much more practical, but as we approached the ruins, I could tell he was at least maintaining the abbey grounds.

I had been rather fond of the Gothic pile of Dryburgh Abbey, and its air of peace and tranquility, of nature merged with the fallen creation of man. But at night, with only the faint gleam of our lanterns to light the way, and the moon casting strange shadows across the faces of the crumbling ruins, I felt less assured.

We skirted the edge of the abbey cemetery, which we were divided from by a row of hedges and then the remnants of the abbey wall. It rose in jagged portions from waist-high to forty feet above our heads before it met up with the decorative rounded arches of the west door.

There, at the edge of the door, lay Dodd's body propped against the stone frame. His head had fallen back to rest between the small niche created by two of the arches, exposing his neck to the light of our lanterns. One hand trailed across the ground beside his body while the other sat cradled in his lap, as if he had tried until his final breath to stanch the blood flowing from the wound in his upper chest and the hand had dropped with his last gasp to where it lay. His eyes were blessedly closed.

"Poor Dodd," Lord Buchan murmured, the first to break the tense stillness.

I glanced up at him, and then Willie, whose cheeks were streaked with silent tears. Biting back an answering surge of emotion, I moved closer to the body, determined to remain unaffected. My tears would do neither Dodd nor Willie any good, but my reluctantly accrued knowledge of anatomy just might.

"Bring that lantern closer," I told Willie, hoping that by giving the young man a purpose, it would help him collect himself.

He sniffed loudly and shuffled closer, nearly treading on my skirts.

I pushed the hood of my cloak back and knelt carefully beside the body. The air was cool enough to mask most of the odors, but I still breathed shallowly through my mouth, as I'd learned in Sir Anthony's surgeries. My finely tuned nose could still smell the old caretaker's musty body odor and the metallic tang of blood. I pushed back the edge of Dodd's coat to see that his coarse woolen shirt beneath was, as expected, soaked with blood. The hole torn into the right side of his chest was quite obviously the cause of the bleeding. I quickly scanned the rest of his torso and his limbs, but could see no other signs of injury.

"One gunshot to the chest," I said, stating the obvious in case one of the gentlemen could not see.

I reached a hand around Dodd's shoulder, trying to pull his body forward to see his back. Willie passed his lantern to one of the other men and leaned over to help me.

"No exit wound."

Willie and I gently rested Dodd's body back against the stone arches. I surveyed the stone and the ground around the corpse and then made to rise. Trevor's hand cupped my elbow, assisting me to my feet. Pressing my now blood-smeared fingertips together, lest I unwittingly touch anything, I turned to thank him, and then wished I hadn't. The tight line of my brother's mouth and the stark look in his eyes told me just how little he appreciated seeing this side of me.

I inhaled quickly and stepped away, returning to the task at hand.

"It doesn't appear that he was shot here," our uncle commented, and I joined him in scanning the grass-choked path through the arches.

A drop of color at the base of the stone caught my eye. "Bring the lantern closer," I urged. Stepping through the doorway, I cautiously pivoted to the right. "Here. See the blood?" I pointed to the splatter on the stone arches just inside the door, and then backed away, circling wide of the path. "Dodd must have been coming through the doorway when he was shot."

The men followed my gaze to the spot where Dodd must

have been standing. It fit well with what we knew so far. The old caretaker must have come inside the abbey ruins to find out what the source of the light was. I wondered if Dodd had seen the man who shot him or if a lookout had been positioned near the door and stepped out to kill Dodd before he could ask questions. There were shadows deep enough to conceal a man here. And if a group of grave robbers had been working here, and they were any bit as organized as the gangs of body snatchers who plied their trade in Edinburgh and London, they would most certainly have had at least one sentry.

I turned around once again to survey the darkened ruins of the abbey church and the trees and cemetery encroaching on it to the left. At the edge of our lantern light I could see a pile of stones that had once been the base of one of the pillars, but beyond that everything was illumed only by moonlight. About a hundred feet in front of us, the hulk of the remnants of the north transept and presbytery were visible only because they towered above everything else, an island unto itself, separated from the south transept and the remainder of the standing abbey by the loss of the roof and walls that had once connected them. However, even that was only a mass of pale arches and craggy shadows.

Trevor moved forward to stand beside me, his breath condensing in the cold air around us as he sighed. "Willie, where is this grave Dodd pointed you to?" he asked, following the same bent of my thoughts.

Willie shuffled across the grass and pointed toward the ruins of the north transept. "O'er there. Near St. Mary's Aisle."

I glanced over my shoulder at Lord Buchan. His face was creased in a troubled frown, his thin lips almost disappearing. "That's what my uncle always called it," he explained, and then moved forward, his urgent stride lengthening with each step.

I shared a look with Trevor, suspecting the earl knew exactly who was buried in that prime location of the ruins.

The rest of us hurried to catch up with him, dodging the bits of stone still remaining on the abbey floor. We heard him gasp a sigh of relief as he got closer to the transept.

"My Elizabeth," he explained, standing before an undisturbed grave near the ruins, a hand pressed to his chest as he tried to catch his breath.

From the gravestone I could see that his wife had not been dead long, only since 1828, but still longer than twenty months.

I was about to ask after his uncle when at the edge of the lantern light I saw it. The mound of dirt. And beyond it the yawing hole of a grave.

Lord Buchan followed my gaze and gave another gasp, though this one was horrified. "My uncle." He stumbled forward and then halted abruptly, as if he wasn't certain he wanted to peer down inside the empty tomb.

I could sympathize. I felt a fluttering in my stomach at the same thought. It seemed rather like tempting fate.

Willie did not have similar qualms. Or perhaps he'd already faced them earlier. His foot sank into the loose soil, releasing the pungent scent of the earth into the night air, as he looked down into the grave. Feeling silly that this young man, barely out of boyhood, was braver than the rest of us, I moved closer, and the other gentlemen followed suit.

I'm not sure what I expected to find. A fully dressed corpse? A ghost? A vampire like Lord Ruthven in Polidori's story? I was not normally given over to fancy. And I knew that in twenty months the body would have decayed so significantly as to be not much more than bone.

But when I looked down into the grave and into the open coffin and saw only a pile of discarded clothing, I was momentarily shocked speechless.

The effect on my uncle was much the opposite. "What the devil!" he spluttered in outrage and then turned to glare at me. "They took his body, but not his clothing. Who does such a thing?"

"From what I understand, it's very common," I replied softly. "After all, theft of property, whether from the living or the dead, is a more serious crime than merely snatching a body. Or at least, according to common law, it is." I took another step closer to the edge of the grave, trying to get a better look at its contents. Trevor stepped up next to me, wrapping his hand around my upper arm to steady me and pull me back. "A grave robber who steals something as simple as a corpse's waistcoat can be sentenced to death or transportation. A body snatcher only faces a fine or a short imprisonment if he's caught."

"But why?" Lord Buchan demanded, his hooked nose quivering in indignation. "Why would they steal his body, his bones, and not take his effects? What could they possibly be worth?"

He was right. It didn't seem to make any sense. The eleventh Earl of Buchan's discarded fine-woven suit, silk waistcoat, and gold pocket watch alone would have fetched more than fifty pounds. I wasn't currently aware of any market for stolen bones. Maybe the teeth could have been made into dentures. Or the smaller bones of the hands and feet into trinkets. But what did they propose to do with an entire skeleton?

And why this skeleton? Why this graveyard? There were plenty of other cemeteries less conspicuous and easier to reach. And for that matter, plenty of other graves that were easier to dig up, even in this graveyard. I could see from the scuff marks and the gap in the earth above the coffin that the Earl of Buchan's enormous headstone must rest partially over the grave, which made it difficult for the robbers to get to the top of the coffin. They'd been forced to dig a foot of earth out from the bottom of the coffin and shift the entire thing backward in order to open it. That had not been a simple feat of manual labor, and had risked the stability of the gravestone.

It seemed someone had wanted to get into this grave in particular. But why? If they hadn't come for his effects . . .

"Do you know for certain they didn't take anything but your uncle's bones?" I questioned Lord Buchan. He blinked at me in confusion. "Do you remember everything that was buried with him?"

He stared down into the grave, his brow wrinkled in thought. "I . . . I'm not sure," he admitted. "I would need to think about it."

"It's not written down anywhere?" I pressed.

"It might be."

"We need to find out. Perhaps these men did take something else. Something you've forgotten about." I frowned. "Though, I still can't see why they would take the bones. Unless it was to confuse us."

I looked to Willie to see that he had been observing our conversation in silence, his gaze still trained on the empty grave. Though, from their tortured expression, his eyes seemed to be seeing something else.

"It seems very likely that whoever dug up Lord Buchan's grave also shot Dodd."

Willie's gaze rose to meet mine.

"That's not to say it's impossible that someone else did it. But it seems impractical to suggest otherwise, given the fact that Dodd was coming here to investigate a suspicious light, and he pointed Willie toward it when he arrived to help. And these men clearly left in a hurry . . ." I gestured to the disturbed earth ". . . leaving the grave exposed and their shovels behind." Most body snatchers at least attempted to cover up their crimes.

Trevor turned to Uncle Andrew and Lord Buchan. "Do either of you know who these grave robbers might have been?"

Lord Buchan shook his head.

"I can check my magistratical records and speak with my colleagues," Uncle Andrew replied, his eyes troubled. "But I must say, I haven't the slightest idea who might have done this."

I nodded, sympathizing with his obvious distress. My uncle and I might not be close, but I knew how seriously he took his responsibilities. The fact that a murder and body snatching had occurred in his jurisdiction, and on the same night, would never sit well with him.

"I suppose it will be difficult to keep this quiet," Lord Buchan said.

After Willie's frantic arrival at the Hogmanay Ball with the first-footer, it would be nigh impossible. But Uncle Andrew only replied solemnly, "I'm afraid so."

"Although we can endeavor to keep the details quiet," I suggested, looking at each of the men in turn, including Willie. "It would help with the ensuing investigation."

I could see my estimation rise even higher in my uncle's eyes. "Kiera's correct, of course. There's no need for any of us to speak of specifics with anyone who isn't authorized to have the information."

"True." Buchan nodded thoughtfully. "Lady Darby, you are acquainted with Captain Lord Gage, are you not?"

I was stunned for a moment by his query. Though, in hindsight, I should have expected it. I fumbled for words. "I . . . have not had the honor. But I am acquainted with his son."

"Acquainted" was perhaps too innocuous a word for what lay between us, but I was not about to explain that to these gentlemen.

"I've heard that Lord Gage sometimes assists the king and his high-placed friends when they find themselves in . . ." he arched his eyebrows significantly ". . . troubling circumstances."

"Yes," I replied, letting him know I understood what he meant. "'Troubling' could be used to describe anything as simple as a gambling debt or as serious as the murder of one's mistress. "As does his son."

"Who is still in Edinburgh, I hear."

I was startled by his knowledge of that detail, but did my best not to show it. "As far as I'm aware."

"Would you write to him? Ask him to come to my aid?"

When I didn't answer immediately, Buchan begged. "I don't know what else to do. And I can't simply allow these men to get away with stealing my uncle's bones and shooting my caretaker."

I understood his predicament. None of the surrounding villages had any sort of organized police force, and though my uncle, the local magistrate, would try, he had very little experience with this sort of thing. Lord Buchan's best option was to hire a private inquiry agent, and he would find no gentleman better than Sebastian Gage.

But still I hesitated to reply, knowing I stood at the brink of a decision I should have seen coming. If I wrote to Gage, even on Lord Buchan's behalf, and asked him for his assistance, I knew he would also see it as my asking him here for myself. To him there would be no difference, no matter how carefully I worded the request.

I had no doubt he would come. He had promised as much the last time we parted. All I need do was ask, he'd said, and he would come to me. Such a small thing, and yet so immense. And I didn't know if I was ready for it.

My feelings were still confused when it came to Gage, and I wasn't certain I was prepared to face them yet. It was true I had needed time and space to heal from the loss of my friend Will, but I also had needed that same time and space to sort through my emotions when it came to Gage. And though in some ways I had done just that, in others I hadn't. I still felt Will's loss so keenly. I didn't know if seeing Gage would make things better or worse, whether his presence would give me comfort and clarity, or cause me more heartache and frustration.

Trevor's feet shifted in the loose earth beside me, recalling me to the present. I felt the sting of a blush in my cheeks that had nothing to do with the wind. How long had Lord Buchan been waiting for my answer? It had likely been only a matter of seconds, but gauging by the taut silence, that had been long enough to become awkward.

I offered the earl a smile of apology. "Of course. I'll write to him as soon as we return to Clintmains."

Lord Buchan's shoulders sagged in relief. "Thank you."

I nodded and turned away to strip off the bloodstained gloves, doing my best to conceal the fact that my hands were shaking.

# CHAPTER FOUR

When Uncle Andrew, Trevor, and I returned to Clint-mains Hall in Buchan's carriage, we were surprised to see that many of the guests had already departed, though perhaps we shouldn't have been. Normally the Rutherford Hogmanay Ball lasted long into the night, almost until dawn, but not this year. It seemed Willie's disruption of the first-footer ceremony had dampened the festive spirit.

Most of those guests who remained were staying the night at Clintmains, but even many of them had retired. Aunt Sarah waited for our return in the ballroom with a few stragglers and two pickled men who had yet to be carried up to their assigned chambers. When Trevor asked if, under the circumstances, we might spend the night at Clintmains instead of making the fifteen-mile journey back to Blakelaw House, she readily agreed. She already had rooms made up for us and our servants were bedded down with some of her household staff.

I excused myself to Uncle Andrew's study and sat down to write my letter to Gage on Lord Buchan's behalf. With my uncle hovering over me, I didn't have time to agonize over my choice of words, which was perhaps a blessing, as I certainly would have, given the opportunity. Instead I jot-ted off a quick missive, providing him with only a brief account of events, and stamped it closed with my uncle's seal. He already had a rider waiting to depart to deliver the message to Edinburgh by the swiftest route.

I didn't sleep well that night, and the fault for my restlessness did not lie with my aunt. For despite the short notice and the house overflowing with guests, she had still managed to provide me with a lovely little room facing the gardens. No, the fault lay in me. I had never slumbered easily, but my insomnia had only grown worse in the months since Will's passing. My mind simply would not allow me the undemanding peace of a deep sleep. It was always on guard. And this night's new worries over Dodd's murder and the eleventh Earl of Buchan's missing bones, coupled with my anxiety over Gage's pending arrival, only added to the burden.

Consequently, I was up almost with the sun and down to the breakfast parlor before I expected to see any of the other guests. But I was wrong. Two young men sat conferring with one another in hushed voices at one end of the table. The tone of their voices would have seemed suspicious but for the fact that one of them was very clearly nursing a thick head from a long night of drinking. It was he who jerked upright at the sound of my approach from where he had been draped over the table and then winced, brackets of pain forming around his mouth and eyes. I recognized Lord Shellingham at once and waved him down, lest he try to rise and cast up his accounts. I couldn't imagine why on earth he would be out of bed at this hour in his condition.

My gaze swung to take in the man beside him, who was eyeing me with some misgiving, though I couldn't think why. Unless, having heard the rumors concerning me, he thought I was about to lure him to his death before selling his body for dissection. If that was the case, the man must not be very bright.

"Good morning," I murmured, moving to the sideboard. A yawning footman stood to the side, ready to assist, and I smiled at him in sympathy. A servant's duties were never done, even the morning after a ceilidh.

I settled across from the two men, observing that Lord Shellingham had nothing more than a cup of black coffee before him, while the other man's plate of food had barely been touched. I sipped my tea and eyed him curiously. In my experience, young men of his age practically inhaled their food. He didn't appear to be suffering the ill-effects of a night of overindulgence, but I supposed he could simply be hiding it better.

"Forgive me. I've forgotten your name," I said. Trevor had introduced us the previous evening, but though Lord Shellingham's name had stuck, thanks to his friends' manner of calling him Shelly for short, this fellow's had not. "Remind me."

He cleared his throat. "Archibald Young, my lady."

I nodded. Now I remembered. Though only two or three years younger than I, thanks to his rather puppy-doggish looks, he seemed younger still. Even now he was staring at me with his big brown eyes like I was about to scold him for piddling on the carpet.

Lord Shellingham, on the other hand, was quite the fop—his clothes and hair arranged just so. Although this morning that was definitely not the case. I found him to be handsomer without the artifice. If you looked beyond the green cast to his true complexion, that is.

If I remembered correctly, the pair were cousins, and I thought I could see a shared familial trait in the strength of the jaw and the shape of the eyes, though there the similarities ended.

"Are you off early?" I inquired, taking in their riding attire.

"Er, yes," Mr. Young stammered, darting a glance at his companion. "We're due back in Edinburgh for a dinner."

"Blasted dinner," I heard Lord Shellingham mutter as I took a bite of toast, and bent my head to hide my answering smile.

"And you?" Mr. Young asked politely.

I shrugged one shoulder. "I'm up early most mornings, regardless of how late I retired."

I studied Mr. Young as he picked at the food on his plate and Lord Shellingham as he cradled his head in his hands, and decided they were as good a place to start as any.

"So what are your impressions of what happened last night? Quite an odd way to begin the new year, don't you think?"

Mr. Young darted another nervous glance at his cousin, who merely parted his fingers to look at me through them.

Neither man spoke, so I clarified. "The interruption of the first-footer."

"Oh, yes." Mr. Young gasped, almost seeming relieved.

What else had he thought I referred to?

"That was odd," he confirmed.

Clearly interpreting my probing gaze, Lord Shellingham added, "We both got a little more foxed than we intended, Lady Darby. I think Archie, here, has been worried he might have gotten into some trouble he shouldn't have."

"I see," I replied neutrally, not at all sure there wasn't more to it than that. But before I had a chance to question them further, another guest entered the room.

"Good morning," he announced loudly with good cheer.

Lord Shellingham winced so sharply I thought he might collapse under the table.

I turned to smile at the newcomer, a gentleman about my uncle's age with a wisp of very fair, thinning hair. "Good morning."

He halted at the edge of the table rather abruptly and, after examining my features quite thoroughly, offered me a dazzling smile. I began to worry there was some smudge on my face or that my hair, which was never really tamed, had already fallen from its pins. But he quickly disavowed me of my fears.

"There is nothing quite like the sight of a lovely lady in the morning to brighten one's day," he declared, a slight nasality to his accent betraying his country of origin.

I blushed at his outrageous flattery, and he swept around the table to take my hand, bowing before it.

"Gentlemen . . ." he urged the two men sitting across from me ". . . please introduce us."

"Oh, er, Lady Darby, may I present Mr. Stuart," Mr. Young stammered.

"Lady Darby." Mr. Stuart rolled my name over his tongue like it was a savory treat. "I have heard of you." His silver eyes twinkled. "And, I must say, the pleasure is all mine."

I arched my eyebrows at the old roué, but couldn't suppress an answering smile. "Thank you, Mr. Stuart." Then I glanced down at where his hand still held mine. "But perhaps you might let go of my fingers now. I *would* like to finish eating."

He chuckled. "Of course." He nodded to the footman standing by the sideboard, who moved forward to pour him a cup of coffee, and settled into the seat beside me.

I watched him out of the corner of my eye as he inhaled and then took his first sip of the beverage, preferring it black and bitter. He sighed contentedly.

I grinned at his obvious enjoyment. "Have you been in Scotland long?"

"A few months only. A lovely country. And such fascinating customs! The singing, the bonfire, the first-footer. I have never been here before to celebrate what you call Hogmanay in your country."

"But you've visited Scotland before?"

He nodded briskly as he took another sip of his coffee. "My first visit was in 1812." He paused, a strange expression tightening his features. "So long ago now, it seems," he murmured, almost wistfully. But before I could ask him about it, he hurried on to say, "But I'm afraid I did not stay long. I soon set sail for Philadelphia."

Mr. Young perked up at this bit of news. "You've been to America?"

A smile returned to Mr. Stuart's lips. "I have. And quite the adventure it was. I saw the city of Washington burned by the British. Even visited the frontier."

Mr. Young leaned forward eagerly. "Did you see any Indians?"

"I did. I was even able to speak to a few of them." He paused dramatically, a knowing twinkle in his eyes telling us he had more to share. "Davy Crockett introduced us."

This finally caught Lord Shellingham's interest, as he lifted his eyes to the man, still carefully cradling his head in his hands. "The frontiersman?"

Mr. Stuart relaxed back in his chair, clearly enjoying the attention. "Fascinating man. I even witnessed him dispensing what he liked to call 'justice' by shooting a man who was attempting to steal his horse in the b—" His gaze strayed to mine, as he seemed to recall the presence of a lady at the last moment. "Er . . . an uncomfortable place."

I hid a smile, knowing Mr. Stuart was eager to share more, but had halted out of respect for me. Taking the cue that none of these gentlemen would be so impolite as to actually express, I excused myself from the table. It was unlikely I would be able to glean any useful information about the night before from them anyway.

I couldn't help but chuckle as I exited the breakfast room, wondering if I should believe a word Mr. Stuart said. He simply did not seem the type who would go off on these sorts of adventures. He might have visited America. He might have seen the city of Washington burn—from a safe distance. But the rest seemed more like embellishment.

"I see you've made Mr. Stuart's acquaintance," Aunt Sarah remarked, correctly interpreting my amusement when she intercepted me at the doorway. Dark circles rung her eyes, but they twinkled with good humor as she peered over my shoulder at the Frenchman. I suspected she had only managed to snatch a few hours of sleep, but being hostess, she would feel it was her duty to be up early to see to her guests.

"Yes," I replied. "He's quite a colorful character."

"Telling tales of his exploits, is he?"

"Davy Crockett."

"Ah," she said knowingly, and then slipped her arm

through mine, striding with me a few steps away from the door into the hall. "Well, he is charming. And perhaps a bit . . ." she wrinkled her nose as if searching for the right word ". . . eccentric."

I smiled. That word could encompass any number of odd behaviors. I myself was called eccentric, but I was nothing like Mr. Stuart. However, I knew what my aunt was trying to say as tactfully as possible.

"I'm glad you found me," I admitted.

She arched her brows in query.

"I wanted to ask you whether anyone mentioned if they'd seen anything strange last night—before, during, or after the ball."

Her face tightened. "You mean, other than when that poor young man stumbled in during our first-footing?"

"That upset quite a few people, didn't it?" I asked, thinking of how superstitious some Scots could be.

She sighed. "You saw how quickly everyone left." She lifted a hand to her forehead wearily. "It was not exactly an auspicious ending to the evening."

"No. It wasn't."

Pressing a hand to her stomach over her lavender morning dress, she tilted her head to study me. "Your uncle told me you sent for this investigator, Mr. Gage."

I nodded. "Lord Buchan asked me to."

"Well, hopefully he can get to the bottom of this nasty business." Her eyes narrowed in scrutiny. "And I suppose you mean to assist him."

"If I can," I answered demurely, though I had already determined there was no way I was going to let Gage or my uncle leave me out of the matter.

A warm smile spread across her face and crinkled the corners of her eyes. "I expected nothing less. You are Greer's daughter after all."

At the mention of my mother's name, and the implication of her infamously stubborn nature, I couldn't help but return my aunt's smile with one of my own.

"Well, then, your uncle should be in his study, if you wish to speak with him. As for the other, I'm afraid, I have nothing to tell you. None of the guests mentioned anything out of the ordinary . . ." she frowned ". . . besides their superstitious nonsense." She shook her head. "But you're welcome to question those guests who stayed the night. And I can provide you with a copy of the guest list."

"Thank you."

She waved it aside. "It's only common sense. If someone saw something, I would hope they would come forward of their own accord, but people are not always sensible about such matters, are they?"

I knew her question was rhetorical, so I did not reply.

"I'll ask my staff if they saw anything, so that will be one less thing for you and Mr. Gage to do. But should you wish to question them yourself, just say the word."

I was extremely grateful for my aunt's practical nature. I knew from experience that most other ladies of the manor would have declared that the murder and grave robbing at Dryburgh Abbey had nothing to do with Clintmains Hall and refused to assist me. But then again, the damage had already been done last night when Willie stumbled in during the first-footing. What further harm could questioning a few guests or servants about what they'd seen cause?

In any case, I was more interested in returning to Dryburgh Abbey and the earl's neighboring manor house. If anyone had seen anything suspicious, it was more likely to be one of Lord Buchan's staff. After all, the grave robbers must have traveled in a carriage or on horseback. Perhaps someone had seen them coming or going.

I found my uncle in his study, just as my aunt had suggested. However, he wasn't alone. My brother was seated before our uncle's heavy oak desk, his brow furrowed in either fatigue or frustration, I couldn't be certain which, maybe both.

When I informed them of my intentions, neither man

spoke for a moment, leaving me perched awkwardly on the edge of my chair.

"Don't you think it would be wiser to wait for Mr. Gage?" my uncle finally asked.

"I do not," I replied, trying to keep the sharpness out of my tone. "I assure you, Mr. Gage would expect me to begin investigating immediately. Time is often of the essence. Evidence is lost. Witnesses change their stories. I need to return to the abbey and speak to Lord Buchan's staff."

Uncle Andrew glanced at Trevor and then sighed. "If you're so determined, I cannot stop you. But I recommend taking your brother with you."

"Of course," I replied, having no intention of arguing. Trevor was intelligent. I was sure his presence would prove quite useful. In any case, I knew it would be wasted breath to protest. I could read the stubborn set to his chin. He was not going to allow me to investigate alone.

Uncle Andrew nodded in approval and explained his intentions to send out riders on the roads leading north toward Edinburgh and Glasgow—the likeliest directions the grave robbers had gone—to ask about the travelers who had stopped at the inns and pubs last night along those routes. Perhaps someone had noticed something unusual or could at least give us a description of a group or several pairs—for they may have split up—of men traveling together.

So while our coach was made ready, Trevor ate some breakfast and I gathered my cloak and gloves, having already dressed in a warm, deep blue serge gown borrowed from my aunt. Trevor was silent as we pulled out of Clintmains Hall's drive and the carriage gathered speed on the road to Dryburgh Abbey, but I knew better than to think this would last. He may have held his tongue in our uncle's study, but there was no reason for him to do so now that we were alone.

"Why are you doing this?"

I looked away from the window I had been staring out of at the weak winter sun to find him watching me with stern resolve.

"Doing what?"

He arched a single eyebrow in impatient chastisement. "Throwing yourself headlong into this investigation."

I wasn't sure how to answer him. With his jaw hardened like that, and his legs spread, his feet planted firmly on the carriage floor as if prepared for battle, I knew Trevor would not be placated by a dismissive answer. He was determined to have the truth from me, even if I wasn't certain precisely what that was.

"I . . . want to find Dodd's killer."

"Yes, but Mr. Gage and Uncle Andrew could undoubtedly handle it."

"Maybe," I admitted reluctantly. "But I want to help."

"Why?" When I didn't immediately answer, he leaned forward and braced his elbows on his knees. "It's not as if you have any personal investment in this inquiry. You're not trying to prove your innocence or protect your family. You're not attempting to salvage a friend's reputation," he rattled off, listing the reasons behind my interference in the last two investigations. His bright lapis lazuli eyes, so like my own, searched my face. "Why are you so determined to be involved?"

I crossed my arms over my chest and turned once again to stare out the window, unable to still meet my brother's probing gaze. Irritatingly, he was right. I did want to bring Dodd's killer to justice and give Willie some peace, but that wasn't my sole motivation. It couldn't be.

"Kiera," Trevor murmured, gentling his tone. "You don't sleep. You barely eat. And since you arrived at Blakelaw House, you've hardly lifted a paintbrush."

I opened my mouth to protest, but he forestalled me.

"I know you pretend. But you've been working on the same landscape since you arrived, and it looks worse than that painting in Uncle Andrew's receiving room."

I scowled at him, but he ignored it, continuing on relentlessly.

"You hate painting landscapes, Kiera. So why are you even attempting one?"

I stared blindly out the window at the countryside passing by.

"Kiera?"

"Because every portrait I begin is rubbish," I finally snapped.

"Why?"

I shrugged, unable to put it all into words. The last portrait I had completed had been of my friend Will, just after he died. And once it was finished, it seemed, so was I. It was as if my desire and my ability to capture the essence of people on canvas, which had always been my solace in times of distress, had deserted me also.

Trevor sat back in his seat. "Then do you really think you should be getting involved with another investigation after everything that happened with the last one?"

"It wasn't the investigation."

He arched his eyebrows in skepticism.

"It wasn't," I insisted. "If I hadn't gotten involved, then William Dalmay might never have been cleared, and that . . . *blackguard* . . . might have gone on to harm more innocent people. I don't regret that. I can't." I swallowed the lump of emotion gathering in my throat. "What I regret is that Will had to die. And in such a horrible way."

Trevor reached into his pocket and offered me his hand-kerchief, but I shook my head at him angrily.

"I don't like feeling helpless," I said, glaring at him. "And this is something I can do. Something I happen to be good at. So if it makes me feel better to be useful, even if it involves a murder investigation, isn't that better than the alternative?" I shook my head. "I can't go on as I have been. I know I can't. *You* know I can't."

My brother studied my features, as if trying to read my thoughts. "You do know that you're simply distracting yourself from the real problem?"

"Well, maybe that's just what I need," I countered. "Remember when Father died?" His gaze dropped from mine. "Did anything truly make you feel better? Except when you found something to occupy your thoughts long enough to make you forget for a little while how sad you were."

From the stark look that had entered Trevor's eyes, I knew I had caused him pain, but I could think of no other way to make him understand.

"If helping with this investigation allows me to forget for a time," I asked him more gently, "then what's so wrong with that?"

He inhaled deeply and nodded.

I gave a small sigh of relief. Not that I actually thought Trevor would have forbidden me to assist with the inquiry— he was accompanying me back to the abbey, after all—but it would be much easier to proceed with his approval.

"But that doesn't mean you can go off on your own," he warned, reassuming his role as big brother. "This is a murder investigation. We don't know what kind of criminals we're dealing with. And I have your safety to think of."

"I understand," I replied, having become accustomed to the protective stances of the males around me when it came to these investigations. Not that that had always been effective in keeping me safe . . . but I knew better than to argue.

"If you wish to investigate something, I will make myself available to you. And once Mr. Gage arrives, there will be two of us to accompany you."

My breath caught at the reminder of Gage's impending arrival, and when I felt the carriage turn into the drive for Dryburgh House, I was grateful for the distraction.

Several of Lord Buchan's servants were already at work in the ruins of the abbey when we arrived. Dodd's body had been taken away, and Willie was down on hands and knees scrubbing at the bloodstains left behind. My heart clenched at the sight, and I touched a hand gently to his shoulder. He looked up at me, and I could see the stark tracks his tears had left behind on his grimy face. He sniffed and nodded, and then bent back to his task.

I thought it was cruel that Willie should be assigned this distressing job, but then I realized the guilt-ridden young man had probably requested it. An apology for not accompanying the older man to the abbey the previous night. I knew it would do no good to point out that, had he done so, Willie would likely also be dead. Guilt did not often answer to common sense.

Two other men were employed near the eleventh Earl of Buchan's yawning grave. I had to admit that the sight still made a chill run down my spine, even with the pale winter sun shining peacefully on the ruins, chasing away the night's lingering shadows. Barren creepers and ivy covered the cold stone walls of the north transept, a bleak backdrop to the scene.

Our footsteps crunched across the frosted grass, alerting the men to our approach. One fellow stood down in the grave while the other kneeled beside it. A pile of the deceased Lord Buchan's discarded clothes, retrieved from the coffin, lay next to the headstone.

Trevor and I introduced ourselves and quickly learned that both men were employed by the earl as gardeners and had been at the ceilidh the night before.

"Did either of you notice anything strange, either at the bonfire, or before or after?" I asked.

Both men shook their heads.

"An unfamiliar carriage on the road or a group of men on horseback?" Trevor pressed.

"Aye, well, we seen plenty o' unfamiliar carriages, but they was all headed t'ord Clintmains," the man kneeling by the grave said as he rose to his feet. "Saw a fair number o' lads on horseback as well. But they 'tweren't no strangers."

"And what of here?" I glanced significantly at the grave. "What have you recovered?"

The man shifted to look at the pile of belongings. "His

clothes and shoes, a handkerchief—though I dinna ken what he'd need tha' for—a watch, and some sort o' jeweled pin. What ye call it?"

"A stickpin," the man in the grave replied in his deep, gritty voice.

"Aye."

"No bones?" I clarified.

"Nay."

So the robbers had been careful to retrieve all of the bones—even the tiny ones in the hands and feet—but had left behind the valuable items. Such circumstances were very odd. All of the items in that pile were worth a good deal of money, including the gentleman's handkerchief, and yet none of the robbers had taken them. Not even the stickpin, something small and easily concealed.

Either this group of men had considerable confidence in the amount of money they would be receiving for stealing the bones and nothing else—and the self-discipline not to be tempted to take one of the other objects to make a couple of extra quid—or they weren't in need of the money. Their motive was something else entirely.

Of course, we still needed to verify with the current Lord Buchan that all of his uncle's effects were accounted for. Maybe something buried with the body had been taken—a ring, a medal, a jewel-tipped walking stick. At least now we knew what had not been taken and could move forward from there.

"Did either of you see the late earl laid out in his coffin before he was buried?" I asked the men, curious if they would remember anything.

"Aye, m'lady. We all did. Had his coffin restin' on a table in the parlor so we could all pay our last respects."

"Can you recall whether anything he was wearing then is missing from this pile?"

The man standing beside the grave glanced down at his companion, and then shook his head. "Sorry."

I nodded, knowing it had been unlikely they would remember.

"But ye might ask Mrs. Moffat in St. Boswells. She be the one who cleans and lays oot the bodies o' our dead."

I had not thought to confer with such a woman, but she might prove an invaluable source of information. I thanked him and took Trevor's arm to allow him to lead me across the abbey ruins and through the west door, past Willie, who was still scrubbing almost desperately at the stone. I tried to push the image from my mind, but the vicious scraping of his brush against the sandstone dogged our steps as we moved away from the sheltered arbor of the abbey and down one of the paths that led toward Dryburgh House.

# CHAPTER FIVE

The Earl of Buchan's staff consisted of the usual assort-
ment of characters—butler, housekeeper, cook, footmen, maids of every stripe, a valet, and even a governess who
tutored the earl's young son. We'd already questioned the
stable hands and coachman with no luck, but I had hopes
that one of the indoor staff would have something to tell us.
Most of the servants present had attended the bonfire and
ceilidh at Clintmains Hall, though the butler, valet, and
governess had remained behind, the latter to care for her
charge, I suspected.

"I did see a light at the abbey when I pulled the window
drapes closed in my room," the governess admitted in some
distress. "But I'm afraid I didn't think much of it. It wasn't
my concern, in any case. The young master was. And he
wasn't very happy to have missed out on the Hogmanay
festivities."

I nodded, understanding the woman had likely had her
hands full dealing with the boy. The others might have
enjoyed their Hogmanay, be it at the ceilidh or quietly on
their own, but if the boy had been sullen or unruly, she may
not have.

"What of the rest of you?" I asked, scanning their faces
where we stood clustered in the large entry hall. "Did you
hear or see anything strange at any time yesterday or even

in the days before? Did you see anyone on the roads or near the estate who seemed out of place?"

Their blank faces and shaking heads did not encourage me. At least half of them seemed to be nursing thick heads, including the otherwise stalwart-looking housekeeper, and I wondered if that portion of my audience truly comprehended what I was saying.

Then a petite maid with corkscrew auburn curls inched forward from where she had been cowering near the staircase. She glanced about her anxiously, and I knew she was working up the courage to speak. I smiled at her encouragingly, repressing the excitement that surged in me at the prospect that she might have something worthwhile to tell.

"Is . . . is it true then?" she stammered.

"Is what true?" I asked, curious just what story had been circling the manor about Dodd's death and the goings-on at the abbey.

She swallowed before replying haltingly. "They say the ole earl rose from the grave. Th-That he's come back to haunt us."

"Or drain our blood," another maid whispered beside her.

I frowned at the two maids and then surveyed the others gathered around them. Some seemed as apprehensive as they were, while others smirked at their naïveté and superstition.

"No. The late earl has not risen from the dead," I replied.

"But Dodd . . ." the maid persisted.

"Was shot. So unless Lord Buchan was buried with a pistol, then Dodd encountered a very living, breathing human in the abbey cemetery." I could hear that my aggravation had crept into my voice, and I took a deep breath. Scolding the staff would not convince them to share any information they had with me.

"Maybe it was the Nun of Dryburgh," the second maid whispered, her eyes wide as she glanced around at her fellow servants.

I barely resisted rolling my eyes at the girl's mention of the mythical figure Sir Walter Scott had written about in one of his poems. I decided it would be best to switch tactics before anyone else named a creature of fantasy as the murderer.

"What of Dodd? Had he argued with anyone recently? Would anyone have had a reason to wish him dead?"

This question seemed to shock the servants more than anything I'd asked, for they began murmuring to each other with astonished looks on their faces.

The cook, a formidable-looking woman with white hair, harrumphed. "Ole Dodd was cantankerous, teh be sure. But no one 'd want teh harm 'im."

I had known the query was probably pointless, for it was likely the caretaker had simply been in the wrong place at the wrong time, but it was best not to make assumptions, and so the question had to be asked.

While the staff slowly filed out of the hall, seeming reluctant to go now that the questioning had passed, Trevor and I followed Lord Buchan into his study. The earl told his butler to have tea sent in, and then closed the door on the curious eyes of the lingering servants. He motioned for us to take a seat in the pair of burgundy wingback chairs before his heavy oak desk.

"I wish my staff could have been more helpful," he replied in regret. His heavy brow was furrowed, and deep grooves etched his forehead between his eyes. His chair creaked as he settled into it. "I've been thinking over the matter, and I must say I'm as baffled as ever."

I glanced out the tall windows at the swiftly flowing current of the River Tweed, feeling the same bafflement. So far I had no suspects, and I desperately wanted some direction on where to look.

"I asked the servants about Dodd," I told Lord Buchan. "And I apologize, but I also must ask about your uncle." I paused, not wishing to offend him. "Did he have any enemies? Anyone who might have wanted . . . revenge?"

The earl frowned.

"I know it seems an odd question." In fact, it sounded ridiculous. "But none of this makes sense."

"No, no. I appreciate you're simply trying to understand it yourself." He closed his eyes as if thinking hard, and then shook his head. "I'm sorry. I can't think of anyone who would do such a thing. Don't get me wrong. My uncle was no saint. But he was more likely to annoy you than anger you. He was too vain and self-important to be concerned with others."

"What of you?" Trevor asked him. "Is there anyone who might try to strike at you by stealing your uncle's bones?"

I tensed, worried he might be insulted, but he only cradled his chin in his hand as he gave the matter some consideration. I turned to Trevor, thanking him with my eyes for asking the sensitive question. He dipped his head in response.

Lord Buchan's mouth curled in chagrin. "I'm sorry. Perhaps I deceive myself, but I can think of no one who would wish to harm me in this way."

A tiny rap on the door signaled the return of the butler, and we fell silent while the tea tray was settled on the edge of the desk nearest to me. Once the door had closed behind the servant, I reached forward to pour the fragrant brew.

"Then maybe we should approach this from a different angle," I said while I added the cream and sugar the earl had requested to his cup. "Is there any way someone could benefit from the theft of the earl's body?"

The earl's brow dipped low again as he accepted his cup. "How would someone benefit from it?"

"I don't know," I admitted. "It was simply a thought. If your uncle's body was targeted specifically, then maybe the motivation was not revenge, but an attempt to gain something?" I finished uncertainly. That was the problem with this entire matter. It didn't feel like we could be certain of any aspect of it.

I handed Trevor his tea, prepared how I knew he liked it, and both men sat back to think while I poured my cup.

"Were you able to find a list of everything that was buried with your uncle's body?" my brother asked, reminding me I had failed to question the servants on that matter.

"No, I didn't. But I will keep looking." He lifted the edge of a stack of papers on his desk to look under it and then set it back down. "If nothing else, it may be noted in one of the ledgers."

Trevor nodded, clearly understanding the earl's line of thinking. "If all else fails, follow the money."

The earl took another sip of his tea and then his eyes widened. "I've just recalled. I did have a gentleman from Edinburgh visit me maybe three, no, four months ago. Perhaps it's unrelated but . . . he was curious to know whether a certain item had been buried with my uncle."

I sat forward. "What item?"

"It was a gold torc. Like the type of necklaces the Celts used to wear. Apparently, his family had discovered it on their estate and his aunt donated it to the Society of Antiquaries of Scotland. My uncle was a founding member."

"And this man thought your uncle had the torc?"

"Yes. He was quite agitated. He claimed the torc was supposed to be part of the society's collection, but it was missing. He accused my uncle of accepting the donation under false pretenses and then stealing it for himself."

I glanced at Trevor in surprise. "That's quite a serious charge."

"Yes. And completely unfounded," Lord Buchan replied in indignation. "My uncle would never do such a thing. In any case, I would clearly recall if he'd been buried wearing a torc around his neck."

I stared down at my cup of cooling tea. "What if he was wearing it under his clothing?"

The earl opened his mouth to hotly deny the possibility, but then he stopped. His mouth slowly closed as he brooded over the thought. "I don't deny that my uncle was quite eccentric," he answered carefully. "Or that the idea of being buried in a torc might have appealed to him. They were worn by the Celts as a sign of nobility and royalty, were they not?" He looked to us to confirm. "But I balk at the idea that he would have stolen one to do so."

"What if this man was mistaken? What if your uncle purchased the torc?"

"Well, I suppose that's possible," Lord Buchan admitted. "But as I said, he wasn't buried in it. You can be certain that if my uncle was buried wearing a torc, he would have wanted it to be seen, not hidden away underneath a shirt and cravat."

I couldn't argue with his assessment of the man. I had not known the late earl, but if he was as vain and self-important as he was portrayed, then his nephew's opinion was undoubtedly correct.

"The man who asked about the torc. What was his name? Do you recall?"

"Lewis Collingwood," he declared, lifting his chin into the air. "I remember because I went to school with a Collingwood, and a more disagreeable man you will never meet." He sniffed. "It must run in the family."

"I wonder if I sent a message to Gage asking him to track down Lewis Collingwood whether he would receive it before he left Edinburgh," I pondered aloud as our feet crunched down the gravel drive leading toward our carriage.

"Probably not," Trevor replied.

I tilted my head in thought. "I suppose I could ask Philip to locate Collingwood, but I do hate to bother him with our sister in such a delicate state. I know she's doing well, and the baby isn't due for another three months, but she's not to have any excitement, and I doubt Philip could keep my request from her." I turned to smile at our brother. "You know how Alana can be."

"I do." He looked up, squinting into the sun. "She takes an inordinate amount of interest in everything her younger siblings do."

"Yes." But my amusement fled as I began to wonder just what our sister had written to Trevor about me. And Gage. I peered up at my brother out of the corner of my eye. I had seen the letters she had posted to him. They were always folded together with mine, and she never failed to ask after Trevor in her missives to me, and speculate on some aspect of his life, whether it was the estate or his need to find a wife. What information, other than their shared concern over my grief, had she been sharing with him about me?

"It must be killing her that she's in Edinburgh while we're both down here at Blakelaw." A self-satisfied smirk stretched the corners of his lips. "But write to Philip anyway. She'll discover you've got yourself embroiled in another inquiry sooner or later. It may as well be from you."

"True. And we do need to find out what we can about this Mr. Collingwood. At this point, he's our most viable suspect."

"Then, write on, dear sister," he teased as he opened the carriage door for me. "I'll enclose it with the letter I have ready to send to Philip. Who knows? Maybe he can convince her it's filled with nothing more than my boring estate business."

I arched my brows, letting him know just how successful I thought that would be, and he laughed.

# CHAPTER SIX

The church bells rang out crisp and clear in the chilly morning air. So loud, in fact, that I grimaced at the sound of their bright ting as Trevor and I passed through the doors and out onto St. Cuthbert's front steps. I shielded my eyes against the sudden glare of the sun and rubbed my temples against the headache that had been building all morning.

Upon our return to Blakelaw House late the previous afternoon, I had spent the remainder of the evening searching our library for any mention of uses of human bone, be it superstitious or more practical, but had little luck. I knew that the ground-up remains of Egyptian mummies had been used in some paint pigments as early as the sixteenth century, but I had never heard of more modern human bodies being used in that manner. I didn't think it was possible. The body composition would not be the same.

In any case, I had not fallen asleep until just before dawn, and when my new maid, Bree, had woken me for church, I had been tempted to remain abed. But then I realized that if I missed Sunday service, the next week would be filled with visits from well-meaning villagers, worried about my health or curious what had kept me from church. After all, we were the highest-ranking family in Elwick, so our comings and goings seemed to naturally concern those around us, whether I wished it to be so or not.

I greeted Vicar Grey, who was a gentle, mild-mannered man, barely older than Trevor and me, and a recent addition to the parish. Trevor spoke highly of him, and said that his energy and eagerness to help had done much good for the tiny community. For my own part, the attribute I appreciated most in the vicar was his temperance. Too many people had rushed to judge me since the scandal over my involvement with my late husband's work broke in London nearly two years prior, including clergymen. So I did not fail to value those who would not be swayed by the gossip.

He asked whether I had enjoyed my aunt and uncle's Hogmanay Ball and then turned to speak to Trevor about some local matter. I nodded to Mrs. Heron as I crossed the churchyard toward the cemetery, distancing myself from the building and its parishioners. I was grateful for the warmth of my fur-lined winter cloak, but even so, the bitter wind sliced through me. Somehow it seemed fitting to my mood.

I paused at the gate and glanced behind me at the solid block of rough-hewn stone that was St. Cuthbert's. I knew if I truly wanted to be left alone, I would need to venture into the graveyard. The villagers would assume I was visiting my parents' graves and leave me to my solitude. But still I hesitated. I supposed after the disturbance at the Dryburgh Abbey cemetery two nights prior, I was a bit wary.

However, when out of the corner of my eye I caught sight of Mrs. Stamper, a notorious busybody, moving toward me, I knew that word of the disturbance at my aunt and uncle's Hogmanay party had spread. Having no desire to rehash the event with her, I opened the gate and slipped inside the graveyard.

The ground was still soft from the recent rains. I nestled deeper in my cloak and picked my way carefully around the graves toward the tall oak under which my parents rested, side by side. I huddled close to the tree, using to it block some of the wind, and stared down at my mother's gravestone. It was rather simple, by most nobility's standards, but lovingly rendered with flowers and vines. Father's was plainer still, but it suited him.

I tilted my head back against the tree bark to look up through the oak's barren branches at the winter blue sky. Clouds raced across its expanse, driven hard by the blustery wind. It was not a bad place to spend one's eternal rest, with the flat stretch of fields to the south, and the curve of the River Tweed to the north. There would be the sound of church bells and singing, of farmers toiling in the fields, and children playing in the river to mark the seasons.

I knew Father and Mother had both loved Elwick, and Trevor showed every sign of following in their footsteps. But, of course, he owned Blakelaw House, so his home was here. I, on the other hand, felt as adrift as ever.

I had left my sister's household because I knew I couldn't stay there indefinitely. It was true, I had needed to get out of Edinburgh and find a place to heal after Will's death, but I had also been escaping a situation I knew no longer suited me. Alana had her own family. She didn't need me constantly underfoot, no matter her protests to the contrary.

So I had come to Blakelaw House. But I knew my childhood home was not the place for me either. Trevor had welcomed me with open arms, and shown me every consideration. I knew he was grateful for the companionship, no matter how poor my company had been in the past seven weeks. But I could not settle here—there was a restlessness in my spirit—and I suspected that once this investigation was concluded, it would be time to move on. Whatever healing I had been looking for, I had not found it at Blakelaw.

I would return to Edinburgh to help my sister with the birth of her fourth child in a few months' time, but once she was safely delivered, I knew I couldn't remain. Where I would go was still a mystery to me, but I felt the surety of the decision in the depth of my bones. I had three or four months to decide what to do. Perhaps I would know by then.

Sir Anthony had left me almost nothing. Even the dowry I had brought to the marriage had been spent. I had the proceeds from the sales of my artwork, done mostly under an assumed name, so I was not without means, modest as they were. I could live comfortably on my own if I was careful with my money.

I rarely played the game of "what if." It was futile. But standing before my mother's grave, I couldn't seem to help but do so. I wondered what my life would have been like had she lived. Would I still have married Sir Anthony, or would my mother have seen the truth about him that my father and I had missed? Maybe she would have insisted I have my London season rather than allow my father to arrange my marriage as I'd requested, too consumed with my art to be bothered to meet eligible gentlemen.

For all of my father's properness, my mother had been the one who most easily related to people of all classes, high and low. She had been the one to force my head out of my sketchbooks, to make me accompany her on calls so that I might learn to socialize, to insist I take better care with my appearance when I would have been happy to go about covered in charcoal dust. At the time, I had disliked her meddling, but now I could see the truth for what it was. Left to my own devices, as my father had done upon her death, I retreated into the safety of my art. It was satisfying to paint such skilled portraits, but it was also a rather lonely existence. I observed others and captured them on canvas, but I rarely interacted with them in any meaningful way.

I thought that was what I wanted. But now I wasn't so sure. And maybe my mother had seen the truth of that long before the rest of us.

The sound of approaching footsteps alerted me to my brother's presence, for I knew no one else would disturb me here. I didn't look up as he came to stand beside me, his hands clasped behind his back. I wasn't sure what he would see reflected in my eyes, so I kept them trained on my mother's gravestone, lest he read too many of my thoughts.

"I miss them," he surprised me by admitting. "Mother's been gone almost seventeen years, and Father for just three, but I still miss them both." He huffed a laugh. "Whenever

I enter the study, I still expect Father to be seated behind his desk working."

I smiled in response and said quietly, "I thought the same thing when I first returned."

Trevor nodded. "Sometimes I catch myself thinking about some bit of estate business I want to ask him about, and then I realize . . . I can't."

I shifted closer, linking my arm with his.

We stood there silently staring at our parents' graves while the others filed out of the churchyard behind us. The howl of the wind blocked most of the noise of the voices and the crunch of the gravel from the departing carriages. I knew our servants would be waiting to depart, but still I was reluctant to leave.

And then Trevor spoke.

"You always go to Mother's grave." Our eyes met for the first time since he'd joined me, and I frowned. "When you come here," he clarified. "You always go to Mother's grave. You seem to barely be able to look at Father's."

"Don't be silly," I scoffed uncomfortably. "Mother's is just closer to the tree, and thus out of the wind."

"But it's not always windy when you visit here."

"True. And I stand before Father's grave then."

"But you don't." His voice was gentle, but certain.

I scowled, angry that he had even taken note of this. "What does it matter whose grave I stand before or . . . or look at? I'm visiting them both."

"Kiera. You have every right to be angry at Father for arranging your marriage to Sir Anthony. But you need to let it be."

"What are you talking about? I'm not angry," I snapped, backing away from him. I hated the tone of voice he was using on me, as if I were a child he wished to soothe.

"Then why won't you look at his grave?"

"I do! I am!" I turned to stare pointedly at his gravestone and then back to Trevor. "See!"

He reached out to take my arm, but I backed away. "Kiera, I'm sorry Sir Anthony was so brutal to you. If I could . . ."

"No!" I said, holding up a hand to stop him. "No! We are not discussing this." My mouth tasted sour, as if I was going to be sick.

"But, Kiera . . ." he pleaded.

"No! You do not get to foist this upon me." I pushed past him, hurrying across the graveyard toward the gate.

"You're right," he relented, catching up with me. "You're right. That was badly done of me."

I wrapped my arms tighter around myself, trying to stop the quaking his accusation had started inside me, making me confront things I didn't want to face. Why had Trevor used the word "brutal" to describe my late husband? I thought I had hidden the worst from him, but maybe he knew more than I realized.

I breathed in deep, trying to push the image that was forming from my mind.

"Kiera. Kiera!" My brother grabbed my arm, forcing me to come to a stop. He looked down at me, reading the naked emotion in my eyes, for I was too shaken to hide it properly. "I apologize for upsetting you. But at some point, we do need to talk about this."

I shook my head, but he insisted.

"Well, maybe *you* don't, but *I* do."

I blinked up at him in surprise, seeing for the first time the pain in the depths of his gaze. I swallowed hard at the sight, not having realized that as much as I was hiding things from him, he was also hiding things from me.

"Trevor," I began, but a movement behind him drew my attention. My brother turned to see what I was looking at.

"Is all well?" Vicar Grey asked, offering us a worried smile as he opened the cemetery gate.

I looked away, trying to compose myself while Trevor assured him everything was fine. He said that the anniversary of our mother's death was soon, and it was always a difficult time. The vicar accepted the excuse readily, but I could feel his concerned gaze still trained on me even as I climbed into our carriage.

The conservatory at Blakelaw House projected out from the northwest corner of the manor toward the River Tweed, so that the ceiling, and the east, north, and west walls were all covered in glass. On sunny days like this one, it was often the warmest room in the house, even in the dead of winter. And the perfect location for my art studio.

Upon my return to my childhood home seven weeks ago, I had reclaimed the farthest corner of the conservatory as my art studio. I had spent a week shifting and adjusting things just so, and another preparing canvases and pigments, but truly I'd been stalling for time, hoping my desire to paint would return. It seemed I'd been finding one way or another to stall ever since. The days I did manage to put brush to canvas usually ended with a terrible headache and a gnawing pain in my gut, if not an outright temper tantrum.

I so desperately wanted to recapture my ability, my passion for painting, and I hated myself for losing control of my emotions when things did not go my way. But most of all, I lived in fear and dread that my talent wouldn't return, that it had deserted me forever. My entire life, since the moment I discovered I could copy the people around me on paper, had been devoted to this one pursuit. If it had deserted me, like my mother, like Will, then I didn't know what I was going to do.

I stood at the edge of my studio space, with the late afternoon sun shining brightly down on it, and delayed again. I could turn around and go find something else to occupy my time—play the pianoforte or my viola, or answer my correspondence. Avoid the confrontation and the prospect of my failure another day. Or I could force my feet forward, don my apron, and mix my paints.

I breathed in deep, the gentle scents of the plants and flowers behind me competing with the sharp odors of turpentine, gesso, and linseed oil in my studio. I felt queasy at the prospect of picking up a paintbrush, but my brother's words kept ringing in my ear. I could hear the concern, the confusion. The accusation. There was no choice. I had to find my way past this. And if that meant painting until the muscles in my fingers would no longer grip a brush, practicing over and over again every skill I'd ever learned, then so be it.

I forced my body forward, breathing through the swell of nausea as I slipped my apron over my head and tied the strings behind me. After securing the kerchief I used to protect my hair, I flipped back the covering over the canvas on my easel and smiled in reluctant agreement. Trevor was right. This landscape was worse than the one hanging in Uncle Andrew's receiving room.

I lifted it from the easel and moved toward the corner to prop it against the wall out of the sun. Why I took such care to preserve its color, I'm not sure, except out of habit. I chose another canvas instead, this one a portrait I had begun a few weeks prior of the cook's granddaughter. The rudiments were there, the basic outline. Now I simply needed to fill in the details, I told myself. Nothing to be concerned with. I'd done this hundreds of times before.

I was bent over mixing the paints I would need for the little girl's dress when I felt a now familiar brush against my legs.

"There you are," I said, acknowledging the gray tabby. "I wondered when you would turn up."

He purred as he rubbed his body against my ankle one more time before crossing the room to what had become his usual spot in the corner of the wicker settee at the edge of my studio space. He hopped up and circled twice before settling in the bed of blankets I had given him during one of my more fanciful moods. After dark it grew cold in the conservatory, and I'd worried that on the nights he failed to find his way into my bedchamber, he would be chilled. It was silly really. The house cat was one of our mousers, and was supposed to stay belowstairs with his other mouse-hunting compatriots. But he was a sly one. It didn't matter how many times he was banished to the kitchens, he still found his way back upstairs, and attached to my side.

I didn't know why. I hadn't been the most welcoming of humans when he first turned up in my studio during the week I returned to Blakelaw House. I'd never had a pet. And though I didn't dislike animals, I wasn't particularly fond of them either. I appreciated them more for their usefulness—like the horses we rode, or my brother-in-law's two greyhounds he used to hunt, or the mouser cats in our kitchen—than for their companionship.

But the tabby hadn't seemed to mind my surly disposition, and simply ignored my attempts to banish him. He didn't even seem to mind my temper tantrums. So I let him be. He rarely got in the way. And, I had to admit, I sort of enjoyed his silent company. It did make the day and the night a little less lonely.

I smiled at the mouser, who watched me with his golden eyes. I could have sworn he wore a satisfied smirk.

I lifted my palette and approached the canvas. Then after dipping my brush in the Prussian blue, I took a deep calming breath, and carefully began to apply the color as the base to the folds of the little girl's dress.

I worked quietly that way for some time, conscious of every nuance of my brushstrokes. I couldn't seem to help myself from keeping tally of every stroke I got right, and every time my touch had been too heavy or too light, the wrong angle, the wrong depth of pigment. In the past when I painted portraits, I simply lost myself in the process, reveling in the beauty of each touch, each layer, each bit of shading as the subject's image began to take shape, to unfold before my eyes. I was barely conscious of each step, knowing instinctively from many years of practice exactly what to do.

But now I could not block out these intrusive thoughts. I could not find that space I went to inside myself, the place I so desperately wanted to locate again. I felt barraged with doubts, and the internal tally of things I'd done wrong versus things I'd done right seemed to be tipping heavily to the negative. I tried to forget that, to ignore it. Yet it was ever at the back of my mind, nagging me, driving me to make the next brushstroke perfect. But it so rarely was.

And then my hand began to shake, and no matter how many deep breaths I took, I could not force it to stop. My fingers quavered, smudging a fold of the little girl's skirt, and I snapped.

I tossed the palette and the brush down on my worktable with a cry of frustrated disgust. Breathing heavily, I planted my hands on my hips, trying to control the urge I felt to lash out at the offending canvas. It was either that or I would begin to cry.

Then I heard a footstep shift behind me and a deep voice tsked. "Temper, temper."

I gasped and whirled around to find Sebastian Gage standing there, looking as handsome as ever.

## CHAPTER SEVEN

"What are you doing here?" I demanded in shock when I could find my voice.

He arched a single eyebrow and crossed the remaining distance between us. "You wrote to me and asked me to come."

"Yes, I know," I stammered, wiping my paint-smeared hands on my apron. "But what are you doing *here*? That is to say . . . my studio."

His winter blue eyes twinkled, and the corner of his lips quirked into a crooked grin, telling me he was enjoying my flustered state.

"I . . . I wasn't expecting you yet."

"I beg your pardon, my lady," Crabtree, my brother's butler, wheezed, hurrying across the conservatory. "I would have announced Mr. Gage, but the gentleman simply would not wait." He glared at Gage's back.

"It's all right," I told Crabtree, arching my eyebrows at Gage in gentle reproach. "Mr. Gage often doesn't stand on ceremony."

Gage grinned at me unrepentantly.

"Please tell my brother our guest has arrived when he returns from his business."

Crabtree nodded and retreated, disappearing behind a stand of ferns.

Gage stood watching me with his hands clasped behind

his back and that gleam still in his eyes. He looked very well in his riding attire—the navy blue coat and tight buff pantaloons. His golden hair was ruffled from the wind, and his boots were still covered with the dust of the road, making me suspect he'd ridden here on horseback.

"I suppose I should offer you tea and a chance to freshen up." I glanced about me. "But I'm afraid my art studio is not exactly the ideal place for such a thing." I brushed a hand down the sides of my drab brown kerseymere gown where it showed at the edges of the apron. "Had I known you would arrive so soon, I would have been better ready to receive you."

Gage's smile softened at my fidgeting and he stepped closer, crowding into my space. "You look charming."

"I . . . I do?"

"Yes."

I felt my cheeks begin to flush with color under his regard, but I couldn't stop it. Nor could I look away. I knew I had missed him, but I hadn't really let myself admit that until now. It had somehow been easier to deny it than acknowledge that I longed to see his face. He'd distanced himself from me twice now, though, admittedly, the second time had been as much my doing as his. There was still so much I didn't know about him, so much I didn't understand. It had seemed foolhardy to long for him, and yet I had. I could feel the truth of that now in the racing of my heart and the ridiculous urge to giggle.

He reached up to touch my face, and for a moment I thought he was going to kiss me, but his callused thumb rubbed along my jawline instead. "You have a little something . . ."

"Oh," I gasped and used my fingers to swipe at the offending dab of paint myself.

He smiled at my embarrassment and then glanced down at our feet, where the cat was winding its way around his legs. "And who is this?"

"That's Earl Grey," I answered absently as I yanked the

kerchief from my head, having forgotten it was there, and tried to smooth my unruly hair back from my forehead.

Gage laughed. "You named your cat after the Prime Minister?"

I turned to see he had squatted down to scratch behind the cat's ears, who was lapping up the attention.

"He's not my cat," I protested. "He's just a mouser from the kitchen."

"And yet you named him."

I frowned. "Well, he wouldn't stop pestering me, and eventually I decided I had to call him something. He's a gray tabby and quite imperious." I shrugged. "The name seemed to fit him."

Gage rose to his feet, shaking his head as he smiled a rather secretive little smile.

"What?" I demanded as I paused in untying my apron strings.

"You."

I furrowed my brow in confusion. "Me, what?"

He just shook his head.

I studied his features a moment longer, still trying to understand, and then turned away to drape my apron over an empty easel. When I turned back, he had paced across the room toward the windows, taking in the details of my space. Earl Grey had returned to his pile of blankets.

"My uncle's rider must have made excellent time in reaching you for you to arrive so soon," I commented, still a bit stunned to find Gage in my childhood home.

He glanced back over his shoulder. "I thought there was some urgency."

"Well, yes, of course. I only meant that the fastest I'd hoped for you to arrive, after putting all your things in order in Edinburgh, was tomorrow."

He picked up a jar of pigment to examine it. "I was preparing to leave for London. So my preparations for travel had already been made."

"Oh, London," I remarked in some surprise, a knot forming in my stomach. "Are we keeping you from—"

"No, no," he replied quickly. "Just a small matter I needed to see to. It can wait."

I watched as he continued to study my shelves of pigments, feeling sure he wasn't telling me something. "You're certain?"

"Yes." He glanced up then and must have sensed my suspicion, for he offered me a sheepish smile. "It concerns a matter on which my father and I disagree. And my letters don't seem to be swaying him."

I nodded, knowing relations between Gage and his father were often tense. "Does he still wish you to return to London?"

"That's part of it."

I waited for Gage to say more, but he seemed determined not to, so I didn't press him. I had never met Captain Lord Gage, so I wasn't certain exactly what type of personality we were dealing with. But knowing his son, and from the things I'd heard about him, I could only guess that Lord Gage was a formidable man used to getting his own way. Gage seemed tired of living by his dictates and under his shadow.

"Shall I show you to your room, or would you prefer tea first?" I asked, recalling my duties as hostess.

He crossed the room to rejoin me. "I'm afraid I rode on ahead of my carriage carrying my valet and my luggage, and I doubt they've arrived yet. So I hope you'll forgive my bedraggled appearance a little while longer."

He flashed me one of his charming smiles and I arched my eyebrows in reply. He hardly looked bedraggled, and he knew it. I suspected covered in mud he would still look devastatingly attractive. But I was not about to pay him the compliment he was fishing for.

"Tea, then," I replied.

"Kiera," my brother called, emerging from behind the ferns that shielded the door from my view. "Crabtree told me Mr. Gage has arrived." His gaze locked on the man in question over my shoulder and his posture stiffened slightly.

"Yes," I said turning so that I could see both men. "Mr. Gage, allow me to introduce my brother, Trevor St. Mawr."

Gage's relaxed charm was as evident as ever when he shook hands with Trevor, but I could tell he'd noticed my brother's slight shift in bearing. It was there in the watchfulness in Gage's eyes. He had also armored himself, though in subtler manner, one I doubted many others could detect, but it was hovering in the air about them.

I eyed both men with some misgiving, hoping they weren't about to begin posturing. I should like them to be friends. Perhaps they simply needed to size each other up without my being in the way.

"Trevor, will you escort Mr. Gage to the drawing room while I finish cleaning things here. And have tea brought up."

I didn't miss the way Trevor's gaze darted over the portrait on the easel and the mess I'd made on the table, not seeming to miss a detail.

"Of course," he replied, leading him away.

I cleaned my brushes and palette, and wiped up the paint as best I could, but as the table was already splattered with odd bits of color here and there it didn't much matter. Then I dashed into the washroom to scrub at my hands and check my face for any stray splotches of paint. I repinned my hair and studied my appearance in the mirror, wondering if it would seem odd if I ran upstairs to change gowns. I decided against it, as too much time had already passed, and who knew where the discussion would wander if I left Trevor and Gage together alone for too long.

Fortunately, I found both men seated across from each other conversing congenially. I smiled in relief and noticed the tea things were already there, but they had waited for me to pour.

It wasn't until I crossed the room that I realized what subtle, but clever battle lines they had drawn. Each man sat on a settee, Trevor on the sage green damask and Gage on the cream and gold toile, with the tea table positioned between them. No other chairs were drawn close enough to the table to reach the tea things, so they would force me to choose. Would I sit next to my brother or the man with whom my relationship was undefined?

A less observant person might have thought nothing of the arrangement, but I knew better. I could see the way their eyes cut to one another, the twitch of their fingers on the arm of the settee, especially Trevor's, who was far less skilled at subterfuge than Gage.

I slowed my steps, dismayed and then frustrated that they should do this to me. I could not choose without upsetting someone. It was impossible.

I could feel my smile tightening on my face as the choice was upon me. So I selected the man who had least offended, settling beside Gage on the cream and gold toile. I glared at Trevor over the tea set. Gage was a guest in our home. My brother should know better than to try to discomfort him.

I'm certain Trevor knew what my glare meant, but far from being chastened, he scowled right back. I resisted the urge to roll my eyes, and I set about preparing everyone's tea.

Once we had each settled back with our cups of tea and the little lemon cakes our cook prepared that I so adored, Gage introduced the topic for which he'd been summoned to Blakelaw House. I filled him in on the details we'd gathered so far concerning Dodd's murder, and the theft of the eleventh Earl of Buchan's bones. Gage listened thoughtfully, asking the occasional question, but mostly just absorbed the information I related. The data I imparted about Lewis Collingwood and his interest in the late earl's burial seemed to intrigue him particularly.

"Though," he puzzled, leaning his fair head back against the settee, "if the grave robbers had only wanted the torc, why would they also go to the trouble to steal the rest of the body?"

"I wondered the same thing," I admitted. "But what if

they took the bones to distract us from the fact that they took the torc?"

A slow smile curled his lips. "Devious."

I couldn't help but smile in return. "Yes."

Trevor leaned forward to take another cake from the tea tray. "But all of that hinges on the assumption that the torc was buried with the earl, and so far we have no proof of that." He arched his eyebrows to make his point and then popped the cake in his mouth.

"Well, our best bet for discovering the truth about that is to speak with Mrs. Moffat in St. Boswells. She prepared the earl's body for burial."

"Then we shall have to pay her a visit tomorrow." Gage lifted his head, sitting up straighter in his seat, and crossed one booted foot over his knee. "Now," he declared, eyeing us both closely. "I'm afraid there's something I must tell you that may have bearing on this investigation."

I shared a look of astonishment with Trevor and then leaned forward from my corner of the settee toward Gage. "What do you mean? You've uncovered something already?"

He tapped his fingers against the leather of his boot. "Indirectly. It relates to another inquiry I conducted recently. One that is disturbingly similar."

"How so?"

"It was another body snatching. This one of a grave that was over eleven years old."

"So nothing but bones," I clarified. "And the deceased's effects? They were left behind?"

"Yes. The same circumstances. Except . . ." He paused, glancing at both of us again.

I strained even closer, curious what he would say.

"About a week after the theft . . . the family received a ransom note."

# CHAPTER EIGHT

"A ransom note?" I gasped in disbelief. "For a corpse?" Gage nodded. "Yes. Very odd."

I sat back, slightly stunned, and then amazed as the possibilities began running through my head. "And fiendishly clever." The gleam in Gage's eyes told me he had also considered the implications.

"What do you mean?" Trevor demanded, frowning in confusion.

"I take it the family of this other victim is wealthy?" I asked Gage, just to be certain that my speculation lined up with the facts.

"Very."

"Body snatchers can't earn more than maybe a dozen guineas per corpse," I explained to my brother. "And now that the public is aware of their actions and has tightened security at the graveyards in and around Edinburgh and London and the other medical schools, setting watches and using mortsafes and such, it's much more difficult for them to steal bodies without being caught. Especially since Burke and Hare's trial two years ago." The actions of those men were still fresh in the minds of everyone in Edinburgh, particularly the poor, who rightly believed they were more susceptible to similar such schemes.

Rather than risk being caught while performing the difficult labor of disinterring bodies from the heavily guarded local graveyards, Burke and Hare had begun inviting victims to their lodging house, plying them with alcohol, and smothering them to death. They then sold the bodies to the Surgeons' Hall at the Royal College of Surgeons of Edinburgh, hoping the anatomists would not recognize the bodies they were dissecting as missing persons. There was some speculation that the surgeons had known what Burke and Hare were really doing, but it could never be proven. In any case, Burke and Hare were finally caught in November 1828, but not before they'd murdered sixteen people.

That Sir Anthony's death and the revelation of my involvement with his work had occurred less than six months after Burke and Hare's trial had only added fuel to the fire of my scandal. The shock of the discovery of a gently bred female participating in such a gruesome undertaking as human dissection appealed to the morbid fascination of the citizens of London, making it all too easy for vicious rumors about me to begin circulating. I had never prowled the streets, luring unsuspecting young gentlemen to their deaths, or dined on their choicest organs. I was no cannibal, nor did I have anything to do with the procurement of my late husband's dissection subjects. I merely sketched what he told me to. But the truth did not matter to the public, and soon they were whipped up into such a panic that there was nothing for me to do but leave the city. It simply wasn't safe for me or my family to stay.

I still felt bitter that no one had considered my feelings in the matter. Everyone had jumped to the conclusion that I had wished to assist with Sir Anthony's work, when the truth was that I had been forced to do so. I'd had no desire to take part in the grisly business, and for three years I'd suffered in silence. I'd made the best of it—I'd had no other choice—learning from my late husband's pompous tutelage, as he still continued to lecture as if speaking to an entire medical theater full of students rather than an audience of one. When Sir Anthony had died, any tears that had stung my eyes had been in relief, not grief, though of course, I'd never let them fall. I couldn't. Not then.

I shook away the memory, hoping Gage and Trevor hadn't noticed how downtrodden my thoughts had become.

"But older bodies would not have been guarded. Just as Lord Buchan's wasn't. Everyone believes they're safe from any criminals," Trevor guessed, beginning to understand what Gage and I had already realized.

"Yes," I replied. "Think how much more money they could earn ransoming a body back to wealthy relatives. So much less effort and risk, and such a greater reward."

"I doubt the laws against kidnapping contain any mention of corpses," Gage added with an ironic lift to his brow.

"Or would the corpse, the bones, be considered stolen property?" my brother pointed out.

Gage nodded his head to concede Trevor's point. "An interesting conundrum."

"Do you mind telling us whose body was stolen . . . kidnapped . . . whichever it is?" I asked Gage.

"Sir Colum Casselbeck. I was asked to investigate by his son, Sir Robert. Sir Colum's body was taken from the graveyard at their parish church in Musselburgh."

"That's east of Edinburgh, near the sea, isn't it?"

"Yes." He frowned down at his boot where it rested against his knee. His hand flexed where it gripped his ankle. "I'm afraid I wasn't much help. I was asked to investigate just a few days before the ransom note arrived. I wasn't able to uncover anything of use, so we decided to follow the ransom note's instructions and try to catch them that way." He looked up at me and I could tell he was angered by whatever had happened. "But they were clever. Fiendishly. Isn't that the word you used?"

I nodded.

"They directed us to put the money in a bag wrapped in sealskin and place it in a tiny rowboat that we were to set adrift where the River Esk meets the North Sea in the Firth of Forth at a specific time. We couldn't follow it by boat, not too closely, or we knew they would never attempt to retrieve the money. So we positioned men along the shore of the headland to watch, and tried to keep the rowboat in our sights from a fishing boat we had taken out into the firth. But the day was already misty and rainy, and as the afternoon progressed, it only grew worse. Soon we couldn't see farther than a few hundred feet in the fog, and the visibility for the men on land was even worse. Our boat captain said we had to turn back or we risked running into serious trouble ourselves.

"At first I wondered if the little rowboat had been lost to us all. But then, two days later, Sir Colum's bones were found in a bag in a pew in their parish church, just as the thieves promised." He shook his head. "They must have known what the weather was like on that part of the coast, and where the sea currents usually ran. That's the only way I can figure they would take such a risk collecting the ransom in that manner."

I leaned forward and began setting our teacups and saucers back on the tray. "I assume you're thinking what I'm thinking. That somehow these two robberies might be connected?"

"If it's worked once, why wouldn't they try it again?"

Trevor handed me his cup and saucer. "I suppose we'll know for sure if Buchan receives a ransom note."

"But . . ." I paused, staring at the delicate, china teapot. "What of Dodd?" I glanced at Gage. "I suppose no one was hurt when they robbed Sir Colum's grave?"

"No," he admitted. "But maybe they weren't interrupted."

"So Dodd truly was just in the wrong place at the wrong time," I murmured, thinking of Willie, of the guilt he clearly felt for not accompanying his mentor.

"That would be my theory. That is, if the same group of men perpetrated both body snatchings."

"So if the criminals are the same," I mused, sitting back against the settee, "how are they choosing their victims? Do the late Earl of Buchan and Sir Colum have anything in common?"

Gage pivoted so that he could see me more fully, draping his arm across the back of the settee. "I don't know. But I did wonder about this Society of Antiquaries you mentioned. You said Collingwood's torc was supposedly donated to the group, and that Lord Buchan was a founding member."

I nodded in confirmation.

"I wonder if Sir Colum was also a member."

"It's as good a place as any to start. And we can ask the current Lord Buchan whether he knows when we visit him tomorrow. I thought you would wish to see the disturbed grave and the spot where Dodd was killed as early as possible."

"I would." He glanced at Trevor and then back to me. "I also want to write to a friend of mine in Edinburgh. He's a sergeant in their new police force, and I'm curious whether he can tell me if there have been any other similar grave robberies."

"You think there might be more?" I asked in surprise.

"Maybe. There's no reason to think that Sir Colum was the first. And if there have been more, then that gives us a wider circle to search for clues and connections. These body snatchers have to be choosing their victims somehow, even if their motive is only greed."

"It's often as good a reason as any," Trevor remarked.

I noticed he was more relaxed than when our conversation had first begun. I hoped that meant he was finished antagonizing Gage, and that whatever had troubled him about our guest had been put aside. I knew my brother viewed himself as my protector, but if that was the way he intended to exert his role, then I planned to protest. Surely he knew that our brother-in-law, Philip, considered Gage a friend, and normally Trevor trusted Philip's judgment.

But I also knew that our sister, Alana, had been writing

to him, and I had to wonder once again just what she had told him about the relationship between Gage and me. Which called into question how much Alana actually knew. For instance, did she realize that Gage had visited me in my bedchamber both at Gairloch Castle and Dalmay House, innocent as it had been? Did she know we had kissed? Several times, in fact. I had told her nothing of these things, but my sister was nothing if not resourceful, and disturbingly accurate at reading my expression. With the way he'd acted upon Gage's arrival, I was only too grateful that Trevor was out of practice with that skill.

Crabtree knocked on the drawing room door to inform us that Gage's valet and his luggage had arrived.

"Then please show Mr. Gage up to the Evergreen Room," I told him, rising to my feet with Gage.

"Wouldn't he be more comfortable in the Sunset Suite?" Trevor interrupted.

I turned to my brother in surprise. "Grandmama's old room?"

Trevor cleared his throat. "Er . . . yes."

I arched a single eyebrow at him in chastisement. That room was frosted in ivory and lace, with ribbons and furbelows to match, and well he knew it.

"No, the Evergreen Room will do nicely," I informed Crabtree.

Our stoic butler nodded and led Gage from the room.

"Is that really appropriate?" Trevor hissed.

"What do you mean? Your old bedchamber is really our only bachelor quarters. Unless you want to give up the master bedchamber? But won't that be a little awkward?"

Trevor scowled at me. "We still have Alana's chamber . . ."

"It's pink," I snapped, before he could add to that ludicrous statement. "Trevor, what is going on? Why are you acting this way?" He turned his head aside, but I continued on, wanting an answer. "And why do you care which bedchamber he sleeps in? He'll be at the opposite end of the house from you, if that's what bothers you, across the hall from . . . Ohhh," I groaned in annoyance. "Is that why? Because he'll be across the hall from me?"

His gaze was sharp and angry. "Kiera, I've spent time in London. I know Mr. Gage's reputation. He's a rake."

I rolled my eyes and turned away. "He's not a rake."

"Kiera, as a man, I think I know just a little bit more about these things than you do," he declared, following me across the room.

"Then you realize that some people's reputations are unearned. That rumors are often false," I shot back at him. After everything I'd been through, the scandal and the name-calling, I'd thought my brother would have learned to be a little slower to rush to judgment.

I saw that he knew what I was referring to, but far from being chastened, his mouth set into even more mulish lines. "He has a history of dawdling with widows."

"And so, because I'm a widow, you think he wishes to dawdle with me?"

"I know he does."

I had opened my mouth to respond, but the certainty in my brother's voice startled me into silence.

"I see the way he looks at you," he persisted. "And it's not innocent."

I felt a blush beginning to burn its way up into my cheeks, and hated that betrayal of my reaction to such a statement. "Gage has behaved nothing but honorably toward me."

Trevor's eyes searched my own, the bright lapis lazuli color softening to a more muted hue. "That doesn't mean I have to trust him."

"Trevor!" I protested.

"No, Kiera," he told me gently. "You may believe his intentions are good, but I have the right to withhold my confidence until he's proven it to me." He reached up to chuck me playfully under the chin, a gesture I'd hated as a child, but now accepted as the endearment it was. "I'm your brother. If I don't look out for you, who will?"

I sighed and reluctantly nodded. I knew he was right. I couldn't force him to trust Gage, not when it had also taken me some time and persuasion to do so myself. Gage was not one for confidences, and he preferred to charm people and fool them into thinking they were close, when in actuality he'd shared next to nothing of his real self. He'd slowly begun to let me in, and as relieved and flattered as I was by that, I was also frustrated by his unhurried pace to do so. He was the most secretive person I'd ever met. Except for, perhaps, myself.

# CHAPTER NINE

Monday dawned bright and nearly cloudless. The sun's rays streamed through my bedchamber window as Bree threw back the drapes. I groaned and rolled to my side, while she persisted in humming some ditty she'd undoubtedly danced to at the ceilidh three nights past. Normally I didn't hold my new maid's perpetual cheerfulness against her, but this early in the morning, after another night of fitful slumber, I was a hairsbreadth away from snarling at her.

Then I recalled the reason she was waking me so early. My heartbeat quickened in remembrance that Gage was in the bedchamber across the hall from mine. Though I'd half expected him to, he had not visited my chamber the previous evening. At least, not to my knowledge. And I'd been awake until after the clock struck three. I should have been relieved that he'd decided to follow the rules of propriety—and I was—but I would be lying if I didn't admit I was also a little disappointed. Apparently, Gage was still able to keep me off my guard, even when that meant not appearing when I was prepared for him to do so.

I pushed myself upright, scraping my wild hair back from my face. From his corner at the bottom of the bed, Earl Grey cracked open one golden eye to see what was happening and then settled back into slumber.

"Good morning, m'lady," Bree proclaimed brightly as

she bustled across the chamber carrying a gown from my dressing room, which she laid over a chair.

I mumbled my greeting in reply, unable as yet to bestir myself more.

She carried over a tray filled with toast, jam, and chocolate—my normal morning repast—and set it across my lap. "It looks teh be a lovely day."

I nodded, still squinting at the brightness of the morning sun, and poured my chocolate into a cup. After taking a drink of the bittersweet liquid, I sighed, and settled back against my pillows to watch Bree move about the room, laying out my clothing for the day and tidying up what I had discarded the night before.

When I had arrived at Blakelaw House seven weeks prior, I had selected Bree from the other housemaids to attend me as my lady's maid mainly because she had seemed the least frightened by me. Her deep dimples and sparkling brown eyes had said she was not unsettled by me—or my macabre reputation—and her neat appearance and trim posture suggested she would be efficient and uncomplaining. And for the most part, I'd been right. She was cheerful and tolerant of my recent crankiness, but she was also bright and resourceful, two qualities I admired greatly.

Things had not gone well with my previous maid, and though Lucy and I had parted amicably, I was still somewhat disillusioned by my discovery of her disloyalty, and hesitant to trust a new maid. Whether or not Bree understood the reason behind my reticent behavior, she seemed to accept it. As this was her first assignment to such a position, perhaps she didn't know any better. But regardless, I was grateful for her forbearance.

I was still uncertain whether I would ask her to come with me when I left Blakelaw House, but I felt the arrival of last night's guest might swiftly help me to a decision. After all, Lucy's behavior had caused me no qualms until we departed Gairloch, where she'd spent her entire life, and encountered the attractive, but treacherous, Donovan, a servant in the employ of the Dalmays. I couldn't help but wonder about Bree's reaction to Gage's valet, Anderley. After all, the girl was quite young and pretty, with her strawberry blond curls, carefully tamed, and her sunny disposition, and I knew Anderley was not unattractive. His dark hair and eyes made quite a decent foil to his employer's golden good looks.

However, I could think of no way to introduce the subject without sounding suspicious, and had resolved to find a plausible excuse to ask her later when she unwittingly broached the topic herself.

"You're sure ye dinna wish to eat any more?" she asked, pointedly staring at the piece and a half of toast I had left on my plate.

"I'm finished," I replied, dabbing my face with a towel after washing it.

Bree's eyebrows briefly creased with concern and then straightened again as she moved to place the tray on the table near the door. I set the towel aside, lifted my nightgown over my head, and picked up my shift. By the time my head had emerged from the fine lawn fabric, Bree was there holding out my looser daytime corset, ready to help me fasten it.

"Everyone belowstairs is excited aboot our visitors," she remarked.

I watched her in our reflection in the mirror, seeing her head bent over her task behind me. "Oh?"

"'Til you arrived, Master St. Mawr had ne'er had any. And you bein' his sister, ye arena' really a guest. So this is the first they've seen in some time. Since I've worked here anyway."

I frowned, trying to recall whether I'd ever asked her before. "Remind me, how long have you been employed at Blakelaw House?"

"Oh, goin' on seven years noo." She looked up in the mirror, catching my look of surprise, and grinned. "Aye," she said, answering my unasked question whether she remembered me. "I worked in the kitchens when I first come. Barely fourteen, I was. And quiet as a mouse."

"I'm sorry," I said, shaking my head in regret. "I don't think I . . . Wait! Are you the girl our former cook was always railing at?"

She nodded, flashing me another smile.

"But . . . I thought her name was Marie."

"'Twas what Cook decided to call me. She said Bree was a stupid name."

"Then you're the maid . . ." I stopped, but not before she realized what I was thinking of.

"She beat with her rolling pin and almost crippled?" The sparkle in her eyes faded. "Aye. And if it weren't for yer father, she probably woulda."

I had been married to Sir Anthony by then, but I had heard something of the incident, though none of the details. "What do you mean?"

"He's the one who stopped 'er. Heard the shrieks from his study and came doon teh find oot what all the racket was." She finished with my corset and handed me my stockings. "He sent Cook packin', and fetched the surgeon from Kelso for me."

"I'm so sorry," I murmured, sinking down on the vanity bench, horrified that I hadn't known she was the same girl.

She brushed it aside. "No reason for that. Yer father didna ken what the ole harpy was doin', and he sent her away as soon as he did. I canna blame 'im, or you, for what ye didna ken."

"Yes, but . . ."

She shook her head and turned to pick up my nightgown where it lay on the bed, adding it to her pile of dirty garments by the door. I focused on my stockings and then rose to allow Bree to drop a warm, carnelian red woolen walking dress over my head. By the time she'd buttoned my gown up the back, any sign that the story she'd told had distressed her was wiped clean from her face. I had to admire her resolve and her resilience.

I settled on the bench again so that she could run the brush through my unruly hair. It crackled with each pass through the thick tresses.

"Tell me," I said, deciding to take a chance. "What did you think of Mr. Anderley?" I reached out to pick up a bottle of floral-scented perfume my sister had sent me for Hogmanay. I rarely, if ever, wore fragrances, but I decided to dab some on my neck. It gave me something to do with my hands. "I've been told he's rather vain and pompous," I supplied when she remained silent. "And I was just curious how you found him."

I lifted my eyes to her reflection, just in time to see the grin of amusement that warmed her features.

"Aye. I suppose you could call 'im that." She proceeded to divide my hair into several sections and begin to plait each one.

"But you wouldn't?" I prodded, wondering at her reticence.

"Well, I'd say it's more likely his armor. Ye ken? The way he wishes teh be seen rather than seem vulnerable. It canna be easy enterin' a strange household."

I studied Bree in the glass, realizing she had an amazing capacity for empathy. If she'd seen so quickly to the heart of Anderley in one evening, I wondered how much of my hidden pain she'd already guessed at.

She must have sensed my unease, for she looked up from her task, meeting my eyes in the reflection of the mirror, before returning to my braid. "Everyone's got their hurts. No matter who they are. It's easy teh forget that when we're no' willin' teh look too deep."

I stared down at the vanity, considering what she'd said while she finished styling my hair in a tight coronet. It was easy to assume that people were uncomplicated, that the face they showed the world was their true selves, but I knew, perhaps as well as anyone could, that this was not true. I did not share myself easily. I never had. And neither did Gage. Sometimes I thought that was part of the reason I was drawn to him. He intimately understood, in a way most people couldn't, just why I was so reluctant to let others see the truth.

Normally I was attuned to sense the sides of people that they would prefer to remain hidden, with a few notable and detrimental exceptions. It was what made me such a good portrait artist. I saw the truth behind the facades they so painstakingly erected. It was almost always the eyes that gave them away, even if only in the flicker of a fraction of a second. It was impossible for me to know the depth and breadth of their secrets, whether they were big or small, whether they hid them from others or just themselves, but I could see the truth of who they were, good or bad. And people didn't always like it.

However, since William's death I'd grown out of practice, or perhaps just uncaring. I'd been so consumed by my grief, my worries, my fears that I'd blocked out everyone else, including my maid. And to some extent, my brother.

It was no wonder he was so worried about me. I'd always been able to unerringly read him, but since my return to Blakelaw House, I hadn't really bothered to try. I knew there were things that were troubling him, and they didn't all revolve around me, but I hadn't even made an effort to probe them. His pestering little sister hadn't been pestering him. I could understand how unsettling that would be.

Bree finished my hair, and as she'd already laid out my kid leather boots and gloves, she made ready to leave, but I stopped her. She faced me with her hands clasped before her, an uncertain expression on her face. It was perhaps the first time I'd seen her look unconfident, and I hastened to reassure her.

"As I'm sure you know, it's Handsel Day. And although I know it's customary to give all the servants their gifts together, I wanted to give you yours here."

Bree instantly relaxed, and a very becoming flush of pleasure brightened her face as I handed her three packages. "Thank you, m'lady."

I felt an answering blush heat my cheeks as I indicated the largest of the three. "That contains two dresses I asked Miss Little to alter for you. She said she had your measurements, but if for any reason they don't fit, she'll fix them." It was customary to give the servants a new uniform every year on Handsel Day, but as Bree was now a lady's maid, she was allowed to wear cast-off gowns from her employer and other finer apparel. I hoped the two dresses I'd selected and asked our seamstress to alter would suit her.

Bree beamed with happiness, and I urged her to open the other two packages, hoping she would like them just as well. One was a package of scented soaps, as I'd noticed how much mine seemed to please her when she helped me to wash my hair. The other was a set of hairpins with small, finely worked metal flowers on the ends. I had seen them in a shop in Kelso and immediately decided they would be perfect for Bree's curls.

She gasped at the sight of them, and I knew I'd chosen well.

Once I'd ushered the joyful girl out of my room, who insisted she could juggle her presents, my breakfast tray, and the laundry all at once, I joined my brother downstairs. He arched his eyebrows at my bright smile, but I ignored him, unwilling to let anything spoil Bree's infectious cheer.

We passed out gifts to the remainder of the staff, and then Trevor told them they would have the remainder of the day to do as they wished. The coachman and footman who would accompany us to Dryburgh Abbey were promised they would receive an extra day off sometime that week.

Gage, who had viewed the ceremony from the doorway of the drawing room, waited until the three of us were inside the carriage before asking about Handsel Day.

"It falls on the first Monday of the new year, and is when the Scots prefer to give their presents to each other," Trevor explained. "As most of our servants are Scottish, and perhaps, more importantly, Mother was Scottish, it's always been the tradition we follow at Blakelaw House."

"So you don't celebrate Christmas or Boxing Day?" he

asked, naming the holidays on which Englishmen usually gave each other gifts.

"Not in the way most English do. Though we do attend church service and enjoy a nice dinner." Our father *had* been English, after all, and we did live on the English side of the Border, arbitrary as that was much of the time.

The Border region was almost a country unto its own—had always been, even during the time of the Border reivers—and Scots and English mixed freely. Because of the tales that had been handed down through the ages about the fierce Border Marches, outsiders often assumed there were nasty ongoing feuds between Scots and English along the boundary between the countries. But more often than not, a Borderer would side with his neighbor—no matter which country he was from—than some distant government in London so far to the south or Edinburgh to the north. Now, that wasn't to say there weren't still feuds between rival clans, but they, as often as not, pitted Scot versus Scot, or English versus English, as English versus Scot.

It would be almost impossible for an outsider like Gage to understand the strange dichotomy of concord and rivalry that made up the backbone of the Borders. Most of the people who populated it were descendants of those who had suffered through centuries of war and pillaging and reiving. It had taken a stubborn, hardy disposition to survive, and their descendants were understandably no different. They had their own traditions, their own way of doing things, and woe to those who tried to stand in the way.

This was something it would behoove us to remember as we made our inquiries, especially as Gage was an outsider, and a Londoner, at that.

# CHAPTER TEN

When we arrived, Dryburgh Abbey was already awash with midmorning light. The stones where Dodd had died were scrubbed clean, though I suspected Willie had rubbed his hands raw in doing so. I huddled deeper in my fur-lined cloak as we paused at the spot on our way into the abbey, wondering where the young caretaker was on this cold morning. I could feel Gage's eyes on me as I explained the location's significance, but as we passed through the west door, he was distracted by the late Lord Buchan's yawning grave.

I'd asked the current earl not to fill it in on the chance that Gage was able to uncover something that the rest of us had missed. He circled the plot and bent down to examine a few things while Trevor and I stood by watching. I shifted closer to the headstone, a red smudge on the marble having caught my eye, and when I turned back, it was to find Gage actually climbing down into the grave.

My chest squeezed uncomfortably, seeming to force all of the air from my lungs. Gage's actions were quite justified and perhaps even necessary, but the sight of him down in that grave made a chill of foreboding run down my spine. I wanted to reach out and snatch him back, to order him out of there, but I seemed frozen, unable to speak.

Neither of the men seemed aware of my reaction, as

Trevor inched closer to where Gage stood with his head lowered, scrutinizing something in the grave. They both murmured something, but I could not hear them, didn't want to hear them. I just wanted Gage out of that ominous hole in the ground.

Thankfully, he found nothing to interest him and quickly climbed out with the aid of my brother. Once his feet were firmly planted on even ground again, I turned away, unwilling to let him see how rattled I was. The air came rushing back into my lungs, and I breathed deeply for several moments of the sharp winter air, trying to regain my composure.

It was silly of me to become upset. Just two days prior I had seen one of Lord Buchan's gardeners down in the grave and it had not unsettled me. There was no reason I should be upset now seeing Gage down there.

But irrational as it was, I couldn't seem to shake the disquieting feeling that had overcome me. That Gage had just placed one foot in his own grave.

Still oblivious to my distress, Gage moved forward to stand beside me. "Have you already searched the rest of the abbey ruins?"

I turned to him with a start and he nodded at the stairs leading away from the abbey church down into the cloister. "I . . . no." I fumbled, mentally castigating myself for not thinking of it. "I can't believe we failed to do so."

Gage turned back to me. "I'd glad you didn't."

I bit back the self-recriminating thought I was about to utter and scowled at him. Just what did he mean by that?

"It would have been dangerous to conduct a search on the night the crime took place," he replied, clearly trying to placate me. "Those stairs look none too steady, and I can't imagine the rest of the abbey is in much better condition."

"And the morning after? When Trevor and I returned?"

"Well . . ." He paused uncomfortably. "It's unlikely your efforts would have turned up much."

I arched my brows angrily. "But we still should have looked."

I turned to stride across the distance toward the staircase, frustrated with myself for not having done so earlier. Here I was trying to prove how capable an investigator I could be on my own, and I'd neglected to do something so obvious. Gage was right. It was unlikely we would have found anything to assist with our inquiry—there was no reason the grave robbers should have visited the other parts of the abbey—but it still needed to be searched. And now that three days had passed since the murder and robbery, it was doubtful we would find anything even if something had been left to find. The rain and wind and time would have washed it away.

Gage caught up with me before the stairs, taking hold of my elbow as we picked our way down the chipped sandstone steps. We passed through an archway overgrown with creeping plants and into the cloister, now completely open to the sky. The roof had long ago fallen in, probably during the destruction wrought by Henry VIII's army in the mid-sixteenth century. The stone and wood had been carted away to be used elsewhere, but the holes in the walls where the roof beams had once been supported still remained. Now a patch of green grass spread out across the enclosed courtyard, with trees and shrubs hugging the walls.

Trevor followed behind us and we all paused, studying our surroundings before turning to the block of buildings on our left. We passed a large arched ledge built into the wall and strolled by several rooms, some of which were in too much disrepair to enter. The library, a narrow barrel-vaulted room with only a few decorative accents remaining, was empty.

But the Chapter House was not.

Gage and I cautiously crossed through the doorway flanked with ornate pillars and halted at the top of the stairs that led down into the echoing chamber. The musty stench of mold assailed our nostrils. As our eyes adjusted to the darkness, I could see that the room featured several lovely Gothic pointed-arch windows. However, the heaviness of the stone walls and vaulted ceiling and the trees shading the abbey ruins made it next to impossible for these meager light sources to brighten the chamber.

I couldn't help but admire the plaster ornamental arches and scrolls on the walls at the far end of the chamber, even as I shivered from the chill that seemed to pervade the room. Staring up at the rounded vaulted ceiling as we descended the steps into the gloom, I could almost hear the canons' voices resonating around us in the space. It must have been a glorious sound when they were alive, but now the memory of those reverberations only prickled over my skin, as if the canons' ghosts were brushing past me.

Gage pulled me closer as I shivered a second time, but then his attention was captured by something to our left. A bundle of cloth rested on the low stone ledge that spanned the length of the walls where the canons had sat in contemplation.

Gage guided us toward it, enabling me to see that the bundle appeared to be made of a course woolen cloth of some kind. I did not object when Gage released my arm and reached out to examine it, not wanting to touch it myself. I leaned in cautiously as he folded back the cloth, half afraid some woodland creature bedded down inside would leap out. When all he uncovered was the fine pink muslin of a lady's gown, I rocked back on my heels in confusion.

Gage glanced back at me, his brow furrowed, sharing my puzzlement. Then he carefully lifted the dress to find a set of women's undergarments, including a frilly shift and petticoat. At the bottom of the pile rested a dainty pair of women's slippers.

Neither of us seemed to know what to say, and ultimately it was Trevor who broke the silence.

"Who the devil's clothes are those?"

We both turned at the sound of his disgruntled voice.

"There isn't another disturbed grave in the cemetery, is there?" Gage asked in dismay.

I shook my head. "I . . . don't think so. But I suppose we

should check. Although . . ." I glanced at the pile of clothing ". . . it would need to be a very recent burial. If I'm not mistaken, and I often am when it comes to fashion, that gown was purchased rather recently."

Gage lifted the gown by the shoulders so we could see the bodice better. "No. You're right. These wide puffed sleeves haven't been *en vogue* for long."

I couldn't help pursing my lips. Two months prior, I had eyed those sleeves in the shops in Edinburgh with distaste, and they certainly hadn't grown on me since. Stylish they might be, but they were not conducive to painting. The big, floppy things would simply get in the way and hinder my movements.

"But I thought Lord Buchan said his uncle's burial was the most recent, and that was twenty months ago," Trevor pointed out.

Which made it unlikely this gown had come from a grave in the abbey's cemetery.

My brother shifted closer, his face creased in a troubled frown. "So if those clothes are not from a corpse, then where did they come from?"

We all turned to stare down at the pile of strange garments.

"And where is the girl to whom they belong?" Gage added grimly.

After searching the remainder of the abbey ruins that were safely accessible, we retraced our steps through the west door and then turned to follow the path that led away from the abbey out across the wide lawn toward Dryburgh House. The Earl of Buchan's manor was relatively young by most standards, having been built barely a century earlier, and also charmingly modest considering the previous earl's eccentric reputation. Fashioned from the same reddish-brown sandstone as the abbey, it somehow seemed natural that the Palladian mansion should be situated there, even with its grand pillars and arched windows. I suspected this had more to do with its size than anything else, for rather than dominate the landscape, it seemed to simply settle neatly into its space, enhancing the setting instead of altering it.

The current earl greeted us warmly as we were ushered into his study. He was clearly glad to see Gage, and I tried not to feel slighted, though it was impossible not to feel some sting. It was a reminder that I was merely the assistant. Gage was the inquiry agent, with his own extensive reputation and that of his father's to back him up. I'd merely helped solve two investigations—two *tricky* investigations—but only two, nonetheless.

"Lord Buchan," Gage began, settling into a chair. "We may have uncovered something significant."

"Oh?" Buchan murmured, leaning forward eagerly.

"Yes. But first, I must ask, have you received any communication from the men who took your uncle's bones?"

Buchan sat back suddenly, his heavy brow arched high. "Communication? Why, no. Of course not."

Gage's eyes flicked to my own. "I'm afraid there's no 'of course' about it." He related the story of the similar abduction of Sir Colum Casselbeck's body and the ransom note the Casselbeck family had received. All the while, Buchan's eyes widened farther and farther with each new detail until I thought they might be expelled from their sockets.

"Oh, my. No. I haven't received anything of the like. Should I be expecting it?" he asked.

"I'm not certain," Gage admitted. "But there is a possibility the two body snatchings are related." He sank back in his chair, resting his linked fingers over his abdomen in a gesture I'd become very familiar with. Then he tilted his head to the side to ask, "Do you know if your uncle was acquainted with Sir Colum?"

"Why, yes. They were friends. And both founding members of the Society of Antiquaries."

Gage's posture straightened, the only outward indication

he gave that his interest had been piqued along with mine. "This society is the same one to whom Mr. Collingwood alleged his aunt donated his family's gold torc?"

Buchan glanced over at me for the first time since we'd taken our seats, clearly realizing I had shared this information with Gage. "Yes. Do you think Mr. Collingwood also accused Sir Colum of theft?" he asked Gage.

"I don't know. But I shall find out." He studied the earl before posing his next query. "I suppose your uncle considered many of the other members of the society to be his friends."

Buchan nodded. "He was quite enthusiastic about the subject, and many of the other men thought very highly of him. They still speak of him so."

I straightened in my chair as Gage voiced the same question I was thinking. "Are you a member?"

"I am. Which reminds me . . ." He turned toward me eagerly. "Lady Darby, after you expressed so much interest in the location of Collingwood's gold torc, I wrote to the society's treasurer to discover whether there are any records of such a donation, and if so, where the artifact is currently stored. I should have done so the moment Lewis Collingwood darkened my door with his accusation, but how could I have known it would come to this?"

I exchanged a look with Gage.

"Now, let's not be too hasty to rush to judgment," he cautioned the earl. "Mr. Collingwood is our most promising suspect, but by no means do we have sufficient evidence to prove he is in any way involved. There are still numerous other avenues to explore."

"Such as?" Buchan demanded, his brow darkening. He clearly did not appreciate being chastened.

"Well, for one, can you tell us whether any young ladies in the area have passed away recently?"

Buchan's eyes widened at the question. "None that I'm aware of. Why?"

Gage shrugged his shoulders. "Just idle curiosity. Perhaps unrelated."

I frowned, curious why he'd chosen not to tell the earl about the clothes we'd found in the abbey. When we exited the house a quarter of an hour later, it was the first thing I asked him.

"Sometimes it's best to keep one's cards close to one's chest," he answered obscurely, adjusting the angle of his hat on this head.

"You don't trust him," I persisted.

"I don't know him well enough to decide whether to trust him."

I nodded, thinking I understood his logic. I glanced out of the corner of my eye at my brother, walking on the other side of me, recalling how we had had a similar conversation just the evening before.

"And so in the meantime," Gage added, "I intend for us to do all of our own questioning. Which means we shall be contacting the members of the Society of Antiquaries ourselves."

So that we could be certain Lord Buchan was not omitting any pertinent information to our inquiry. I squinted against the bright sunlight as I made plans to once again call on Philip's assistance. He knew everyone who was anyone in Scottish society, government, and industry. Surely he was acquainted with at least a few of the society's members.

As we passed the corner of the manor to join the drive down which our carriage was parked, a dark-haired maid stepped out of the shadow of the building. The gravel crunched loudly as we halted in surprise. She eyed us warily, twisting the apron over her skirts, and for a moment I thought she would bolt. But then she inhaled deeply, as if finding her courage.

"My lady," she murmured with a wobbly voice.

I nodded in encouragement, taking a step closer to her to separate us from the men. Even so, she studied them through the screen of her lashes over my shoulder. I sensed that she wished we were alone, and I was about to tell the men to go on ahead when she inhaled shakily again and spoke.

"Ye said if we remembered anythin' else teh tell ye."

"I did," I confirmed, trying to place her in the crowd of servants gathered in the entry hall of Dryburgh House two days prior. I thought she might have been one of the small maids cowering in the back, perhaps nursing a thick head from all of the drinking the night before.

"Weel, I didna remember the other day, but then Tally, she's another maid like me, ye ken." I nodded, trying to follow her thick brogue as she began talking faster. "And, weel, we got teh talkin', and we remembered we saw these lads doon at the abbey."

My face must have shown my interest, for she hastened to add, "'Twas through the trees, ye mind, where we was beatin' the rugs. And we didna ken they might be up teh trouble. Or we'd o' said somethin' for sure."

"I understand," I assured her. "When was this?"

"Hogmanay morn. We was hurryin' to get our tasks done so we could go teh the ceilidh."

I resisted the urge to turn and look at Gage and Trevor, who I knew must be sharing my anticipation, and focused on the maid. "How many men were there? Did you get a good look at them?"

She unwound and then twisted her apron again. "Two— that we could see." She shook her head. "But we couldna see 'em weel. Though we did try." She blushed. "They was very dashin'."

"How do you mean?"

"They was dressed teh the nines. Even their horses were the prime article."

I frowned. "You mean they were gentlemen?"

"Oh, aye."

This was something I hadn't been expecting. "You're sure?"

She nodded in certainty and I thanked her and sent her on her way.

"What do you make of it?" I asked Trevor and Gage as we turned our steps toward the carriage again.

"It could mean nothing. Many people stop to visit the abbey ruins," Trevor pointed out. "Perhaps they were simply a pair of young gentlemen out on a lark."

I lifted my carnelian red skirts as I stepped over a particularly muddy patch in the drive. "Maybe. But in that case, they likely also attended the Rutherford Ball. Every gentleman for miles around was there, and many from farther afield."

"Then your aunt and uncle should be able to give us a good idea who they might have been," Gage chimed in, pausing at the side of the carriage. "St. Mawr is right. They might have been doing nothing but indulging in a bit of idle curiosity."

I arched my eyebrows, not fooled by his display of indifference. "*Or* they were scouting the location for a digging expedition later that night." Taking Trevor's proffered hand, I climbed up into the carriage before Gage could respond.

My brother followed me inside, sitting beside me, as he had on the ride to Dryburgh. Which left Gage to take the seat across from us, forcing me to either look out the window or meet his laughing gaze. He had known that I wouldn't be able to resist countering his argument, even though I knew he was as aware of the alternative possibility as I was.

The carriage swayed slightly from side to side as it slowly rolled forward over the gravel, bumping Trevor's shoulder against mine. I looked up as Gage removed the bundle of clothing we had found in the abbey from inside his black greatcoat, where he'd stored it during our interview with Lord Buchan. He rested it on the seat beside him.

Trevor inhaled as if coming to some decision. "How did you know that dress belonged to a young lady?" he asked

Gage. Though I knew he'd meant for the question to sound casual, I realized it was far from that. I suspected Gage did, too, if the subtle manner in which his nostrils flared was any indication.

"The gown is pale pink," Gage replied as if that was answer enough. And it would have been for any woman, or a fashion-conscious man. But a dandy my brother was not, and neither was he particularly observant when it came to women's clothing choices.

"Only debutantes wear pale pink, Trevor. It's insipid on older women."

He turned to me in chagrin. "Oh."

I couldn't help but smile. "It's all right, dearest. Had you known that, I would have worried you were coming down with something."

He grinned sheepishly. "Yes, well, half the time I don't even notice what color waistcoat Shep is handing me. Is it blue or green?"

"Today it's slate gray."

He arched a single eyebrow in irritation. "Well, if we're being precise."

I shrugged and turned toward the window. "You should have known better than to ask an artist."

# CHAPTER ELEVEN

Uncle Andrew, Aunt Sarah, and their family and few remaining guests were just sitting down to luncheon when Gage, Trevor, and I arrived at Clintmains Hall. They insisted we join them. So as chairs and place settings were added to the already crowded table in the family parlor, I introduced Gage, suddenly grateful that only a handful of the many members from my mother's side of our family were in attendance. He was apparently already familiar with my cousins Jock and Andy, and Miss Witherington also appeared to have made his acquaintance. She curtseyed very prettily for him and offered him her hand with a sickeningly sweet smile. I would have liked nothing more than to trans-form it into one of her withering glares, as it always made her lips tighten into an ugly little moue, but my aunt had news for me.

She linked her arm with mine and pulled me a short distance away from the others. "I'm afraid none of the guests or staff had anything of interest to tell me." She offered me a sad smile in apology. "I don't know whether that is because they truly didn't see anything of importance or because they're unwilling to admit it, but either way, I'm sorry I don't have any information to add to the investigation."

I patted her hand where it rested on my arm. "I under-stand, Aunt Sarah. Thank you for trying."

"Of course, dear." Her eyes rose to just over my shoulder, and I looked up to see that Gage was also listening to our conversation. "But should you wish to question them yourself, please do so. Here is the list of Hogmanay guests I promised you. I made a few helpful notations beside some of the names. Those who are invalids, or were too sotted at the ball to have gotten into much mischief."

I returned her playful smile and slid the list into the pocket of my walking dress.

"Thank you," Gage told her and my aunt nodded.

We all settled into our chairs around the table and tucked into the meal of crusty bread, cold meats, cheeses, pickles, and apples—simple fare perfect for my ravenous appetite. It was not until partway through the meal, as I was laughing at something my cousin Jock had said and trying not to spray a mouthful of bread and cheese across the table, that I realized how significant the moment was. I'd glanced at my brother, who was watching me with a curious look in his eyes that I couldn't decipher. But when his gaze dropped to my plate and I looked down to see half the food I'd heaped upon it gone, I suddenly understood.

I was actually hungry. But perhaps more important, I'd eaten. Not once had the meal turned to sawdust in my mouth or made my stomach clench in knots as it had normally done in the past few months when I tried to dine. I finished chewing the food in my mouth slowly and swallowed, wondering what it meant, and whether I should even be trying to comprehend it.

Did it mean my grief was gone? No. The heavy weight I felt in my chest when I thought of William Dalmay was still there, but it was perhaps a fraction lighter. Just a sliver. Nonetheless it was something. Maybe.

I took a deep breath and forced my attention back to the conversation swirling around me.

"So Young picked up the rifle and fired. Missed the axe by a good ten feet," Jock gasped, laughing so hard he could barely get the words out. "And . . . and almost shot Shellingham's ear off. The puir man was as green as this table-cloth." He slunk lower in his chair, swiping tears away from his eyes as everyone joined in his amusement.

"And what did Mr. Stuart do?" Trevor asked between chuckles.

Jock swallowed and tried unsuccessfully to recompose himself. "He . . . he shook his head and said, as calm as ye please, 'Well . . . well, at least, Crockett wasna here teh see it.'"

I laughed along with them this time. Apparently, Mr. Stuart's stories about Davy Crockett hadn't been enough. Mr. Young had to actually attempt one of the man's more famous tricks, presumably under Mr. Stuart's "capable" tutelage.

"Who is this Mr. Stuart?" Gage asked.

"A gentleman from the Coldingham area," Aunt Sarah replied. "Rutherford met him in Edinburgh."

Her husband nodded in confirmation, his mouth full of roast beef.

"The silly man claims to be the grandson of Charles Stuart, the Young Pretender," Miss Witherington muttered under her breath, just loud enough so that we could all hear. I'd noticed she had been the only one to not find Jock's story amusing.

"Yes, well," Aunt Sarah murmured, a frown forming between her brows as she looked across the table at her future daughter-in-law. "Let's leave the man his eccentricities. After all, he's not harming anyone."

Jock spluttered. "Except maybe Shellingham."

Following luncheon, Uncle Andrew escorted us into his study along with his son, Andy, who'd been groomed since childhood to one day take over the massive estate. Apparently, my uncle also hoped those duties included magistrate. I didn't mind. Andy was a likable, easygoing fellow. Perhaps a bit staid, but that was to be expected with a father like his.

Gratefully, Uncle Andrew got directly to the point.

"My riders didn't discover anything useful from the inns and taverns along the roads to Edinburgh or Glasgow." He steepled his fingers in front of him on his desk. "So either the innkeepers and stable lads were paid well for their silence, these men were more stealthy than we anticipated and traveled by back roads, or they did not journey north as expected with the body."

Gage rubbed his hand over his jaw as he considered the matter. "You're right. It could be any of those possibilities. And it doesn't make sense to waste resources sending riders in other directions when we have no credible information to tell us they did anything but travel north. Perhaps later." He sighed and shook his head. "But not now."

Uncle Andrew nodded.

"What of the guests?" I asked. "Aunt Sarah said that none of them had any useful information to provide us. But were any of them acting suspiciously?" I glanced between my uncle and my cousin. "Were any of them conspicuously missing from the ball at any point?"

Andy and his father exchanged a look, their brows furrowed as they considered the matter.

"Not that we can recall," Andy replied. "But there were almost eighty guests here that night. We could have easily missed seeing one leave. Or not."

"As for not having anything to tell us," Uncle Andrew began hesitantly. "You'll notice that my wife said they didn't have anything *useful* to inform us." He grimaced and I wondered just what he was so loath to mention. "Several of the staff, and a few of the guests, suggested the culprit might be . . ." He sighed and muttered, "The Nun of Dryburgh."

I nodded, having heard this suggestion from Lord Buchan's staff as well.

"Who?" Gage demanded in justifiable confusion.

"The Nun of Dryburgh," I repeated. "A fanciful myth they tell . . ." I broke off when I saw my uncle shake his head.

"It's not just a myth," he said.

My eyes widened in surprise.

"There's a real woman who lives in a tiny hut on the property adjacent to the abbey. Though she's never been a nun, as far as I'm aware, and her sanity is somewhat questionable."

I glanced at Gage and then my brother, curious if they were as uncomfortable with this new information as I was.

"But she's harmless," he hastened to add. "Nothing more than an old woman who prefers to keep to herself."

"You've met her?" Gage asked.

"Yes. Several times. But . . ." he paused, studying Gage and me in turn ". . . although I believe her to be blameless, it might be good for you to meet with her." He spread his hands wide in explanation. "She may have seen something. Something everyone else has missed."

Gage placed his hands on the arms of his chair as if to rise. "Then we shall go to see her now."

"You can't."

Gage sank back with a start.

Uncle Andrew cleared his throat. "That is . . . she's nocturnal."

From what I remembered of the myth, I had half expected this answer, but it still startled me. "She . . ."

"Only goes out at night. And as far as I can tell, she only answers her door after dusk."

Gage's face was awash with an interesting mix of emotions. He seemed unable to decide whether to frown or laugh. Eventually, he decided on a scowl, just a slight one, that tightened the corners of his eyes. "Then we shall visit her this evening."

My uncle nodded. "Very good." He made to rise, but it was Gage's turn to foil that.

"Are you acquainted with a Lewis Collingwood?"

He sat back in his chair with a frown and lifted his eyes to the ceiling as if the answer were written there. "No. I don't believe so. Should I be?"

Gage shook his head. "Just curious. He's a man Buchan mentioned in passing."

I turned to stare at Gage, surprised he was being so

vague with my uncle. The man was a magistrate, after all, and my relative. Did he suspect him as well?

"One last thing . . . Are you aware of any of your guests visiting the abbey ruins earlier in the day on December thirty-first?"

My uncle seemed to have been taken unawares by the question, for he glanced at his son. "I can't say with any certainty. I know several of the guests took their mounts and carriages out. And, of course, I wouldn't be aware what the guests who only arrived that day did on their journey here. That was their matter."

"Certainly," Gage replied in an effort to placate my frowning uncle. "But would you give the matter some thought and make a list of those who you remember taking their horses out? It might clear them of any suspicion."

Or do the exact opposite. I resisted the urge to glare at him, knowing he was only telling my uncle what he needed to hear to get the information he required, for indeed, Uncle Andrew nodded and agreed to consider the matter.

"What was that?" I demanded of Gage as he climbed into the carriage after me.

He stared across the space between us as if he didn't know what I meant.

"Don't you trust my uncle either?"

His gaze dropped, suddenly finding something of great interest on the dark fabric of his greatcoat. "To a certain extent. After all, Lord Rutherford's reputation precedes him. He's been a magistrate for this Border region for over twenty years."

I narrowed my eyes. "Then why the subterfuge?"

"Well, Lord Rutherford is also known to be quite . . . strict. Starchy. I thought it best to leave him as much in the dark as possible regarding my methods." His eyes rose to probe mine. "Was I wrong?"

I swallowed, recalling how reluctant Uncle Andrew had

been to allow me to assist in the investigation. How he still disapproved, I'm sure Gage had deduced as much. "No."

His gaze continued to search my face, and I began to look away when he spoke. "I started to think your brother was a man of the same stripe, but then he allowed you to come away alone with me."

I, too, had been surprised when Trevor sent me off to the village of St. Boswells alone with Gage. I had expected him to insist on accompanying us, but instead he'd declared he had business to discuss with our uncle. Not for the first time, I'd been left with the uneasy feeling that all was not well with my brother's estate. It was something I should have been more attuned to before now, but being so wrapped up in my own grief, I'd ignored it. My brother's demeanor had been oddly solemn since I'd arrived, and I suspected now that it wasn't only because of my own distress.

"I may have misjudged him," Gage said, interrupting my thoughts. He lifted his eyebrows in query. "Perhaps he's just playing the protective older brother."

This time I did look away to stare out across the winter fields outside the window. "Maybe."

The silence stretched between us, heavy with our unspoken thoughts, and I suddenly realized this was the first time we had been alone, without the potential of interruption, since Gage had climbed into my carriage in Edinburgh to say good-bye. I swallowed the sticky residue of nerves that coated my throat and mouth and wondered just what he was thinking.

And then I wished I hadn't.

"Kiera, why did you send for me?" His voice was gentler than normal, but determined. As if he'd been initially hesitant to ask the question, but changed his mind.

Though I'd known it was coming, it was the question I had been dreading. Mostly because I did not know how to answer it. Or perhaps more fairly, did not want to answer it.

"Because of the investigation, of course," I replied, unable to look at him. "Lord Buchan asked me to."

My gloved fingers clenched tighter together in my lap during the pause that followed.

"Is that all?"

"I . . . I don't know what you mean." I stared blindly out the window while I braced for the onslaught of whatever his response would be, if there was any response at all. After all, I'd risked wounding the man's pride.

"Liar."

I jolted at the quietly teasing tone of his voice. I turned to see his pale winter blue eyes twinkling at me as if in jest. But I would've been a fool not to also notice the hard edge to his stare, the fierceness.

I sat immobile, not knowing how to reply. Was I glad to see him? Yes. But would I have ever sent for him of my own accord if I had not been prodded into doing so? I didn't know. Everything inside me was jumbled when it came to Gage. I didn't know how to sort it out.

So ultimately I settled for the truth.

"You confuse me."

I could tell I'd surprised him, for some of the surety vanished from his expression. "I confuse you?"

"Yes."

When he simply stared at me as if willing me to elaborate, I sighed and lifted a hand to my forehead.

"I don't know what else you want me to say," I snapped in exasperation. "I don't seem to know anything when it comes to you."

His gaze softened, though that edge of fierceness remained. "Surely that's not true."

I glared at him.

"You know how I feel about you."

I blinked at him in astonishment. Was the man daft?

I shook my head. "No, I don't."

His eyes flashed. "Then I'll just have to remind you."

The next thing I knew I was in his arms, and he was kissing me with all the devastating thoroughness I'd come to expect from him. And yet under all of his skill, there was also a note of urgency, of desperation—and it was that emotion that resonated with me most of all, for it matched my own.

When he pulled back, I could not open my eyes, not with my emotions so stirred up inside me, shimmering on the surface. But I clung to the front of his greatcoat, unwilling to let go. So he pressed his lips to my forehead and held me close.

I had just decided to venture looking up at him when a shout from outside the carriage forced us to separate. We turned to see a man outside the window hailing our coachman as the carriage began to slow and the first row of cottages at the edge of what must be the village of St. Boswells came into view.

Our first stop was at the Abbot Inn, presumably named for the past heads of nearby Dryburgh Abbey. My uncle had recommended we stop there, recalling an altercation the innkeeper had with a pair of body snatchers several years back. He had not been specific about just what type of confrontation, so I was more than a little anxious about hearing the innkeeper's tale.

So with my nerves still shaken from Gage's kiss, I grabbed my sketchbook and let him help me out of the carriage in front of the inn at the edge of the wide village green. The inn stood in a row of whitewashed stone buildings with charcoal gray shingles, sparse and unassuming except for the sign hanging out front featuring the figure of an abbot in his habit holding an overflowing tankard of ale.

We entered the inn's front room, which also clearly served as the village's pub, and I was first struck by the scent of wood smoke, barley, and stale ale. The room was steeped in dark shadows, lit only by the fireplace, a few braces of candles, and the sparse light filtering through the room's two dusty windows. Probably better to mask the sticky substance that coated the floor fashioned from sturdy planks of wood. The same wood the gouged and chipped tables and chairs were fashioned from. I suspected the establishment had seen its fair share of rowdiness.

The room was empty save for two men hunkered around a table in the corner with their tankards of ale. They stared at us in curiosity as we crossed the room toward the counter. A tall, burly man hobbled through the door behind it, favoring his left leg.

He wiped his hands on a towel, looking us up and down in our obviously well-made and expensive winter attire. "Will ye be needin' a room then?"

"No. I'm after information, actually," Gage said.

The man's gaze immediately turned suspicious. "Oh?"

"Lord Rutherford hinted you might be a good man to talk to."

He set down the towel and crossed his arms over his chest. "About?"

I tensed at the man's belligerent stance, but Gage continued on unaffected. He pulled a coin out of the inside pocket of his coat and placed it on the counter. "Tell us about your run-in with that pair of body snatchers."

Whether because of the money or Gage's nonthreatening manner, the innkeeper abandoned his surly demeanor, pocketed the coin, and offered to pour us a drink. Gage asked for ale, but my stomach was too tied up in knots to imbibe anything. Besides, a lady never drank in the public room of a tavern, not if she could help it, and that proved to be a more difficult convention to break than I'd expected.

The innkeeper slid a foaming tankard of ale across the scarred counter to Gage and then leaned against it with his not inconsiderable bulk. "'Twas two summers ago. Mr. Harden 'n I was on our way back from Galashiels Fair when we saw this trap comin' t'ord us." He shook his head. "Somethin' 'twasn't right aboot it. An' I said as much to Harden."

"What wasn't right?" Gage asked after taking a drink of his ale.

The innkeeper's eyes narrowed in emphasis. "There was three men in that trap, but the one in the middle looked funny, all slouched o'er and pale. And he seemed familiar."

I clutched my sketch pad tighter to my chest, suspecting what was coming.

"Weel, I yelled at 'em to stop, and the two on either side leapt oot o' the trap and ran off into the night. I woulda' chased 'em, and likely caught 'em. But there was the third one left to deal wi'. And he was sittin' there motionless. We saw why when we got closer." The innkeeper leaned in closer. "'Twas ole Peter McCraig, who'd been buried two days past." He nodded sagely. "Those men were body snatchers."

I suddenly felt the urge to laugh, inappropriate as it was. But the innkeeper had clearly been called upon to relay this story numerous times, and had calculated its delivery for maximum effect. I lifted a gloved hand to my mouth to cough, smothering my humor. Out of the corner of my eye, I could see Gage's mouth twitched. Apparently, I wasn't the only one amused.

He cleared his throat. "Yes. Were they ever apprehended?"

The innkeeper shook his head. "Nay. Though the horse was collected by a dealer in Kelso, who said he hired it oot. Last spring there was talk that the trap was claimed, but no one ever came for it." His eyes hardened, staring off into the distance. "And noo, there ain't nay more trap for 'em teh claim."

What that meant, I could only guess.

"Did you get a good look at the men?" Gage asked, distracting him from whatever thought was giving him such spiteful pleasure.

"Aye. I saw 'em weel enough."

"Would you be able to describe them for us? Perhaps well enough for us to make a sketch?" He dipped his head toward me and the sketch pad and charcoals I'd brought at his suggestion.

"Aye. Sure I could," the innkeeper declared.

"Do you mind?" Gage asked me, a bit belatedly.

How could I say no? After all, it was one skill set I possessed that he did not, and I did want to be useful. Even if that meant sitting in this sticky taproom for another half hour.

I nodded.

The innkeeper pushed himself up from his slouch. "Does this have somethin' to do with the goin' ons o'er at the abbey a few nights past?"

"Something," Gage answered obscurely.

The three of us settled down at a table near the bar with a rather large gouge in it. One that I thought looked suspiciously like the shape of an axe-head. Just what went on in this pub?

I tried to ignore whatever substance was stuck to the table—figuring the towel the innkeeper had set on the bar was probably not much cleaner—and balanced the sketch pad in my lap. Thankfully the innkeeper seemed to have a distinct memory—that, or he was making it up—for the session moved quickly. Once or twice I looked up to scowl at Gage where he sat rocking on the back legs of his chair, still nursing his tankard of ale. I hoped the glass was cleaner than the rest of this inn, or he was in for an unpleasant surprise. Or perhaps I should have wished the opposite.

In any case, I finished quickly and Gage thanked the innkeeper, passing him another coin for the ale.

After we climbed back into the carriage, I turned to him with displeasure. "Do you honestly believe these drawings are going to prove helpful?" A year and a half after the incident, with only a short glimpse of these two men in the dark, how on earth could the innkeeper's description of them prove accurate?

"I don't know. But there was no harm in trying. Perhaps he got some of the details right. Like that scar across the one man's forehead. Or the second man's crooked teeth."

I continued to frown. He did have a point.

"I know it's long odds. After all, Peter McCraig's corpse was stolen by traditional body snatchers, while with the late Earl of Buchan's body, we don't know who we're dealing with."

"But they could still be the same men," I said, finishing the thought for him. Perhaps they'd stumbled upon a more lucrative plot themselves. Or been hired by someone else for their experience in such matters—both with the snatching and the area. Either was a possibility.

I sighed and turned to stare out the window at the village.

Gage nudged my foot with his own, waiting for me to look at him. He grinned. "Cheer up. Or Mrs. Moffat will think I'm bringing her another corpse."

I arched a single eyebrow in annoyance. "Very funny."

CHAPTER TWELVE

M rs. Moffat lived in a tidy little cottage at the edge of
the village. Barren bushes sat neatly trimmed beside
the doorway, and trellises were attached to the walls on
either side of the windows. I suspected in spring and summer the home was nearly covered in creeping roses and other
flowering plants. Even in the dead of winter, one could sense
the promise of the greenery and blooms to come.

I'm not sure what I expected of the person who cleaned
and prepared the bodies of the deceased, but it was not this
charming home. Or the smiling middle-aged woman who
opened the door to our knock. She could not have stood
taller than five foot, even with her hair piled up under her
neat white cap.

When Gage informed her of the reason for our visit, she
stepped back to usher us inside. "Oh, come in. Come in."
She closed the door behind us and took our coats. "And
please dinna mind the mess," she said hustling us toward a
door on the other side of the parlor. "Children will be children after all."

What mess she was referring to, I could not tell, for the
inside of her cottage was as tidy as the outside. Perhaps it
was the overabundance of china shepherdesses decorating
every available surface above three feet high, or the cluster

of toy soldiers in one corner of the room. In either case, those things only proved the house was lived in.

I'd half expected her to escort us into her work space where she prepared the bodies, but it was merely a sunny kitchen with white lace curtains. A loaf of bread sat cooling near the stove, its yeasty fragrance filling the air. She invited us to take a seat at the tartan-covered table to one side of her back door. I pulled out my chair and then hesitated, suddenly wondering if this was the flat surface she used to lay out the bodies. Though I thought I was being subtle, Mrs. Moffat noticed.

"Lore, no, m'lady. The bodies ne'er come in here."

I flushed. "I'm so sorry. I shouldn't have—"

"Nay, lass," she interrupted, reaching out to place a hand over my own where it rested on the chair back. "It's all right. I ken what I do is a bit ghoulish. And I wouldna be doin' it either if it didna pay such good money."

She patted my hand one more time for good measure and turned to cross the room toward her stove. "When my Albert died, leavin' me with four young bairns teh feed, I didna ken how I was gonna keep food on the table." She set a kettle of water on the stove and began to spoon tea leaves from a tin on the counter into a plain white porcelain pot. "Then Vicar Timms came teh me with the offer of this position. The woman who'd done it afore had died. And perhaps it's sad teh say, but it seemed like a godsend."

She turned and smiled, her hands pressed together over her skirt. "I ken it must be hard to understand, gruesome as the work seems—"

"No," I said gently, it being my turn to interrupt her. "It's not hard to understand at all."

She regarded me thoughtfully, and I was certain she sensed more than I was saying, but she was gracious enough not to mention it. She simply nodded and turned to gather up a set of cups and saucers.

I felt slightly ashamed of myself for making assumptions

about the woman before I'd even met her. The fact that people did the very same thing to me had made me sensitive to the subject. But apparently that didn't mean I was incapable of committing the same ignorant sins myself.

I glanced at Gage as Mrs. Moffat set the cups before us and then pulled out her chair. He offered me a sympathetic smile, making me suspect he'd guessed where my thoughts had gone.

"Noo, what can I do for you?" Mrs. Moffat asked.

"We've been told you prepared the late Earl of Buchan's body for burial," I said.

She nodded. "I did. 'Twas an honor." She paused to look between us. "Does this have teh do wi' his body bein' snatched from his grave the other night?"

Gossip did travel fast, especially in small villages.

"Yes."

She sighed and shook her head. "I've ne'er heard o' the like." She tipped her head to the side. "'Course, there was that incident wi' ole Mr. McCraig. Ye've heard o' it?"

We nodded, having just come from hearing the details at the Abbot Inn.

"Aye. Well, apparently, because o' that, I have the unique distinction of havin' prepared the same body *twice* for burial." She scoffed. "As if that's somethin' to be proud of."

The kettle began to whistle and Mrs. Moffat rose to pour its contents into the teapot. "Have they found him then?" she called over her shoulder.

"Uh, no. And if they do, it's unlikely your services will be needed."

"I figured no'. The man'd be nothin' but bones." She set the teapot down on the table. "So what is it ye wish to ask me?"

"Do you remember what was buried with him?" I asked, suddenly hopeful this efficient woman would be able to give us an answer to this question once and for all.

She nodded decisively. "I do. Keep a record o' all my clients' effects, doon to the buttons on their shirts."

I breathed a sigh of relief. Finally.

"I'll be happy teh fetch the list for ye soon as we've had our tea."

"Thank you."

"Sure," she replied and then asked how I liked my tea.

Once we were all settled back with our cups, she turned to regard me again. "Was there an item in particular you're curious aboot?"

I smiled. Mrs. Moffat missed nothing. I imagined she'd make quite a formidable investigator herself, if she ever tired of preparing bodies for burial.

"There is." I set my cup down in its saucer with a clink. "I know this may sound odd. But was the earl buried with any unusual jewelry? A gold torc, perhaps?"

Mrs. Moffat began to laugh. "Lore, that is somethin' his lordship would do." Clearly she understood the jewelry's implication. She shook her head and giggled once more, as if imagining the deceased earl wearing a torc. She cleared her throat. "But nay, m'lady. The only jewelry I placed in the coffin wi' him was a stickpin and a gold watch. I'll check my records to be certain, but I'm fair sure. And I'd certainly remember a torc."

I nodded and took another sip of tea, staring at Gage across the table. If the earl wasn't buried with the torc, then just what were the body snatchers looking for? Did they truly only come for his bones? It made no sense to me.

"Although," Mrs. Moffat mused, interrupting my thoughts. Her mouth pursed. "That disna necessarily mean he wasna buried in it."

"What do you mean?"

"Well, once I was finished, the coffin was taken to Dryburgh House and reopened for the viewing before the funeral. Someone could o' put it on him then."

So, truly, we had no way of knowing. Perhaps Mrs. Moffat and the earl's nephew had not placed the torc in the coffin with him, but the old earl could have entrusted the task to a servant or friend. There was no way of knowing for sure unless we tracked down every person who had viewed the body before the burial, and even then there was no guarantee they would tell the truth.

Gage and I thanked Mrs. Moffat, taking the list of the late earl's effects she'd copied for us to compare with those that had been found, but just from a glance, I could tell there was nothing missing. Nothing but the earl's bones.

"Well, this is proving to be a fruitless excursion," I griped.

"Not necessarily," Gage replied with infuriating calm.

"What do you mean?"

"Well, if the late earl was buried with a torc, it was done with some sort of subterfuge. Which makes it more likely that Collingwood's claim is true. Or else, why hide it?"

"Yes. But that only matters if it was, in fact, buried with him. How are we going to find that out?"

"Patience. There's still much to discover."

I considered throwing my boot at his head.

When questioning my aunt Sarah, we had discovered that most of the local aristocrats and gentry had attended the Hogmanay Ball, but there had been one person conspicuously absent—a Miss Musgrave, who lived with her parents on the western edge of St. Boswells. Their large, classically designed home sat but two hundred yards from the River Tweed and, interestingly enough, across the water from Dryburgh Abbey. From the south shore you could see nothing of the abbey ruins through the screen of trees along the north shore except the top of the abbey church's south transept and a sliver of the west wall of what had been the refectory, but it was there all the same.

The butler, a rather puffed-up man, reluctantly showed us into a parlor at the back of the house, where we were forced to wait for several minutes. As early as darkness fell in January, the sky had already begun to deepen toward dusk, and it was barely teatime. I studied the gray ribbon of the river outside the window rather than the ornamentation of the room around me. Mr. Musgrave—we'd been warned his wife was dead—was clearly more interested in displaying his wealth than comfort or aesthetics. The chair I perched on was covered in a lovely gold and cream toile, but hard, stiff, and garish given its position next to a canary yellow sofa.

The man himself seemed to prefer simple black. He wore trousers and a double-breasted, calf-length frockcoat with what I suspected were padded shoulders, for I highly doubted the round man sported such a physique naturally. Fashionable Mr. Musgrave might be, but there was no comparison between him and Gage, even though Gage wore only a pair of buff riding breeches and a hunter green tailcoat—no padding necessary.

Mr. Musgrave paused in the doorway to examine each of us before striding across the room to shake Gage's hand. "Sorry to keep you waiting," he declared in a manner that told us he was not. "Business to attend to." He gestured for Gage to take a seat next to me. "Noo, what can I do for you?"

Clearly the man had no desire to indulge in idle small talk, so Gage got directly to the point. "We understand your daughter was ill on Hogmanay and could not attend the ball."

"Aye. Just a touch of the ague."

Gage cleared his throat. "Yes. Well, we wondered if we might have a word with her and any servants who stayed with her that night." He nodded toward the windows. "We noticed part of your home faces the river, and the abbey, and we wondered if they might have seen anything regarding what happened there."

Mr. Musgrave sat forward on his chair. "I'm afraid I canna help ye. As I said, my daughter was ill with the ague. She wouldna seen anything."

"But if we could just confirm that with her," Gage pressed before the man could rise to his feet.

He narrowed his eyes. "I told ye. She didna see anything."

"And how do you know that?"

Mr. Musgrave's mustache began to quiver. "She woulda told me. Noo . . ."

"I'm sorry, sir," Gage said, a hard look entering his eyes. "But I'm afraid we must insist."

Mr. Musgrave's complexion began to grow red.

"Or I can ask Lord Rutherford to pay you a visit, and he can speak with her."

It was a viable threat and Mr. Musgrave knew it. My uncle *was* the local magistrate, and there would be curious questions from the townsfolk about his visit.

He nodded jerkily. "Give me a moment."

"You know he's going to interrogate his daughter now before she talks to us," I leaned closer to tell Gage after the door closed behind our host.

He smiled grimly. "Yes, but it can't be helped."

About five minutes later, Mr. Musgrave returned with a young lady of about eighteen dressed in a pale lavender gown with puffed sleeves. They were trailed by a maid perhaps a dozen years older than her charge, her hands clasped tightly before her turning her knuckles nearly white. I couldn't tell whether the woman was generally anxious around her employer or if she was nervous about the questions she knew we were about to ask.

The girl looked even less confident—darting glances between us and her father, her face pale and drawn. I nearly told Gage we should excuse ourselves, and not bother wasting their time or ours. The women weren't going to give us any information, whether they had any to share or not. And we would never be able to tell whether their nerves stemmed from withholding this information or Mr. Musgrave having threatened them into silence.

But I held my tongue and rose to my feet this time, more to put the maid and the girl at ease than in deference to our host. I outranked them all, after all, and little as I cared to use that privilege most of the time, I wouldn't mind exerting it over Mr. Musgrave.

"Noo, tell them what ye told me," Mr. Musgrave prompted his daughter. When she didn't respond quickly enough for him, he nudged her in the back. "Tell them, Alice."

"I . . . I was ill in bed all of Hogmanay." Her voice was soft and cultured, clearly well educated, as many wealthy merchants' daughters were, in hopes of catching a titled husband.

"I see." Gage offered her a sympathetic smile. "You must have been very disappointed to miss out on the ball?"

Her eyes blinked wide. "I . . . Yes, I was."

"I'm sure you were looking forward to dancing and laughing with your friends. I'm sorry you missed it."

She darted a look to the side where her maid stood just behind her and nodded.

Curious.

Gage seemed to have noticed it as well. "So you never got up? Never looked out the window?" he tried again.

Miss Musgrave opened her mouth to answer but her father cut her off. "She said she didna."

Gage turned to the maid. "And what of you Miss . . ."

She glanced at her employer before replying. "Peggy, sir."

"Peggy," Gage replied, offering her a smile as well.

A slow flush began to burn from the neckline of her brown serge gown up into her cheeks.

"Surely you must have been up and down, tending to Miss Musgrave so admirably, missing out on the Hogmanay festivities yourself."

Miss Musgrave frowned, not seeming to like his supposition.

"Did you by chance hear or see anything unusual when passing a window?" Gage persisted.

The maid stood silent, as if considering her words, and I thought for a moment she might be about to share something. But then she replied simply, "No, sir."

I withheld a sigh. There was certainly something Miss Musgrave and Peggy were not telling us, but now was not the time to press. Not with Mr. Musgrave present, in any case.

So we excused ourselves, gathered our outer garments, gloves, and hats, and made our way back out to the carriage. However, the maid had one more surprise for us.

I turned to say something to Gage when I heard a hiss from the corner of the building. Peggy darted her head around the corner and gestured to me before ducking back behind the wall, lest she be seen by the pretentious butler still standing by the doorway. I looked up at Gage to see if he'd seen the maid as well.

"Oh, let's stop and admire the view for a moment. It's such a lovely one."

Catching on to my ploy, Gage flashed me a secret smile. "Yes, shall we." He grinned broadly at the butler, who I swore sniffed before closing the door.

We strolled unhurriedly toward the corner where Peggy stood, in case we were being watched through a window.

"I canna be caught . . ." she stammered, glancing behind her ". . . or it'll mean my post."

"We understand," I said.

She looked behind her once more and nodded. "On Hogmanay, I did step ootside once. For fresh air."

I suspected it had more to do with escaping her charge.

"And . . . and I saw lights. O'er at the ole abbey."

I exchanged a knowing glance with Gage. It was nothing more than we already knew, but it was confirmation, nonetheless.

"Do you know about what time that was?" he asked.

"Eleven? Half-past? 'Twasn't yet midnight."

"Thank you," I told the maid and she nodded and turned to go. "Peggy."

She looked back over her shoulder at me.

"If ever you should find yourself in need of a position, go to Clintmains Hall. Tell them I sent you."

Our eyes held for a second longer in mutual understanding and then she was gone.

I sighed and allowed Gage to escort me back to our carriage. "Do you think she was seen?" The wind lifted the hems of my cloak and his great coat, tangling them around our heels.

"No. But perhaps it would be better if she had been."

The look in his blue eyes told me he'd observed as much as I had. Mr. Musgrave would not be an easy man to work for. Or an easy man to call father.

"Do you think Miss Musgrave was really ill?"

Gage tilted his head, considering the matter. "I don't know. But you're right. There was something she was keeping from us. Something she was anxious her maid would reveal."

"To us *and* her father."

Gage's gaze sharpened. "Yes."

## CHAPTER THIRTEEN

"This is the place, is it not?" Gage murmured in a hushed voice.

Clinging tightly to his arm, I narrowed my eyes trying to pierce the shadows under the trees, but the darkness here was absolute. "Yes," I whispered, following his lead. "My uncle said the hut was surrounded by a stand of ancient yew trees."

The wind sliced through the night, whistling and clattering through the branches. Like icy fingers, it crept over my shoulders and up under my skirts, making me shiver with dread. I had not enjoyed visiting the abbey on Hogmanay night, when Dodd was murdered and the late Earl of Buchan's grave was disturbed. And I was not happy to be here again, in the cold and the dark, searching for the Nun of Dryburgh, a woman many believed to be nothing but a spirit haunting the ruins and mourning her lost love.

I had heard tales of the brokenhearted woman who had taken to living in a vault in the abbey after her lover was killed during the Jacobite rising of 1745. In the absence of her man, she swore never to again look upon the light of day. Some said she was the lady of a local nobleman and had taken up with one of her husband's kinsmen. When their treachery was discovered, the wife was banished and the lover sent to die on a battlefield.

Whether there was any truth to the story, I did not know. But if the Nun we searched for was, in fact, a living, breathing woman whose lover had died in '45, then she must be ancient, certainly the oldest person I had ever met.

Rationally, I doubted the macabre tale. If my uncle had spoken with the Nun, and she lived in a wooden hut next to the abbey ruins, not inside one of the vaults, then the rest of the story was likely either fabricated or embellished, perhaps to keep people away from the unstable ruins after sunset. Or maybe to prevent scavengers from stealing any more of the abbey's stones for their own building projects.

But standing here in the dark and cold of a winter night, with the howl of the wind and the shifting shadows playing tricks on my eyes and ears, it was far easier to believe the ghoulish tale.

"I think I see something," Gage said.

I gripped his arm tighter, my fingers pressing deeper into the woolen fabric of his coat. My heart leapt in my chest, pounding against my rib cage, as I tried to locate what he was seeing. When I realized he was only talking about the hut, which I could now glimpse the outline of as he lifted the lantern higher, I exhaled in relief, loosening my grasp on Gage's arm. I breathed deep the scent of yew and the sharpness of the wind, which burned my lungs, as he pulled me closer.

The hut was built of rough-hewn wood with no windows, and looked to be barely lashed together against the weather. It couldn't be a comfortable place to live, even sheltered among the trees. Especially if the Nun was as old as she was rumored to be. I frowned. Why wasn't she better cared for? Where was her family?

Or did she not have need of one? After all, if she were a spirit, I doubt she felt the cold.

I swallowed and glanced over my shoulder as Gage reached up to rap gently on the door.

The pale light of a fire spilled out from beneath it, letting us know someone inhabited the abode. Someone who felt the bite of cold and needed the light by which to see. When there was no answer, he knocked again, but no one came to the door.

"Madam," he called out hesitantly. "We're sorry to disturb you. We're friends of Lord Rutherford." He paused, but there were no sounds of movement from within. "If we could just have a word with you, we'll be on our way." Gage's plea was greeted with more silence. "Madam?"

"Maybe she's not here," I whispered.

He frowned and nodded.

If she only emerged at night, then surely she must run her errands under the cover of darkness as well. But where had she gone? To the village? Or was she much closer?

Gage pivoted us so that we could see the craggy outline of the abbey in the pale moonlight penetrating through a break in the clouds.

My heart began to beat faster again at the thought of entering the ruins, but I knew there was no help for it. They would have to be searched. Given the Nun's propensities, it was the likeliest place to find her. And, in fact, the place we hoped she'd been three nights past when the grave robbers were at work.

Gage and I did not speak, both knowing what must happen, and that I would insist on joining him, no matter his protestations to the contrary. He merely nodded in resignation, and we set off down a path through the trees.

This time we approached the abbey from the southeast. Gage hesitated at the entrance to the covered stone passageway that led through the eastern wall. It was thick with darkness, and though we could see some moonlight at the other end, there was still a good fifty feet of blackness before us. We turned toward the south, but the ditch that ran southeast to northwest along the southern edge of the abbey blocked us from reaching the other side of the ruins. There was no choice but to pass through the slype or retrace our steps to our carriage and find our way around to the West Door.

"Follow me," Gage ordered, nudging me behind him.

His hand reached inside the pocket of his greatcoat and extracted the pistol I'd grown accustomed to seeing in the back waistband of his trousers.

I followed suit, edging my hand into my reticule to wrap my fingers around the Hewson percussion pistol my brother-in-law, Philip, had purchased for me before I left Edinburgh. After the two spots of danger I'd found myself in during the last two investigations I'd assisted with, I'd vowed never to go anywhere unarmed again. Trevor had not been happy when I asked him to teach me how to use it, but he'd complied, knowing I would have stubbornly tried to teach myself, risking injury in the process.

Hefting the lantern high, Gage inched his way through the tunnel, twisting from side to side to sweep the darkness for any movement. I followed a short distance behind, my shoulders up around my ears as I periodically glanced behind me, mistrustful that something was tailing us. As before, the cloying scent of mold and must surrounded us, reminding us how old these buildings were, and how long they'd been exposed to the elements.

When we reached the other side, Gage still did not put his pistol away, but kept it at the ready. I wondered if he felt the same uneasiness I did. We searched the rooms to our left and to our right, open to the elements, and then the ruins of the refectory directly in front of us. The soaring western wall of the room remained mainly intact, with its beautiful twelve-lighted rose window.

Turning to the right, we climbed the chipped flight of stairs up to the cloister.

"Mind your step," Gage told me.

I hefted my skirts, trying to recall where the uneven patches of stone were from descending them earlier that day.

At the top we turned to survey the open grassy area just as the moon passed behind a bank of clouds. I shivered, clinging to his side and the ring of light cast by the lantern. Everything was silent, save for the gust of the wind and the creaking of the lantern.

And then a short tapping sound reached us, like that of metal against stone.

We turned as one to stare at the doorways to our right opening off the cloister. Side by side we moved forward, listening for the sound. It was several moments later, as we were considering entering the Chapter House, that we heard it again, coming from a room farther down the wall. We paused at the entranceway to the library and then realized it was emanating from the next door. The one leading to the room we had not searched earlier that day for fear that it looked too dilapidated. The vault.

Gage lifted his hand, telling me to stay back, and then inched closer to the door. The sound had stopped, likely because whatever was making it had seen the light of our lantern approaching.

"Is someone there?" he called.

I could not hear an answer and so inched closer to be able to see around Gage's shoulder inside the blackness of the open doorway.

"We mean you no harm," he tried again. "But if you do not come out, I will come in after you. And I warn you, I am armed."

Several seconds passed, and I began to worry that Gage would indeed have to go in after them, when suddenly a form in gray seemed to materialize out of the darkness.

I gasped and shrank backward, pressing a shaking hand to my mouth.

When the visage before my eyes began to take on more depth and texture, I realized it was human. An old woman, to be exact, with long, flowing gray hair and a wrinkled face that still managed to retain some of the great beauty it must have shown at a younger age. She stood with her hands wrapped in the folds of her coarse gray garments, silently observing us as we observed her, the only difference being that her countenance appeared unconcerned, even accepting of our presence.

I took another step closer, drawn by the serenity and sorrow that seemed etched into the lines of her face, almost at odds with one another. Her eyes were a pale crystalline gray, like the ice at the edge of a loch. They regarded me, first with indifference and then growing curiosity, as if she saw in me more than she expected.

"You're the woman they call the Nun of Dryburgh," I said, interested in her reaction to the sobriquet.

But there was none. "I am." Her voice was oddly flat, but still pleasing.

"My uncle, Lord Rutherford, suggested we speak with you."

"About the diggers." It was a statement, not a question.

I turned to look at Gage to see his reaction to the woman before us. He had dropped the pistol to his side, but had not replaced it in his pocket. And his eyes, they seemed . . . muddled, as if uncertain what he was seeing. But when he caught me looking at him, he righted himself, his gaze turning firmer.

"You saw them then?" he asked her. "On Hogmanay. The men disturbing the late earl's grave."

Her eyes trailed into the vault through which she'd emerged, and she spoke, not to us, but to herself or perhaps someone else. "I told you to be buried here. Where you're safe. But you did not listen."

I glanced at Gage again, not knowing what to make of her words.

He shook his head. "Did you get a good look at these diggers? Did you hear any of them speak?"

She turned to look at us, her expression resigned. "No. It was best to stay away."

I couldn't argue with her about that—not when poor Dodd had been shot to death for disturbing them—but it was still frustrating to hear.

"So you noticed nothing that would help us identify them?" Gage persisted, aggravation stretching his voice. "The type of clothes they wore? The number of men?"

Her head tilted to the side as she studied his features more closely and answered abstractly. "Four. They spoke oddly. It hurt my ears, so I didn't listen."

What that meant, I couldn't have guessed, though he tried.

"You mean, they didn't speak English?"

"No. It was English. Just not the way I speak it. And not like the man with cotton in his nose."

Gage's brow creased in confusion. "Was it harsher? Coarser? More genteel?"

She shrugged, as if the matter no longer interested her. "Tell me, have you seen Sir Godfrey?" She turned to stare out over the dark cloister, her voice fading. "I've been waiting for him so long."

My eyes widened, but I shook my head when Gage's uncertain gaze pleaded with me to make sense of her words and I could not.

"No, madam," he replied hesitantly. "I'm afraid I have not."

She sighed with such heartbreak that I wished there was something I could do for her. Something I could say. How had she come to this?

But before I could offer her any comfort, she began to murmur under her breath. "Young lovers, young lovers everywhere. But mine is lost to me." Then she lifted her gaze and spoke more directly. "They're a plague, you know."

"Young lovers?"

"Yes."

"They come here?"

"Some do."

I thought of the bundle of lady's clothing we'd found that morning. "Do they go to the Chapter House?" Out of the corner of my eye, I saw Gage's stance sharpen in interest.

But the Nun's attention had already wavered, and she was staring forlornly off into the distance. I opened my mouth to ask again, but Gage shook his head, moving forward to take my arm.

"Thank you for your time, madam," he told her politely, recapturing her attention. "If you think of anything else, well . . ." He paused, clearly recalling the difficulty of receiving communication from her. "If you can get word to Lord Rutherford, he'll let me know."

She nodded slowly and I reluctantly allowed Gage to turn me away.

"Hold him close," she spoke to my back, and I stopped to look over my shoulder. Her serene face was creased into lines of worry. "That one has a shadow hanging over him."

My heart stilled at the pronouncement, but before I could ask more, she was gone, disappeared back into the darkness of her vault.

"What was that?" I asked Gage as we climbed the stairs into the ruins of the abbey church.

"Nonsense." His voice, like his footsteps, were sure, unshaken by the Nun's words.

But I didn't feel so confident.


In contrast to the dark shadows of the abbey, Clintmains Hall was bright with light when we returned. I welcomed the glow of the warm candlelight and the heat of the fires, still trying to shake away the chill of the night and the Nun of Dryburgh's words. We were invited to stay for dinner, which we were told would be quite informal, saving us embarrassment since we had no evening clothes to change into.

We informed Uncle Andrew of our discoveries, which were few. It was frustrating to know we'd achieved almost nothing but to confirm information we already had, and wheedle some unclear statements about the body snatchers' odd manner of speech from the Nun. The day felt wasted.

I hoped to steal a moment alone with my brother, but he seemed determined to avoid me. Whenever I entered a room, he was drawn to another one, or asked to turn the pages of my cousin Gilly's sheet music, or requested as a fourth for a hand of whist. There was no obvious evasion on his part, but some deft maneuvering was made, nonetheless. It only made me worry all the more that I had missed something important while so preoccupied with my anger and grief. I considered questioning our uncle, but this was a private matter between Trevor and me. He deserved the chance to tell me before I expressed my concern to anyone else.

At dinner we passed around the sketches I had made of the body snatchers from the innkeeper's recollections. No one remembered seeing them, but my cousins did have fun speculating on the criminals' more interesting features, with Jock offering the wildest conjectures, of course, despite our Uncle Andrew's efforts to turn the conversation.

"Now, look at that knob. Must've walked into a door lintel."

"Nay. His wife probably corked him wi' a frying pan."

"Are you daft? That face is too ugly for a wife. I bet he got kicked by a horse."

"Oh, that reminds me." Miss Witherington gasped eagerly.

I looked up in surprise, not having expected her to join in the conversation. Even the others fell silent, slightly startled by her pronouncement.

She smiled at her fiancé and then the rest of the table. "Did I tell you I received a letter from Miss Holt? She's just become engaged to Lord Wilmot."

"Why, how delightful," Aunt Sarah replied, while the rest of us lost interest.

I even caught sight of Jock rolling his eyes and had to stifle a laugh in my napkin. Which somehow Miss Witherington failed to miss, for her eyes narrowed to slits. She pointedly turned to Gage with a calculating gleam in her eye.

"Did you know that Miss Holt is the cousin of Lady Felicity Spencer?"

"Is she?" Gage replied, forking a bite of pheasant.

"Yes. They're quite close." She tilted her head to the side

in much too innocent a display. "Aren't you acquainted with Lady Felicity?"

He did nothing but flick an annoyed glance at her, but it was still enough to make my stomach sour.

"Yes. We've been introduced."

"Oh, there's no need to be so circumspect," she declared with a trill of laughter, before leaning forward. "I heard you danced with her twice at the Snowdon soiree and twice at the Cheltenhams' Midsummer's Eve Ball."

"Did I? I can't recall." His tone of voice was perfectly neutral, but I knew better. If he was making such an effort to sound as if he were uninterested, then he was. But why?

However, Miss Witherington clearly did not know this about him, and disappointed with his answer, her mouth puckered into an insipid pout.

"Have your friend, Miss Holt, and Lord Wilmot set a date?" Aunt Sarah asked, stepping in once more to redirect the conversation.

I knew Miss Witherington did not like me—she had made that abundantly clear—and so she was only trying to upset me by mentioning the more socially acceptable ladies of Gage's acquaintance. A fact she needn't have pointed out. I was well aware how popular Gage was among good society, and how far below him in estimation I was, at least in that regard.

As the only son of a newly minted baron and a baronet's widow, we might have been equal in rank, but not in wealth or standing. On his father's death, Gage would inherit a title and estates worth several hundred thousand pounds, while I was an artist with barely two thousand pounds to my name. I would bring almost nothing to an alliance, but a soiled reputation.

Miss Witherington's dart had certainly found its mark by making me recall this truth at a time I would have preferred not to, even though it was not something I was likely to forget for long.

Though what was most unnerving was Gage's reaction—

his determined indifference. Why had he felt the need to appear uncaring? Was it simply an effort to discourage Miss Witherington's questions? Or was there something more to his relationship with Lady Felicity? Something he didn't want explored?

I stirred the beans around my plate, trying to convince my now disinterested stomach to take a bite.

"Trevor, aren't you acquainted wi' Lord Wilmot?" Jock leaned forward to ask my brother.

Trevor stiffened, seeming startled by the question. "Uh . . . yes."

"Ye should invite him doon to Blakelaw," Jock continued on, oblivious to the quelling look my brother sent him. "I hear he's a capital fellow. Great fun."

Trevor's eyes darted to me and then away. "Perhaps another time. Now isn't really the best."

Jock nodded, speaking around a bite of bread. "Right. Wi' the murder and missing bodies and all."

But I knew that was not what Trevor had been referring to. I set my fork down by my plate, unable to stomach even the thought of another bite.

I had known my brother's reputation had not been helped by his relation to me, but I had never suspected he was embarrassed. I had never really given much thought to any of the hardships my brother might have suffered because of me. Perhaps that was unworthy of me—being so wrapped up in my own worries and self-pity—but that didn't blunt the sting it caused to think that my brother was too ashamed to invite his friends to visit while I was present.

After the investigation was finished and Alana's baby was born, maybe I *should* consider finding a little cottage of my own. I would be able to afford one with the money I'd saved from the sales of my artwork. If I lived modestly in a home near London or Edinburgh, I should be able to live off the proceeds from my portrait commissions. I would visit my sister and my brother, but neither would be burdened with the obligation of supporting me.

It would be somewhat lonely living on my own, but perhaps that was for the best. I would have quiet and solitude, and company only when I wished it. And Alana and Trevor would be free to live their own lives again without worrying over me.

## CHAPTER FOURTEEN

We did not return to Blakelaw House that night until nearly midnight. It had been a somewhat tedious carriage ride home as both men had dozed in their respective corners while I sat rehashing the case, and the lack of progress we'd made. After such a long day I should have been worn out, but I was not.

I thought to ask my brother if I could speak with him, but before I had even finished removing my outer garments, he'd declared himself exhausted and wished Gage and I a good night. I watched him climb the stairs, wondering if I should insist, but his steps did seem incredibly weary. Perhaps it would be best to wait.

Gage halted in his ascent and turned toward me. "Aren't you retiring?"

"I'll be up in a minute," I replied, and he nodded.

Once he disappeared around the corner, I began to aimlessly wander the rooms on the ground floor—the drawing room, the study, the library, the dining room. It was something I'd found myself doing often since my return two months prior. I still wasn't sure what I was looking for.

Eventually, I ended up in my little corner of the conservatory, standing before one of my easels. I hesitated, just for a moment, before reaching out to lift the cover off the portrait sitting there. It was the cook's granddaughter, the same painting that had caused me to fling down my palette in frustration the previous afternoon. But here in the shadows, which were broken only by the pale waning moon, painting the portrait didn't seem so intimidating.

I carefully lit two lamps and positioned them to better illuminate the portrait. Surprisingly, it was not as badly executed as I'd expected. No, it was not up to my usual skill, but it was certainly far from an abomination. Perhaps with a little more work, and a little more patience, it could be salvaged. Or I could try something new.

I glanced at the blank canvases I had prepared stacked in the corner. My fingers twitched with eagerness.

I began to shake the thought away, as I'd done for weeks, but this time I stopped. Should I not at least give it some consideration? I'd been suppressing the desire to paint Gage for months, it seemed, though I'd sketched him countless times. It had made sense when I was trying to avoid thoughts of him, to push him from my mind. But now that he was here, sleeping across the hall from me in my childhood home, what was the use?

The same fear that had nagged me since finishing William Dalmay's portrait began to crawl up inside me, but this time I took a deep breath and angrily squashed it. I was tired of letting it control me. Perhaps if I gave in to the urge and painted a portrait of Gage, it would be the worst thing I'd ever created. But chances were, it would not. Just the fact that I was itching to hold a brush between my fingers, to breathe in the noxious bite of turpentine, to find the exact mixture of pigments that would duplicate the color of Gage's eyes, gave me a sudden thrill of hope.

I closed my eyes and pressed a hand to my speeding heart. And as if my thoughts had conjured him, I felt the heat from the very man materialize behind me.

"I thought I'd find you here," he murmured, his deep voice brushing against the side of my neck and raising gooseflesh.

"Must you always walk so stealthily?" I demanded, glancing up at him over my shoulder.

He merely smiled in his enigmatic way, his eyes warm and teasing. "I didn't know I was being so quiet. I'll remember to stomp next time."

I arched a single eyebrow in chastisement and turned back to my easel. "What are you doing here?" I asked, my voice sounding more breathless than I'd expected.

"Looking for you."

"Yes. I gathered that. But why?"

"Do I need a reason?" he asked, turning me to face him.

"No," I admitted, feeling somewhat flustered by his presence so close to me. "But you usually have one."

His gaze told me he sensed just how I was feeling. "Maybe it's only for this." And he pulled me close, cradling my chin in one hand, and kissed me. I fell into the moment, eagerly returning his affection. He smelled of sweat and starch and the spicy yet woodsy scent of his cologne, and tasted like the whiskey we'd placed in a decanter in his room. But as time stretched, I became urgently aware of our exposed location, of the doubts and questions still unaddressed between us, and pushed him back.

"Wait." I gasped, still wrapped in his arms. "What if Trevor sees us?"

I was pleased to hear that his breathing was just as ragged as mine. "And?"

I blinked, confused by his lack of concern. "He . . . he won't approve."

Gage stared down at me for a moment, as if gathering his thoughts. "Yes, I've noticed your brother can be rather protective of you. Though I think he could have done a better job of it five years ago when you wed Sir Anthony Darby," he added, his eyes turning hard.

I was momentarily shocked by the repressed fury in his voice. "Stop. My disastrous marriage was not his doing."

"No. But he should have looked after you."

"He . . . he did," I protested. "It's not his fault I didn't confide in him what Sir Anthony was doing."

Gage's gaze softened at my obvious distress, and he gently caressed the back of my neck, the rough calluses on his hands rasping against the delicate skin there. "Kiera. You cannot convince me he didn't realize something was horribly wrong. Your brother is not an ignorant lout."

I opened my mouth to argue, but his words had stung something inside me I did not want to touch. I swallowed and shook my head. "It doesn't matter. If he finds us here together like this now, he will feel it's his duty to demand satisfaction. And I don't want you and my brother to duel."

"Perhaps a duel would not be necessary."

My breath caught and I stared up into Gage's searching eyes. He couldn't mean . . .

Clearly sensing my confusion, he pulled me closer and brushed a stray hair from my cheek. "Kiera, I'm tired of denying this. Tired of pretending there isn't something between us. You know there is."

I nodded slowly. I couldn't refute it. Though I didn't know exactly what it was.

"I left Gairloch Castle thinking in a few weeks' time I would forget you. But I didn't. I couldn't. And believe me I tried."

I frowned, not certain I liked the sound of that, but he was still speaking.

"When I let you go that second time, after Dalmay's death, I already knew there was no use. That it would take a lot more than time and distance for me to stop thinking about you. But I knew you needed time, away from me, from everyone."

"Is that why you abandoned me in Edinburgh?" I whispered.

His eyes were stricken. "Is that what you thought?"

I nodded.

"Kiera, I'm sorry. I suppose I didn't want to get in the way of your grief for Dalmay. I know you cared for him a great deal. And perhaps I was a bit jealous."

"Of Will?" I asked in bewilderment.

His pale blue eyes darkened in color, and the depth of the emotion reflected there made my breath catch. "No man wants to watch the woman he cares for grieve for another man so intensely."

I didn't know what to say, but I thought my eyes might be telling him more than enough. I lifted one of my hands from his chest to press it against his cheek. It was warm and bristled with evening stubble.

He lifted his hand and pressed it to mine where it rested on his cheek then slid it around and gently kissed the center of my palm. His lips were soft and his breath hot. When he closed my fingers over it, I squeezed them tightly, as if I might brand the kiss into my palm.

"Kiera, I'm finished trying to forget you. And dare I hope that since you sent for me, you're finished trying to forget me, too?"

I knew what he was asking, and I knew it was in my power to give. But the pit in the center of my stomach—the part of me I had always relied upon to tell me when something wasn't right—dropped, and whether or not it was only fatigue or simple anxiety instead of outright fear, I knew I couldn't hand him what he wanted. At least not yet. I could see he sensed that, for the light in his eyes dimmed a little before I spoke.

"Gage, you know I care for you. I do." My eyes dropped to the folds of his cravat. "I never thought that someone . . . that I . . ." I stumbled over my words. "But I . . . I don't know. There's just still so much you haven't told me."

"You're right."

I lifted my gaze to his, relieved to see his expression was far from injured. In fact, it looked frighteningly determined.

"There is still a great deal I should share with you. And I will try. But I ask that you be patient with me. I'm no more used to sharing myself than you are."

I offered him a weak smile.

"Will you do that?"

"Yes," I replied softly.

"Which I assume means that, though you aren't ready to admit anything yet, you are willing to explore what this is between us. To let me woo you?"

I opened my mouth in surprise.

"I won't press you, Kiera, but you have to let me try. And I refuse to dishonor you by sneaking around like this and not at least announcing my intention to pay you court."

He was right. Thus far there had been no formal declaration between us, and I had been letting him kiss me like I was simply another merry widow, happy to accept his attentions without the benefit of matrimony. The fact that I was inexperienced in those ways did not mean I was not aware of them. Unsure of myself, I had let Gage take the lead. And though I'd known he was honorable, and he would never have coerced me past my own moral and religious compass, I had still relied upon him to guide us.

That he would actually admit to even more honorable intentions where I was concerned had never crossed my mind. Marriage between Gage and me seemed impossible, even foolish for me to contemplate, and yet here he was asking to court me. I was stunned.

"Kiera?" he pressed.

His gaze was so open, so hopeful, I couldn't help but feel a trill of happiness in my heart. And suddenly it seemed even more foolish for me to deny him.

"Yes."

He smiled, a flare of pure joy I couldn't help but return, and then pressed a kiss to my lips and then another.

"I will leave you then. Before your brother, or his dutiful butler, happens upon us."

I watched as he left, lifting my hand in farewell when he turned back before he disappeared behind the potted palm.

Something warm had taken root inside me, and though I felt the tangled branches of my anxieties trying to worm their way inside, for the moment I pushed them back. Unable to wipe the grin from my face, I turned to pull my apron down from its hook.

I woke the next morning to a feeling of warmth pressed to my left side, while the right side of my body was frozen. I shivered and curled in closer to the heat source. It was soft and pliable. But when it moved on its own, I blinked open my eyes.

I squinted against the sudden glare of sunlight and stared into the slits of Earl Grey's golden eyes. Above us the glass ceiling of the conservatory was bright with the morning sun. Clearly, I had fallen asleep on the wicker settee in my art studio and curled up in Earl Grey's blanket, and sometime during the night the friendly feline had decided to join me. He lifted his hind quarters, scooting an inch closer to my torso. I yawned and brushed my hand down his back from head to tail.

"That cat has become quite devoted to you," my brother said, startling me. I hadn't even known he was in the room.

I turned my head to see him standing before my easel, studying the portrait I'd left sitting there to dry. I flushed as I suddenly recalled just whose portrait I had worked on last night. I'd painted long into the night and made far more progress than I'd expected.

"What time is it?" I muttered, trying to distract my brother from the canvas.

His gaze shifted to meet mine. "Half past ten."

I opened my eyes wide and pushed myself into an upright position. "Truly?"

"Yes."

Earl Grey rumbled a protest as I jostled him and the blankets trying to swing my feet out from under them. I smothered another yawn as I sat up and reached over to pet his sleek fur in apology.

"I see you're painting again," Trevor said, taking us back to the subject I wished to avoid.

I smiled self-consciously. "Trying to anyway."

He continued to study the painting as if he couldn't take his eyes off it, and not wanting to know exactly what he was thinking, I opted for a more direct diversion, one I'd been attempting most of the previous evening.

"Trevor, is everything all right?"

He glanced up in surprise. "Yes. Of course."

"Because I know I haven't been the best of sisters since I came home. I've been consumed by my own concerns, to the exclusion of all else. I thought maybe you had problems of your own you wished to share," I murmured hesitantly.

The corners of Trevor's mouth turned up in a tight smile. "No, Kiera." He sat down next to me and patted my hand. "I am well."

"Are you sure?" I asked, avoiding his eyes by continuing to pet Earl Grey. "There's nothing troubling you about the estate?"

Trevor gave a short laugh. "There's always something troubling me about the estate." He offered me a reassuring smile, but it did not reach all the way to his eyes. "But nothing in particular."

I suspected he was lying, but it was clear he didn't wish to confide in me, and I could not force him to. But there was something else I could ask him about.

"You know you are welcome to invite Lord Wilmot or any of your friends to visit. I don't mind."

His face immediately creased into a frown. "No, I cannot."

My stomach clenched. "Be . . . because of me."

"Yes," he replied without hesitation.

Feeling a burning begin at the back of my eyes, I dropped my gaze to my feet and wrapped my arms around my churning stomach. Though I had suspected this was the reason, I hadn't expected my brother to confirm it so baldly. He must truly be ashamed of me then.

"I'm sorry. I should have thought," I murmured in a low voice.

"Why are you apologizing?" Seeing my confusion, he

elaborated. "You couldn't have known what a bad lot Lord Wilmot is. Could you?"

"Bad lot?" I blinked against the wetness in my eyes, trying to understand what he was saying. "You mean, you're not ashamed of me?"

"Of course not," he declared, and I felt the ball of dread that had gathered inside me release.

"So you're not embarrassed to introduce me to your friends?"

His gaze turned sad. "Oh, Kiera. If I'm embarrassed of anyone, it's myself."

"Why?"

He paused, as if considering what to tell me. Heaving a heavy sigh, he turned to stare out the glass wall of the conservatory. "I fell in with some bad people a few years ago. Gentlemen I'm not proud to be associated with."

"After the scandal broke over my involvement with Sir Anthony's dissections?" I guessed, and he nodded. "They shunned you as well?"

He sighed again. "Not at first. But after going one too many rounds of fisticuffs in defense of your honor, and calling one of the society matrons a shrew, well, you understand."

"Oh, Trevor." I gasped, oddly touched by his poor behavior.

He held up his hand. "I could have ignored their spiteful words. I should have. But I was too angry with them all. With myself."

I reached over to link my arm with his, sinking my head down on his shoulder.

"When I was no longer welcome at society's best events, I started attending those that were more questionable. Which is how I fell in with Wilmot and his cronies."

"Are they really so terrible?" I ventured.

"Yes. They're scoundrels and reprobates. And I don't want you to have anything to do with them." He glared down at me until I agreed. "I pity this Miss Holt. Even if she's as supercilious as Miss Witherington, she deserves a better husband."

I smiled. "Ah, so you've noticed that as well?"

"How can one miss it? She clearly has a bee in her bonnet where it concerns you." Then he muttered under his breath, "I seriously hope Andy has considered what he's in for if he marries the chit."

I squeezed his arm and he looked down at me.

"Do we understand each other now?"

I offered him a smile. "Yes."

He nodded and turned to stare at my easel. "I have questions for you about your Mr. Gage. But I suspect you don't wish to answer them now, do you?"

My cheeks began to heat at his description of Gage as "mine," and I cursed my fair complexion for being such a telltale.

He only grinned at my discomfort. "We'll save that for another time then. But don't think I'll overlook it forever."

I scowled. "I know you won't. Though, I admit, I was surprised you left us alone to question the villagers and the Nun."

He shrugged. "How much trouble could he get you into on the way to St. Boswells and back?"

"We could have stopped at an inn," I goaded him.

He arched his eyebrows in chastisement. "I already know you did. I was aware of the plan, remember. And our coachmen kept me abreast of your every movement."

I shook my head. I should have suspected as much.

"Just doing my duty by you, my dear."

# CHAPTER FIFTEEN

As we'd all slept late into the morning, Trevor, Gage, and I did not gather in the dining room until almost a quarter after noon. While the footman cleared away my remaining breakfast things, leaving the tea, at my request, Gage began to lay out all of the facts we had so far, which were disturbingly few.

"We know that on the night of Hogmanay a group of four men who spoke 'oddly' dug up the late Earl of Buchan's body and stole his bones, leaving everything behind, save maybe a golden torc. In the process of exhuming Buchan's body, it's likely they were disturbed by the Dryburgh groundskeeper, whom they shot and killed to keep silent."

"Very succinct," Trevor quipped. "What of Kiera's drawings?"

"Well, we knew that more traditional body snatchers have worked in the area before," I interjected. "So these could be the same men working on their own, or under someone else's direction."

Gage nodded in agreement. "We also have that bundle of lady's clothing we found in the Chapter House to consider. Though I can't see how they fit in."

I sat back to contemplate the matter, sipping from my cup of sweetened tea. I could make no sense of the clothes either.

Trevor tapped his fingers on the table and leaned forward. "And what of the connection with the body snatching of Sir Colum Casselbeck? Is it too early to have heard anything from your friend with the Edinburgh City Police?"

Gage crossed his arms over his chest. "I suspect it'll be at least two more days before I receive word from him. He'll need time to investigate. Depending on the families involved, these crimes may not have been reported."

I groaned. "We've learned almost nothing new."

"Patience," Gage soothed. "Sometimes that's the way investigations are. They're not always solved in three or four days. Most of my inquiries last weeks or months. There's no reason to become discouraged until we've exhausted all lines of inquiry."

I inhaled deeply and nodded. He was right. There was no reason for me to become so frustrated. We would find Dodd's killer and the late earl's body. It just might take a little more time than I was accustomed to. As confusing as this inquiry was, it was infinitely preferable to my two previous investigations, the first being a race to prove my innocence and find a killer before he struck again, while the second had been to find a missing girl and prove my friend Will Dalmay was sane and not a murderer.

"Now, I suggest we start by searching other local graveyards to see if any other graves have been disturbed. Lord Buchan's might not be the only one."

I agreed, grateful to have something to do to distract me from more unpleasant thoughts.

However, two fruitless days of searching turned up nothing. We could find no evidence that any of the other local graveyards had been disturbed by body snatchers in recent years. We even stopped by the tiny cemetery in Elwick, though I insisted I would have noticed if anything there was amiss. I showed Gage my parents' graves, and we spent a long time talking under the branches of the old oak standing sentinel over their final resting places.

More often than not, it was just Gage and I who made these excursions. Trevor would excuse himself, saying he had estate matters to attend to, but sometimes there was a look in his eyes that made me wonder if there was more to his absence than that. Regardless, I was pleased to see that my brother seemed to trust Gage, or that at least he was giving him the benefit of the doubt, for my sake.

And Gage was giving him no reason to regret it. True to his professed intentions, he behaved like a proper suitor. Well, most of the time. He did sneak in a kiss here and there. But I would have expected no less. And truth be told, I would have been disappointed had he not.

They were lovely, golden days, and even our lack of progress in the investigation did not dim my quiet joy. But they would not last forever.

It was late in the afternoon, and Gage and I had just returned from our walk to Elwick. The sun hung low in the sky behind us, casting long shadows on the road in front of us. I remarked on the odd flatness of the sky that evening, wondering if we might receive a dusting of snow soon.

Trevor heard us come in, and emerged from his study as I was removing my cloak. I could tell from the look on his face that something had happened.

"Trevor, what is it?"

He lifted a folded piece of paper. "It's from Lord Buchan. He's received a ransom note."

"Just two days. That doesn't give us much time," my uncle exclaimed, pacing back and forth before the hearth in Lord Buchan's drawing room. I didn't think I'd ever seen him more agitated.

Gage looked up from his perusal of the ransom note. "I would surmise that was intentional."

"Do they honestly expect Lord Buchan to have that much cash readily available on such short notice?" Uncle Andrew bellowed. "It's preposterous."

"Do you?" I asked the earl, who had sunk into one of the Chippendale chairs next to the wall of windows looking out on the lawn. Cold rain drummed against the glass, accented by the sharp ping of sleet.

He looked up from his dejected perusal of the Aubusson rug. "I do."

Uncle Andrew grumbled under his breath, but did not cease pacing. I suspected he was more agitated by the fact that such a crime was being committed in his jurisdiction than anything else.

"Under the circumstances, that's a very good thing," Gage said, handing me the note where I perched on the settee in front of where he stood. I ran my fingers over the paper. It was made from very good stock, though embellished with no markings. I opened it to read it while the conversation continued to flow around me.

"Why? You're not actually going to pay the ransom?" Uncle Andrew said.

"How else am I going to get my uncle's remains returned to me?" the earl argued.

Quality paper it might have been, but the handwriting was atrocious. I didn't know whether this was an attempt by the sender to disguise his identity or the general state of his penmanship. I suspected a mixture of both. The words were sloped and cramped, and the grammar was generally good, but here and there a word choice or phrase seemed off. Another thinly veiled effort at concealment, or the writing of a less educated man?

"That will be Lord Buchan's decision to make," Gage interjected, rounding the settee to sit down beside me. "But either way we are going to be there to meet that horse in two days' time, and we are going to at least make the thieves *think* we're paying the ransom."

The earl frowned. "What do you mean?"

Gage leaned forward over his knees. "The ransom note has given us very specific instructions. We're to place the money in two leather satchels and strap them to a horse that will be waiting for us at Shotton Pass. But I'm not about to send that horse on its way and not attempt to follow."

"But they said they'll be watching. That they'll know if we try to track the horse."

"How exactly? If they can see us, then we'll also be able to see them."

"Yes, but . . ."

"My lord, this may be our only chance to catch these men, to bring Dodd's killers to justice," Gage argued, sitting taller in his seat. "Had they merely stolen your uncle's body, I might be more open to persuasion. But they've already proved themselves willing to commit murder. And given the fact that they've likely done this before, and are apt to do so again in the future, I think it's imperative that these men be apprehended before they can cause more harm."

"So you think these are the same men who ransomed Sir Colum Casselbeck's body?" I asked.

There was a deep well of restrained anger behind his eyes. "Yes. The planning and the pattern of movements are too similar. Though they have moved the timetable up a bit. The Casselbecks had almost a week to gather their ransom money."

"But their exchange was conducted over water," I pointed out simply for the sake of argument.

"Because Musselburgh is near the forth. Maybe they thought asking Buchan to travel to the forth was too far away. Or perhaps we came too close to catching them the last time. I don't know. But I must say I prefer this payment location to that of one over water."

"Yes, but the ease of this location is deceptive," my brother murmured, tapping his fingers against the arms of his chair.

Our uncle nodded in agreement, finally settling into a chair near the warmth of the fire.

"Shotton Pass is at the edge of the Cheviot Hills, and that Border terrain is riddled with old reiver trails. It's broken country, dreary and desolate. Easy to lose your way and wander into a moss or a bog if you don't know where you're going. There's no way to know which trail the horse will have been trained to follow."

Gage's brow furrowed in frustration. "Yes, but surely it's been mapped."

Trevor shook his head. "They're all incomplete. How do you think the Border reivers were so often able to evade the wardens and each other? The terrain and twisting passes are known only to those who live on it. That's how it's always been. And that's how they mean to keep it."

"Then I suppose we'll need someone to ride with us who knows the area."

Trevor nodded to me. "Kiera and I have both ridden through the Cheviots. Though we're by no means experienced enough to claim we know the terrain, especially in the dark. I'll ask around. See if I can find someone willing to guide us."

I was both surprised and pleased that Trevor and Gage were not trying to leave me out of this part of the investigation, as I'd fully expected them to. I supposed they thought me safe enough trailing a horse through the desolate loneliness that was the Cheviot Hills. That or they simply recalled how little good it did to leave me behind. In both prior investigations, I had been left behind for my own protection while Gage and others pursued important leads, and yet I'd still ended up in danger.

"I'm sure my son and some of my nephews would also be willing to ride out with you if you think it would help," Uncle Andrew offered.

Gage rubbed his chin in thought. "No. I think four riders are plenty. Many more and we might just become confused in the darkness. After all, to follow the thieves' horse, we may have to rely more on the sound of the horse's hooves than on sight." He flicked a glance at me. "When we happen upon the culprits, we'll proceed with caution. If there are too many for us to safely apprehend, then we'll simply have to follow them or set a watch over their location." He turned to my uncle.

"But if your son and nephews would be willing to wait at an inn close to the location of our initial exchange, then we could send word to them should we need assistance."

He nodded. "It will be done."

Gage shifted in his seat so that he could better see Lord Buchan, who had been quietly listening to our plans. "I'll need you to position some men around the abbey on the evening of the exchange and for several days and nights after. When Sir Colum Casselbeck's ransom was paid, his bones were returned to the church attached to the graveyard where he was exhumed." His jaw hardened. "If they somehow manage to elude us while the ransom is being paid, perhaps we can catch them when they return the body."

## CHAPTER SIXTEEN

Though the light of day had not yet completely vanished from the sky, the waning crescent moon already shone on the horizon as we crested the ridge of land that would lead us down into Shotton Pass. Once the pale pink and yellow light of dusk faded from the sky, there would be little natural light to guide us. The thieves had chosen their time well.

I shivered as the wind whipped through the valley between the two rises. The rough land was speckled with scrub and rocks and bracken. If not for the unpleasant reason behind our visit, I might have found the vista before us rather beautiful, in a bleak and melancholy way. The sky above was streaked with low wispy clouds tinted red by the setting sun, and the almost desperate loneliness of the Cheviot Hills stretched out before us. Even the bitter gusts of the winter wind rattling the skeletal branches of the low-lying scrubs added to the landscape's desolation.

I huddled deeper into my royal blue woolen riding habit and brown fur-lined cloak. The rain had finally ceased a few hours before, and I was grateful to only be contending with the cold and not the wet. I could not say the same for Figg, my strawberry roan filly, whose pale legs were already coated in icy mud.

Figg seemed to pick her way along easily enough, despite the shifting, uneven ground beneath her hooves. Her ears twitched from side to side occasionally as the stumbling sounds of our progress echoed between the ridges, but she remained calm and collected following behind Trevor's bay stallion. Gage and his beautiful chestnut gelding brought up the rear.

Being a market day, my brother had been unable to find a guide to lead us into the hills on such short notice. A fact I was certain our thieves had also counted on. These men were far too intelligent for my comfort, and so I rode on deeper into the wilderness with some trepidation.

Trevor reined in his horse as we rounded a curve in the pass, allowing us to pull up beside him. Up ahead in a sheltered nook stood the yew tree the ransom note had described, and next to it, with her leather reins twisted in the branches, stood the sorrel mare nibbling at the tufts of grass at her feet. We all scanned the ridges above us, looking for any sign of someone watching from above, but the light was fading fast. It would not have taken much effort to remain hidden.

"Do we proceed?" Trevor asked.

The lines of frustration and grim determination that had marred Gage's brow all day deepened still. "Yes. But remain observant."

We followed him as he guided his horse forward, down the rise and deeper into the pass. The sorrel mare's ears perked up, followed by her head as she watched our approach. She did not seem overly wary, and I could only assume she was accustomed to encountering strange horses and people.

I remained on my horse, my eyes trained on the ridges above and my ears attuned to any strange sound—a cough, a sneeze, a slide of loose dirt or rocks, or worse still, the click of a pistol cocking. But no noise came to me beyond the gust of the wind and the shifting of Gage and Trevor's feet as they hefted the leather satchels filled with Lord Buchan's ransom money onto the back of the sorrel mare. The leather straps creaked as they were tightened.

Gage nodded for Trevor to mount and then reached up to untangle the mare's reins from the tree. I tensed, tightening my grip on my own reins, prepared for the thieves' horse to take off at a gallop. Instead, when Gage pulled the reins over her head, knotting them loosely behind her neck, and tapped her on the flank as directed, she grunted and slowly ambled forward, as if disgruntled to be forced to move from the warmth of this nook in the rocks. Gage had plenty of time to mount before the mare made any sort of effort to leave Shotton Pass.

She trotted lazily through the pass, taking us out of Scotland and into England. I turned to look at Gage, riding just over my right shoulder. Was it truly going to be this easy? At this pace, we could easily keep up with the mare and follow her to wherever the body snatchers were waiting for her.

But my thoughts had raced too far ahead. For when we cleared the last twist of the pass and an open stretch of moorland appeared before us, the mare suddenly lengthened her stride, cantering across the black expanse. In the weak light of the moon, it was difficult to see more than a few dozen feet in front of us—the rest was steeped in deep, tangled shadows.

Even so, the sounds of the mare's hoof strikes were easy enough to hear, but they also became distorted by the noise of our own horses. Every few hundred feet we were forced to pull up and listen for the swiftly departing cadence of the mare. With each pause, the mare traveled farther away from us, and as much as this frustrated me, it frustrated Gage more. I could feel his aggravation rolling off him in waves, tautening the already tense atmosphere.

Looming before us to the left and to the right, I could see the dark outline of the two ridges where my cousins and uncle had positioned themselves. I was becoming increasingly grateful the men had altered their plan. Uncle Andrew and my cousins were to act as lookouts only, so as not to confuse our pursuit with the sounds of their horses' hooves. But if they heard the mare pass by without the sounds of our own horses following near enough behind, they were to take over the chase.

Gage pushed his gelding faster, overtaking Trevor in his determination to catch the mare.

"Slow down," Trevor yelled at him over the rushing wind. "It's not safe."

Gage knew this well enough, for we'd visited the day before in the cold winter rain that had plagued the Borders for the past three days. He'd seen the uneven ground, the loose pebbles and shifting mud, the holes overgrown by heather and bracken ready to trip up an unsuspecting horse or human. The harder-packed trails were relatively safe, but they were difficult to follow in the dark with their sudden twists and turns, and with all the rain, even the trails' dirt had become unstable.

He pulled up so quickly, I worried his gelding had stumbled. "We're losing her," he snapped.

He was right. I had to strain to hear the horse's lope in the distance.

When Gage set off after the mare again, Trevor shouted after him, "It won't matter if you break your neck."

I held my breath as Gage's horse sped off ahead of us, daring to actually break into a gallop. I wanted to follow, but I knew to do so only meant suicide. If not for me, then for the beautiful roan beneath me. How easy it would be for her to step into a hole and snap a leg bone. Trevor would be forced to put her down.

Gage disappeared over a rise, and I was certain I didn't breathe again until Trevor and I crested it to see him stalled at a fork in the pass. His gelding danced left and then right, uncertain which way to go. I could no longer hear the mare's hoofbeats above the wind. The skin prickled along the back of my neck. I scanned the landscape around us, wondering if we were being watched, and whether the observers were friend or foe.

"Which way?" Trevor asked as something familiar caught my eye.

"I don't know," Gage replied through gritted teeth.

"We could split up."

He nodded and was about to spur his horse onward when I spoke.

"It'll do no good." I nodded toward the hillock on our right. "I recognize that cairn. The path to the right splits again in another hundred feet. Are Trevor and I going to go separate ways as well?"

I knew the question was futile. Neither man was going to let me ride off into the desolation of the Cheviot Hills by myself, even if, as I strongly suspected, I was more familiar with its landscape than either of them.

"This is a waste of time," Gage barked. "We're all going left."

He rode off before either Trevor or I could argue, and once again at too hasty a speed. Although the loose down-hill terrain did force him to slacken his pace somewhat. We raced onward into the night, letting Gage choose which direction we went. I didn't even offer an opinion, knowing the likelihood of our stumbling onto the correct track the horse had taken was growing slimmer with each fork and cross path we traversed. I did try to note which trail we followed, so that I could return us to Shotton Pass when Gage finally realized the futility of continuing our search, but with each mile farther we traveled, the lower my confidence became of even being able to do that.

I could only hope that Uncle Andrew or one of my cousins had picked up the pursuit once they realized how far we'd lagged behind. Maybe one of them had been able to track the sorrel mare to wherever her ultimate destination was.

Trevor seemed just as dejected as me, hanging back and allowing Gage to lead. That was, until we reached the edge of an expanse of land I strongly suspected of being a bog. The cloying musk of damp and moss and decay reached out to claw at my nostrils even through the biting wind.

"Gage, stop!" he yelled.

I watched in horror as the gelding stumbled, giving a piercing cry. Gage grappled with the reins before being pitched over the side of the horse into the brush beyond.

My heart leaped into my throat. "Gage!" I shouted as Trevor and I urged our mounts forward.

I couldn't see him beyond the tall grass and scrubs. Had he broken a bone? Cracked his head open on a rock? There were a number of terrible possibilities.

Trevor and I pulled our horses to a stop and dismounted, still calling Gage's name. Trevor grabbed the gelding's reins and led him away from the spot where Gage had fallen, lest the horse trample him in his distress.

"Gage!" I cried again, and was finally met with an answering groan coming from the scrub to my right. I hurried forward to find Gage struggling into a seated position. His breath wheezed in and out of him.

I fell to my knees beside him and cupped his elbow to help him sit upright. "Are you hurt? Is anything broken?" I ran my hands over his extremities, searching for blood and fractures.

He brushed me off. "No. I'm well," he rasped. "Just . . . got the wind . . . knocked out of me."

"Is he hurt?" Trevor asked, coming to stand over us.

"I'm well," Gage reiterated in irritation. "Just . . ." he lifted his hands, his face screwing up in disgust ". . . wet." He flicked his arms outward, flinging brackish water off them.

I turned away from the cold spray and scrambled to my feet. Trevor leaned down to assist Gage in his attempt to stand.

Gage hobbled a few steps forward, favoring his right leg before his gait straightened out. He reached back to brush mud and water from the back of his greatcoat. "Is Titus injured?" he asked, looking for his horse.

"It doesn't appear so," Trevor replied. "But I checked him quickly. He seems to just be spooked."

"Good," he declared, approaching his mount with just a slight hitch in his step. "Then if we hurry, we might still be able to catch up with the mare."

"No!" I gasped in unison with my brother.

"Just stop, Gage," Trevor snapped, his patience clearly waning. "The mare is long gone."

Gage shook his head stubbornly. "She's not. I heard her hoofbeats just a few moments ago. Just over that way." He pointed with his finger out into the heart of the bog.

"Then you're imagining things. No horse went that direction."

His voice was hard. "It did. I know I heard it. So if you think I'm imagining things, then don't follow me."

"Gage," I pleaded, grabbing hold of his arm before he could mount. "That's a bog. Please, you'll only kill your horse, and maybe yourself."

He halted, turning to look out over the dark landscape. Our overworked horses' sides heaved, their breaths condensing in the cold air. The night was silent around us beyond our breathing and the icy wind. But still, if I strained hard enough, like Gage, I thought I could hear the pounding of the horse's hooves. It was a trick of the landscape, of our minds, and that made it all the more unnerving. We so desperately wanted to catch the mare, and the people she was hurrying home to, that we could convince ourselves of almost anything.

I felt rather than heard Gage curse himself as his entire body tightened and then released as if expelling something. I let go of his arm and glanced at Trevor, having learned long ago that sometimes it was better to allow a man to vent his spleen on himself than to interrupt, especially when I was certain my words would do no good.

His internal struggle over, Gage turned to face us. His eyes were angry, but resigned. "Do either of you know where the horse might have ultimately gone?"

I shrugged. "There are a number of villages on the eastern edge of the Cheviot Hills, as well as several farms and homesteads scattered throughout." I gazed out at the shadowed hillsides. "Without knowing exactly where we are, I couldn't even begin to guess."

Gage followed the direction of my gaze, seeming to realize for the first time that we were almost certainly lost. Not that we couldn't find our way back out again. But at the moment, I didn't know whether we were closer to Yetholm or Wooler, Kilham or Harbottle.

He sighed. "I suppose we should begin trying to pick our way back to Yetholm." It was the nearest village to Shotton Pass, where we had agreed to meet at the inn when our part in the evening was finished.

Trevor helped me to mount and I pressed my knees to Figg's flank to urge her forward, unwilling to let Gage take the lead this time. I didn't know if Trevor had been memorizing each of our turns, but with his sometimes poor sense of direction, I knew I was our best bet of escaping the hills before dawn.

Town Yetholm rested about a mile west of the border with England and a mile south of Shotton Pass, in the shadow of several craggy ridges at the edge of the Cheviots. Its wide main street was lined with most of its businesses, including The Plough Inn, which, due to my cousin Jock's recommendation, we'd settled on as our meeting place.

It was close to midnight before Gage, Trevor, and I found our way out of the bleak hills and back to the center of Town Yetholm. Light shone brightly through the two front windows of the solid, stone building, and smoke puffed cheerily from the double chimneys. Desperate to get warm, I dragged myself off the back of my horse, nearly tumbling into the mud, and hobbled on frozen legs into the front room.

Several men very solicitously settled me before the bright flames in one hearth, where I shivered and lifted my hands toward the heat, trying to thaw my fingers. A mug of something hot was pressed into my hands and I sipped it gratefully, savoring the warmth of its spicy flavor as it slid down my throat. My nose immediately began to run, but I did not care. A man knelt to rest a hot brick wrapped in flannel under my booted feet, finally giving me the presence of mind to observe the party around me.

Uncle Andrew and my three cousins were already there. They had made room for Gage and Trevor to get closer to the fire, but they still huddled about us, now putting cups of the warm beverage into the men's hands and adjusting the blanket that had been thrown around my shoulders. My spirits plummeted, and I suddenly realized just how much hope I'd held out that a pair of these men had been able to track the sorrel mare all the way to its owner.

"When you took so long to return, we thought for certain you had successfully tracked the mare to her destination," my uncle was telling Gage in reply to his dejected pronouncement that we'd lost her.

Gage shook his head, his face grim with acceptance. "They eluded me again."

No one spoke for a moment, probably sensing like me that he had no wish for platitudes. Though I was anxious to catch these murderous body snatchers, it was clear Gage was even more determined, especially in light of his failure to capture them the first time he encountered them.

"Well, whoever they are," my cousin Jock mused. "They're canny. We couldna see more than dim shifting shadows, and no' even those verra clearly. And wi' the howling wind and the echoing rocks, it was hard to tell whether the horses were coming or going."

Trevor frowned into his glass. "They must be familiar with the landscape."

"But they were also familiar with the Firth of Forth," I pointed out, speaking up for the first time since my entrance. There was still a slight quaver in my voice from my continued chill. "I think it's far more likely they simply did their research."

"Which doesn't sound like the typical body-snatching ruffians I've encountered," Gage said, looking up from his unhappy contemplation of the fire. "So either we're dealing with a group of men far more resourceful and organized than the typical grave robber, or someone has hired these resurrectionists to do their dirty work for them."

Several of the men nodded and murmured to each other in agreement. Out of the corner of my eye I could see the innkeeper wiping down the tables nearby, his ears turned our way, clearly eavesdropping on our conversation. It was likely the most interesting discussion he'd heard in quite some time.

"And we still don't have any clue as to why?" I added.

Gage's eyes met mine, and his mouth flattened into a humorless grin.

If these body snatchers were more than simple street thugs stumbled onto a scheme to earn more cash, then the likelihood of money being the motive, or at least the only motive, was looking more dubious.

I stared into the depths of my mug. If the thieves were this clever, then how were we ever going to catch them? What if they decided to play it safe and quit now before they were caught? Had we just missed our last chance?

CHAPTER SEVENTEEN

The ride back to Blakelaw House was nothing but misery for me. I'd just gotten comfortable in front of the fire at The Plough and had nearly dozed off in my warm nest of blankets, when the gentlemen decided it was time to go. Trevor offered to return home and send the carriage after me, but that would mean rousing the coachman and a footman or two from their beds. I could take a room for the night at the inn, but again that meant waking the innkeeper's sleeping wife to ready a room—one with a cold hearth—for me.

Instead, I forced myself to my feet, spurred on by the promise of a warm bedchamber and the comfort of my own bed. Even so, every muscle in my body ached from the chill and the exertion of the long ride we'd already taken that night. At several points on our journey home, I nearly begged to turn back, too exhausted to go on. Gage and Trevor flanked me, blocking me from as much of the wind as they could manage, even though I knew they must have been just as cold and sore as I was. I endured, only because I really had no other choice.

They helped me down from my horse and into the house, where they handed me off to the capable hands of my maid. Bree, it appeared, had been up waiting for me all night, and it could not be many hours until dawn. She hustled me upstairs and out of my clothing, stiff with cold and the occasional mist of chilling rain we'd encountered during the last leg of our journey. I shivered in delight as she dropped a warm woolen nightgown she'd been heating by the fire around my shoulders and helped me push my arms into the sleeves. Then tucking me up under the thick coverlets on my bed, she went to answer the knock at my door.

I stretched my feet down toward the delightful heat of the hot cloth-wrapped bricks she had placed under the sheets. Earl Grey had already found that source of warmth and curled up at the bottom of the bed. Bree returned to hand me a steaming cup of tea, helping me to drink my first sip as my hands were still shaking. After they'd stilled, she left me to rest back against the pillows while she gathered up my discarded clothes.

I watched her bustle about, savoring the warmth of the bedding and the fragrant tea as it settled into my bones. But as the moment stretched on, I couldn't help but compare it to a similar situation which had occurred just a few months earlier, when my previous maid and the Dalmays' housekeeper tried to comfort me after Will's death, and my own brush with mortality. The thought left a cold lump in my chest.

I set the half-full teacup on the nightstand, no longer able to stomach the drink.

It had been days since I'd thought of William Dalmay in more than passing, and that realization unsettled me more than anything. It was a good thing, a necessary thing, I knew, for my healing, but it still made me anxious. After all, it had been only a little over two months. Should it be this easy to forget such a tragedy, to forget a friend?

I swallowed hard against the sudden urge to be sick, and looked up in surprise when I felt Bree's cool hand press against my forehead. I had not even noticed her approach.

"Not comin' doon wi' somethin' from the chill, are ye?" she asked gently.

I shook my head.

Her warm, whiskey brown eyes were kind as she searched mine. "Sure?"

"Yes."

She nodded and turned away, tossing another garment over her arm.

"I'm sorry you had to stay up so late to wait for our return," I said. "I should have told you that you needn't wait up."

"Well, seein' ye in the state ye were in when ye arrived, I'm glad I did. Men dinna ken how to handle such things." She smiled, flashing her dimples. "A'sides, I had a nice long nap last evening after dinner. Another few hours this morn and I'll be right as a trivet."

I yawned and nodded. The warmth of the bedding and the soothing sound of Bree's voice combined with my own weariness were beginning to have an effect on me, despite my apprehensions.

"Did ye catch 'em then?"

I blinked up at her, momentarily stumped by the conversation's change in subject. "The thieves?"

Her bright eyes danced with excitement. "Ye were gone so long, I was certain ye mun' have caught 'em."

"No," I replied, deflating her enthusiasm. "Though we trailed their horse for quite some distance." Or had attempted to.

She nodded and offered me a tight smile, sympathizing with our disappointment. "These men mun' be canny."

I knew she was trying to cheer me, but reminding me of their cleverness didn't exactly help. I frowned at the fire burning in the hearth in the wall opposite the foot of my bed. "They are."

When Bree did not respond or move from her position beside the bed, I looked up to find her fingering a loose thread along the seam of one of my garments. Her brow was furrowed in thought, and I could tell she was debating something with herself. When she finally glanced at me, I knew it was with some indecision.

"I wasna goin' to say anything, especially if ye caught the men responsible. But since ye havena . . ." She sighed.

"Bree, what is it?" I asked, my muscles tightening.

"My friend . . . do I have to give her name?"

I shook my head, figuring I could coerce her into telling me if it became necessary.

"She's a maid o'er at . . ." She shook her head, cutting off whatever revealing information she was about to share. "In another household. And she was also at the Rutherfords' Hogmanay Bonfire."

I tipped my head in encouragement.

"She told me she saw Sim's Christie sneaking away from the bonfire afore midnight."

"Where?"

"Oot into the field. Noo, I should warn ye," she hastened to add. "My friend used to dandle after Sim's Christie. She may just be talkin' oot o' spite. 'Specially if he was goin' to meet another girl."

I nodded, understanding what she was trying to say. The information could be completely false, and even if it wasn't, this Sim's Christie may have just been in the middle of conducting a tryst. But even though he may have nothing to do with the murder and the body snatching, being farther away from the light and the noise of the bonfire, he may have seen something the others had not.

"Thank you," I told Bree. "I'm sure Mr. Gage would like to at least question him."

She dipped her head, still clearly uncertain she should have said anything. Considering how few clues Gage and I now had to follow up on, I was grateful she had. But I could also respect her dilemma. She did not want to create unnecessary trouble for her friend or Sim's Christie.

She turned to go and then swiveled back. "I thought you'd also like to ken, 'cause ye asked aboot him the other day, Mr. Anderley, Mr. Gage's manservant, has been askin' after ye doonstairs."

"Asking after me?" I asked in some surprise.

"Aye."

I frowned, wondering just what the valet wished to know. And whether he was acting alone or on behalf of Gage.

"Did you tell him anything?"

"Nay," she replied quickly, but did not elaborate. Her mouth was sealed in a tight line.

She may have been telling the truth, but I suspected someone had talked, and she knew who. However, I decided it was unfair to ask her to betray the other servants, so I simply thanked her and sent her to find her bed for whatever remained of the night.

Perhaps it would be best to confront Gage about his valet myself the following day.

W hich was exactly what I did, as our carriage stumbled along through the deep ruts all of the wet weather had created in the roads. The mud had hardened in the near freezing temperatures overnight, casting the earth into rough shapes. It jostled us back and forth on our seats, making it impossible for us to rest back with any comfort.

"Did you know your valet has been questioning my staff about me?" I demanded of Gage after we plowed through one particularly teeth-rattling portion of road.

He looked up from his survey of the scene outside the window. The gray rippling ribbon of the River Tweed lay beyond, paralleling the road. He didn't reply immediately, but his mouth quirked up at the corners.

"Anderley can be rather . . . protective of me."

I scowled. "What does he think? I'll poison you? Dissect you in my secret operating theater?" I demanded, irritated by the ridiculous rumors that still persisted about me.

"No, no." Gage twisted the hat he cradled in his hands round and round. "It's far more likely he's worried you'll try to trap me into marriage."

"Oh." My cheeks began to heat and I shifted awkwardly.

Gage looked up at me through his lashes, his expression

far more serious than I'd expected. Here was the perfect opportunity to tease me, but he didn't take it.

I cleared my throat. "Has . . . has that happened before?"

Now it was his turn to squirm. "A . . . few times."

"Oh." Clearly my conversation skills were becoming stunted.

I turned to look out the window, relieved to see we were approaching the bridge that would lead us over the river and into Kelso. The weak afternoon sun illuminated the village's rooftops in the distance, including that of the Armstrongs', where Sim's Christie worked in the stables.

No one had been more surprised than I when I slept through almost to noon, with Earl Grey tucked snuggly against my side. I couldn't recall the last time I'd slept even close to seven hours. And neither could my brother, which was why he and Gage had elected not to disturb me and attended church at St. Cuthbert's on their own. I'd scolded them for letting me doze, but neither seemed the least repentant. I only hoped that Trevor's assurances of my health had been convincing enough to prevent a tide of local well-wishers from visiting Blakelaw House in the coming week.

Still waiting for word from Lord Buchan on the return of his uncle's bones, and with no other information to immediately pursue, Gage had agreed to accompany me into nearby Kelso to question Sim's Christie. He appeared even less hopeful than I was that the stable hand would have any useful information to give us, but there was no harm in inquiring. Sometimes the smallest things led one to the truth.

The Armstrongs lived in a large gabled home near the river. Rather than pull up to the house in our carriage, alerting the Armstrongs to our presence and necessitating a social call as well as an uncomfortable explanation that could potentially get their stable hand in trouble, we decided to disembark near the bridge and stroll along the river. There was a well-tended path that provided beautiful views of the English countryside across the river, including the old royal burgh of Roxburgh. But in the bracing cold wind, we didn't see much of it, preferring to tuck our heads down and huddle together as we hurried forward.

Fortunately, the stable yard was sheltered somewhat by the surrounding buildings. The crunch of our footsteps must have been heard inside the stable, for a man emerged, the sleeves of his shirt rolled up to reveal muscular forearms. As expected, he smelled strongly of hay and horses.

"Canna I help ye?" he asked.

"We're looking for a man called Sim's Christie," Gage replied, though I didn't think he had any need to. With his thick curly hair and swarthy good looks, I strongly suspected this was the man Bree's friend had dandled after.

"That's me," he replied only after a moment's hesitation.

I'd already explained the Borders' convoluted naming system to Gage, who had only looked more confused when I finished, and I hoped he wasn't about to ask for a repeat from the stable hand. However, Gage refrained, choosing to quickly introduce us instead.

"We were told you left the bonfire at Clintmains Hall at one point on the night of Hogmanay," Gage informed him casually. "Can you tell us where you went?"

Sim's Christie's eyes narrowed. "'Twas Callie, weren't it?" he demanded. "She's the one who told ye."

Gage and I exchanged a look.

"I don't know who Callie is," Gage answered honestly. "Did you leave the bonfire?"

The stable hand huffed out an angry breath and turned his head aside. "Aye," he answered gruffly. "I was . . . meetin' a lass."

As I'd suspected. I pulled my cloak tighter around me, resigned to hear the rest.

"How long were you gone?"

He shrugged. "Quarter, maybe half an hour."

My eyebrows rose.

"You were in the field?"

"Yes."

Gage tilted his head, watching the man closely. "Did you

see anything odd while you were away from the bonfire? Anything out of the ordinary?"

Sim's Christie's head darted to the side again and he stared off toward what must be the back of the Armstrongs' house. I couldn't tell whether he was simply anxious for us to leave or he knew something he wasn't sure he wanted to tell. People from the Borders were secretive folk, and not inclined to share with outsiders like Gage. His gaze shifted to focus on me, and I kept my expression carefully neutral, hoping he would choose to trust us.

"Aye," he finally muttered. "I saw two men leavin' Clintmains."

I glanced at Gage in surprise.

"Did you get a good look at them?" he asked the stable hand.

"Nay. They were too far off. But they was dressed like toffs. And they were in a hurry."

"Which direction did they go?"

"Doon the road." He paused, looking Gage up and down. "T'ord the abbey."

His brow furrowed in confusion. "And they were on foot?"

Sim's Christie nodded. "Aye."

Gage thanked him and hooked his arm through mine, leading me back toward the river path.

"Who do you think they were?" I asked once we were out of earshot of the stable yard.

"I don't know."

I frowned down at the hem of my cloak. "My aunt said that no one could remember anyone leaving or missing from the ball. Is it really possible that no one noticed?"

"Well, the gathering was fairly large. And didn't you say that many of the guests were already deep in their cups?"

"True." It wasn't as if anyone was worried about having to account for their fellow revelers' whereabouts. Most of the people at the ball likely couldn't tell me half of the people they danced with, let alone where that person went once their set was done. Most people only noticed what directly affected them.

"But what on earth were they doing walking away from the ball on foot? And why? Were their accomplices picking them up away from Clintmains to avoid suspicion?"

"Possibly," Gage mused. "Though it seems an odd way to go about it."

I heaved a sigh. "None of this is making any sense."

"I know." His voice was tight with the same frustration I shared. "And it's about time it did."

The eleventh Earl of Buchan's body was not returned to the abbey. It was left in a pew at the back of St. Mary's Church in St. Boswells. An unhappy present for the parishioners to find as they filed into church that Sunday. The bones were stuffed in a crude canvas sack with no discernible markings or extraneous objects except a note addressed to the current earl with nothing written inside.

There was no way of knowing if the bones truly were those of the eleventh Earl of Buchan and not another departed human being, and given the shrewd and callous behavior of the body snatchers, it was difficult to trust that they were. But we had no choice. The ransom had been paid. The current earl had insisted upon it, in case just such a thing as our losing the horse had happened. He wanted his uncle's body back, whatever the cost, and given the outcome, I couldn't blame him.

Regardless, I had recommended that Lord Buchan ask Dr. Carputhers to examine the bones. He should at least be able to tell him if the skeleton was the right size and if the skull was consistent with the late earl's features. He should also be able to tell if any of the bones were missing, and if they had been damaged in any way since being stolen from the grave.

Gage was furious. He'd felt certain they would return the bones to the abbey, that the men Lord Buchan had posted there would afford him one last chance to catch the culprits. But whether they had noticed the guards or foreseen his ploy, they had not fallen for it.

I was more concerned for young Will, who looked dejected when he realized our last chance of capturing the men who killed Dodd had failed, and angry with myself for disappointing him.

So it was with heavy hearts that we returned to Blakelaw House that Monday evening. I didn't know where to turn next, and Gage seemed equally stifled. All we had was a bunch of seemingly random facts that led to nowhere. I wanted to ask him what he'd done in the past when he'd found himself in a similar situation, but the forbidding expression on his face told me the question could wait.

It was lucky that Trevor had the solution to our quandary waiting for us in his study. Gage almost dismissed his summons when we entered the hall—I could see it in the tense line of his back—but he followed me into the dark-paneled room that I didn't believe I would ever be able to enter without thinking of my father. It always made my breath tight for the first few seconds after I crossed its threshold.

"You have a letter," my brother told Gage, motioning toward the sideboard under a landscape of Knellstone Manor, the St. Mawr family seat down in Sussex, near where my father grew up.

Gage's shoulders squared. He flipped the missive over. "It's from Sergeant Maclean."

Trevor and I watched as he broke the seal and began to swiftly peruse its contents. I assumed this was the friend he'd written to who was a member of the Edinburgh City Police. Maybe the sergeant would have news for us. Something more concrete than a few scattered facts.

I stood straighter against the back of the chair I rested my hands on as Gage's expression changed from one of intense concentration to that of satisfaction. When at last he looked up, my fingers were digging into the brocade upholstery below me in anticipation.

"There was a third body snatching."

"What?" I gasped, glancing at my brother, whose wide eyes said he shared my shock.

"Before Sir Colum Casselbeck's."

"Who? Where?"

Gage glanced back down at the letter. "An . . . Ian Tyler of Woodslea."

"I know his son." Trevor moved around his desk to join us. "Their family home lies just west of Edinburgh."

"Do you think they're all connected?" I asked Gage.

"I think it would be foolish to assume they aren't. According to Sergeant Maclean, the theft followed the same pattern. He's making further inquiries to discover if there are other similar crimes."

I pressed a hand to my chin in thought. "We should speak to the Tylers. And the Casselbecks."

He nodded. "I agree. We seem to have reached an impasse here with Buchan's snatching. Maybe there will be new information for us to uncover in Edinburgh."

His words gave me pause, though I didn't know why they should surprise me. "So . . . you think we should go to Edinburgh?"

Gage's brow furrowed. "Yes. How else would we question the families?"

I turned away, rubbing my suddenly sweaty palms down the woolen skirt of my gown. "You're right. Of course. I just . . . hadn't thought."

"You could stay with your sister, couldn't you?"

I crossed my arms over my chest, nodding absently as I peered up at the portrait I'd painted of my mother and father when I was just sixteen. My mother's likeness had largely been done from memory, as she'd been gone nearly eight years at the time, but my father had still chosen to hang it in pride of place above the hearth. I thought I'd done a satisfactory job of reproducing her image, but I could never be certain. It was like seeing something out of the corner of your eye, but when you turned toward it, it was always gone.

I wasn't sure why the thought of leaving Blakelaw and returning to Edinburgh so unnerved me, but it did. Perhaps because it still held memories of William Dalmay's passing. After all, I'd made the opposite journey just two short months ago, hoping to escape those thoughts and emotions, looking for some sense of peace. In so many ways, I still hadn't found it, and yet I couldn't stay in this place forever. I refused to allow myself to hide here, like I'd done at Gairloch, to close myself off from the world. That would do me no good.

Perhaps it *was* time to leave.

"I'm sure Alana and Philip would be happy to see her," Trevor was telling Gage.

"And you?"

"I'm afraid I need to remain here at Blakelaw," he protested, making me wonder yet again if there was something more my brother wasn't telling me.

But Gage was unfazed by it. "Kiera," he persisted gently. "Are you content to travel to Edinburgh? I suppose I could go there myself, but I confess, your presence would be most helpful."

I swallowed the trepidations swirling around inside me and turned to face the men. "Yes. Of course, I'll accompany you. It's just . . . a long journey to make in the cold," I finished lamely.

They both eyed me up and down, making me aware that my response had not been the least convincing.

Gage's eyes were tight with concern, but he did not voice whatever worries he felt for me. "Can you be ready to leave at first light?"

I pressed my lips together and nodded.

"If we make good time, we'll be in Edinburgh by tomorrow's nightfall."

# CHAPTER EIGHTEEN

"Sergeant Maclean must have been waiting for your note," I remarked as Gage's carriage pulled away from my brother-in-law, Philip, the Earl of Cromarty's town house on Charlotte Square, its pale stone gleaming in the midmorning sunlight.

Gage looked up from his contemplation of an article in the *Scotsman*. "He's nothing if not efficient."

"Have you known him long?"

He tapped the folded newspaper against his leg as he thought back. "Perhaps three months. He assisted me with an inquiry."

This must have taken place during the time after he left Gairloch Castle and before he visited the Dalmays. I realized I knew very little about those few months, except that he had been called to Edinburgh on business for his father, and had been trying to avoid me.

I stared out the window at the carriages parked along George Street, ready to collect their passengers and their purchases. A trio of footmen stood outside one shop, chatting while they waited for their employers. My sister, Alana, had expressed a desire to do some shopping while I was in town, but with Gage's summons this morning it appeared that would have to wait. Not that I was all that eager to purchase new frocks, but to please my sister, I knew I would join her. Especially after witnessing her tears of happiness last night when I appeared in her front hall.

It had been nearly midnight before we reached Edinburgh. After a long day crowded inside a carriage with Gage, Bree, and Anderley, jostled about by the rough roads and even rougher winds, I'd wanted nothing more than to fall into a warm, soft bed. I knew Alana and Philip well enough to expect that the bedchamber I had used before moving to Blakelaw House would still be ready for me.

Philip had been working before a cheery fire in his study and, after a warm embrace, immediately ushered me inside. A tea tray was sent for, and a maid dispatched up to my room to light the fire and show Bree about. We'd barely broached the topic of the reason for my visit when we heard Alana calling down the stairs from above. We'd gone to meet her, worried that in her haste to descend she might trip.

I was surprised by the force of her grip as she pulled me to her, burying her face in my hair. She professed her joy to see me, though the tears streaming down her cheeks seemed to belie her words. I stared wide-eyed over her shoulder at Philip, but he merely smiled and shrugged. Apparently, this extreme show of emotion was normal. I guessed it had something to do with the child she was carrying, who was now evident in the gentle swell of her stomach pressed against my side.

I was pleased to see how healthy she looked. Gone was the wan complexion and hollow eyes from her queasy stomach and fatigue, and in their place she showed a healthy glow and slightly plumped cheeks, as well as the encouraging bump at her abdomen. I could feel myself breathe a sigh of relief. Much as she and Philip had insisted in their letters that she was doing well, I realized I had not fully believed them. But here was confirmation.

Alana wanted to join us in Philip's study, but late as the hour was, and as uneager as I was to answer the questions I knew my inquisitive sister would ask, I instead wrapped my arm around her waist and urged her back upstairs. She argued for a moment, but when I pled weariness, she reluctantly gave in, insisting we would speak the next day.

Gage's arrival that morning as we were eating breakfast had postponed that conversation a few hours longer, though I could tell from my sister's expression as we left that I would not be allowed to put it off indefinitely.

When the carriage veered down Princes Street instead of following the road up toward the Old Town, I turned toward Gage in surprise. "Aren't we meeting him at the police house off Old Stamp Office Close?"

His eyebrows arched high. He was clearly stunned I knew such a thing, though he shouldn't have been. "No. Sergeant Maclean thought it best to meet us somewhere a little less conspicuous."

I frowned down at the deep forest green skirts of my gown.

He chuckled and shook his head. "You truly thought I was going to take you inside the police house?"

I felt my cheeks begin to heat at the sheer ridiculousness of the idea. "I know it's no place for a lady. Especially one of my reputation. But yes. I was."

"It's nothing to see," he informed me, the softened tone of his voice clearly communicating that he sensed my disappointment.

I nodded, both of us knowing that was far from the truth.

"And in any case, I don't think your presence was the only reason Sergeant Maclean directed us elsewhere."

"What do you mean?"

Gage turned to look out at the shops passing by. "Maclean's superior may or may not have agreed to let him pursue this investigation."

"But why would he object?" I asked. "Clearly there are crimes being committed."

"Yes, but they're not necessarily within Edinburgh's jurisdiction, and I'm sure the Superintendent of Police would rather his men pursue active investigations in Edinburgh."

I scowled. "So because these body snatchings are occurring in different locations outside of the city, he's not interested in seeing them solved?"

"Oh, I'm sure he's interested," Gage replied, glancing out once again as the carriage rolled to a stop. "But without one of the high-ranking men who had their ancestor's body stolen making a complaint—and they won't, seeing as they have their ancestor back and they have no wish to involve the police—it's not his highest priority." He pushed open the carriage door and climbed down before reaching in for my hand to help me out.

"That's ridiculous. If they're refusing to investigate such crimes, then who is going to catch these criminals?"

He tucked my arm through his and grinned. "That's where we come in."

A warm feeling spread throughout my chest in spite of the nip in the wind. I looked away, lest I stand there all day smiling stupidly at him. The shop before us served tea, and although it was still quite early for most to stop in and enjoy the beverage, the "Open" sign hung prominently in the window. Gage escorted me inside, and we were immediately surrounded by the herbal aroma of tea and the sweet scent of pastries baking. The smells were so heavenly that I believe I actually sighed in delight.

Eight tables were scattered about the little shop, draped in pristine white lace. A cup and saucer sat in front of each chair, and at the center of the table stood a tiny bud vase, holding one brightly colored flower. Amid the gleaming wood and blinding white, the little blooms provided just the right amount of charming whimsy the shop needed.

At the table farthest from the entrance, near the door that must have led into the kitchen, sat a tall, brawny man. So brawny, in fact, that I couldn't believe he was comfortable perching on the tiny chair below him. His bearing was restrained and awkward, as if he was worried about gesturing too broadly and damaging something, but he laughed easily enough with the woman standing near him.

He rose from his seat as we approached and reached out to shake Gage's hand. "Mr. Gage, it seems ye've been keepin' yerself busy," he remarked with a welcoming smile, which also looked awkward on his face, as if his cheeks would only lift so far. Perhaps this was related to the injury to his nose, which from its crooked appearance had clearly been broken sometime in the past, probably on multiple occasions.

"That I have," Gage replied, and from the ease of his demeanor and the gleam in his eye, I could tell just how much he liked the sergeant. "And yourself?"

"Aye. There's always someone up to no good." His eyes shifted to me, and I could see the spark of curiosity, though he did make some effort to hide it.

Gage introduced us. I was sure Sergeant Maclean must know who I was, or at least have heard of my reputation, but he said nothing.

Instead he turned toward the woman still hovering near us. "My sister-in-law, Mrs. Duffy."

She smiled and nodded. "Welcome. I'll bring ye some tea shortly. Please make yerselves comfortable."

This better explained Sergeant Maclean's decision to meet here rather than the police house. At such an early hour, the likelihood of other patrons entering was slim, especially with us seated near the back of the shop, far from prying eyes. And with his sister-in-law presiding over the establishment, we could be assured of privacy. It was the ideal situation for an officer of the Edinburgh City Police who needed to meet with higher-born citizens loath to enter a police house.

Gage hung our outer garments next to the sergeant's gray greatcoat on a rack in the corner while the sergeant pulled a chair out for me. I noticed his knuckles were scabbed and scarred, indicating he'd been in a fight fairly recently. Had the altercation been in the course of his duties or something else? Perhaps the sergeant enjoyed boxing. He certainly had the physique for it.

Sergeant Maclean caught me looking at his hands and

shifted them self-consciously. "Broke up a fight doon on Cowgate last night. Had to throw a few punches myself."

"Not that you minded," Gage remarked with a smirk.

"Aye, well, there are few consolations wi' this job. But, I admit, bustin' the jaw o' longtime brutes is one o' 'em." His eyes hardened. "'Specially if they been preyin' on lassies and bairns."

Gage settled into his chair, his long legs stretching out beneath the table. Between his big feet and the sergeant's, there was little room for my own. "Any word on other body snatchings similar to the three we already know about?"

He shook his head. "But I sent queries oot to Glasgow and Dunkeld. If they're workin' as far south as the Borders, there's no tellin' how far west and north they've operated."

"Do you know anything more about this Tyler family?"

"No' much."

The sergeant paused as Mrs. Duffy emerged from the kitchen with a tray of tea and a plate filled with heavenly-smelling scones dotted with sultanas and a towering pile of clotted cream. My mouth began to water. She smiled as she set the dishes down, and then disappeared back into the kitchen. Sergeant Maclean resumed his explanation while I poured.

"The victim, Ian Tyler of Woodslea, died in 1818, and was apparently a well-respected man. Left his fortune and his property to his eldest son, Owen Tyler. Fairly straightforward. No suspicions o' foul play at his death. And even if there was, twelve years is a long time to wait to dig him back up."

Gage took a sip of his tea and nodded. "Where is he buried?"

"Glencorse Parish Kirk. Oot past Seafield Moor."

He nodded, apparently knowing the location. "Have you spoken with the family?"

Sergeant Maclean shook his head as he chewed and swallowed a bite of his scone. "I couldna manage it. 'Tis too far oot for me to travel wi'oot good reason."

I studied the burly policeman. So he *was* pursuing this investigation without official approval.

"Asides, I thought that's where you fit in. Or am I gonna do all the work myself?" he jested.

Gage gave an ironic lift to his eyebrows. "Let's not forget who brought the matter to your attention in the first place."

The sergeant chuckled in his deep voice.

Gage nodded at me. "Lady Darby and I will pay them a visit then, along with the Casselbecks in Musselburgh, the family of our second victim. In the meantime, we've some sketches we'd like you to show around. Maybe someone will recognize them."

I reached into my reticule and extracted the two sketches I'd made from the St. Boswells innkeeper's descriptions.

"There's no need," Sergeant Maclean remarked with a frown after looking at them. "I know both of 'em." His gaze rose to meet mine. "You've a rare talent. Looks just like 'em."

"Who are they?"

He set the two drawings on the table and pointed to the first man, who sported a scar across his forehead. "This one goes by the name o' Curst Eckie. And this one is Sore John. They're both part o' Bonnie Brock Kincaid's crew. Or used to be anyways. I havena seen 'em aboot in the last few months, and I'm usually rousin' 'em oot o' one pub or another."

"Who's Bonnie Brock?" I asked when it appeared Gage would not.

Sergeant Maclean glanced at Gage, as if asking how much to share.

"Bonnie Brock runs one o' Edinburgh's largest gangs o' criminals. You name it, if it's illegal, Bonnie Brock's probably got his fingers in it."

"If you know that, then why hasn't he been caught?"

His gaze turned weary. "Because the man is too canny. Even when we ken he's behind a crime, we canna pin it on him. His men are too loyal, 'cuz they ken he'll find a way to break 'em oot o' jail, or rig the jury during their trial. The one time we did have him locked up, the city rose up in protest and another man came forward and took the blame."

"Why?"

"He owns too many o' 'em. And the rest view him as some sort o' hero, their verra own Robin Hood."

Though I knew the sergeant's words were supposed to horrify me, I couldn't help but feel reluctantly curious about this Bonnie Brock. Who was he and why had he chosen a life of crime?

"Interestingly enough," Sergeant Maclean added. "It's rumored that Bonnie Brock started oot as a body snatcher."

I shared a look with Gage.

"And he still runs crews aboot the city when the price is right." His chair creaked as he leaned back in it. "If Edinburgh criminals are a part of this bodies-for-ransom scheme, I'd wager he's involved somehow."

Gage tapped his fingers against his teacup, frowning down at its dregs. "Any way you can find out? Will some of his men talk?"

The shop door chimed and a pair of ladies entered, slowly removing their gloves.

Sergeant Maclean leaned forward, speaking more softly. "I'll put some feelers oot, see what I can find."

Our conversation quickly broke up. While the ladies were distracted by Mrs. Duffy, Gage and I slipped out, allowing the sergeant to take his leave later, perhaps through the back door, depending on how inconspicuous he wished to be. In his gray greatcoat with a baton strapped to his belt, it was easy enough to recognize him as a policeman.

I was silent for most of the ride back to Charlotte Square. Was it really that simple? Were the culprits merely an enterprising gang of Edinburgh body snatchers who had stumbled on a more lucrative way to make money, and Dodd had gotten in the way?

But then who were the gentlemen who visited the abbey the morning of Hogmanay? And what of the two men Sim's Christie had seen leaving the ball? Were they unrelated?

Was the lady's clothing also unconnected? And how exactly were these criminals choosing their victims? It wasn't as if they'd picked them out of a newspaper obituary. Two of them had been dead for over a decade.

I wasn't satisfied with this solution, and until we found the connection between the three men, I doubted I ever would be.

# CHAPTER NINETEEN

My sister was waiting for us when we returned to the town house. Reclining on a settee positioned near the bow window at the front of the house, she had an optimal view of the square and all its passersby. I felt somewhat sorry for her, knowing the doctor had ordered her to limit her outings. Alana was a social person, and being cooped up in the house most of her days had to be trying for her. But I was also conscious of the fact that, bored as she was, now she would be more interested in my activities than ever before. Little as I liked to share about myself with anyone, this would be very taxing for me.

I smiled anyway as we entered the drawing room, still pleased to see her looking so well after the hellish early months of her confinement. I leaned down to kiss her on the cheek and tell her she looked lovely, for she did, seated in the sunshine in her yellow frock with a soft white blanket draped over her legs.

She brushed the compliment off, but I could tell by the light in her eyes that she was happy. Gage seconded my opinion, making a blush rise in Alana's cheeks. She gestured for him to take a seat near her and then turned to me.

"Now, your nieces and nephew had been asking after you all morning, so you must go up to see them. But first, I'm claiming you for luncheon. And you as well, Mr. Gage."

I knew when it was best not to argue with my older sister, so I simply nodded. But, of course, Gage could never be so mundane. "I wouldn't dream of denying such a beautiful lady," he murmured.

My sister demurred, but once again her cheeks blossomed with color.

"Flattering my wife, are we, Mr. Gage?" Philip remarked as he entered the room. He arched a single eyebrow in mock warning. "I think you're treading on dangerous ground."

"Oh, Philip," Alana scolded as he made a great show of leaning down to kiss her on her cheek.

I smiled at the familiar sight of their natural affection, realizing I'd missed seeing it these past months. In the years since my marriage to Sir Anthony, I'd learned just how uncommon a loving marriage was, but whenever I was tempted to become jaded, the sight of my sister and her husband together always pulled me back. It was rare, but not impossible. And that thought couldn't help but give me hope.

Philip joined me on the settee, pushing aside a mound of pillows someone had piled in the corner of it. "Now, if I sensed the mood right, Alana was just about to interrogate her sister."

I couldn't help but laugh while Alana reproached him again. Oh, how well my brother-in-law knew his wife.

"I was going to do no such thing." She smoothed her hands over the blanket covering her lap. "I . . . simply had some questions for her."

Philip raised his eyebrows. "And just what exactly is the definition of 'interrogate'?"

"I believe it has something to do with asking a person multiple questions," Gage replied, joining in the banter.

Alana glared at them both, but the effect was ruined by the smile curling her lips. "Yes. Very humorous. Are we finished now?"

"Of course, my dear." Philip gestured to me with a flourish. "Proceed with your interrogation, er, questions."

I choked back a giggle, grateful to him for, if nothing

else, lightening the mood. Seeing him this relaxed and playful only confirmed how well Alana must be doing, a welcome sign as she entered the last few months of her confinement. She'd had a difficult birth with her third child, and we were all nervous about the delivery of her fourth.

"How is Trevor?" my sister asked, clearly choosing to be diplomatic first.

"Very well," I was able to reply easily. Though I did look to Philip, wondering if he knew something about my brother's secretive business. I knew Trevor admired his brother-in-law and respected his opinion, so it only made sense that he might seek Philip's advice. I decided it would be worth asking him about later. No need to worry my sister with it.

"And the Hogmanay Ball. You said you enjoyed it."

I nodded, having written her so in my most recent letter.

Her eyes narrowed. "Up until the moment that boy arrived covered in blood?"

I grinned sheepishly. I'd left that part out.

"Word travels fast, especially something as shocking as that. And imagine my surprise when our neighbor Mrs. Cready tells me all about it while my sister has made no mention of it in her letter."

"I didn't want to upset you," I tried to explain.

"Well, I assure you, hearing it from Mrs. Cready was certainly upsetting."

I sighed, glancing at Philip for help, but it seemed he'd decided to stay out of the fray with this one. I could have pointed out that Trevor and I had written her husband about it, and he could have told her, but I decided it was unfair to drag him into my quagmire.

Even so, I was irritated. "What was I supposed to say, Alana? Oh, by the way, another dead body dropped in front of me."

Her lips tightened. "You could have at least forewarned me. So I didn't look a complete fool."

Realizing this argument was going nowhere, I swallowed

my frustration. "Yes. You're right. I apologize. I should have forewarned you."

She looked as if she wished to say more, but my apology and capitulation barred her from doing so, unless she wished to look petty. I'd been embarrassed by Gage's presence during this spat, but now I was grateful. It prevented my sister from airing all her grievances.

She nodded and then added, "Remember that next time."

I hoped I wouldn't ever *need* to report another boy arriving covered in blood to tell us of a murder, but I took her point, and I elected not to further anger her with such a sarcastic remark.

The butler appeared at that moment, interrupting the tense scene to announce luncheon. We all filed downstairs into the dining room, located at the front of the town house's ground floor. A fire crackled in the hearth as we sat down to a meal of warm soup, cold chicken, and crusty bread. I sipped from my glass of white wine, feeling oddly misplaced.

The last time I'd sat down to a meal in this room had been the evening before I left for Blakelaw House after Will's death. I turned now to stare blindly up at the painting on the wall above the hearth, trying to rebury the grief that was bubbling up inside me. I didn't want to think about my lost friend, or any of the pain his passing had caused me. I just wanted to enjoy this meal. Or as much of it as I could stomach.

Philip had politely asked after Gage's father, which Gage answered obscurely, as always, and then surprised us all by addressing the main issue at hand.

"So this Lewis Collingwood you wrote to me about," Philip began, ripping off a chunk of bread and dunking it in his soup. "I believe I've found him."

"Really?" I replied, glancing at my sister to figure out whether she had any idea what we were talking about. "Where?"

"Here in Edinburgh. At least for the time being. I can

give you his direction. I assume you and Mr. Gage would like to speak with him."

"Yes. Thank you."

Alana swirled her spoon around in her bowl. "Is this Mr. Collingwood a suspect?"

I couldn't tell from the tone of her voice whether she was irritated or not.

"Yes. Or, at least, a person of some interest."

She nodded and lifted the spoon daintily to her mouth.

"Cromarty, how well are you acquainted with the Tylers of Woodslea?" Gage asked.

Philip paused in reaching for another bit of bread. "Well enough, I suppose. Why do you ask?"

Gage quickly informed them of the connection we'd found between the three body snatchings for ransom, leaving out many of the pertinent details. We were eating luncheon, after all. "So I wondered if there was anything of interest we should know about the Tylers. Or whether you could think of any connection between the three men whose bodies were ransomed."

Philip sat back in his chair, giving the matter some thought. "Well, I can tell you that Ian Tyler was a somewhat noted historian, and an avid supporter of Scottish music and poetry. He was a member of the Society of Antiquaries, likely a founding member."

I leaned forward at that pronouncement, sharing a look with Gage. There was that group again. Why did it keep coming up?

Philip paused in his resuscitation of facts. "What?"

"The Society of Antiquaries. Lord Buchan and Sir Colum were also founding members," Gage informed him.

"It's not surprising. It was rather the rage at the time."

"What do you mean?"

"Well, most Scotsmen of some rank wished to be a part of it. Much like being a member of the latest gentlemen club opening in London. Preserving Scotland's heritage was suddenly *au courant*, regardless of your sympathies."

Thirty-some-odd years following the Battle of Culloden, I could understand the titled gentlemen's sudden wish to protect what was left of their homeland's treasures.

"My father was even a member, albeit not a very active one."

"So you think the fact that all three of these gentlemen were members of the society is not very significant?" Gage asked for clarification.

Philip shook his head. "I'm afraid not."

My shoulders sank in disappointment, but Gage didn't appear quite so daunted.

"Even so, it could still be our answer to their connection, if someone was working from a list of old members."

Like Lewis Collingwood.

Philip took a sip of his wine. "They could certainly expect most of the families on that list to have the income available to pay such a large ransom."

"The immediate family anyway," Alana remarked off-handedly.

Gage and I turned to her in curiosity, though Philip seemed to already know what or whom she was talking about.

"What do you mean?" I asked.

"Only that Mr. Fergusson, who's a cousin or nephew or some kind of relation of the family, voiced quite a loud complaint about his limited income when he came of age last year. Claimed the family had cheated him of his fair share."

"Yes. But you should know that this Mr. Fergusson also has a rather large gambling problem," Philip added. "It's difficult to know just how much he thought was a fair share, considering he's rumored to have pockets to let."

Alana gestured to her husband. "Precisely. Not your most reliable source."

Maybe not, but it presented some interesting possibilities.

Had Mr. Fergusson orchestrated the body snatching of his relative in hopes of pocketing the ransom money? And if he was really in such deep debt as Philip insinuated, how long would that money last? Would he stoop to committing more body snatchings for ransom just to fund his gambling habit? I couldn't say, but it was certain that if he had some part in the crimes, he wasn't working alone. Maybe he'd hired Bonnie Brock's crew of resurrectionists to disinter the bodies.

Regardless, it would be a good idea to speak with this Mr. Fergusson.

"What of the other families?" Gage questioned my sister and her husband. "Did either the Casselbecks or Lord Buchan have any disgruntled relatives?"

Alana stared up at the chandelier suspended over the table in thought and then shook her head. "Not that I can think of."

"There was that matter with the Erskines," Philip remarked. "But that was more of the wife's doing."

Gage frowned, clearly trying to place the names. "The Erskines?"

"The late Lord Buchan's youngest brother and his family. When Buchan died without issue and left the title to his nephew Henry, his second brother's child, the wife of his youngest brother complained because her son received nothing. She thought the estate should be split between the two nephews. But she wasn't born into the aristocracy, and didn't understand how the rules of inheritance work," Philip added, waving the matter aside.

I supposed I might be displeased, too, if my older nephew inherited an earldom, several estates, and a large fortune, while my son was given nothing. It seemed the late earl could have left the boy something. But I wasn't privy to all the details of that family's affairs. Perhaps the earl had gifted the younger nephew before he died.

In any case, Gage didn't appear concerned with the matter, and Alana had already moved on to talk about the upcoming balls, dinner parties, and other events occurring over the course of the next week. I was not particularly interested in attending any of them, but I also had to admit they would be good places to collect information. I was aware of the irony in my seeking out gossip for potential evidence when I hated the insipid conversations and petty blather that made up such society gatherings. Especially as I'd been chattered about in just such a manner since the day I entered society, and even more so since the revelations after Sir Anthony's death. But I bit my tongue and surrendered to Gage and my sister's better judgment as they selected which events they would write to the hostesses of and beg an invitation for Gage and me. There was no doubt of Gage being obliged—he was one of the most sought after gentleman guests in the country—and most would be willing to accommodate the request of my sister, a countess, on my behalf.

We had just finished luncheon and exited the dining room when there was a knock at the door. The butler went to answer it as we all began to climb the stairs to the drawing room, but a familiar voice made Gage and me stop and turn. It was Anderley, bundled up in a dark greatcoat and hat.

"I beg your pardon, sir," Anderley murmured as his posture stiffened, clearly startled by the sight of all of us. "But this message just came for you. It said that it was urgent." He held out a letter, beaten and soiled by its journey.

"Excuse me." Gage released my arm and descended the stairs to take the letter. He flipped it over to examine the seal. His jaw hardened.

"Gage, you're welcome to use my study," Philip began, but fell silent when Gage forcefully broke open the seal and unfolded the missive.

We stood awkwardly by as he perused its opening contents, his expression growing stonier with each line. Before he'd even reached the middle of the page, he lowered the papers and began to refold them angrily.

"I apologize," he bit out crisply. "But I must see to this."

"Of course," Philip replied, his voice echoing the same confusion I felt.

"Does it have to do with the investigation?" I ventured hesitantly.

He took a deep breath and returned to the base of the stairs to look up at me. "No. Just . . . a personal matter."

I nodded slowly, unsure exactly what that meant.

His lips flattened in a self-deprecating smile. "I've told you how little my father likes his orders being disobeyed."

And Gage had postponed his return to London in order to take on this inquiry.

I indicated my understanding, but I couldn't help but wonder if that was really all there was to it. I knew Captain Lord Gage had been instructing his son to return to London for almost four months now, so surely he wasn't still waiting for his son to take over an investigation for him. Was he really so autocratic, or was there another reason for his urgency that his son return?

Gage climbed the few steps separating us and pressed a kiss to my hand as he promised to call for me early the next morning for our trip to Woodslea. I said I would be ready. I watched as he and Anderley departed, their two tall frames, one golden-haired and one dark, descending the front steps of the townhome side by side.

When the butler closed the door on the sight, I turned to follow Alana and Philip up the stairs, only to be surprised to find them still standing near the top, watching me. The pleased smiles that stretched their faces left me with no doubt that they understood the significance of Gage's leave-taking. Heat began to rise into my cheeks, and I hurried up the stairs past them.

"I believe you said the children wanted to see me," I muttered, moving on before either of them could say anything.

But all the same, I could hear Alana's happy laughter as it followed me up the next flight of stairs. And I couldn't help but smile, despite my embarrassment.

## CHAPTER TWENTY

Woodslea stood on an eastern slope of the Pentland Hills, nestled within a small wood that had grown up around a burn. Traveling across empty Seafield Moor as we were, we could see the Pentland Hills rising before us for miles, and then the pale stone facade of Woodslea as it stood out against the darkness of the trees. The sun was hidden behind low gray clouds, which scuttled across the sky as if racing toward some goal—perhaps a warmer clime.

I tugged the hood of my cloak up around my ears, trying to block the bite of the wind as we made our way from the carriage into the mansion. The solid oak door stood open just wide enough for us to slip through, and then the butler slammed it shut.

I jumped as the sound echoed through the vaulted space.

"Apologies," the majordomo said with a warm smile. "The wind often makes closing the door quite difficult." He gestured to a footman hanging back near the wall to take our coats and gloves. "You are here to see Mr. Tyler."

It wasn't really a question, but Gage answered it as such anyway. "Yes. He should be expecting us."

The butler nodded. "Right this way."

We followed him up a staircase, around a corner, down another short flight of steps, and then down a long corridor to a room near the back of the house. From our approach,

Woodslea had appeared to be a rather irregular pile of stone, with several additions made on different dates, and our convoluted path to this, what must amount to the drawing room, only confirmed it.

Owen Tyler and a rather plain woman, who I suspected might be his wife, rose from their seats as we entered. Introductions were swiftly made, and we settled down on opposite sides of the long table positioned between two settees. The drapes over a large window had been drawn back to show the garden, which must have been lovely during the summer. Now there were only barren branches and shrubs, and towering evergreens to look at.

"I hope my letter arrived in good time, and adequately explained the reason for our visit," Gage started off by saying.

"Yes," Mr. Tyler replied. He glanced at his wife, whose hands were tucked demurely in her lap. "And, I must say, we were rather unsettled to hear there've been other such thefts."

"We're still making inquiries to discover if there have been even more, but from what we've ascertained, yours may have been the first. You understand why we would want to find out all we can about the incident."

"O' course. Whatever we can do to help."

Gage joined me in studying the couple—their rather austere clothing, void of all ornamentation, and the severe style of Mrs. Tyler's hair fastened almost ruthlessly into a tight bun. "If you don't mind me asking, why didn't you report the crime when it happened?"

"Well, to be honest, we thought it was an isolated incident. Some local lads fallen on hard times, or a passing family of gypsies and the like. We never dreamed they'd do it again, to someone else." Mr. Tyler paused, drawing a deep breath. "And we didna want to call attention to it. My father was a good man, a righteous man, for his body to be desecrated in such a way . . . Well, perhaps it was my pride talkin', but I felt that the fewer who ken, the better it would be."

It was clear just how horrified the Tylers were by the

entire affair. I suspected they feared, as many did, that the fact that Ian Tyler's body had been disturbed meant that he would not be able to rise from the dead on Judgment Day. Having married an anatomist who routinely conducted dissections of human corpses—and forced me to assist him—I'd heard the argument many times before. I had no answer for them, but I could attest to the fact that whatever energy, whatever force gave us life—a soul, a consciousness—it no longer inhabited our bodies after death. There was nothing behind a cadaver's eyes but nerves and tissues and fluids, and all of it was quickly decaying.

Whatever had made Ian Tyler the man he'd been was no longer present in his bones. It had gone to somewhere better, or worse, depending on the type of man he really was. Or, at least, that was what I believed. It was the only thing I could believe, faced with all I'd seen.

Gage shifted forward in his seat. "Can you tell us exactly what happened, from the moment your father's disturbed grave was discovered to the day his bones were returned to you? I'd just like to hear it all again in your words. No detail is too minor."

The disturbed grave was found on a Tuesday morning. Initially they'd worried it might have sat open for several days because they'd had guests over the weekend, and so had not visited the graveyard on Sunday as was their custom. But the rector had assured them that he had walked the kirkyard on Monday morning and nothing had been out of place.

Unlike at Dryburgh Abbey, the thieves had taken the time to re-cover the grave, but from the state of the ground, it was obvious it had been tampered with. Mr. Tyler had ordered the coffin dug up, to ensure that everything was in order. When they opened the wooden coffin, the body of Ian Tyler was gone, while all the rest of his clothing and effects were left behind in a disordered pile.

The family was understandably distraught, but they had no idea who could have done such a thing. It was ghoulish. No one had seen anything strange on Monday evening or the morning after, until the caretaker became suspicious of the loose dirt over Ian Tyler's grave.

It wasn't until the ransom note arrived almost two weeks later that they began to suspect that the entire crime had been committed for the money. What other explanation could there be? They had followed the thieves' instructions, leaving the cash on a hilltop in a more remote part of the Pentland Hills. The next day a bag of bones was left inside the kirk door with a note attached saying they were the remains of Ian Tyler of Woodslea.

"So there's no one in particular you suspected?" Gage asked. "Maybe someone who had pressured you for money before? Like Mr. Fergusson."

Mr. Tyler sat taller. "My cousin? Thaddeus?"

"I was told that Mr. Fergusson complained he'd been cheated out of part of his inheritance. And that he has a tendency to play too deep with his cards."

Mr. Tyler nodded, rubbing his hand over his jaw. "Aye. It's true. But I canna imagine he would ever stoop to something like this. 'Tis well below him."

In my experience, people who were desperate were often willing to do some pretty unsavory things. If Mr. Fergusson was far enough in debt to the wrong people, he just might stoop to body snatching. But Gage appeared willing to let the matter drop. Perhaps because the Tylers were not likely to give us any assistance in supporting such a theory.

"Did you save the ransom note?" he queried.

Mr. Tyler began to shake his head, but his wife surprised us all by saying, "Yes."

"I'm sorry," she told her shocked husband. "I ken you told me to burn it, but . . . I was worried someone might try such a trick again. And if so, I wanted to be sure we could compare the handwriting."

I couldn't tell whether he was displeased or grateful his wife had disobeyed him, but when he spoke to her in such a gentle voice, I suspected it was the latter.

"Where is it?"

Mrs. Tyler rose from her seat and crossed over toward the bookcase on the far wall. She reached up on tiptoe and pulled down a book from the second to top shelf. Paper rustled as she thumbed through the pages, and then pulled a folded white sheet from inside. She handed it to Gage, and I leaned closer to get a better look.

I couldn't be sure without examining them side by side, but the horrible handwriting appeared to be the same as that on the letter Lord Buchan received. The text was also quite similar, as if sections of the later note had been copied from this one.

Gage refolded the note and passed it to Mr. Tyler. "Are you aware of any connections between your father and Lord Buchan and Sir Colum Casselbeck? Were they friends?"

"I dinna ken aboot friends, but they were certainly acquaintances. They had similar interests."

"Yes. We're aware they were all members of the Society of Antiquaries of Scotland, but as of yet, that's the only direct connection we can find."

Mr. Tyler sat back deeper into the settee, his brow furrowed in thought. He sighed and shook his head. "I'm sorry. I canna think of anything else."

Gage tilted his head to the side. "Are either of you acquainted with a Mr. Lewis Collingwood?"

The Tylers looked at each other, but from the confused expressions on their faces, it was clear they were not. "I'm sorry. Should we be?"

I could tell from the dip in Gage's shoulders that he was disappointed by their answer. "No. He's simply a man Lord Buchan mentioned to us. He made some accusations about the Society of Antiquaries and a gold torc."

Mrs. Tyler suddenly sat forward in her seat and gasped to her husband. "He must be that man I told ye aboot!"

Mr. Tyler looked grim.

"What man?" Gage asked.

Mrs. Tyler screwed up her face in dislike. "Oh, a rude man came here one day, demanding to see my husband. He kept carrying on aboot a gold torch. Or, at least, that's what I thought he was saying. I told him my husband wasna here, and that we certainly didna have a gold torch. He left in quite a huff."

I could barely suppress my excitement. So Lewis Collingwood had also come here looking for his aunt's gold torc. I wondered how many other members of the Society of Antiquaries he'd visited. Had he gone to see the Casselbecks as well?

"Do you think he has something to do with it?" Mrs. Tyler asked, clearly interpreting our interest.

"Maybe," Gage replied cautiously. "It's too soon to tell. Would you mind if we visited your father's grave? We understand it's at Glencorse Parish Church."

Mr. Tyler nodded. "Aye. And the rector should be there should you have any problem locating it."

We shifted to the edge of our seats, prepared to take our leave, when something in the Tylers' faces made me pause. There was an uncertainty there, an uneasiness.

"Is there anything else we should know?" I risked asking them.

Mrs. Tyler's eyes dropped to her lap, where her hands were clasped tightly together, and Mr. Tyler cleared his throat, glancing at his wife before finally speaking. "Weel, there is one thing. When the thieves returned my father's bones to us, it appears there was one missing."

I couldn't help turning to Gage in surprise.

"We had the local surgeon check, you see," Mr. Tyler rushed on to say. "We wanted to be sure. And, well, he told us a finger bone was missing." He reached to take hold of his wife's hand. "It may not mean anything. The thieves may have accidentally dropped it. It is a wee bone."

"One of the smallest," I confirmed, especially if it was one of the bones at the tips of the fingers.

"But . . . we would like it back. If at all possible."

I nodded, understanding their discomfort. They wanted to be certain all of Ian Tyler was buried together, as it should be.

"We'll do what we can," Gage promised them.

"Now I'm really glad I told Lord Buchan to have Dr. Carputhers check to be sure all of his uncle's bones had been returned," I remarked as we exited Woodslea and climbed back into Gage's carriage.

"I know. I could kiss you for that stroke of brilliance," he replied, and then, with a twinkle in his eye, he leaned forward. "And I think I shall."

I giggled a moment later when the carriage rolled forward, forcing Gage to drop back in his seat.

"Cheeky coachman," he muttered. "I shall have to have a word with him later."

I shook my head. "It's not his fault you have no agility."

His eyes narrowed in challenge. "Oh, I haven't, have I? Well, we shall just see."

Several rather pleasurable moments later, he'd most emphatically proved me wrong. And I told him so.

"That shall teach you to doubt me," he murmured. And though playfully said, I thought there might be some emphasis behind his words.

I lifted my eyes to his golden hair, unable to continue to meet his gaze. His tresses, normally so artfully tussled, were a bit more of a tangled mess than usual from my fingers. I reached up to try to push the hairs I'd disarranged back into place, distracting myself from the intensity of his gaze. I grimaced. Unfortunately, I seemed only to be making it worse.

Gage laughed and I disentangled myself from him so that he could see to the matter himself. One swipe of his fingers through his locks and then back down, and they seemed to fall directly into place.

I reached back to secure two tendrils I could feel loosening from my coil of hair, thinking back to the subject at hand before Gage could broach anything more serious. "Do you think the thieves left out the bone on purpose?"

He watched as I pinned a curl. "Are you asking if I think they kept it?"

"Yes."

"I don't know. I suppose that depends on whether the same or a similar bone is missing from Lord Buchan's skeleton." He turned to look out at the passing countryside and frowned. "If it is . . . then we might be dealing with an entirely different beast."

"What do you mean?"

His eyes were troubled. "If our thief is keeping bones from each of the skeletons, then he's collecting trophies. And that says there's a far different motive for his actions than simply money."

I nodded, pretty sure I understood. "Could it be Mr. Collingwood?"

"Not unless he's a particularly vindictive man. If he's behind these body snatchings, then he just wants his torc back. Albeit he's willing to go to extreme measures to get it. But he would have no reason to retain tokens of his victory over these men. The victory would be in obtaining the torc."

We sat silently contemplating the matter, because thus far we didn't have any suspects who would have such a motive. Collingwood wanted the torc, and Fergusson and the Edinburgh body snatchers the money.

We seemed to be finding more questions instead of answers, and I was heartily tired of it.

The rector at Glencorse Parish Church had nothing to tell us that we didn't already know, and neither did the grave. It had already been recovered, and Ian Tyler's remains secured underground again. The graveyard was located just behind the ivy-covered church and surrounded by thick, tall trees, shielding it from the outside, and making it an ideal place to conduct a body snatching. In the late summer and early autumn, the foliage would be so full on the trees that it was unlikely someone from the outside would even see the light of a lantern or two.

Given the secrecy of the setting, we decided not to question those who lived nearby, assuming they would have come forward long before now if they'd actually seen something suspicious. Any other evidence had long since disappeared or been washed away, so we left the church no closer to the truth than we had been before.

We said little on the journey back north, each of us pondering the strangeness of this case. Or, at least, that's what I was thinking about. But when I began to notice by the increasing number of buildings and the cramped space they were built into that we were rolling into Edinburgh instead of headed east toward the sea and Musselburgh, I turned to Gage in confusion.

"I apologize. I should have told you earlier. There's been a change in plans." He braced himself against the carriage wall as we turned a sharp corner. "Sergeant Maclean sent word last night. He thinks he may know where we can find this Bonnie Brock tonight." He turned to look out the window, avoiding my gaze. "So our trip to Musselburgh will have to wait until tomorrow."

"I see," I murmured, trying to keep my voice carefully neutral, though I could hear my vexation creeping in. "And am I to assume, based on your demeanor, that I'm to be excluded from this excursion?"

"It would be best," Gage replied, still not looking at me.

I turned to scowl out the opposite window. I hated being left out of such things because Gage or some other man was fearful of my safety. Normally such circumstances worked to the opposite effect, leaving me in danger, but I bit my tongue. Given the situation, perhaps it would be best for me to remain behind. If they were searching for a criminal as notorious as Bonnie Brock was rumored to be, then who knew what type of unsavory establishments they would find themselves in, or what miscreants they might be forced to skirmish with. Even with my pistol, I would still be in the way.

There was also my reputation to consider—that which I was protecting from becoming further tarnished and that which I couldn't escape. Gage and Sergeant Maclean would likely find themselves in West Port at some point, Burke and Hare's old haunt, and should anyone learn who I was and recall my reputation while I was there, things could turn ugly quickly. The citizens of Edinburgh Old Town were still very much afraid that more murderers were at work in their streets, selling the corpses to the anatomists at the Surgeons' Hall. To discover a woman nicknamed the Butcher's Wife walking among them would incite a riot.

In any case, as bitterly cold as it was today, tonight would be even worse, and I would not enjoy shivering while I traipsed through dirty, dark, cramped closes in search of this Bonnie Brock.

Or, at least, that's what I told myself.

"Well, be careful," I bit out, hoping this Sergeant Maclean could be trusted to watch Gage's back.

When he didn't reply, I turned to find him watching me with a mixture of surprise and suspicion. But when it became apparent I wasn't going to argue or ask him further questions, he simply nodded. "I will."

I turned back to the window to study the cramped streets of the Old Town and said a silent prayer that he truly would.

When my sister discovered I would be available that evening, she immediately decided I must attend the theater with them. It was one of the few things that Alana's physician had not restricted her from, as long as she remained in Philip's theater box and off her feet for the majority of the performance. I made a weak protest, more interested in spending the evening sketching than watching a play, but upon seeing the joy and excitement my sister felt at the prospect of our outing, I could not deny her long.

So that evening while Gage searched the closes and wynds of Old Town for a criminal, I found myself in a box on the second tier of the recently renovated Theatre Royal watching Thomas Arne's ballad opera *Love in a Village*. No one was more surprised than I to discover that I was actually enjoying myself.

Rather than crowding his box with friends and notables, Philip had invited only a single colleague, the Viscount Strathblane, and his wife. I had dined with Lord and Lady Strathblane more than once at my sister's home, and so felt comfortable in their presence. They had always been remarkably affable, and though polite, not overly talkative, which allowed me to relax and enjoy the performance rather than be forced to socialize.

I had never seen *Love in a Village*, though I was aware of its popularity seventy-some years before. The music was lovely and lyrical, and the soprano who portrayed the heroine, Rosetta, quite impressive. I also found myself sympathizing with her. To escape marriage to a man she'd never met and whom she feared would make her miserable, she instead chose to run away and accept a position as a chambermaid at a nearby manor.

I admired her courage, and that made me curse my own folly. My father had supported Sir Anthony's suit, but he hadn't forced me to marry him. I'd done that on my own. There was an important distinction.

So lost was I in the romance developing between Rosetta and Thomas, another runaway who'd become a gardener in the same household, that I failed to notice how often Alana shifted in her chair. When I turned to her as the lights came up during the second intermission and saw how pale and uncomfortable she looked, I reached for her hand.

She smiled sadly. "No worries, dearest. This happens from time to time. I simply need to rest."

I glanced up at Philip as he came to stand over us. His eyes were shadowed with worry, but by his resigned expression and calm demeanor, I inferred this had happened before. Poor Alana. I knew she hated to be cooped up, but apparently even tonight's minimal excitement had been too much for her.

"I've sent for the carriage," Philip told her. "But I think we should wait until the end of intermission when the lights go back down. There will be less talk, and fewer people to navigate around. Will you be well enough until then?"

Alana inhaled deeply. "Yes. Of course."

I began to gather up my things, but my sister pressed a hand to my arm to stop me.

"Oh, no. Kiera, you should stay. You were enjoying the play so much."

"I'm sure I can see it at another time," I protested, but Alana spoke right over me.

"Philip, you could send the carriage back for Kiera, couldn't you?"

"Of course. It's only a few minutes' ride between here and the town house." He leaned down to press a hand gently to my shoulder. "Stay. There's no reason for you to rush off as well. I'll see Alana home and get her settled."

"Well . . ."

"Strathblane," Philip raised his voice to address his friend, ignoring me as well. "Would you see Lady Darby safely to my carriage after the performance?"

"Certainly," he replied, offering me a smile. "No trouble at all."

His wife, a mother herself, had leaned over to commiserate with my sister on her aches and pains and nausea.

"Then it's settled," Philip declared. Seeing how pleased he looked to have worked this out for me, it felt churlish of me not to simply thank him and accept.

So at the beginning of the third act, Alana slipped out of our theater box with Philip's arm supporting her, and I settled in to watch the remainder of the opera. Early on I had figured out that Rosetta and Thomas were each other's intended spouses, whom they'd each run away from, but that did not spoil my enjoyment of the ending when they discovered this for themselves.

I followed the Strathblanes out of the box and down the

central staircase crowded with other audience members. From time to time either Strathbane or his wife would stop to speak with someone, so our progress was slow, but I didn't mind, taking the time to observe everyone around me. Most of the ladies were wearing gowns with those newly fashionable puffed sleeves I so abhorred, with varying degrees of success. One blond girl with ringlets looked quite lovely, while the excess fabric only appeared to widen the figure of the girl next to her. Contrasting fabric might have helped, for the poor young lady was simply drowning in lavender.

"A rather unfortunate choice, I agree," a familiar nasal male voice said beside me. Mr. Stuart lowered his quizzing glass and smiled, bowing shortly from the waist in greeting. "Lady Darby, I did not know you were in Edinburgh."

"I arrived only a few short days ago. Have you been in town long yourself?"

"Only since I left Lord and Lady Rutherford. Such sad business what happened with that caretaker," he added with a shake of his head. "Did they ever find his murderer?"

"I'm afraid not. Though they did recover the body that was stolen."

"Really? How peculiar."

He turned away to stare out at the crowd, and I tried to place what I'd seen in his expression that had not quite fit. But before I could do so, I heard Lady Strathblane call my name. She and her husband had been pulled along with the tide of bodies moving toward the doors and I would need to hurry to catch up with them. I excused myself from Mr. Stuart's side and wound my way through the crowd to where the Strathblanes stood waiting to collect their outer garments.

Once we were bundled up against the cold, Lord Strathblane guided us both outside. We found their carriage immediately, and the viscount saw his wife safely inside before we went in search of Philip's coach. We located it finally, at the very edge of the crush of carriages parked in front of the theater on Princes Street, almost in the alley running between two buildings. I suspected the coachman had been waiting some time and tried to pull out of the way of the traffic.

Philip's footman hopped down from the back of the carriage to open the door. I thanked Lord Strathblane for his escort, who accepted my gratitude with a smile and nod and turned to go as I took hold of the footman's hand to allow him to help me up inside the coach. It was dark inside, and I wondered if the light from the lantern had bothered Alana on their ride back to Charlotte Square, so Philip had blown it out.

I'd perched on the edge of the seat and barely had time to register that something was wrong when the door was slammed shut and the carriage took off like a shot, tipping me back against the squabs. I heard shouts from outside, complaining about the speed of the carriage. Righting myself, I reached up to rap on the roof to signal the coachman when a rough voice spoke out of the darkness.

"Oh, I wouldna do that if I were you."

## CHAPTER TWENTY-ONE

I slowly lowered my arm, trying to peer into the blackness I faced across the carriage. The curtains had been drawn, allowing no chance of a stray beam of light to pierce the coach's interior. I could just make out the shape of a human seated in the corner of the bench across from me. From the sound of his voice, he was male, and not so much menacing as confident his implied threat would be followed, and willing to back it up if it wasn't.

I heard my pulse pounding in my ears and I realized I was holding my breath. Determined not to let fear overcome my good sense, I forced myself to exhale as the carriage rocked unsteadily around another corner.

"Who are you?" I demanded, pleased to hear that my voice didn't quake. "And what are you doing in my carriage?"

"My apologies," he replied almost ironically. He leaned forward and I shrank farther back against my cushions, sliding my hand toward my reticule on the seat beside me.

When a match flared to life, I took advantage of our shared momentary blindness to slip my hand into my bag and extract my pistol, hiding it in the folds of my skirt. As my eyes adjusted, I could see that the man across from me was lighting the lantern, which he had most likely blown out, not Philip. He was not overly tall, but broad in the shoulders and trim about the waist. He wore no greatcoat, despite the freezing cold temperatures outside, only a rather plain frockcoat over a white linen shirt. His hair was much longer than fashionable, and tumbled to his shoulders, sweeping against his collarbones. I had initially thought it to be dark, but as my eyes became more accustomed to the light, I realized it was tawny, and I wouldn't have been surprised if there were streaks of red visible through it in the sunlight.

Closing the lantern door with a click, he sank back against the squabs and turned to look at me. His eyes traveled over my features, before trailing down my form. I did my best to hide my anxiety, trying to go to that place of numbed emotion inside myself I'd so often visited while married to Sir Anthony. But I found I couldn't return there and retain my willingness to fight. So I tightened my grip around my pistol instead and stoked the anger I felt begin to burn in my gut.

Just when I thought he wasn't going to speak, only sit there staring at me with his smug smile, he finally replied.

"Word is you've been lookin' for me," he drawled. "I mun say, I'm flattered. So I thought I'd save ye the trouble and introduce myself." His eyes twinkled roguishly. "Bonnie Brock Kincaid at your service."

I was not as shocked as perhaps I should have been, for given the circumstances, the possibility had already dawned on me. The man certainly was bonnie, though I still felt Gage, with his golden good looks, far outmatched him.

"*I* haven't been looking for you," I replied defiantly, hoping to wipe the arrogant expression off his face.

"Oh, I ken that weel enough. It's Sebastian Gage and Mean Maclean who been askin' for me, causin' no small bit o' ruction. Ye should hear the number o' runners who come beatin' on my door t'night to warn me." He'd crossed his arms over his chest and now tilted his head to the side to scrutinize me. "But yer Gage's partner, noo ain't ya?"

"Yes," I bit out, realizing it would do no good to deny it. Especially when all I wanted to know was whether he'd harmed Gage or the Sergeant.

"Ye seemed an odd choice, but noo that I seen ye, I can imagine the . . . *partnership* has its compensations."

I narrowed my eyes at his insinuation. "I see. Well, now that you've solved that quandary, you can go." I lifted my pistol and cocked the hammer for good measure to be sure he knew I was serious.

However, far from being shocked or frightened, Bonnie Brock's lips only curled upward in a smile. "Oh, I wouldna do that if I were you."

I was beginning to hate that sentence, especially delivered from his arrogant lips.

"And why is that?"

"Because if my men ridin' up top wi' your coachman and footman hear a gunshot go off inside, there's no tellin' what they might do."

I wavered, not wishing for Philip's coachman or footman to be injured, but also not wanting to lose my upper hand. Taking a deep breath, I steadied my grip. "But that won't matter much to you, will it, when you're dead."

A chill ran down my back as Bonnie Brock's eyes began to harden. They were not the eyes of a man who took threats lightly. I could see now that he had a ridge of scar tissue running along his nose, for its white stood out sharply against the angry red flush of his face.

But I swallowed my trepidation and firmed my resolve. If I'd learned nothing from my last two confrontations with dangerous men, it was to take advantage of the opportunities that were presented to me. If I backed down now, it was unlikely I would get another chance to defend myself, and I had no way of knowing just what he intended for me. I prayed I wouldn't have to shoot him, especially with Philip's servants in danger, but I would if I had to.

Bonnie Brock's tense shoulders slowly began to loosen, and the mottled shade of his skin lightened. A new light entered his eyes, one that was less stomach quavering than the glare he'd fixed on me a moment before.

"True," he reluctantly admitted. "So why dinna you and

I make a deal, hmm? I promise to let you and your brother-in-law's servants return to his town house unscathed—you'll walk right through the door just like I watched Cromarty and your sister do earlier this evenin'."

Something tight wrapped around my rib cage and squeezed at the thought of this man anywhere near my sister and her family, let alone watching them.

"If you'll put doon the pistol," he finished, arching his eyebrows.

The carriage shuddered and rocked as we sped over a portion of rough road and then around another corner, forcing me to press my other hand against the wall of the coach to steady myself. Even so, my gun hand wavered.

Bonnie Brock glared up at the ceiling with a fierce scowl. "Slow down," he snarled.

I stiffened at the sound, but was grateful when the coachman obeyed.

Brock's gaze returned to me, still tight with anger as he waited for my answer.

There was no way of knowing if I could trust him. I could just as easily set aside my gun and then he would attack me. He could clearly read my hesitation.

"I've ne'er given a man a reason to doubt my word, and skewered many a man for questioning it," he warned me. "But yer no' from my world, so I'll make allowances. Given ye dinna realize I could have that gun oot o' yer hand and ye doon on your back afore ye could even think o' pullin' the trigger."

I truly didn't like the look he fastened on me now, and my hand began to shake. I forced myself to take a deep breath to calm my nerves.

Was he telling the truth? Could he really do that? Even if he couldn't, was I really certain my shot would kill him? What if it hit his shoulder instead, or his side? The man could still tackle me and choke the life out of me while his men killed Philip's servants.

I realized I couldn't chance it. But that didn't mean I had to admit defeat.

I locked eyes with him, hard as that was to do, and nodded before uncocking my pistol and resting it across my lap.

He lifted his hand palm up, asking for it.

But I simply lowered my hands to my sides. "If your word is true, then you're as safe with it lying here as you are with it in your possession."

I knew I was testing him, tempting the snake to strike, but there was no way I was going to hand over my only weapon without a fight.

However, he surprised me again when he merely offered me a half smile. "Fair enough."

I breathed a silent sigh of relief and spared a moment to wonder just where he was taking me. We'd been driving for several minutes now, long enough to travel a fair distance at our speed. Distracted as I'd been from the first and with the curtains pulled tight, I couldn't even begin to guess our location.

Shaking the worrying thought aside, I lifted my chin. "Why have you kidnapped me? I know you're not here for an introduction." I tilted my head. "Not unless you just wanted to frighten Mr. Gage and Sergeant Maclean by making them realize you could get to me at any time and they couldn't stop you."

Bonnie Brock's mock outrage did not fool me. "What a terrible thought. 'Specially when I'm here to give ye information."

I eyed him doubtfully. "Information about what?"

"Your body snatchers."

I tried to mask my interest, but from the sardonic quirk in his lips, it appeared I had not done well enough.

"That is what you're investigatin', isn't it? A couple a snatches for ransom?"

"And how do you know so much about it?"

He leaned sideways into the bench cushions, bracing himself with one arm while he draped the other over the knee he'd lifted up when he propped his dirty boot on the seat. His eyes sharpened on me, narrowing slightly at the corners.

"I ken aboot everythin', lass. Nothin' happens in my city wi'oot my ken."

I suspected his relaxed pose was to demonstrate how little he feared me, and his penetrating gaze to show how much I should fear him. They weren't necessary. I'd been battling against the instinct to run since the moment he revealed himself, even though the fact that we were inside a speeding carriage made that option impossible.

I wished I could appear as unruffled, as uncaring, as he did, but my limbs would not obey. So I sat stiffly across from him, grateful for the weight of the pistol over my knees, hollow as the promise of its protection might be.

"Where are you taking me?" I finally dared to ask.

He considered my question for a moment, and I couldn't tell whether he was deciding to answer or he was thinking up a lie. "We're just goin' for a drive aboot the city." My expression must have been skeptical, for he then added, "Listen. Ye can hear the cobblestones beneath the wheels."

He was right. It did sound and feel like the jarring texture of cobblestones. If he was taking me somewhere out of the city, we should have run into dirt roads already. So perhaps he was telling the truth.

And perhaps he wasn't. It wasn't as if, at the moment, it made a difference.

"So what information do you have about the body snatchers? I know they're your men."

"Noo that ye have wrong."

"Come now," I replied, unwilling to be duped. "Sergeant Maclean recognized them as being part of your crew."

"And how did he do that?" Bonnie Brock tipped his head back. "Ah, yes. How could I forget? You've quite a talent for drawin' people. Alive *or* dead."

I gritted my teeth against the urge to snap back at him. He was baiting me. That was abundantly clear from the nasty curl of his lip.

"Weel, Mean Maclean is wrong this time. They dinna

work for me." His eyes hardened again. "No' anymore. They slipped town aboot two months ago."

"Skipped out on you?" I guessed.

"Aye. And ain't *nobody* who gets away wi' that."

His anger was clearly directed at these men, but I had a hard time convincing my nerves of that.

Was he telling the truth? Sergeant Maclean had said he hadn't seen the men in a few months, and this would seem to corroborate that.

"Do you know where they went?"

He arched his eyebrows. "Noo if I knew that, we wouldna be havin' this friendly conversation."

"But you think they're the men we're looking for?"

He scrutinized me again from head to toe. "What do you think?"

I watched him carefully, trying to decide why he was testing me. "I think they're not clever enough to plan these ransoms." Not if they had lived in Edinburgh all their lives, under the thumb of this man. Bonnie Brock was far from stupid. If these men had shown anything more than average intelligence, I imagined they would have been assigned more challenging tasks in his organization than simple grave robbing.

His lips curled upward in a worryingly pleased smile. "You're right. But then a plan like this needs men to do the mindless dirty work. And they're certainly capable o' that."

"Then who's the one giving them directions?" I tried to read his maddening expression. "Do you know?"

He rested his head back against the squabs, his posture lazy and unconcerned, but there was a watchfulness in his gaze that I didn't make the mistake of ignoring.

"Noo, ye wouldna be wantin' me to solve your crime for ye," he drawled.

I scowled, tired of this man playing games with me. "I would be quite content with that. If it meant bringing Dodd's killer to justice. And *if* your information was accurate." I knew I was prodding the beast—as the flash of something sinister in his eyes confirmed—but I couldn't help it. He either needed to tell me what he knew or let me go.

"The caretaker?"

I blinked in surprise, trying to follow the bent of his thoughts. "Yes. Dodd was the caretaker at Dryburgh Abbey. And we assume the body snatchers murdered him when he stumbled on their activities."

"And that's what you're worried aboot?"

"Well, yes. Of course, I want to stop the body snatchings, too. But isn't the murder of a man more important than the theft of the dead's bones?"

He lowered his knee, sitting straighter in his seat. "No' all would say so."

I frowned. Was he referring to their differences in rank? I supposed it was true that some would care little for the life of an old caretaker, especially when opposed to the desecration of an earl's grave, but for me there was no comparison. I sympathized with the families whose loved ones' remains had been stolen, particularly those who were more religious—like the Tylers—and worried about their ancestor's resurrection, but there was no contest for which crime more justly deserved punishment. Murder trumped grave robbing any day.

Bonnie Brock casually lifted aside the curtain over the window with two fingers. "Perhaps you're lookin' at it all wrong."

"What do you mean?"

He shrugged, his gaze still on the shadowy world passing by outside as we rounded a corner. "Perhaps ye should be lookin' into the victims' pasts. Maybe they werena the saints everyone wishes ye to believe. Maybe they werena such friends to Scotland as ye think."

I considered his words. Somehow I didn't think he was referring to the possible theft of Collingwood's torc.

He turned to gaze at me, allowing the curtain to drop. "No' all crimes are bad. No' if the motive is just." He leaned toward me, and I instinctively pressed back deeper into the cushions. "Sometimes the victims are the real villains."

I suspected at this point he was talking about more than just the body snatchings, but when I opened my mouth to question him about it, he cut me off, leaning even closer. I covered the pistol with my hand, lest he try to take it.

"You've the bonniest eyes."

Facing his charming smile and the sudden change in the direction of our conversation, I was momentarily at a loss for words.

"They're like jewels, but no' sapphires."

"Lapis lazuli."

"Is that what they are? They flash when yer angry. I like that." He tried to reach out and touch my face, but I turned aside. "I bet Gage likes it as well."

I had a strong suspicion they were flashing now.

"Mr. Kincaid . . ."

"Ah, lassie, call me Brock."

I considered ignoring his request, but then decided it would only delay matters. "Brock, you've given me your information and proved your point. Will you please return me to my brother-in-law's home now?"

His lips quirked upward, but he sat back, allowing me more breathing room. "But we're no' quite finished, lass."

I scowled. I knew there would be a hidden cost to our agreement. With men like him, there always was. He wouldn't share such information with me without expecting something in return. That would be completely out of character.

"What do you want?" I asked, hoping he would get directly to the point.

His gaze shifted to stare at the carriage wall just over my head and became oddly flat. I began to suspect he was suppressing some strong emotion. It made me more able to patiently wait out his silence.

"I have a sister," he replied finally. His eyes focused on me again, allowing me to see the anger and worry reflected behind them. "She started to dandle after one o' the men yer lookin' for. I told her to stay away from him. He's no good. But she didna listen. And when they skulked off, she went wi' 'em."

"And you're worried she's come to regret that decision."

He nodded, one sharp bob of his head.

I tilted my head, trying to suppress the sympathy I could feel welling up inside me. For all I knew, Bonnie Brock could have been an ogre to his sister and that was why she ran off. But somehow, seeing the real concern he seemed to feel, I suspected he was no worse than any other brother.

"How old is she?"

"Aboot sixteen."

So young. "What do you want me to do?"

"Like I told ye, if she was in Edinburgh, I woulda found her in a matter o' hours. But she's no'. I want ye to find her. To send her back."

I supposed that was easy enough. Chances were she was with these rogue body snatchers, if we ever caught up with them. But I hesitated to make such a promise, especially knowing as little as I did.

"I'll find your sister," I told him, and his shoulders relaxed. "I'll speak with her and find out if she's truly well. And *if* she wants to return to Edinburgh, I'll make sure she returns here, safe and sound. But I can't agree to more than that."

His gaze hardened. "She's no' of age."

"I'm aware of that. And I'll do my best to convince her to return to you. But if for whatever reason she does not want to, I will not force her."

When the vein in his forehead began to throb, I thought it best to do a little more to reassure him.

"Come now. Do you honestly think I would leave a young girl in a situation that I did not think was suitable? For any woman," I added, in case he thought I would think a brothel was appropriate for the sister of a notorious criminal like him. "Perhaps she's found a respectable position for herself somewhere. If she's safe and well cared for, I'm not going to force her to leave."

Bonnie Brock studied me, clearly considering my words. I knew it had been dangerous to defy him, but I simply could not commit myself to something without knowing all the facts, especially when dealing with a man like him.

"I dinna like my requests to be denied," he bit off. "But considerin' how confident I am that Maggie 'll wish to return if given the chance, I'll let your foolishness slide."

"Thank you," I replied, unable to keep the mocking edge from my voice.

His eyebrows rose, but he said nothing. He reached his hand up and rapped on the roof three times and then settled back against the squabs.

I felt the carriage immediately pick up speed again, and then make a turn to the right and then the left. I still had no idea where we were, so the quick changes in direction meant nothing to me, but apparently they did to Bonnie Brock.

He sat forward on the edge of his seat and slid closer to the door. "'Twas a pleasure to meet ye, Lady Darby," he declared.

I felt some of the muscles I'd been holding so tightly begin to release at the realization that this unasked-for interlude was almost over. "I'll give your regards to Mr. Gage." I sneered.

His eyes flashed. "Oh, dinna bother. I'll offer them myself verra soon."

"Don't you dare." I gasped, grasping the implication. "You got what you wanted from me. There's no reason to disturb him."

He chuckled darkly. "Aye. But I dinna get everything I wanted from you."

I frowned. "Because I wouldn't guarantee to send your sister to you?"

He stared at me levelly, his eyelids heavier than they had been before. "Just be glad ye brought yer pistol. And I was convinced ye might try to use it."

The carriage halted abruptly, throwing me forward in my seat. By the time I'd righted myself, Bonnie Brock was already leaping out of the carriage.

"If you touch so much as a hair on his head . . ." I shouted before the door was slammed in my face.

The coach rolled forward again, and I inhaled deeply, sinking lower on the cushions while I tried to come to terms with what had just happened.

# CHAPTER TWENTY-TWO

When I had myself more in hand, I risked a glance out the window, and upon seeing the classical buildings of the New Town, I reached up to rap on the ceiling. The coach immediately slowed, and a few minutes later the footman appeared in the doorway.

His eyes were wide in his face. "My lady, are you well?"

"Yes, yes," I assured him. "What of you and the coachman? Did they harm either of you?"

"No more than our pride, m'lady."

I nodded, relieved to know that at least we'd all come through our encounter with Bonnie Brock unscathed.

"I'm sorry, m'lady. They ambushed us on Charlotte Street. And they told me if I said a word to you at the theater, they'd shoot you."

"It's all right. They put us all in an impossible situation." I pressed a hand to my forehead. "Where did they leap out at?"

"Near The Mound, m'lady."

At the intersection of the Old and the New Town.

The coachmen yelled down something I couldn't hear, but it made the footman glance up and down the street. "Do you wish to return to Charlotte Square, m'lady?"

"Not yet," I replied, giving him an address on Princes Street and instructions on who to fetch once we were there.

He nodded and closed the carriage door before moving to the front to relay my message to the coachman. There must have been a small bit of squabbling over my orders, but eventually they were obeyed.

I huddled inside the carriage, shivering within my cloak. The hot brick Philip and Alana had left had long since cooled, and most of the heat had escaped when the footman had opened the door earlier. As the minutes ticked by, I couldn't stop myself from peering out the window toward the darkness of the trees lining the opposite side of the street. The shadowy outline of the castle on its rock outcropping towered over the scene, offering no deterrent to the criminals that might lurk below it.

When finally the carriage door opened, I jumped, having spent too long imagining terrible scenarios. Gage peered inside at me, a confused expression on his face.

"Kiera. What's happened?"

I gestured him inside and once he'd settled on the seat and closed the door behind him, I couldn't stop from flinging myself into his arms. He held me close and allowed me to bury my face against his neck. I breathed in deeply, comforted by his scent and the solidness of his form, and the steady beat of his heart beneath my palm.

My own pulse began to slow and I turned my head, feeling the scrape of his whiskers against my forehead. It was then that I realized his cravat was missing. I opened my eyes to see that Gage's shirt was partially unbuttoned, allowing me a glimpse of the wiry hairs growing at the top of his chest. My fingers brushed against them where my hand pressed to his hard pectorals. His dark greatcoat was draped around him, but he had not buttoned it before hurrying out to me.

"Kiera," he murmured, reaching up to cradle my jaw and lift my face so that I could meet his concerned gaze. "What is it? Tell me."

"I . . . I just needed to be sure that you were safe."

His brow furrowed. "Of course, I am. Why? What's happened?"

I inhaled deeply and pushed myself upright, so that I could better see him. I brushed my hair back from my face. "Bonnie Brock came to see me."

Gage's eyes widened in shock. "What! When?"

I explained how I'd attended the theater with Alana and Philip, and how they'd left early. When I got to the point of the evening when Bonnie Brock kidnapped me in this very carriage, Gage began stifling curses. He demanded I tell him everything, and I did my best to relay all that had been said, minus the comments about my eyes. Unfortunately, Gage seemed far less concerned with the man's threats to "pay his respects" to him than I was.

"I take it you and Sergeant Maclean were unsuccessful in your search," I added, perhaps unnecessarily.

"The entire town closed ranks as soon as we mentioned his name. They're all either profiting from him or afraid of him."

"Do you think he told me the truth? About the men who used to work for him?"

Gage glared at the wall across the carriage. "I don't know. On the one hand, there was no need for him to confide in you. Not to mention the bit about his sister. On the other, I don't trust him any more than I trust that a stray dog won't steal my steak if given half a chance."

"He's not a nice man, Gage."

Hearing the worried note in my voice, he turned to look at me.

"I don't think you should take his threat so lightly."

"Kiera, I'm not going to come to any harm," he replied, lifting a hand to brush it against my cheek.

I took hold of his hand, gripping it between my own and running my thumbs over his rough calluses. "I just want you to take precautions."

"I will," he promised. "But I'm also not going to allow the

man to intimidate me." His eyes hardened. "He might think he owns Edinburgh, but I'm not without my own contacts."

"Gage . . ."

"Let's get you home. I'm sure your servants are freezing by now." He leaned out to yell at the coachman and then settled back against the seat next to me, wrapping his arm around me. I rested my head sideways against his shoulder, grateful for his warmth and the comfort of his presence.

Philip's town house was only a few blocks away, so in a matter of minutes we were pulling up to its front. As the footman opened the carriage door for me, Philip emerged from the town house, his face creased in lines of worry.

"Oh, thank heavens," he exclaimed as he saw me emerge. "When you didn't return, I thought something had happened to you."

"Something did," Gage replied harshly as he stepped down behind me.

Before the two men could begin to argue on the doorstep, I asked them if we could please go inside out of the cold. They obliged, and soon I was warming myself before the fire in Philip's study while he and Gage quarreled. I decided it would be a miracle if Alana managed to sleep through the racket they were causing. I knew it was merely fear and worry talking, two emotions I had experienced aplenty that night, but after a few minutes of their bickering, I decided I'd had enough.

"Stop!" I snapped, stepping between them. "Philip didn't do anything wrong. He took measures for my safety. There was no way he could have known Bonnie Brock would circumvent them. And there's no use in blaming yourself," I told Gage. "You had no way of knowing the man would be so devious. No one came to harm. Can we not just leave it at that?"

The two men still eyed each other with mistrust and anger, but they did not disagree.

"Now, tell me," I said, turning to Philip. "How is Alana?"

He uncrossed his arms, and moved toward the sideboard. "Resting comfortably."

"Good."

He poured himself a tot of Matheson whiskey from his own distillery and downed it in one swallow. Then he turned to tip his glass at Gage, asking if he would like one.

Gage shook his head. "No, thank you. I should be going." He reached up to brush a hand through his golden hair. "It's been a long evening."

"Take the carriage," Philip told him.

"Thanks, but I prefer to walk."

"No," I interrupted. "That's exactly what Bonnie Brock would want you to do."

He turned to me wearily. "Kiera, the man is not going to ambush me tonight. He's probably at home already, tucked up warm in his bed."

"All the same, you said you would take precautions. And the carriage will be much warmer than walking."

"I have my precautions," he declared, lifting aside his greatcoat so that I could see his pistol tucked into the waistband of his trousers. He looked to Philip. "Thank you for purchasing that Hewson for Kiera."

Philip nodded. "Though you'll have to thank her brother for teaching her how to shoot it. I'm afraid I never got the opportunity." His gaze shifted to me. "Did she use it?"

"Only in threat. But it worked well enough."

I scowled. They didn't need to speak about me as if I wasn't here.

"Gage, please take the carriage," I begged, deciding to try a different tack. "I'll worry all night if you don't."

"Kiera," he murmured, wrapping his hands around my upper arms. "No." Then he dropped a swift kiss on my lips and turned to go.

"Bloody stupid man!" I cried after him, wishing now I'd never gone to see him after Bonnie Brock had released me.

I heard the front door of the town house open and close

with a thud, and I felt like throwing something. Philip stood by the sideboard, smiling in commiseration.

"You could have stopped him," I snapped, before stalking up to my room to pass what was certain to be a long, sleepless night.

As it turned out, I spent more than half of the night tucked up in my makeshift art studio in a small room at the back of the top floor. Worry and anger turned out to be marvelous distracters, and I was able to make significant progress on the portrait of Philip's cousin Caroline I had left behind when I departed for Blakelaw House. I would have preferred to work on Gage's portrait, but I had not brought it with me when we journeyed to Edinburgh, the recent paint I had added to it making it too fragile to transport.

When Gage called for me the next morning in his black lacquer carriage, I was peering out the window, watching for him. I was so relieved to see him that I didn't even wait for him to disembark and come inside to collect me, but simply grabbed my reticule and bounded down the steps. He must have seen me coming, because he had not yet emerged, and in fact sat stiffly on the far side of the carriage while the footman helped me inside.

He made only the most perfunctory reply to my greeting, seeming far more interested in the antics of the neighbor children playing in the square under the watchful eyes of their governesses and nannies. Malcolm, Philippa, and Greer usually joined them sometime around midmorning, after their first course of lessons. Their shouts and laughter could be heard even over the sound of the carriage wheels, as we rounded the square and headed east.

When the organized streets of the new town were behind us, and the towering form of Calton Hill rose to our left and Salisbury Crag to our right, and yet Gage had still not spoken more than two words to me, I became concerned. I turned away from the sight of the new burying ground begun south of Calton to stare at his profile. His firm jaw was as smooth and as hard as granite above the expertly folded draping of his snowy white cravat.

"Maybe you're waiting for an apology from me for my being so angry with you last night," I began. "But you're not going to get one. Not when I was only thinking of your safety." When he didn't even turn to look at me, I became irritated. "You cannot expect to give orders and demands about my safety without my being able to do the same." I frowned at his silence. "I'm glad to see you're unharmed. But that doesn't mean you're invincible."

Gage sighed heavily and closed his eyes. When he opened them again, he turned to look at me.

I gasped as the light from the window illuminated the nasty contusion over his left eye. Leaning forward, I reached out to touch it, but he only turned away.

"I'm fine," he grumbled.

"Let me see it," I ordered him. When he still resisted, I gripped his jaw between my thumb and forefinger and forced his head to the side. Finally he relented.

The bruise was a mottled circle of purple and red extending over his eyelid and down to his cheekbone. There were no lacerations, and the damage would most likely heal without any serious complications, but that did little to soothe my distress.

"What happened?" I demanded.

He pulled away from me and I let him. "You know what happened."

"I told you . . ."

"Yes. I know," he snapped. "But you should see them. They look worse off than I do."

I glared at him. Somehow I doubted that.

"Are you injured anywhere else?"

"Nowhere you need be concerned with."

"Gage!"

"Just a bruise on my shin and another on my shoulder.

And these." He stripped off his gloves to show me his battered and scraped knuckles.

I was happy to see that Bonnie Brock and his associates hadn't gotten away without receiving at least a few blows in return.

I turned to stare out the window, fighting the twin urges to punch the man myself and also throw myself into his arms and beg him never to take such a risk again. No one needed to remind me that he was lucky to have emerged from the fight without more serious wounds. Bonnie Brock could have pulled a knife or a pistol. Gage could have bled out on a cold Edinburgh street.

I shook the terrifying thought aside and concentrated instead on how furious I was with him for not listening to me. The fact that he would not have been walking home alone down the deserted street after midnight if I had not run straight to him after hearing Bonnie Brock's threat also helped to stoke my rage. I couldn't help but feel I had played straight into the scoundrel's hands.

The remainder of the ride to Musselburgh was spent in tense silence, neither of us willing to break the angry standoff. By the time we pulled up to the Casselbecks' manor house along the banks of the River Esk, I was in such a foul mood that I found it difficult to be polite to the servants. All my smiles and comments felt forced and fraudulent, particularly next to Gage's easy charm. But then he also had to endure their openmouthed stares at his black eye. Next to that, I suspected they barely noticed me.

"My goodness, Mr. Gage," Sir Robert gasped when he came forward to greet us. "What happened?"

"Just a minor altercation." Gage's posture was stiff, not inviting comment.

"He walked into a door," I supplied, I thought, rather helpfully.

He turned to glare at me. I ignored him in favor of offering Sir Robert my hand, which he politely took, though it was clear he was baffled by our exchange.

"Lady Darby, it's a pleasure to meet you," he murmured, bowing over it.

"Likewise."

He gestured us toward a grouping of furniture near the fireplace, choosing an orange and brown checked wingback chair for himself. I allowed Gage to sit in the other chair while I perched on the end of the silk brocade settee closest to the hearth. The wind had been bitterly cold again this morning, and the grass and rooftops were dusted with a light covering of snow that had fallen sometime near dawn.

"I understand you've uncovered more information about the theft of my father's bones," Sir Robert said, crossing one long leg over the other. His dark hair was liberally sprinkled with silver at the temples, giving him a rather distinguished look.

"Yes," Gage replied, and proceeded to explain about the other body snatchings and our suspicions that they were all connected in some way, or at least committed by the same criminals. Sir Robert listened silently, and though his eyes widened several times, other than that there was no discernible reaction.

When Gage had finished, he clasped his hands before him. "I'm acquainted with Mr. Tyler and Lord Buchan. What can I do to help?"

Exactly what we'd hoped to hear.

"Are you aware of any connections between your father, the late earl, and Ian Tyler, other than the Society of Antiquaries of Scotland? We've been informed they were all founding members."

Sir Robert's eyes rose to the ceiling, seeming to consider the matter.

"Anything at all," Gage prodded. "Even something that might seem small and inconsequential."

He shook his head. "I'm sorry. I'm sure they knew each other, though I wouldn't have called them close friends." He tipped his head to the side. "Several of them were writers, usually something to do with Scotland. Perhaps they researched or published something together."

Gage nodded. "That's certainly worth looking into."

"Do you think there will be more thefts?"

He glanced at me, a frustrated look in his eye. "I don't know. But I worry there may."

I hadn't heard him state it so baldly before, and it made my stomach tighten with dread.

"Terrible," Sir Robert muttered, a crease forming between his eyes. "What is our society coming to?"

None of us had a good reply to that.

Gage shifted in his seat. "Can you tell me, have you received a visit from a Mr. Lewis Collingwood recently? Perhaps in the last six months."

"No." Sir Robert tapped his fingers. "But I did receive a letter from him."

Gage's disappointed expression immediately transformed to one of interest. "Really? Do you still have it?"

"If I do, it's been filed away somewhere by my secretary. But I can tell you he was asking after some family heirloom. Something Celtic."

"A gold torc?" I suggested.

He pointed at me. "Yes. That was it. Seemed to think my father had somehow acquired it. I told him I had no knowledge of it, and it was not currently housed in our family's private collection."

"Did he try to argue with you?" Gage asked, for that would seem more like the Mr. Collingwood we'd become familiar with.

"If he did, my secretary handled the correspondence."

I turned to stare out the tall window just beyond the men's shoulders. We really needed to speak with Mr. Collingwood. His name simply arose too often in this case for us not to heavily suspect the man. How many other family members of the founders of the Society of Antiquaries had he pestered? And would their ancestors' bones turn up missing, too?

Something bright caught my attention on the opposite side of the window. I narrowed my eyes to see better as a pair of riders ambled up the lawn. The one on the left was sporting the brightest, and quite possibly the ugliest, yellow waistcoat I had ever seen. And he looked vaguely familiar.

I stood to move closer, and Gage and Sir Robert broke off whatever they had been saying to watch me. They turned to follow my gaze.

"Is that Lord Shellingham?" I asked in some surprise.

"Why, yes," Sir Robert replied, and then shook his head in resignation. "Though why my nephew persists in wearing such garish clothing, I'll never know."

"Who is the other gentleman?"

"My son. Being an age, they've always been quite close."

I watched as the young men disappeared around the corner of the house, presumably on their way to the stables. "I didn't realize you were related," I told Sir Robert.

He smiled. "Yes. His mother is my younger sister. Are you acquainted with my nephew?"

Gage's curious expression told me he was wondering the same thing.

"Very recently, actually. At my aunt and uncle's Hogmanay Ball."

Gage's eyebrows rose just a fraction, telling me he understood the implication.

"Ah, yes," Sir Robert said. "I believe he attended with Mr. Young, a cousin from his father's side. I hope they behaved themselves."

"As far as I know." I decided it would be best not to mention Lord Shellingham's overindulgence. Given the fact that it had been Hogmanay—and over half the party had been foxed—it didn't seem fair to hold that against him. "Why? Are they normally troublemakers?"

Sir Robert laughed it off. "No, no more than young gentlemen their age usually are. In truth, I'm rather proud of how well my nephew has shouldered the responsibilities of his title since his father's death. Didn't leave him much, I'm afraid. But then again, his grandfather didn't leave his father much either." Sir Robert shrugged. "His parents' marriage was a love match—otherwise I don't think my father would have allowed it."

I found it very difficult to keep my eyes trained on our host through this speech, wanting to see if Gage was as interested to hear all of this as I was. When he'd finished and finally I could glance in his direction, Gage sat as calmly as ever, not betraying by the flick of an eyelash that the man had just given us motive for his nephew to commit the crime of body snatching and ransoming his grandfather's remains. But I knew he was thinking of it. As sure as I knew that Sir Robert was now a little embarrassed he'd shared so much about his family.

He cleared his throat and shifted uncomfortably in his seat. "Pardon me. Now, where were we? Ah, yes. Gage, you asked if anything was missing from the grave?"

"From the remains of your father that they returned after the ransom was paid," Gage clarified. "Were there any bones missing?"

Sir Robert seemed slightly taken aback. "Well, I didn't think to check. And, of course, we've already reburied him." His brow furrowed. "Should I be concerned?"

"Just a formality," Gage replied, brushing it aside as if it wasn't consequential. I realized he was trying to spare the man's feelings. There was no use in upsetting Sir Robert over the matter unless we heard from Lord Buchan that a bone was missing from his uncle's remains as well. Otherwise, it might just be a detail limited to Tyler's remains—an accidental oversight by the thieves.

Gage and I excused ourselves soon after. We'd barely made it into the carriage before I pounced on the new information Sir Robert had unwittingly given us.

"I wonder if Lord Shellingham has recently come into a sum of money."

Gage's eyes were also bright with the knowledge of our new discovery. "I don't know. But I would certainly find that interesting."

"We know the Tylers' cousin Mr. Fergusson was having

money trouble. And Alana mentioned a second nephew to the eleventh Earl of Buchan who may have felt he was cheated out of his fair share of the inheritance."

"A Mr. Erskine."

I nodded. "What if the two of them teamed up with Lord Shellingham? Perhaps they thought this would be a quick, harmless way of making some money. No one gets hurt, except their dead relatives."

"That is, until Dodd got shot."

I frowned. "Yes. But I would guess they didn't expect that. They hired a group of Edinburgh criminals to do their dirty work, never anticipating it could go so wrong."

I recalled Shellingham's miserable expression the morning after at breakfast. Had he overimbibed because it was Hogmanay, or because he was trying to forget something awful? Mr. Young, on the other hand, had been skittish. Had he known what his cousin was involved in? Was he part of it, too?

"I can't recall either Mr. Erskine or Mr. Fergusson being at the Hogmanay Ball," I remarked. "But perhaps they were staying elsewhere nearby."

"Yes. I imagine Mr. Erskine was the least eager to be seen. He probably stayed at an inn, possibly under an assumed name." Gage's mouth flattened into a thin line. "But we're making an awful lot of assumptions. We need to look into their finances. Then ask around to discover where they were on the dates of all three thefts. Perhaps they didn't all need to be near the area, but I imagine at least one of them was."

I turned to stare out the window at the dark waters of the Firth of Forth, visible to the right of the carriage as we turned back toward Edinburgh. "We could have questioned Lord Shellingham while we were there."

Gage shook his head, his eyes narrowed as he contemplated something. "It's too soon. We don't have enough information, and if he guesses we're suspicious of him, it might make things more difficult. It's best he remains oblivious for the time being."

"They already know we're investigating."

"Yes. But they don't know who."

I nodded, acceding his point.

"We also need to question this Lewis Collingwood. I don't like how often his name has arisen during this investigation."

I agreed. "Shall we pay him a visit this afternoon?"

Gage looked up from his scrutiny of the burgundy seat cushion. "Actually, I've arranged a visit with several current members of the Society of Antiquaries. I thought they might be able to shed some light on this issue of Collingwood's torc, and tell me more about our three victims."

He was right. They might have some very useful information for us. Not to mention being able to explain why Collingwood was so determined that one of its members had stolen the torc.

However, I had another destination in mind.

"Then, if you agree, I'd like to share what we've uncovered with Philip. He might have some ideas we haven't thought of. And I'd also like to ask him about Bonnie Brock's suggestion that we're looking in the wrong place. That something unsavory in the victims' pasts connects them."

"Brock's words are more than likely lies. Meant to distract us," Gage groused.

I suspected that was his black eye talking more than his common sense. "Yes, well, I think we should at least consider it."

His scowl turned blacker, but he didn't argue.

# CHAPTER TWENTY-THREE

When I returned to the town house, Philip was alone in his study. He was seated behind his desk, head bent over a book of ledgers, his large hand gripping a quill. I rapped lightly on the door frame.

"Kiera," he murmured with a cautious smile, likely remembering the way I had stalked angrily out of this very room last night.

"Do you have a moment?"

"Of course."

I gently shut the door behind me, before moving forward to perch on the edge of one of the red chairs facing his desk. Much like the red chairs in his study at Gairloch Castle. I'd never made the correlation before.

He waited expectantly, his hands folded before him.

"It's about the investigation."

It may have been my imagination, but I thought I saw his shoulders relax. What dreadful topic he thought I was going to pursue, I didn't know, but it distracted me for a moment.

"How can I help?"

I explained about my conversation with Bonnie Brock. About his claims that something in Ian Tyler of Woodslea, Sir Colum Casselbeck, and Lord Buchan's shared past was the reason for the thefts and ransoms of their remains. That they had been the real villains, and not as friendly to Scotland as one would think.

Philip sat back in his chair, staring up at the ceiling as he gave the matter some thought.

"Do you have any idea what he might have been hinting at?"

He shook his head. "I don't."

I exhaled in disappointment.

"But . . . I know someone who might. That is, if there truly is something to find." He stared across the desk at me. "Do you really trust this Bonnie Brock's word enough that you want me to ask?" I lifted my gaze to the portrait of Alana and the children hanging above the fireplace. Greer had still been an infant, cradled in my sister's arms. Soon I would need to paint a new one, with their fourth child added to the grouping. Though, perhaps this one should include Philip as well, no matter how he protested.

"I do," I told Philip. "At least enough to make a few discreet inquiries. If nothing comes of this, I'll let the matter drop. But I can't help thinking the man went out of his way to give me this information and ask me to help find his sister. What reason would he have to do that and then lie?"

"I don't know. But I suppose he's as human as the rest of us. If he truly cares about his sister and wants to find her, he would try to help you however he could. Though why he didn't just give you the culprit's name confuses me."

"Me, too."

And that was the question that bothered me most. Why hint at the truth? Why play games if your sister's well-being is at stake?

Unless it was a question of honor. And Bonnie Brock certainly seemed to value that attribute. He had not liked my questioning it. Maybe his personal code prevented him from revealing the man's name. Perhaps he'd made a promise or a bargain, and now could not go back on it, but he could point me in the right direction.

That was something I hadn't considered before. Sometimes a vow of silence prevented someone from sharing what they wanted.

I studied my brother-in-law's open face, hoping he hadn't taken a vow of silence as well.

"Philip, is everything well at Blakelaw House?"

His brow lowered in confusion. "What do you mean?"

"It's just . . . Trevor has been acting a bit strange lately. And whenever I ask him about it, he tells me there's nothing to worry about and changes the subject. Is . . . he having money problems?"

Philip offered me a kind smile. "This is something you really need to speak to Trevor about."

"But he's confided in you?"

"Well, yes. To a certain extent."

I gripped the arms of my chair tighter. "He isn't going to lose the estate, is he?"

"No, no. Nothing like that," he assured me. "But Trevor is a grown man. He's learning to deal with his failures as well as his successes. And it's really up to him who he wants to know about them."

I frowned. "Does this have to do with the disreputable crowd he fell in with after my scandal broke?"

Philip's mouth tightened while he deliberated over just what to say. He truly seemed torn. "Kiera, I really shouldn't say more. But I can promise you your brother will come out all right in the end."

I allowed the matter to drop. It was unfair to keep pressuring him when I should really be quizzing Trevor. But as reassuring as Philip had intended to be, his words did not comfort me.

I was surprised when I found Alana in my bedchamber with my maid Bree. However, one look at the mounting pile of gowns on my bed told me just what was going on.

"Oh, no," I declared, closing the door firmly. "You are *not* getting rid of any of my dresses." I turned to glare at my sister where she reclined on the chaise situated before my fireplace. "You do this every time. And then I'm forced to purchase new ones."

"Well, that's the point, dear."

"Not this time. Bree, put them back."

"Kiera, be reasonable," Alana said, keeping her voice at soothing tones. "Some of those gowns are three years out of season. Did you have Lucy hide them from me?" she complained, mentioning my former maid.

"These gowns are all perfectly fine. Especially if I'm traipsing across the countryside at Blakelaw or Gairloch. And even when I'm in town, I don't leave the house every day."

"But, dearest, you really should make room for some new gowns. I've just had Bree pull out the worst. Take those down to the rubbish bin."

"No," I snapped. "Bree, hang them back up."

The poor girl stood there clutching a dress before her like a shield, watching our argument.

I stabbed my finger at my sister. "You do not get to throw out my possessions. I'll purchase new gowns when I'm ready. And when they've gotten rid of those hideous puffed sleeves," I added as an afterthought, ignoring the fact that my sister was wearing a dress in that style now.

Her eyes narrowed. "I ordered a new gown for you for the assembly tomorrow night."

"Please, don't tell me . . ."

"It is of the current style," she declared, and I groaned. "Though, out of deference to you, I did ask her to keep the sleeves' diameter to a minimum. I hope it fits, given you've lost weight *again*, while I'm only gaining it."

"You're carrying a baby," I reminded her.

"Yes, yes," she replied, waving it aside. "The dress should arrive by two o'clock tomorrow afternoon, and Madam Avignon has promised to send a girl over to take care of any last-minute alterations. So please return from *wherever* you've gone with Mr. Gage by then."

I wasn't sure why, but a blush suddenly began to burn its

way up into my cheeks. Perhaps it was the manner in which my sister had phrased her remark, as if we were not really traveling about the city, tracking down leads in a theft and murder investigation. Or the memory of the way Gage had kissed me before letting me leave his carriage less than an hour before. All I knew was that I was forced to turn away lest my sister guess something far worse.

Even so, through the reflection in the mirror, I could see her eyeing me suspiciously.

G age's visit with the current members of the Society of Antiquaries turned out to be rather uneventful. None of the men wished to speak ill of their dead members, and hearing high praise about each of them told us nothing about why they had been targeted by body snatchers years after their death. They also swore that they had no record of a donation of a gold torc from a Miss Collingwood, no record of a torc of any kind. Several of them admitted to receiving letters or visits from Lewis Collingwood, but as the man had no documentation to prove his aunt's donation, there was nothing they could do about it.

So we found ourselves armed with at least that knowledge when we appeared on Mr. Collingwood's doorstep. He lived in a town house situated in a row of similar edifices on Broughton Place, and although the exterior looked much like every other town house in Edinburgh's New Town, the interior was something completely different.

Words could not do it justice. Every available bit of wall space was covered in an odd array of relics and artifacts, some of which I was quite certain were not authentic. Spears and daggers, masks and reliquary, arrowheads and coins mounted in glass boxes, fishhooks, old playbills, gold plates. And there didn't appear to be any order to it. A shelf of tiny Egyptian statues hung next to a Roman gladiator's helmet, next to a conch shell from some tropical country.

There was dust everywhere. I didn't know whether Mr.

Collingwood did not employ maids or if he simply didn't allow them to clean properly for fear of them damaging his possessions. Either way I was glad when the man offered us no tea or other refreshments. I wanted to escape as soon as possible.

He received us in his drawing room, which, to my discomfort, sported an entire wall of stuffed animal heads. Their beady eyes stared down at us almost in accusation, much like their owner, who it appeared was not happy with the interruption to whatever he'd been doing. Preparing more artifacts to hang on his walls?

He greeted us affably enough, but there was impatience in his movements and a tightness around his mouth. The man was also a snob. It was clear he had no idea who either of us were, but because I had the title "Lady" before my name, he at least treated me with civility. Gage, he took one look at while he was introduced, glared at his black eye, and instantly dismissed him as unworthy of his time.

"Now, what can I do for you?" he turned to ask me as I perched on the edge of a lumpy horsehair sofa. To coordinate with the animal heads on the wall, I was sure.

"Actually," Gage said, speaking up despite the man's efforts to ignore him. "We've come to ask you about the gold torc your aunt allegedly donated to the Society of Antiquaries of Scotland."

"Not allegedly," he snapped. "She donated it. And they've lost it, or stolen it, one or the other." His eyes traveled over Gage's appearance, which was faultless except for the contusion over his eye, but Mr. Collingwood seemed to find it lacking, even though his own rumpled attire and uncombed hair left much to be desired. "I take it then that you are not here to tell me they found it."

"I'm afraid not," Gage replied calmly.

"And what have you to do with it? You're not a member of the society. You're not even a Scotsman."

"No. But I sometimes act as an inquiry agent—"

"An inquiry agent?" Mr. Collingwood interrupted, scooting forward in his seat. "Then the police have finally decided to take my complaint seriously?"

"Not exactly." Gage tilted his head to the side in interest. "You took the matter to the city police?"

"Yes. Not that they did me any good," he grumbled, his rather prominent eyes shifting to the side. "They told me there was nothing they could do. Not without my having the paperwork to prove my aunt's donation."

"I'm afraid that's true. Otherwise it's their word, or perhaps that of a dead man, against yours."

Mr. Collingwood completely missed the reference to a dead man, and jumped straight to indignation. His nostrils flared. "Are you calling me a liar?"

"Not at all. I simply understand the police's predicament. When did your aunt make her donation to the society? Do you know the year?"

He nodded sharply. "July of 1816."

Before any of the owners of our disturbed corpses had passed away.

Gage laced his fingers together and rested his hands over his flat stomach, a gesture I knew to mean his interrogation was about to grow more serious. "We've been told that you've contacted several of the society's members, either by letter or a personal visit. And that you've even gone so far as to contact the family of past members."

"What of it?" he retorted, growing more belligerent. "One of them stole my family's torc. Something my aunt had no right to give away. And I want it back." His eyes were bright with almost a feverish anger.

Gage was not intimidated. "Did you know that three of those deceased members recently had their graves disturbed?"

Mr. Collingwood's expression was startled, but only for a moment. "Did they find anything? Because if there was a gold torc, it's mine."

I watched the insensitive man carefully, trying to figure out whether he was this good of a liar, or he was genuinely unaware of the thefts.

"The only thing it appears they took were the men's bones," Gage replied.

Mr. Collingwood's face screwed up in an ugly scowl. "Well, what's that to do with me?" He glanced back and forth between us. "I'm only interested in the torc."

I had to struggle not to scowl right back at the dreadful man. Now I understood exactly what Lord Buchan and Mrs. Tyler had meant when they called him disagreeable.

"Well, did you not suggest to at least one of the victims' families that their relative might have been buried with the torc?" The corner of Gage's eye twitched, telling me how impatient he was getting.

"And?"

"And then his grave is dug up and his bones stolen? Am I supposed to believe that's just a coincidence?"

Mr. Collingwood's face was growing an alarming shade of red. "How dare you accuse me of such a thing! I think you need to leave now." He made to rise, but Gage stood his ground.

"I think you need to answer my question."

He glared at Gage as though he were an insect. "I do not go about digging up graves like some common laborer."

"No, but you might have hired some common laborers to do it for you." Gage leaned closer. "Perhaps a group of experienced body snatchers. And given them the idea that they could ransom the bones back to their relatives for as much money as they wished, so long as they brought you the gold torc if they found it."

Mr. Collingwood's lips twisted in disgust. "You're insane." He glanced at me. "Both of you." When I frowned, he sneered. "Oh, yes, I remember who you are now, Lady Darby. Perhaps it's she you should be looking at for these body snatchings. Though I've heard she likes them a bit fresher, with a little more meat on the bones."

My cheeks flamed at hearing the old insinuations. That

I was a ghoul, a killer, a cannibal. I clasped my hands tightly together, prepared to deliver the man a set down, when Gage spoke up.

"That's enough," he nearly shouted. His pale blue eyes were as hard as ice chips. "You will address the lady with the proper respect she deserves, or you and I are going to have a problem. Do I make myself clear?" When Mr. Collingwood did not answer, Gage raised his voice even louder. "Do I make myself clear?"

"Yes," he bit out.

Gage's shoulders relaxed somewhat, but he still looked as if he was ready to plant the man a facer at any moment. I found myself wishing he would.

"Now, you did not answer my questions. Did you have anything to do with the thefts of the bodies of Ian Tyler of Woodslea, Sir Colum Casselbeck, or Lord Buchan?" Mr. Collingwood opened his mouth to reply, but Gage wasn't finished. "I'd think carefully before lying to me."

Mr. Collingwood's eyes narrowed. "Or what?"

The hair on the back of Gage's neck fairly bristled. "Do you really want to find out?"

In the face of Gage's angry glare, made all the more intimidating by his black eye, Mr. Collingwood's bravado slowly melted away, though his voice was still tight with affront. "No. I had nothing to do with it."

Gage eyed him a moment longer and then reluctantly nodded.

We left the odious man soon after, and climbing into Gage's carriage, I turned to ask, "Do you believe him?"

Gage settled onto the seat facing me, his face still creased into a frown. "I'm inclined to. Only because I can't imagine the man actually stooping to speak to 'common laborers.' Nor do I think he's intelligent enough to concoct such a plan."

"But he's certainly obsessed with finding that torc."

"Yes. Which makes him a bit unpredictable. Obsession makes men dangerous. I don't think we can rule him out yet."

I nodded, agreeing with his assessment of Mr. Collingwood. I knew all too well how treacherous a man overcome by an obsession could be. Had we not underestimated that man, William Dalmay might still be alive.

The carriage turned right onto York Place, passing the long rectangular building of St. Paul's Chapel with its four rounded spires on each corner. Two women exited through one of the sets of doors, each dressed in voluminous mantels to accommodate their fashionably puffed sleeves. I grimaced, recalling my fitting, and hoping the modiste had listened to my sister's instructions.

"I'm sorry you had to listen to his claptrap."

I looked up to find Gage watching me with a pensive expression.

"It's all right," I replied, simply wanting to forget it. "I should be used to it by now."

"No, you shouldn't." His voice was insistent and almost angry. "That man had no right to speak to you that way. No one does."

I shifted in my seat, slightly taken aback by his vehemence. "That may be true. But that's not going to stop people from doing so. It's best if I just ignore them."

"No, it's not. You should confront their bad behavior."

I frowned. "And what? Cause a scene? Gage, if I spoke up for myself every time someone snubbed or belittled me, they would be able to write a separate column about it in the society papers. That's not going to help."

"It would be difficult at first. But maybe after a few times, others would take a lesson and stop."

I stared at him, my hands fisting in the fabric of my cloak. "Are you saying it's *my* fault that people are saying nasty things about me?"

"No . . ."

"That if I'd just stood up for myself from the beginning, my name wouldn't have been tarnished?"

"Well, no. Not from the beginning . . ."

I huffed an irate breath and turned aside to glare out the window.

"But if you'd started doing so from the moment your sister's guests arrived at Gairloch Castle five months ago . . ."

"You and everyone else would still have suspected me of murder."

He hesitated, clearly not having thought his accusation all the way through. "Then from the moment you arrived in Edinburgh."

"After Will died? When I could not have cared less what anyone did or said?" Tears began to burn the backs of my eyes, and I turned away. I was grateful to see the green space of Queen Street Gardens giving way to town houses, which meant our turn onto Charlotte Street would come soon.

Gage remained silent, and I had hopes he would abandon the topic. But as the carriage turned left, he leaned toward me. "Well, *now*, then. You needn't be so passive when others insult you. You should tell them the truth."

I glanced up at him wearily, not bothering to point out the fact that I would have defended myself to Mr. Collingwood if he hadn't been so quick to do so. "Gage, no one wants to hear the truth. Not when the fiction is so much more interesting."

He frowned. "Then you must make them."

The carriage turned right onto Charlotte Square, slowing as the black door of my sister's town house came into sight. I could have said nothing, walked away, and hoped he would drop the matter, but I couldn't leave without asking him one question, though it turned my stomach sour to do so.

"Why?"

Gage seemed surprised by my simple query.

"Why does it matter?"

"Because you should not have to endure it—"

"No," I interrupted him. "Why does it matter so much to you?"

He appeared confused.

"Why is it so important to you that I defend myself? That I make them understand the truth?" I could hear the hurt in my voice, and I hated it. I scowled, wanting to hide it any way I could.

The carriage rolled to a stop, and it swayed gently as the footman clambered down.

The movement seemed to urge a response out of Gage. "Because I don't like seeing you upset. I know you like to pretend you don't care, but I can see the pain in your eyes."

I moved to the edge of my seat as the door opened, and I gathered up my reticule. I lifted my eyes to meet his, swallowing a bubble of emotion that seemed to be choking me. "I never said I didn't care."

"Kiera," he said, but I was already halfway out of the carriage, and I didn't stop to look back.

I dashed up the steps and into the town house, trying to squash the hurt and anxiety Gage's words had brought to the surface, but they would not be smothered so easily.

Was Gage ashamed of me? Embarrassed to be reminded of my scandalous reputation? Was that why he was so eager to see me defend myself, even when the situation was impossible? Not every person could be reasoned with—he should know that, perhaps better than most. So why was he so angry with me for not standing up for myself sooner?

At Gairloch I still hadn't been ready. I'd been too beaten down and afraid. It had taken someone insulting my sister's support of me for me to finally speak up. And upon our arrival in Edinburgh two and a half months ago, I hadn't cared. I was too wrapped up in my grief over Will's death. What did it matter to me what others said about me?

Since our return to Edinburgh he'd spent little time with me in public, so how could he know how I handled the slights and insults of others? It seemed grossly unfair that he should attack me for being passive. One incident, in which he'd given me no time to respond before jumping to my defense, hardly seemed like an adequate example.

Gage was not normally so unreasonable, so I had to suspect there was more to his sudden desire that I defend myself than this single confrontation with Mr. Collingwood. Which left me with an unsettling pain in my chest and an unhappy suspicion. A suspicion I'd been trying to ignore from the very first moment I'd accepted that Gage was interested in me in more than just a friendly capacity.

I'd known from the beginning how unlikely a relationship between a man like Gage and myself would be. He was charming and attractive and popular, I was awkward and eccentric and barely tolerated. So what would a man like Gage see in me . . . other than my abilities?

I choked back a sob.

I'd proven myself to be quite able as an investigator—something I'd felt great pride in, but now it brought me only an immeasurable amount of sadness. I almost wished I'd proved to be clumsy and incompetent. Then I might at least know that Gage was interested in me for me, and not for my talents of detection.

I'd already endured marriage to a man who was solely interested in my artistic abilities. By the time I'd discovered Sir Anthony's real intentions for me, it had been too late to obtain an annulment, and I was trapped in a living nightmare. I had no intention of ever allowing myself to enter into such an uncertain relationship again, no matter how tempting it might be. Not without knowing for sure that the man could be trusted, that his intentions were true.

But how could I ever know for sure? How could I ever believe that Gage was truly interested in me, and not the assistance I could give him?

# CHAPTER TWENTY-FOUR

I tried to be cheerful, or at least responsive, as Madame Avignon's assistant made the last few adjustments to my dress. Blessedly, the modiste had followed my sister's instructions, making the sleeves rather short and far less puffed than many of the gowns I'd seen recently. Alana had chosen a lovely deep blue, a shade or two darker than the color of our eyes, and ordered the belt, the trim, and the flounces to be made in a complementary shade of pale blue and white. The neckline was slightly lower than I was accustomed to and, gathered as it was, showed a rather large amount of cleavage. But Alana and the seamstress assured me this was the current fashion in evening dresses, and I bowed to their expertise.

I'd caught Alana looking at me oddly from time to time throughout the fitting, and I tried to shake myself from the sullen stupor that had come over me, but truly my effort was minimal. I was only too happy to escape to my room to bathe and let Bree dress my hair.

She chattered happily while she curled my hair, telling me more things about the running of Philip and Alana's household than I was certain I wanted to know. Nonetheless, I was glad to hear she had settled in so easily with a new staff, especially after the trouble I'd had with my previous maid. It was soothing somehow to just let her words wash over me—undemanding and inconsequential. I suspected Bree knew this as well, for she had never been one to prattle.

She was also excited, her eyes bright and her movements quick, and I realized that, other than the Hogmanay Ball, this was her first chance to truly test her skills as a lady's maid. I tried my best not to dampen her spirits, and even allowed her to style my hair taller than I normally would have permitted. I had to admit she'd done an admirable job imitating the pictures on the latest fashion plates. In an hour my unruly hair would be deflated and falling from its pins, but for now it looked quite elegant.

Alana gasped in delight when she entered my room to find Bree just finishing buttoning up my gown in the back. "Oh, you look lovely!" A knowing smirk crossed her face. "I knew that gown would suit you. Now, if you would only let me replace your other dresses."

I scowled in displeasure, but she merely laughed and waved Bree out of the room.

Moving toward me, she lifted her hands to reveal the sapphire and diamond necklace I had seen her wear on more than one occasion. "This will go perfectly."

"Alana . . ."

"No protests. I'm not going to have you appear at the Assembly Rooms with only Mother's amethyst pendant to adorn your neck. It's not your fault your husband was such a miser."

I pressed my hand to the cold gems she draped around my neck while she fastened the clasp, not wanting to be reminded of Sir Anthony, especially after the events that had transpired earlier.

"There." Alana gripped my shoulders and turned me so that she could see the full effect of the necklace. A warm smile softened her face, making me think I might truly look pretty. "If Mr. Gage doesn't pay you all sorts of compliments, then the man must be blind."

I turned away to straighten the brushes and combs and

other various items littering the top of my vanity table. I knew he was likely already downstairs waiting to escort me to the ball Alana had managed to gain us a special dispensation to attend, that I would have to go down to join him soon. But I suddenly had no idea how I was going to face him.

"Is something wrong, dearest?" my sister asked gently. When I didn't immediately respond, she moved closer, her face appearing in the reflection of the mirror. "Is it Mr. Gage? Has he done something?"

"No," I lied.

She hesitated, and then stepped even nearer so that she was standing at my side. "Then is it William?" The sleeve of her dress brushed my arm as she turned. "You know, you can't mourn him forever."

I sighed. "Of course I do. But it's barely been eleven weeks. Why is everyone so determined to forget that?"

"Because we're worried about you."

"Don't you think I know that?" I snapped. I closed my eyes against the sight of Alana's hurt expression and inhaled deeply. "I'm sorry. That wasn't fair. I know you're only trying to help."

She reached out to press a hand to my elbow above my long white evening gloves. "You know I would do anything for you."

I gave her a sad smile. "I know. But there are some things that even a fierce older sister cannot make better. No matter how much she wishes to."

Tears glistened in Alana's eyes, and I reached out to squeeze her upper arms.

"Cheer up, dearest. I no longer want to smash every dish in sight. Or torch that hideous set of curtains you decided to hang in the parlor."

She gasped a laugh.

I leaned forward to see into her eyes. "That's a positive sign, isn't it?"

She sniffed and nodded. Her hand rose up to smooth a curl back into place. "Isn't it my job to reassure you?"

"Yes, well. Perhaps it's time that changed."

Gage was speaking to Philip just inside the doorway to my brother-in-law's study when Alana and I descended the stairs to the ground floor. It was gratifying to hear how their conversation stumbled to a stop as we came into sight, their words trailing away. I felt Gage's eyes on me before I even looked up to meet them. The intensity of his gaze tingled across my skin. His pale blue eyes, normally an icy hue, warmed to something much less wintry as they trailed over every inch of me before settling on my face. A blush crested my cheeks and I struggled to keep it from blossoming further.

Gage appeared as handsome and impeccably turned out as always in his dark evening kit. His golden curls were artfully arranged, his linens pristine. The only thing to mar his appearance was the dark circle of his black eye. I wondered what the matrons and young ladies at the Assembly Rooms would think of it.

He met me at the base of the stairs, offering me his hand to help me down the last few steps. "You look lovely."

"Thank you," I replied, feeling flustered by the way he was looking at me.

A smile curled his lips. "Are you ready?"

"Yes."

I pivoted to take my fur-lined white evening shawl from Alana, but Gage reached for it first. He held it out for me and I turned so that he could drape it over my bare shoulders. The skin across the back of my neck and shoulders prickled with awareness at his close proximity. I wrapped the soft fabric around me, hugging it close. My heart was beating very fast, and I suddenly felt wildly out of my element. Such a simple thing, to help a woman into her cloak, but no one but my father and brother had ever done so for me. Maybe the movements were the same, but *this* was very different.

I looked up to see my sister beaming down at me, clearly pleased by Gage's attentions toward me. I tried to offer her a smile back, but I was afraid it came out quite timid. Then Gage was taking my arm and leading me down the steps to his carriage. I settled back against the squabs, my breath fluttering very quickly in and out of my chest like I'd run a race.

Gage sat beside me and I was grateful for his warmth, as well as the fact that I would not have to try to meet his gaze. The lantern light cast everything in golden shades, including the stack of papers tossed on the bench across from us.

"What are those?" I asked as the carriage pulled away from the curb and began to round the square toward George Street.

"I made some discreet inquiries into the finances of our intrepid trio of young gentlemen."

I turned toward him eagerly, thankful for the distraction.

"It appears that Lord Shellingham and Mr. Erskine are still as strapped for capital as usual, though there have been a few odd inconsistencies in Mr. Erskine's spending. Mr. Fergusson, on the other hand, has received two large influxes of cash. But without delving deeper, I can't tell you whether that's because he finally gambled and won for once, or if the money came from another source."

The carriage slowed as it joined the queue of vehicles waiting to drop their occupants off in front of the arched portico of the Assembly Rooms. I lifted the curtain aside to see how far we were from the entrance. It was less than three blocks from Charlotte Square to the Assembly Rooms, and we'd been driving for less than a minute.

"Do you think it's worth pursuing? Do we think Mr. Fergusson could have arranged the thefts with the assistance of Edinburgh body snatchers himself?"

Gage's voice was pensive. "Perhaps. Though from what I've observed of the man, I don't think he's nearly so cautious or calculating. Were he working alone, I think his involvement would be much easier to detect."

I nodded, adjusting the shawl over my front and pushing back the errant curl from my face.

He watched me with an amused twinkle in his eye. "But I don't think we should rule out the possibility that all three of them are working together just yet. Shellingham may just be more careful than his cronies. Stop fidgeting," he ordered, pulling my hand down from my face. "You look lovely. Did I not say so?"

"Yes, well." I ran my other hand down the soft fabric of the shawl. "Perhaps you're just being polite."

Gage lowered his head, arching a single eyebrow at me. "I was not being polite." He leaned closer, lowering his voice. "And you know it."

My gaze dropped to his lips. "Well, maybe." I turned away. "I know I'll at least not embarrass myself, or anyone else. Alana and Bree made sure of that."

Gage lifted his gloved fingers to my chin, turning my face to force my gaze back to his. His eyes searched my own, and I was sure he saw every thought that was swirling through my head, even though I tried to hide them. "Kiera, you could never embarrass me." My face must have looked as skeptical as I felt, for he leaned even closer, almost touching his forehead to mine. "You couldn't." He searched my eyes deeper. "Is that what you thought I was saying earlier? Why I was pushing you to defend yourself?"

I closed my eyes, unwilling to continue to meet his gaze, not with all the emotions churning around inside me. They were too close to the surface, too easy for him to read, and I felt vulnerable in a way I hadn't for a very long time.

"Kiera," he whispered, his voice filled with sorrow. He gently pressed a kiss between my eyes. His clothing rustled as he looked away, likely to see how much progress our carriage had made. "This isn't the time, although we *are* going to discuss this later. But Kiera . . ." He paused, waiting for me to open my eyes.

I blinked trying to bring him into focus, his face was so close to mine.

"You are beautiful," he told me earnestly. "Your dress this evening just accentuates that."

A warmth began to spread in my midsection at his words, but before I could thank him, the carriage halted and the door was thrown open. Gage disembarked first, allowing me a moment to compose myself, so that when he reached inside to help me down, I felt almost all the emotions he'd stirred up were safely packed away. All except an elation I could feel radiating from my smile, especially when he met my grin with one of his own.

We passed beneath the arches and then in through the open doors. Our coat and shawl having been checked, we climbed the stairs toward the sound of music spilling out of the ballroom above. The staircase and foyers above and below were filled with ladies and gentlemen adorned in their evening attire, laughing and chattering and sipping glasses of champagne or punch.

Half a dozen people called out to Gage or crossed the foyer to greet him, exclaiming over his injury. They all eyed me with a blatant curiosity that swiftly turned to shocked bewilderment after we'd been introduced. I suspected word of Sebastian Gage's arrival with the infamous Lady Darby on his arm would have made its way around the assembly before we ever reached the ballroom. I waved politely to the few people I was acquainted with through my sister, and while they replied in kind, none of them hurried to greet me.

There was one exception—a Mr. Knighton, whom I'd met at one of Alana's dinner parties. Apparently he and Gage knew each other well, for they shook hands and exchanged a few ribbing comments about Gage's black eye before Mr. Knighton asked after Philip and my sister. He listened attentively, and never once gave me the impression he wished to be elsewhere. He even insisted upon claiming a dance from me later in the evening, signing his name to the dance card dangling from my wrist.

"I apologize if Mr. Knighton was a trifle overeager. I assure you he means well," Gage told me after the other man had moved on to speak with another couple.

"What do you mean?" I asked in confusion. "I thought he was very pleasant."

"Yes. But he should not have forced you to dance if you do not wish to."

I stared at him in surprise, realizing what he meant. "I never said I didn't like to dance. In fact, I'm rather fond of it."

It was Gage's turn to look astonished. "You are? But why have I never seen you dance at the dinners and other soirees I've attended with you?"

I glanced back at him with a sardonic lift to my eyebrows. "No one asked." I turned to survey the crowd surrounding the dancers inside the ballroom, not wanting to see pity in his eyes. But a tug at my wrist pulled my attention back to him. "What are you doing?"

He scrawled his name across my dance card in several places. "Claiming my dances before they're all taken."

I didn't know what to say, but a fierce joy suddenly shot through me, making it difficult to stand still and allow him to finish. He looked up at me and smiled, just a gentle little curl of his lips that I knew was meant only for me.

"Now, see here, young man. Give the rest of us a chance," a genial voice proclaimed. Mr. Stuart grinned widely at us, reaching out to take the card and pencil from Gage. "I don't want to miss my opportunity to dance with the lovely Lady Darby."

I shook my head at the man's flattery. "Mr. Stuart, allow me to introduce you to Mr. Sebastian Gage."

"You visited the Rutherfords recently," Gage said, reaching out to shake his hand.

"I did. And, of course, you would know that because you're investigating that terrible business that happened over at the abbey on Hogmanay." Gage's eyes widened slightly and Mr. Stuart winked at him. "I've heard you're very thorough. I would've expected nothing less." He turned back to my card to write his name down for the next waltz.

Gage seemed slightly taken aback, but he recovered his good humor quickly. "Yes. I try to be."

"Have you apprehended the culprits?"

"Not yet. But we're making progress."

He nodded, looking back and forth between us. "Well, I'm sure you'll catch them in good time. I've heard of your exploits." He offered me a faint bow. "I look forward to our dance, Lady Darby."

We watched as he wove through the crowd, on his way to sign another dance card perhaps. I smiled.

"He's French?"

"Yes," I replied. "Or, at least, partly so. I believe he's quite widely traveled."

"And the grandson of the Young Pretender," Gage added dryly.

I poked him in the side with my elbow. "That's Bonnie Prince Charlie, if you please. Remember, you *are* in Edinburgh."

"Pardon me," he teased.

A handsome couple standing near the corner where the dowagers were seated caught my eye. "I'm going to speak with the Strathblanes," I told him, but decided not to explain that Philip had suggested the viscount would be a good man to speak with about my concerns over Bonnie Brock's hints. Any mention of the criminal was liable to irritate him.

Gage followed my gaze, before leaning close to say, "Then I'll make my rounds through the gaming salons and see if I can track down Mr. Fergusson."

We parted ways, and I wove my way through the crowd, skirting the edge of the dance floor. The wood gleamed underneath the light of the bright chandeliers, and the gold filigree adorning the two cornices that circled the ceiling fairly sparkled. The fast-driving music of a mazurka had just begun when I reached Lord and Lady Strathblane's side.

They greeted me amiably and asked after Alana and the children's health. From the ease of their manner, I guessed they had not heard about Bonnie Brock's abduction of Philip's carriage and me from the theater, and I decided not to enlighten them. Not when there was no reason to alarm them. No harm had been done, at least to me. And Gage's foolhardiness could not be laid at their feet.

When I broached the topic with the viscount that I'd approached them to discuss, he nodded his head readily. "Yes. Of course. Cromarty wrote to tell me you might have some questions for me. What can I do?"

"You know that I'm assisting Mr. Gage with a rather sensitive investigation," I moved closer to say, turning to face outward with the wall at my back, lest someone approach from behind and catch me by surprise.

"Yes. I had heard."

The dancers whirled across the floor before us, executing the quick, intricate steps. With the mazurka's loud, lively music, I could not have picked a better dance to cover our conversation.

"We've recently received information that has led us to believe that something in the gentlemen's past might have been the motive for these body snatchings. Possibly something to do with Scotland." I glanced at him out of the corner of my eye to find him listening attentively. "I know that's extremely vague, but I wondered if perhaps your father had mentioned something to you. I know he was quite active in government in London and here in Scotland." That was an understatement. Lord Strathblane's recently deceased father had served in nearly every branch of government at some point in time, from the Foreign Office to the Home Office to the War Department. He had never served as Prime Minister, but most believed that was a matter of personal choice, for he'd certainly had the experience and popularity to do so.

Lord Strathblane's brow furrowed. "Something to do with Lord Buchan, Sir Colum Casselbeck, and Ian Tyler of Woodslea?"

I nodded. "And possibly others."

He considered the matter for a moment and then shook

his head. "I'm sorry. I honestly can't think of anything. But then my father shared very little with me before a few years ago, and I assume this goes back long before that."

"It would have to be prior to 1818 or 1819, when Mr. Tyler and Sir Colum passed away."

"Then I'm afraid I can't help you. Though I could look through my father's papers."

"Would it be a lot of trouble?" I asked, hating to add to the already busy man's burden, especially on so flimsy a hint as Bonnie Brock had given us.

I could tell from his expression that it would be. "I could peruse his journals for any mention of Buchan, and work from there if necessary. Would that help?"

"Yes it would, as long as it won't take too much of your time," I hastened to make sure he understood.

He smiled kindly. "I'm happy to be of assistance."

I chatted a moment longer with the Strathblanes, but then the mazurka ended and I was whisked off to the dance floor by Mr. Knighton. The Scottish reel was quick and sprightly, and I enjoyed it immensely. Mr. Knighton proved to be a very agreeable partner—accomplished with the steps, but not too stiff to appreciate them.

I had a wide grin on my face when he deposited me at the edge of the ballroom and went off to find his next partner.

"I used to enjoy dancing like that," a voice said to my left.

I turned to see a woman in a cream-colored dress with a gold net overlay seated on a chair watching me. She was perhaps in her late fifties, and still quite attractive, with a long graceful neck and silver hair swirled high on her head and accented with three long white feathers. The twinkle in her eye said she approved of my delight.

"But you must still be able to dance," I protested, taking in her trim, but strong figure.

"Oh, pssh!" she said, waving off my words with her fan. "I'm too old for that."

I smiled at her, suspecting the lady's reluctance had more to do with the assemblage than her age. I certainly planned to continue dancing until my bones simply wouldn't support it anymore. Though I might decide it was best pursued in a smaller gathering as well.

I slid into the seat beside her. "I'm Lady Darby," I told her, gambling that the woman would not be offended by my forwardness.

"The Dowager Marchioness of Bute," she replied, offering me her hand, which I squeezed with my own.

She studied me with interest, and I assumed my reputation had preceded me once again. But this time, it didn't seem to offend.

"I haven't seen you here before," she said, nodding to encompass the Assembly Rooms, I assumed. "Your sister is Lady Cromarty, is she not?"

"Yes."

She joined me in watching the dancers performing the quadrille. "Did she help you choose your gown? I noticed she has impeccable taste, and it seemed like something she would favor. Particularly the color. You both have the same color eyes. Though . . ." she turned to look at me again ". . . I think yours may be a touch more purple."

My smile tightened. "Yes. My sister has quite an eye for fashion."

Her gaze traveled over the fabric of my gown again. "Now, of course, everyone will want to copy it. I noticed them watching you earlier when you were speaking with that handsome young man and Count Roehenstart."

I was momentarily speechless, having never worn a dress that anyone would admire, let alone covet. Surely she was mistaken. But then her second comment penetrated my brain. "Who?"

She turned to me in surprise. "Didn't you know the young man's name who you were conversing with? I saw you come in on his arm."

"Er, yes. Of course. That's Mr. Gage. But I'm not certain I know any counts. Do you by chance mean Mr. Stuart?"

She nodded her head, her feathers bobbing. "One of his

many eccentricities. The man has several titles, has gone by many names, and yet now he most often chooses to be addressed as a simple mister. I suppose out of respect for his grandfather." She leaned closer, flapping her fan in front of her so that the feathers waved in the breeze it created, and her musky French perfume wafted under my nose. "You know, of course, that his grandfather was Bonnie Prince Charlie himself."

"I've heard rumors," I replied carefully.

"Oh, I assure you, it's not just a rumor."

I met her gaze. "What do you mean?"

Her fan snapped shut. "My dear, I'm well acquainted with the family. His grandmother acted as chaperone to my sisters and me when we were in Paris. Before the revolution, of course." She turned back to the dancers, opened her fan, and resumed fanning herself. "And my father acted as something of a financial advisor to the young count when his grandmother passed away."

"So you were childhood friends?"

Lady Bute laughed. "Oh, no. I didn't meet the count until many years later. He came to Switzerland to collect some of his family's old documents and letters. My father had been keeping them safe for him."

"And your father would not have handed them over to him if he wasn't certain he was who he said he was."

She gestured toward me with her fan. "Precisely."

I contemplated the implications of a direct descendant, particularly a male, of the Stuart royal line being alive, and in Scotland. His grandfather's bid to reclaim the Scottish and English thrones during the Jacobite Rising of 1745–46 ended in disaster. Did Mr. Stuart have similar designs?

Surely not. Not only did people whisper about his claimed heritage as if it were a joke, but the man himself did not seem to be making any real effort to gain support for his cause. However, I knew from experience that some men were craftier than others. Though, I would have thought that with Philip's position, he would have at least heard rumblings. It would be impossible to keep such a thing completely quiet.

"Most people seem to think his claimed ancestry is fabricated," I couldn't resist pointing out. "And Mr. Stuart doesn't seem to care to correct them."

She sighed. "I know. It's rather sad, really. But rest assured, he is of Stuart royal blood. Even our government has admitted so."

I turned to her in surprise. "They have."

She nodded firmly. "Why else do you think they went so far as to accuse him of high treason, with their evidence contrived by British agents and even Scottish gentlemen? Fortunately, he was in Paris at the time, and with the help of his friends and the French police, he was able to prove the charges were nothing but outright lies and ridiculous exaggeration." She narrowed her eyes. "Oh, yes. They know exactly who he is. They would hardly have gone to all the trouble otherwise."

A shadow of suspicion was stirring in my mind. "When was this?"

"Twelve, thirteen years ago." She waved her fan as if it were no consequence.

Perhaps before Ian Tyler of Woodslea died? I turned to ask her if she knew who the Scottish noblemen had been, but she was already rising from her chair. I joined her.

"Lovely to meet you, Lady Darby," she proclaimed, before sweeping across the floor toward a pair of older gentlemen standing in the doorway to our right.

I watched her go and then sank back in my chair.

Bonnie Brock had claimed that the victims weren't saints, and that they weren't true friends to Scotland. Was he a Jacobite? Did he believe the Stuarts to be the rightful kings? I would have thought the criminal would care little who was on the British throne, but maybe I was wrong.

So if Buchan and Tyler and Casselbeck were the Scottish gentlemen who conspired to see Mr. Stuart accused of high treason, then perhaps Mr. Stuart wanted revenge.

I frowned. But snatching their bodies for ransom after they were dead seemed an awfully strange way to go about it.

"If I didn't know you better, I would think you were trying to scare people away."

I blinked up at Gage. "What?"

He grinned and pulled me to my feet. "You're scowling. Rather fiercely, I might add."

I glared at him. "No, I'm not."

He arched his eyebrows in skepticism, and I tried to relax my face.

"I was thinking."

"About something unpleasant obviously."

Now it was my turn to arch my eyebrows.

He swiveled so that we were standing almost side by side, both of us looking out over the dancers. "Well, think on this. Mr. Fergusson was betting rather heavily at the tables tonight, and Lord Shellingham was definitely not happy about it."

"Looking out for his friend?"

"Or irritated the man was making such a spectacle of himself and his newly plump bank account."

"Did you try to talk to either of them?"

"No. But Lord Shellingham was drinking whiskey in rather copious amounts. I'm going to give it a little bit longer to loosen his tongue and then try."

"Well, don't wait too long," I cautioned him. "He got foxed at my uncle and aunt's Hogmanay Ball and was barely coherent even the next morning."

Gage nodded.

I opened my mouth to tell him what I'd learned from Lady Bute, when a young lady's voice called out his name. We turned to watch her approach in a gown of cream and sage. Her dark hair was swept up very high on her head, and I couldn't help but wonder how close it came to grazing the top of the doorways. She was very pretty, and also quite young, perhaps just out of the schoolroom, but her fresh-faced good looks belied her razor-sharp interior.

She smiled beatifically at Gage, only sparing a moment to shoot a venomous glance my way. I was under no illusions that this debutante wished me well.

"I didn't know you were still in Edinburgh," she exclaimed, offering him her hand. "I thought you'd returned to London."

"Yes, well, business has kept me in Scotland," Gage replied rather tautly. "But you are looking quite fine this evening."

She preened. "Thank you."

Gage turned toward me, to offer an introduction, but she cut him off.

"But how disappointing for Lady Felicity. I know she's been eagerly awaiting your return." The chit's eyes darted my way again, just for a fraction of a second, as if to gauge my reaction.

I willed myself to remain calm and emotionless, though my stomach was suddenly clenching in dread. I had heard Lady Felicity's name before, during Miss Witherington's conversation with Gage at my aunt and uncle's dinner table, but she had only been baiting him for information. This girl seemed to know much more.

"Has she?" Gage replied indifferently, but I could tell he was far from disinterested. The muscles in his arm had tensed where it brushed against mine, and his voice was a shade higher in pitch than normal.

"But, of course she is. And you know it." She tilted her head coyly. "She's been waiting for months to announce your engagement."

# CHAPTER TWENTY-FIVE

And there it was. The news the chit had been so eager to share. I had been preparing myself for something dreadful, but this surpassed even that.

I couldn't prevent myself from stiffening, even though I knew it would only give the girl pleasure. Her lips curled into a satisfied smile while my heart clenched so tightly in my chest I thought it might burst under the strain.

"I'm afraid you must be mistaken," Gage replied. He was trying to sound authoritative, but the strain in his voice was anything but reassuring.

The girl laughed. "Oh, there's no need to be secretive. Lady Felicity tells me everything. I know your fathers have already had the marriage contracts drawn up. All that's left is for you to sign them and post the announcement in *The Times*."

I wanted to turn away, to move as swiftly and as far away from this as I could. But where would I go? We were in the middle of a ballroom—buzzing with gossiping voices, pierced by prying eyes—and few of them were truly friendly to me. The moment I turned to run, Gage would stop me, and everyone's attention would be on us.

I forced a deep breath into my lungs, trying to control the sudden urge to vomit. Tears stung my eyes, but I blinked them back and swallowed hard, trying to choke down that dark ball of emotion that seemed to be ever present lately.

"I'm afraid there's more to it than that," I heard Gage telling the girl, while his eyes kept darting to me. I refused to look at him, refused to acknowledge him. Gritting my teeth, I welcomed the swell of rage I felt building in my breast. Anything to block out this pain.

And then, blessedly, seemingly out of nowhere, Mr. Stuart appeared by my side. "Lady Darby," he declared cheerfully. "I've come to claim you for our waltz."

I had been so consumed by the scene before me that I was barely conscious of the lull in the music or the dancers drifting off the floor.

I offered him a tight smile and accepted his proffered arm. "Of course."

Gage lifted his arm as if to stop me, but then he must have realized how rude that would be, for it never touched mine. I didn't spare the girl even a glance, but did spend a spiteful moment wishing her ridiculous hairstyle would get caught in a door or catch fire from a low-hanging chandelier.

Mr. Stuart swung me into the steps of the waltz as I did my best to compose the riot of emotions swirling about inside me. There was no reason to take out my anger on him.

He seemed conscious of it anyway, remarking in his slight French accent, "If I am not being too impertinent to say, but that conversation seemed fraught with tension."

"It was," I admitted, deciding it would be silly to deny it. "I'm actually rather glad you appeared when you did."

"Ah, I am your knight in shining armor then."

I couldn't help but crack a smile at the pleasure he seemed to take from that. "Yes. In a way."

"Then may I request a token from the fair lady?"

I arched my eyebrows at his flirtation. "That depends on the token you are requesting."

He clucked his tongue in mock indignation. "No, no, no. Nothing so impudent. What you must think of me?"

"I think you're a flirt."

"Ah, well, guilty as charged. But, I promise, it is nothing so forward. I merely wish to claim your handkerchief, as the knights of old might have done."

"My handkerchief?" I asked doubtfully.

"Yes." He seemed perfectly serious.

"All right," I agreed, deciding there could be no harm in it. "After the dance."

He nodded.

"And on one condition," I added at the last.

His head perked up, waiting for me to explain.

"That you answer a question for me."

"Of course," he replied without hesitation.

I almost felt guilty for using his chivalry against him, but then I decided the investigation demanded it. Especially the justice I sought for Dodd.

"I had the pleasure of meeting Lady Bute just a short while ago. She told me you are well acquainted."

He smiled. "Yes. For many years."

"She also told me how the British government contrived to have you charged with high treason." I watched his expression carefully, but so far he barely flicked an eyelash, though I must have brought up a painful moment in his history. "Did you know the Scottish gentlemen who accused you?"

It was a gamble to approach him this way, and I hoped he didn't close down completely or push me aside in the middle of the dance floor. I prayed that his good manners would at least prevent him from doing the latter.

His smile turned more resigned. "Yes." He swung me into a sharp turn to avoid another couple and then corrected our course. "But what I think you really wish to know is who those men were."

I blushed in discomfort, but didn't reply, hoping my silence would convince him to speak more than any awkwardly worded response.

Mr. Stuart's gaze turned compassionate. "I am not upset, Lady Darby. I know you and Mr. Gage are investigating the unpleasantness at Dryburgh Abbey. You must ask these types of questions, yes?" I nodded.

"It is true, one of the men was Lord Buchan. Is that what you wondered?"

"And the others?" I pressed even as I hated doing so.

He tilted his head, observing me. "Lord Demming and Sir Colum Casselbeck. Those are the only names I am aware of."

Two of the men whose bodies were snatched for ransom, but not the third. Though maybe he had purposely omitted Ian Tyler of Woodslea's name, knowing what I was hinting at. I was not familiar with Lord Demming, but perhaps his family was the next we should contact.

"If you speak with someone in the government, they should be able to confirm the facts. But truly, as horrifying and embarrassing as the accusations and the trumped-up evidence were, that was more than thirteen years ago. And I was cleared of all charges. What reason would I have to disturb Lord Buchan's grave and harm his gardener?"

I studied his features—his expression seemed open and honest, if not a bit defensive. But one could hardly blame the man. I was accusing him of some rather heinous things in a roundabout way. He'd made no mention of the other two men's disturbed graves, so either he was very careful or he didn't know about them. And beyond that, I liked the man. I didn't want to believe he was responsible for these awful crimes, and without any further evidence than what he'd given me himself, I had no reason to suspect him.

So I thanked him for his candor and allowed the matter to drop. Philip or Lord Strathblane would be able to look into the incident for me and confirm the details. If we discovered he'd lied, we could pursue the matter then.

I did my best to enjoy the remainder of the waltz, but much of the joy I normally felt in dancing had been spoiled by our strained conversation and my discovery of Gage's deceit before the song had even begun. By the end, I could tell we were both pleased to escape the dance floor. I asked Mr. Stuart to return me to the side of the room farthest from Gage, and then gave him my handkerchief from my reticule, as I'd promised. He bowed at the waist with a flourish and then was gone, presumably off to find his next partner.

As soon as his back was to me, I turned and fled the room, praying no one would stop me, least of all Gage. I smiled tightly at a couple ascending the stairs as I hurried down them. It took the footman longer than I would have liked to find my wrap, but chilly as it was, I knew I could not leave without it. I pulled it around my shoulders and escaped through the doors into the night.

I was certain the footmen huddled outside waiting to help the guests in and out of their carriages looked at me oddly as I walked past them and then turned down George Street alone, but they could hardly say anything. Not to me anyway.

The air was so bitter cold it almost burned as it entered my lungs, but I welcomed the discomfort. Anything to distract me from the hurt and anger roiling up inside me, threatening to choke me.

I lengthened my stride as I crossed the intersection at Frederick Street. The farther I walked away from the Assembly Rooms, the quieter the night became, and fewer carriages were parked along the curbs. The streetlamps illuminated the sidewalks in this part of town quite adequately, but even they could not pierce the gloom completely.

So when a man pulled away from the shadows clinging to the buildings and fell into step beside me, I was not anticipating it. I made a startled side step, even as I continued to walk, but when I realized it was Bonnie Brock, I merely scowled, too irate to feel any genuine fear.

"Don't even think about forcing me into another carriage," I told him, staring fiercely ahead of me. The ground was hard and cold beneath the material of my thin slippers, but I refused to shorten my stride.

In any case, my fast pace didn't seem to bother the long-legged rogue. His hands were tucked in his pockets as if we were out for a leisurely stroll. "I wouldna dream o' it," he replied. "Just thought I'd join ye on your evenin' constitutional."

I turned to glare at him, catching the flash of his teeth as he smiled. They were remarkably clean and straight for a man who'd grown up on the streets of Edinburgh and lived his life among the rough-and-tumble existence of the lower denizens of Old Town. But then, I really knew nothing of the man's history. Maybe he hadn't grown up on the streets? Maybe he wasn't even originally from Edinburgh?

I considered Brock for a moment. I could understand why he was called Bonnie, for he certainly was handsome, with his tall, trim figure, long hair, and regular features that seemed marred only by his crooked nose, likely from repeatedly being broken. Though tonight he was also sporting a dark bruise across his left cheekbone, hopefully earned in his scuffle with Gage. What I didn't understand was why a man in his position would allow others to call him by such a sobriquet. It didn't exactly inspire fear or awe or respect.

Perhaps that was the point. Maybe he preferred to keep his public face unintimidating, only to lull those who would challenge him into a false sense of security. I had to admit, I'd not found the name to be very menacing when Sergeant Maclean had first told us about him. Maybe that was on purpose. Maybe it was harder to convict a man called Bonnie Brock than it would be if he was called The Butcher, or some other awful name.

"Why are you following me?" I snapped, deciding it would be best for me to remember this was not a harmless gentleman come to walk me home.

He didn't insult my intelligence by attempting to lie to me, though I could tell that he considered it. "Perhaps I find ye interestin'."

I glowered at him, telling him just what I thought of that bit of balderdash.

He easily kept pace with me, even as I hurried across

Castle Street. I could see the dark outline of the green space of Charlotte Square up ahead. Another block and I would almost be home.

"Perhaps I want to ken what progress you've made in findin' my sister."

"Not much," I admitted bitterly.

"Well, perhaps ye need to try harder." His voice had sharpened along with his eyes, but I was in no mood to be intimidated.

"Perhaps it would be easier if *certain people* stopped talking in riddles."

His eyes narrowed to study me more closely, but I turned away, trying to gauge how much farther it was to Philip's door.

"Nay," he declared. "I think it's because yer too distracted by this Mr. Gage."

I stiffened at the mention of his name.

"Although tonight he seems to have angered you something fierce. Or else why would ye leave him and set off to walk home by yerself?"

How long had Bonnie Brock been following me? Certainly since I'd arrived at the Assembly Rooms with Gage, but had he been trailing me before then? What of earlier in the day, or yesterday, or the day before that? I didn't like the idea of being followed about unaware by this criminal or his henchmen.

We had reached Charlotte Street, and I dashed across to the park at the center of the square, hoping Bonnie Brock would not follow me so close to my home. I should have known better. He caught up with me before my feet even stepped up onto the sidewalk. Here, under the ring of trees that surrounded the circle, it was even darker. To the left, I could see the pale dome of St. George's Church through the skeletal branches and the distant circles of light from the streetlamps, but the rest was cast in shadow.

"No denials?" he taunted. "Well, then, perhaps Mr. Gage needs to be taught another lesson?"

I rounded on him then, though I could see the front door of Philip's town house emerging out of the darkness. "You stay away from Gage."

Bonnie Brock stared down at me defiantly and I suddenly had a vision of Gage being accosted in his carriage as he traveled home. Or worse, if he was an idiot and decided to walk.

I leaned closer, pointing at the center of his chest. "If you or one of your men so much as touches a hair on his head, I'll . . . Well, all those rumors people whisper about me . . . I'll make them come true."

He stepped closer and I lowered my finger, but far from being intimidated, his eyes were alight with amusement. "Yer a bloodthirsty wench."

I continued to glare up at him, unable to form a response. So I decided it was past time to go.

But before I could take two steps, he yanked me to a stop, pressing me back against the fence surrounding the square. I stared up into his face several inches from mine. Gone was the laughter of a few moments ago, and it was replaced by an intense ferocity that seemed to burn from his eyes.

"Fair enough," he drawled in a deep voice. "But I'll also warn ye. If you wander into my territory, ye willna leave again."

My heart leapt into my throat. What had I been thinking? This man was a murderer. If I crossed him, he wouldn't have any qualms about killing me.

Then as his face moved closer to mine, I realized he had an entirely different intention in mind. I turned my face to the side just before his lips would have touched mine. They slid across my cheek to my ear.

My stomach turned over, threatening to expel its contents. Something about the situation reminded me too much of the embraces Sir Anthony had forced upon me. When he was angriest with me, he would back me up against a wall and do something very similar. The fury I incited had seemed to excite him somehow, so I had avoided causing it at every turn.

I knew I should scream, should lash out, should do *something*. But for a moment I was back in that helpless state of being in which I'd lived during my marriage. I forced myself to concentrate on my breath, anything but the hard press of Bonnie Brock's body against mine.

He exhaled, gusting hot breath against my neck. "Ye truly do love him, dinna ya?"

He lifted his face away from mine, and his body shifted backward.

The rush of cold air that moved between us was like a jolt of pure relief. I welcomed the shiver that ran through me.

"'Tis a rare thing," he murmured. "But . . . perhaps you already ken that."

I turned to look up at him, his words finally penetrating the haze of my fright. I couldn't reply. I didn't know how to. But it seemed I didn't need to say anything. Bonnie Brock's eyes were lit with understanding.

I swallowed and dropped my gaze to the buttons of his shirt. Unlike the first time we met, tonight he wore a great-coat, but it was not buttoned against the cold that fogged our breath.

"I must go," I finally managed to say.

He studied my face a moment longer and then shifted backward another step. "Find my sister," he told me as I moved to the side.

I looked back at him. His golden eyes were still bright with a concern I strongly suspected he didn't want to feel.

"I'll do my best," I said, knowing I couldn't promise him any more than that.

He didn't object or stop me as I hurried away, crossing the street to the line of town houses on the north side of the square. I pulled open the front door and surprised the foot-man dozing in a chair in the entry hall, waiting to hear the arrival of Gage's coach. I passed him without a word and began climbing the stairs to the next floor. As I rounded the landing headed toward the next staircase, Alana emerged from the drawing room, her hair rumpled from lounging on the settee.

"Kiera, whatever are you doing home?" she demanded. "Where's Mr. Gage?"

"I don't want to discuss it," I told her firmly, lifting my skirts to climb.

She followed me to the base of the stairs. "Kiera—"

I held out my hand to cut her off. "I don't want to discuss it."

I emerged on the top landing, but rather than retire to my bedchamber, I turned toward my tiny art studio at the back of the town house. I knew I would never rest. Perhaps my art would distract me.

Pulling my long white evening gloves from my hands, I tossed them aside and lit the lantern by the door. The warm winter cloak was the next to go, dumped onto a box in the corner, even though it was freezing so far up, without a fire to warm the room. I pulled my old, paint-splattered shawl off the hook on the wall and wrapped it around my shoulders, tying off the ends. I shivered at the touch of the cold, stiff cotton, but I knew it would quickly warm from my body heat.

I considered leaving off my apron, but I was certain my sister would maim me if I stained the fabric of this dress. I had to admit, it really was a lovely gown. In truth, I should go change, but I was in no mood to face anyone, even Bree, and Alana was far more likely to attempt to corner me there than here. She avoided my art studio like the plague, saying the fumes made her nauseous.

So instead I donned the apron and tied off the strings at my back with a yank. I lit a second lantern and positioned it and the first one to allow me the best lighting, and then peeled back the cloth over Caroline's half-finished portrait. I studied it for a moment, noting what colors would be needed, and then set to mixing them.

I stood shivering by the cracked window in my studio, hoping most of the fumes from the crushed pigments and linseed oil I stirred would be coaxed out into the night air. But even so, my eyes and my arms burned, though I suspected the first was at least partially from suppressed tears and the latter was from the exertion.

Images of William Dalmay sitting on the edge of the roof of Banbogle Castle minutes before he died kept flitting through my mind, as well as the crumpled body of the old caretaker Dodd with his young apprentice Willie kneeling over him. But most of all I kept seeing Gage. The way he'd looked at me as I descended the stairs tonight, and then the tight panic that suffused his features as that young debutante had revealed his engagement to Lady Felicity. I didn't know whether to weep or scream.

So instead I stirred—and crushed and ground and pulverized—until the Van Dyke Brown and Mars Yellow I needed were smooth and ready to apply. I worked swiftly, trying to block out all the emotions and unsettling thoughts that threatened to break me apart. I had no idea whether the paint I was applying to the portrait was making it better or ruining it, but for once I didn't care. I just kept brushing it on, stroke by stroke.

I wasn't certain how long I'd worked before someone knocked on the door. I ignored it, but my sister was not so easily deterred.

"Kiera," she called softly, rapping again. "Kiera, I know you can hear me." When I still didn't reply, she sighed. "Mr. Gage is here to see you."

I stiffened, lifting my brush from the canvas.

"Tell him to go away."

"Kiera," my sister chided, though her voice was soft with concern.

"I have no desire to see him." My voice was as hard as chipped ice. "Send him away."

I stood still, waiting for Alana's next argument, but it did not come. A moment later I heard her steps move away from the door.

I turned back to the portrait, staring blindly at the swirls of color. I closed my eyes tightly and bit down hard against the surge of emotion that rose up inside me, pressing on my chest.

I felt like such a fool! Of course Gage would never have any real interest in me. He was the golden boy and I was an outcast. How could I for one moment have believed he could truly want me? What he wanted, what he was enamored of, was the assistance I could give him, the skills I could bring to bear in his investigations. It was just like Sir Anthony all over again. Except Sir Anthony had been interested in my talent with art. And he had been offering marriage.

I must have misunderstood that evening in my studio at Blakelaw when Gage had declared his desire to explore our relationship. Or he had deliberately misled me, knowing all the while that he intended to marry Lady Felicity?

I suddenly didn't know what was worse—the crushing sense of betrayal I'd felt when I discovered that Sir Anthony had married me only to sketch his dissections, or the devastation I now felt knowing that Gage, a man I had allowed myself to trust, and yes, very likely to love, had deceived me in such a cruel way.

I blinked open my eyes, and forced my brush to the canvas, glaring at it through a watery haze. The lump in my throat would not be swallowed, but I continued anyway, refusing to dissolve into sobs. Each stroke became easier, and the slight tremor in my hand had even begun to subside.

That is, until the door to my studio opened with a sharp thrust, stopping just short of crashing into the wall by the strong hand that gripped the doorknob.

I straightened, but did not turn to look at the intruder, too afraid my recent thoughts would be reflected in my eyes. Instead, I stared at the swirls of paint coalescing before me and bit out: "I have nothing to say to you."

# CHAPTER TWENTY-SIX

"What the bloody hell were you thinking walking back here alone," Gage snapped, advancing into the room.

"That's none of your concern," I retorted.

"The hell it isn't!"

"Shhh!" I turned to hiss. "The nursery is just at the other end of the hall. I don't think my sister would take kindly to you waking her children." I glared at him. "Or teaching them such foul language."

He scowled back at me and then turned to close the studio door.

"No." I flung my paintbrush outward, pointing at the door. "You can just leave."

He ignored me. I considered marching across the room to wrench open the door and demand he get out, but the look in his eyes told me I'd never make it past him, so I stayed where I was.

"I have nothing to say to you," I reiterated, turning back to my canvas and pretending to examine it. I swirled my paintbrush in the Mars Yellow on my palette, trying to still my shaking hands.

"That's fine," he said, moving toward me. "But I have something to say."

"I won't listen." My voice rose higher with each step he took closer. Why couldn't he just leave me be?

"Oh, yes, you will," he declared confidently.

I whirled away from the easel and around the table set near it, placing both between me and Gage. "No, I won't." I could hear the panic in my voice, revealing my agitation, but I couldn't control it. "Please," I begged, shaking my head. "Please, just go."

"Kiera, she's not my fiancée!"

I looked up at his wide eyes, his open hands, and shook my head again. "No. You're lying. I . . . I saw the way you reacted."

"Kiera . . ."

"You were headed to London . . . And those letters from your father . . ." My voice was trembling. I flung my paintbrush angrily into the cup of linseed oil sitting on the table, making the glass klink and liquid splash onto the wooden surface. "No. No. No!" I dropped my palette down next to the cup with a clatter and turned away, crossing my arms over my chest.

"Kiera," Gage pleaded behind me. "She is *not* my fiancée. I swear to you."

His footsteps were loud against the floorboards, all of his usual stealth gone. I stiffened as he moved closer, and he stopped several feet from me. I could just barely make out his reflection in the darkened glass of the window before me, standing tall and rigid, his hands fisted at his sides.

"I was headed to London to see my father," he said, his voice tight with frustration. "That part I did not lie about. Or that it was in regards to a small disagreement. I just didn't tell you that the disagreement involved his wanting me to marry Lady Felicity Spencer, and my refusal to do so."

My chin rose at those words, and I supposed he saw it as a sign of encouragement for he moved a single step closer.

"He made the suggestion late last spring, and at the time I had no serious objections, so I let him introduce us and even danced attendance on her for a short while. But before I left London for your sister's house party at Gairloch Castle in August, I had already decided that Lady Felicity was not the wife for me." He hastened to add, "I made her no promises. I confessed no intentions. If she believes I'll make her an offer of marriage, it's not because of anything *I* have said or done."

"But clearly she *does* believe it," I murmured in a small voice.

"Please," he said, shifting half a step closer. "Will you at least look at me?"

I considered denying him. My body quavered with anguish and uncertainty, and I worried that if I looked at him, I might lose what limited composure I still had. But it seemed cowardly not to face him, and petty to do so out of spite. So even though my chest was tight with distress, I turned sideways to meet him halfway, staring up at him through the screen of my lashes.

His shoulders lowered in relief, though his eyes were still stricken. "Despite my resistance, my father is set on the match, and determined to forge an alliance with Lady Felicity's father, Lord Paddington. My father is the one who has kept the suit alive. I've written to him time and time again, telling him I will not marry Lady Felicity. But he will not listen." The last was taut with exasperation. He inhaled deeply. "Which is why I was traveling to London. To make him see reason."

He lowered his head so that he could see more directly into my eyes. "So you see, I am not engaged to Lady Felicity, nor was I ever."

My stomach fluttered with a stirring of hope I wasn't willing yet to believe. "But . . . aren't you honor bound now to offer for her? If your father and Lord Paddington have already drawn up marriage contracts . . ."

"No. I made no promises to the girl. It doesn't matter what my father has done."

"But what of the scandal?"

"There won't be one."

I frowned. Gage might not be concerned, but I knew better. There was nothing society loved more than to criticize and compare. He might emerge from this relatively unscathed, but gossip was always less kind to the females involved.

"And what of Lady Felicity?"

He tipped his head back in realization, seeming to finally understand what troubled me. He lifted his hand slowly and pressed it to my shoulder. "Kiera, do not make the mistake of thinking Lady Felicity is an innocent victim in this. She is not some naïve debutante doing whatever her father tells her. She knew before I left London that I had no real interest in her, and she didn't like it. I've sent her no letters, made no effort to remain in contact with her. If she's chosen to believe whatever nonsense my father has told her to explain my absence and my lack of communication, then she's doing so with her eyes wide open." His mouth flattened into a grimace. "She won't be happy to hear I've rejected her, but she won't be devastated. If I know her, she'll somehow turn this to her advantage, and my detriment."

"Won't your father be furious?"

"Yes. He already is. But I've weathered his tirades before. I suspect I'll do so again."

I nodded, hoping he was right. About all of it.

I looked up into his open gaze, trying to decide how best to ask if there was more. For with Gage it seemed there was inevitably something else he wished to keep hidden.

But before I could question him, his eyes darkened. "What I can't believe is that you would think I was capable of such a thing. That I would make my interest in you known." His voice grew louder with each pronouncement. "That I would *kiss* you, while all the while I was engaged to another woman."

When he phrased it like that, his anger did seem justified. But after all he'd put me through, I was not about to apologize. "Why didn't you just tell me the truth to begin with?"

"I shouldn't have had to."

I scowled. "So I'm supposed to be able to read your mind?"

"No. But you should have trusted me. You should have known better."

"So when women like Miss Witherington or that horrible girl at the Assembly Rooms make tittering insinuations I know nothing about, I'm not supposed to react? I'm not supposed to be hurt?" I dropped my hands to my sides, clenching them into fists. My nails bit into the skin of my palms. "I may be good at pretending I don't care, but I'm not made of stone." It didn't matter this time if he could hear the pain and resentment in my voice.

I crossed my arms and turned away to stare out the partially open window, shivering in its draft.

Gage marched around me, slamming the window shut. "Why is this window open? Are you trying to catch your death of cold?"

"To let the fumes out," I replied softly.

"Oh, well, it's too cold for that," he stammered with a frown. "What are you doing up here painting at this hour anyway?"

I didn't respond, knowing he'd only asked the question in an effort to stall. He already knew the answer. And if he didn't, then he certainly didn't know me very well.

His head turned to the side to stare at the crates in the corner still waiting to be unpacked. I waited, not knowing what to say or where to direct this argument. In one sense, I was relieved to hear that he wasn't engaged to another woman, that he hadn't deceived me in at least that regard. But I was also furious and frustrated with him. We were once again confronted with issues of trust, and I was weary of his stubborn refusal to confide in me until it was too late. Why did he insist on concealing everything about himself, everything that was important? Particularly something like this, something he should have known he would eventually need to explain, especially after Miss Witherington's remarks at my aunt and uncle's dinner table.

"I apologize," he finally said in a calmer voice. His eyes shifted to meet my gaze. "You're right. I should have told you. I just . . ." His shoulders flexed and hunched. "It was an awkward thing to explain. I guess I was embarrassed to admit my father would press such a thing." He grimaced. "It still sounds degrading."

I nodded, supposing I understood. Most men would think nothing of doing such a thing to their daughter or sisters, whether they liked it or not. How much worse would it be for a man to be controlled in such a manner?

"Did your father threaten to cut you off?" I asked, curious how rancorous the disagreement had become.

He huffed in annoyance. "Yes. But it's a hollow threat and he knows it."

I must have looked as confused as I felt, for he elaborated.

"I have wealth of my own, from my mother," he replied almost self-deprecatingly. "So I'm not completely beholden to my father. I'm also his only son and heir, so he knows I'll inherit his estate and his title eventually, even if he cuts me off now." His eyes hardened. "And in any case, whether he admits it or not, he needs me to assist with his investigations and to conduct the inquiries he has no wish to handle. My father may be the inquiry agent with the reputation, but that doesn't mean he's the man doing most of the investigating."

I knew there was much to Gage's relationship with his father that I didn't understand, but I hadn't realized it was quite so contentious. Captain Lord Gage was reputed to be much like his son, charming and highly sought after, friends with the king and scores of high-ranking men, but I had already taken a distinct disliking to him. And I had a strong suspicion that if the day ever came that we should meet, he would not like me either.

Gage moved a step closer to me and I lifted my eyes with a start, realizing I'd been staring at the crisp whiteness of his shirt above his dark waistcoat.

"Do you understand now? Are we well?"

His expression was tender and hopeful, and my resolve nearly crumbled in the face of it, but the tightness remained in my chest and the bitter taste of the hurt and frustration he had caused me still coated my mouth.

"I don't know, Gage." I rubbed a hand over my temple. "You tell me to trust you, but how am I supposed to do that when you're so secretive?" I could hear the exasperation growing in my voice. "You tell me to be patient, that you'll eventually reveal all, but you stubbornly evade all attempts I make to learn more." I turned away to cross the room toward the table where I'd flung my paint-splattered palette. My heart wrenched at what I was about to say. "I don't think I can live like this."

He was silent, and for a heart-stopping moment I worried he would simply turn and walk out the door. But then I heard his soft footsteps cross the room toward me. The skin on the back of my neck prickled as he drew closer and my breath caught. I felt the string of my apron being pulled, and I whirled to look at him.

"What are you doing?"

"I want you to come with me," he told me, calmly reaching out to pull my apron over my head. "There's something I want to show you."

I was so startled by his actions that I was momentarily paralyzed. However, when he reached out to remove the old, paint-splattered shawl from my shoulders, I pushed him back.

"And what if I don't want to go with you?" I demanded.

His eyes saddened, but the rest of him stood still, clutching my apron between his hands. "Please, Kiera." His voice was low and throbbing with resolve, as if he'd made up his mind about something difficult, and he wasn't about to allow himself to back down now. "I wouldn't ask if it weren't important."

He held his hand out to me and I stared down at it for a moment, trying to decide what to do. If I took it, I knew I was committed to learning something about Gage, something he had elected to keep hidden, something that might very well change my opinion of him and our relationship. Now that I was at the brink, I didn't know if I was ready for that. But the pleading in his eyes and the ache in his voice as he said, "Please," again made the choice for me.

With a knot in my throat, I lifted my trembling fingers and placed them in his warm palm. His fingers wrapped around mine and gave a gentle squeeze of thanks.

I shrugged off my old shawl while he gathered up my gloves and the winter shawl. He settled the fur-lined garment over my shoulders while I pulled the tight white gloves onto my hands and up my arms. I blew out the lanterns and pulled the door tight as I locked it. I didn't say a word as he guided me down the stairs and out the door to his waiting carriage, though my heart was pounding. I was surprised not to see Alana or Philip stick their heads out of the drawing room or study door to discover where we were going. They seemed to trust Gage more than I had, but, of course, they also didn't know about Lady Felicity.

The carriage was cold and the night as dark as an hour before when I'd walked home with Bonnie Brock. I peered through the curtains, curious whether he still stood under the trees at the center of the square, watching me depart with Gage. I couldn't see anything, but I suspected he was skilled enough at concealing himself that I wouldn't be able to notice him unless he wanted me to.

The carriage rounded the square and then set off toward Princes Street and the castle.

"Where are we going?"

"You'll see," Gage replied obliquely, though not unkindly. I turned to look at him. "Just . . . trust me."

I felt that I was just about at my limit of trust for the evening, but I held my tongue, knowing it was my nerves talking as much as my head. I pressed my hands tightly together as the coach turned down Rose Street rather than continuing on to Princes Street. It drove several blocks and then turned right into the mews that ran between Rose Street and Princes Street. I realized with a start that we were very likely sitting behind the building where Gage rented his lodgings.

I turned back to him with wide eyes. "I can't go in there," I told him as he opened the door. "What if someone were to see me? I would be ruined."

"That's why we've come to the back door. No one will see you."

"You can't guarantee that."

Gage sat back, seeming to realize for the first time how genuinely distressed I was. "You're right," he replied calmly. "I can't guarantee it. But as I said, I would not have brought you here if it weren't important. So please, Kiera, will you just trust me?" His eyes were begging me to listen to him.

I wanted to be stubborn, to demand he take me back to Charlotte Square, but he was right. I had trusted him up to this point. I should trust him a little bit further.

I nodded and allowed him to help me down from the carriage. He shielded me from any eyes that might be looking through the windows above as best he could as he hustled me in through the back door of his lodging house. But rather than taking me upstairs, he instead directed me down a flight, into what would normally be the servants' exclusive domain. Now my curiosity perked up even further as he approached a door near the base of the stairs.

He hesitated a moment and turned back to look at me. I couldn't see much in the dim light, but I could sense his uncertainty now that the moment was upon him. I was more interested than ever to know what was behind that door, but I waited for him to make the decision, to show me in or change his mind. When he twisted the handle, my heart leapt up into my throat.

The hinges squeaked as he slowly pushed the door open, and immediately I was assailed by the smell of sawdust. I glanced up at him in inquiry as he ushered me inside, but he said nothing. The room was dark save for the small window near the ceiling that looked out on the mews. It cast a muted light on the room's contents, creating more shadows than revealing objects.

I turned as Gage shut the door and then fumbled with what I presumed to be a lantern and matches on the shelf to his left. A light flared to life, momentarily blinding me at his proximity. I heard the creak of the lantern door as he reached in to light the wick, and then a snick as he closed it again. Now that there was a light, I pivoted to view what he had brought me here to see.

It was a woodshop. Several long tables and benches stood in the middle of the floor, and tools of all types hung from pegs and nails on the walls. Along the wall underneath the window, a low shelf held jars and pails filled with what I presumed were nails, pins, screws, and bolts. Several wooden pieces, in varying degrees of completion, were also scattered about the room. A partially finished wooden chair was tipped on its side on one of the tables, while its twin sat on the floor near the door. Two intricately carved shelves held pride of place on the other table, next to a pile of wood.

"What is this?" I asked as Gage moved forward to stand beside me.

I glanced up at him, finding his gaze on the wood rather than me. He reached out to run a finger down a long plank of pale wood, and I suddenly understood. The calluses on his hands, the sometimes woodsy scent of his cologne.

I turned back to the lovingly carved shelves. I didn't know much about wood, but they certainly didn't look like the work of an amateur. Reaching forward, I picked one up, letting my fingers play over the smooth edges. "Did you make all of these?"

Gage finally lifted his head to look at me. "Yes."

"They're beautiful," I replied.

His shoulders were tight with tension, and he didn't respond, instead continuing to run his hands over the wood.

"You know," I told him carefully as I set the shelf down. "I never really believed you got your calluses from fencing." He shifted his weight to his other foot as I reminded him of the explanation he'd given me in my art studio at Gairloch Castle when I'd asked about them. "And I don't really understand why you felt the need to lie." I moved around the table toward the finished chair, figuring Gage would find it easier to talk without my standing there staring at him, demanding answers.

"Gentlemen do not work with their hands. And if they do, they never let it be known," Gage pronounced, as if he'd heard the assertion many times before.

"And you think I care for such nonsense?" I told him over my shoulder. "I willingly married an anatomist, for goodness' sake. I understood what his profession entailed. Though I never expected to take part in it." I muttered the last under my breath.

"Well, I . . ." He seemed momentarily flummoxed, but then he recovered. "No. I did think you would understand. But I'd hid it for so long. It was a bit hard to admit it to anyone."

I pressed my hands on the top rung of the chair and offered him a small smile. "Who taught you?"

"My grandfather, actually." He seemed to speak easier now that the secret was out and I had not derided him for it. "My mother and I lived in a cottage not far from her parents' estate in Devon. I spent a lot of time there as a boy." He grimaced. "Mostly fighting with my cousins." He shifted so that his hip pressed against the table, his eyes growing distant. "One day I stumbled upon a wooden shed near the gamekeeper's cottage, and I couldn't resist peering through the window. Inside I saw my grandfather sawing wood. Well, when he caught me spying on him, he gave me quite the lecture."

"Which is where that pronouncement came from?" I guessed.

"Yes. My grandfather was not a man to trifle with." His brow furrowed as if he still had a hard time believing what came next. "He swore me to secrecy. And then he began to teach me how to build a stool, and then a shelf, and then a chair . . ." He trailed off, but I understood what he was saying. "It was the only place my grandfather and I ever got along."

I watched the emotions flicker across his face as he recalled his time with his grandfather. It could not have been easy growing up with a mother who was constantly ill and a father who was away at sea, at war with France, and only home for barely a fortnight each year. He was an only child and, from the sounds of it, did not get on well with his cousins. I couldn't help but wonder if his mother's family had disapproved of her choice in a husband. After all, until Gage's father received his title from the king six months prior, he had been a lowly mister. I didn't know much about Gage's father's family except that they were from Cornwall, but I strongly suspected that whoever they were, they might not have been seen as good enough for a viscount's daughter.

When finally he looked up from his contemplation of the past, he turned to me with a frown pleating his forehead. "So it truly doesn't bother you that I dirty my hands by building things?"

"No," I replied with a trill of laughter. "Of course not."

"Really?"

I crossed the room toward him and he straightened from his slouch. "Really." I shook my head. "I paint portraits. Does that bother you?"

"No."

I arched my eyebrows in reproach.

A reluctant smile tugged at his lips. "I see your point. But I have one more thing to show you." He turned to pull me toward the corner.

"Oh, no. What will this be? You also sew cushions for your chairs?" I teased.

He glared over his shoulder at me and then reached out to pull an old blanket off something propped against the wall. I turned away and sneezed from the cloud of dirt and sawdust it stirred up, but once the grime had settled, I could see that it was a beautiful bookshelf. There were shelves of all heights, some narrow and some tall, but they all had a nice deep, flat surface. There were even several built-in drawers across the bottom with round knobs. The entire piece was crafted from a dark wood, sanded and varnished.

"It's lovely," I told him, reaching out to run my hand over the smooth surface.

"I made it for you," he said quietly.

I pressed a hand to my chest in surprise. "For me?"

He nodded, but the anxiety had returned to his eyes. "For your art studio. I thought you could use it for your pigments and jars and other supplies."

I turned back to examine the piece in a new light. "It's perfect." I gasped. Tears suddenly welled in my eyes, and I pressed my hands together over my nose and mouth, trying to suppress them. I inhaled sharply. "I don't think anyone has ever given me such a wonderful gift." Certainly not something so customized to me.

Gage reached out to pull me into his arms and I let him. I buried my face in his neck, trying to control the emotions his present had stirred up in me.

"I'm glad you like it," he murmured.

I nodded, the fabric of his jacket rasping against my cheek. "Thank you."

"My pleasure."

I allowed him to hold me for a moment, savoring the feel of him, the scent of him. But then I lifted my head, brushing tendrils of hair away from my face. "You know when you brought me down here, I thought you had something awful to tell me or show me." I couldn't help but recall the last time he'd confided in me, when he'd told me his mother had been murdered. I could see from the sudden sadness in his eyes that he also remembered. "I . . . thought you were going to tell me something about Greece."

Ever since I'd learned that Gage had been in Greece during their struggle for independence from the Turks, I'd been curious to know why. I wanted to understand what had happened to make him so closemouthed about the whole thing. Until now, he had always resisted telling me more. Would he still?

He pushed another loose hair back from my cheek and traced his finger down to my jaw. "I will tell you everything you want to know," he promised me with haunted eyes. "But not tonight. Please. It's . . . too much."

I nodded, wanting to be understanding, but also feeling frustrated at his continued evasion. However, I knew he was right. It *was* late. And if this story was as troubling as I suspected, as the pain in his eyes seemed to indicate, then perhaps it was better to save it for a time when our emotions were not already so raw from everything that had happened this evening.

So I allowed him to put it off a little while longer, hoping I wouldn't later regret it.

# CHAPTER TWENTY-SEVEN

It was almost midday the next day when Gage rushed into the drawing room of the town house on Charlotte Square, where Alana and I were relaxing. Having already quizzed me on what had happened between Gage and I the evening before, she was working on a piece of embroidery for the new baby while I read a copy of *Debrett's Peerage*, trying to work out the tangled web of relations among our suspects in the British peerage. Gage didn't wait to be announced, nor even take the time to remove his greatcoat.

I sat forward at the sight of him, instantly knowing something was wrong. "What is it?"

His expression was grim as he lifted a folded sheet of paper. "Another body."

I shifted to the edge of my seat. "Where?"

"A village called Beckford in the Borders."

I glanced at Alana. "That's just south of Kelso. Not far from St. Boswells."

"I know. I looked at a map," he replied matter-of-factly.

"But what does that mean?" I asked in confusion. "It's so close to Dryburgh Abbey. Is that just a coincidence?"

"I don't know," he admitted. His gaze sharpened. "But I would like to find out. Can you be ready to leave in an hour?"

I looked at Alana again, who had been silently listening

to our exchange. Her eyes were wide, but she said nothing. "I shall do my best."

He nodded and began to back from the room. "I'll call for you at one o'clock."

Even with the help of Alana's maid and another girl from belowstairs, Bree and I were barely ready to leave when Gage came for us. I could only be grateful I'd packed light.

My sister did not help matters by beginning to weep immediately following Gage's departure from the drawing room. Soon she had me biting back tears of my own between issuing instructions for the maids. I'm sure we looked a sad mess when Philip entered my room to find out what the fuss was all about. His eyes were wide with that panicked look some men seem to get whenever faced with an emotional female. Normally he handled my sister's strange moods while she was expecting quite well, but apparently two near-sobbing females were too much for even him.

When Gage's carriage arrived, I embraced Alana tightly and promised her I would return soon, long before her time came to give birth. Even so, it was hard to drive away after seeing her in such a state. I hoped her extreme agitation was only because of the baby and that it would pass soon; otherwise I would feel horribly guilty for leaving her so upset. In the end, it was Philip's reassuring smile that had finally convinced me to allow Gage to help me up into his carriage. I knew he would always take care of her, and that he would send for me if I was needed.

I dabbed at the corners of my eyes with my handkerchief as the carriage passed under the shadow of the rock on which Edinburgh Castle perched. By the time we rounded the crenellation and skirted the Shambles and the Grassmarket on our way out of the city, I had myself much more in hand. I gave one last sniff and stuffed my handkerchief back into the pocket of my dress.

Bree studiously trained her gaze outside the opposite window, but Gage and Anderley both watched me from the seat across from us with varying degrees of uncertainty. Gage was by far the most sympathetic, while Anderley looked mildly unsettled at the sight of a tearful female. I ignored him and focused on Gage.

"Do you know anything more about the body that was taken?"

He nodded, withdrawing the letter he had waved in the air earlier from an interior pocket of his greatcoat. "It was a Lord Fleming." He opened the missive, scanning it for the information he sought. "Your uncle says that he died in 1823, and was succeeded by his grandson, the current Lord Fleming. He was buried at Beckford Parish Churchyard." He glanced up at me over the paper. "Your uncle also mentions he's surprised by the thieves' daring. Apparently Beckford Parish Churchyard is well guarded. It even boasts a watchtower."

My eyes widened in surprise. I knew many of the graveyards in Edinburgh and the surrounding area had built watchtowers and hired men to guard the graves at night, or employed other deterrents to body snatchers, like mortsafes, but I'd not heard of graveyards so far from the city doing so. Of course, I also hadn't initially realized the body snatchers had begun to travel so far afield in search of fresh corpses for the anatomists and anatomy schools.

But these weren't your traditional body snatchers.

"Perhaps Beckford only employs night watchmen when there are newly deceased bodies buried there to guard," I suggested. In such a small parish, I had difficulty imagining they could afford to do otherwise, unless the men were volunteers, another very real probability.

"It's possible," Gage conceded as he tucked the letter back into his pocket. "But certainly something worth looking into."

"Was Lord Fleming a member of the Society of Antiquaries?"

He frowned, squinting through the window into the afternoon sunlight. "We'll have to ask his family. That was something I didn't have time to investigate prior to our departure. I decided a better use of our time would be to arrive there before the ransom note, and perhaps before any evidence they may have left behind disappeared, though the hope of that is slim, since the theft happened three nights ago now."

I remained silent, knowing how badly Gage wanted to catch these men. I wanted them caught as well, but perhaps not with the same fervor. It bothered him that they'd slipped through his fingers twice now. He wasn't about to let them get away a third time.

He shifted to face me. "In any case, I spoke with Sergeant Maclean and he's heard back from a few more of his contacts. It doesn't look like there have been any other similar body-snatching cases, though there's always the chance that a scandal-conscious family might not have reported or been willing to admit to such an incident."

"Did he question you about your eye?" I couldn't resist asking. The deep red and purple of his contusion had begun to fade to a jaundice shade of yellow as it healed.

Anderley looked up from his contemplation of his feet and I felt Bree shift beside me. Apparently they both found this question more interesting than what had come before.

Gage scowled. "Yes."

When he neglected to elaborate, I was forced to prompt him. "And what did he say?"

He simply continued to glare at me, and a thought occurred to me.

"You did tell him the truth?"

A muscle twitched at the corner of Gage's narrowed eyes. "I knew what I was doing when I walked home. I knew *everything* that was at stake."

"So you knew you could be killed and you still chose to do it? But it was so needless."

"It wasn't my life that I was worried about. And it was far from needless."

I frowned. "How could you not have been worried about being killed?"

His gaze traveled up and down my person. "Some things are more important than that," he proclaimed solemnly. "There are some things you simply have to confront in person. And Bonnie Brock needed to be made to understand that he cannot come after you, not without consequences. Not without dealing with me."

I was momentarily stunned by the ferocity I saw in his eyes, especially knowing that it was not directed at me, but on my behalf.

However, his voice had gentled when he spoke again. "Kiera, I will not allow anyone to think for a minute that they can harm you."

I swallowed and nodded, before turning to stare blindly out the window, uncertain how to handle such a revelation. I'd always trusted Gage to look out for me, at least physically. He had saved my life twice, for goodness' sake. But I'd never expected him to place himself in danger simply to ensure my future safety. As little good as that had done, since Bonnie Brock was still having me followed, and had even confronted me again the previous evening. I decided it was best to keep that second encounter with the notorious criminal to myself. There was no telling what Gage would do.

Conflicting emotions twisted inside me as I snuck a glance at him out of the corner of my eye. I didn't know whether to kiss him or kick him, and the presence of our servants did not help matters. His desire to protect me and defend my honor was both touching and noble. And incredibly foolhardy. But I supposed last night I had also been foolish enough to tell Bonnie Brock to his face that I would do the same thing if he ever touched Gage again, so perhaps I understood.

"What can I say?" I murmured, knowing he was still waiting for a response. "Except that if you were killed . . ." I swallowed again, forcing the lump of emotion back down my throat. Even so, my voice shook. "I . . . I would prefer that you were not. That you not take such a chance again, even on my behalf."

Gage's eyes softened, telling me he comprehended far more than I'd said. I turned aside to stare out the window again, trying to quiet the tumult such a simple glance from him could cause inside me.

I was grateful when, rather than pressing the matter, he instead returned to the subject of the body snatching in Beckford.

"There's a much shorter space of time between this theft and the last one. I don't know whether that's because they're escalating, they're growing reckless, or because they know we're investigating and they're worried they won't have time to finish what they started."

"Which would imply that they have a larger plan in mind," I said. "Another aim other than extorting money out of wealthy noble families."

"Precisely." His fingers tapped against his thigh in impatience. "Unfortunately, most of our suspects lend themselves to that theory, so it does nothing to narrow down our list."

"And I've another to add to it."

All three occupants of the carriage turned to look at me at this pronouncement.

"Who?" Gage asked.

"Mr. Stuart." I explained to him briefly the information I was able to gather both from the man in question and Lady Bute at the Assembly Rooms the night before. "He was extremely forthcoming, which makes me inclined to believe him innocent, but he does have motive for some of the body snatchings, slim as it might be. And he could be lying about the number and the names of the men involved. So I don't think we can completely rule him out."

Gage's brow was lowered in displeasure. "Why didn't you tell me about this last night?"

I arched my eyebrows at him in reproach, wanting to know if he really wished me to announce in front of our servants why we'd been arguing. I watched as understanding dawned in his eyes, and his mouth flexed in discomfort.

"I see. Well, I don't suppose there's much I could've done

about it yesterday evening in any case. I'll send Philip a note and ask him to look into it. With his government contacts—"

"I already have," I interrupted. "This morning."

Gage nodded. "Good. Well, I have a few contacts in London I can also press for information, but I'm afraid it will be too late in reaching us if we're to stop the culprits before the ransom is paid on this fourth victim." He rubbed his chin, his eyes narrowing in thought. "Incidentally, had Mr. Stuart just arrived in Edinburgh? I'm curious where he was the night of this latest theft."

I shook my head. "He was at the Theatre Royal. I spoke with him after the performance."

Gage's head perked up. "Really? Just before you left and were abducted by Bonnie Brock?"

Anderley's eyes widened. Clearly his employer had not shared that information with him. I knew Bree was aware of it, though we'd never discussed it. Philip's household was like any other. The servants talked, and I was sure the coachman and footman had shared our ordeal with the others belowstairs.

Even so, I answered hesitantly, "Yes."

"Curious," Gage murmured, turning to stare out the window at the increasingly rural scenery as the buildings became farther and farther spaced out on the outskirts of Edinburgh.

"Why?" I asked in some confusion, and then realized what he was implying. "You think Mr. Stuart and Bonnie Brock are in league?"

"The possibility did cross my mind." His voice was maddeningly calm.

"But then why would Brock point me in the direction of Mr. Stuart? I would never have suspected the man without his veiled comments."

He shrugged. "Maybe he's tired of being under the other man's thumb."

I considered the matter for a moment, unsettling as it was, but then decided it was very unlikely. "I don't think

Bonnie Brock is under anyone's thumb," I said with awed certainty.

Gage grimaced and reluctantly admitted, "I don't either."

I glanced over at Bree, who was watching me. I could tell she had something to say, but for whatever reason, she held her tongue.

I decided I would ask her about it later. My chance finally came when we stopped at an inn just outside Lauder for the night. Bree was helping me to undress when I broached the subject.

"Aye, m'lady," she admitted. "But I wasna sure ye would wish me to mention it in front o' Mr. Gage."

I stepped out of my dress and turned to face her in my shift, shivering in the cold of the room. "What do you mean?"

"Well . . ." She rolled up my warm flannel nightgown and dropped it over my head. She nibbled her lip as I pushed my arms into the sleeves. "It's just that . . . there've been men watchin' the house. Johnny noticed 'em first," she added, naming one of the footmen. "And he thinks they're Bonnie Brock's men." She was clearly distressed at sharing this news.

"It's all right. I already know," I assured her.

"Ye do?" she said in surprise.

I nodded. "Or, at least, I suspected it."

Her brow furrowed in confusion. "But why, m'lady? To warn ye away from the inquiry?"

Hearing the worry in her voice triggered my own. I reached out to run my fingers over the smooth surface of my amethyst pendant where I had set it on top of the old, dented dresser when I began to undress. "Well, if I'm to take his word for it, he actually wants me to solve it."

I looked up into Bree's concerned eyes. "His sister's missing, and he believes she's run off with the men responsible for doing the actual body snatching."

Her eyes instantly softened in sympathy. "Poor dear. I s'pose she'd no idea what she was gettin' herself into."

"I imagine not."

"And he'd no notion where they went?"

I shook my head. "Away from Edinburgh. That's all he knew."

Bree nodded and set about tidying the room, deep in thought. I couldn't help but wonder if she empathized with the girl for more reasons than just a soft heart, but I elected not to ask.

The roads the next day were less than ideal for travel. The snow we had feared when we watched the approach of the heavy gray wall of clouds on the horizon at dusk the day before had arrived. Overnight it had blanketed the ground several inches deep, and although the accumulation was not heavy, it was a nuisance. As the day wore on, and the traffic as well as the temperatures increased, the muddy slush of the roadways made travel slow and messy. Twice Gage and Anderley were forced to climb out and assist the footman in pushing the carriage out of a boggy mess.

We had left the inn before dawn, in hopes of reaching Marefield House before noon, but it was late afternoon, closer to teatime, before the carriage lumbered up the drive. The manse was a two-story speckled stone building with what looked to be mostly symmetrical additions made to each end. The dark gray slope of the roof was covered in snow, but smoke puffed from several of the chimneys. I wrapped my arms tighter around myself inside my cloak, anxious to get inside. The hot brick I'd been given at our last stop had long since grown cold, and my toes were freezing inside their kid leather boots.

Fortunately, the butler had either been expecting us or was kind, for he ushered us inside the relative warmth of the entry hall quickly. He gathered Gage's and my winter things while Bree and Anderley were escorted downstairs to the servants' quarters by a footman. I watched them go, wondering if they would be able to gather more information from the servants than we would of their employers. The butler flicked a glance down at Gage's mud-splattered boots and the knees of his breeches, but as there was nothing that could be done about it, he clearly thought better of mentioning it, and instead escorted us to the drawing room.

The first thing that struck me was the extreme coziness of the space. A fire burned in the hearth at the opposite end of the room, casting flickering light across the warm burnt orange walls. The lovely silk wallpaper bore a swirled pattern that gave the surface a textured appearance that made one wish to run their hand across it. The plush chairs and settees and ottomans, in various autumnal shades of red and orange and golden yellow were stuffed with pillows and all arranged so that one could easily hold a conversation without raising one's voice.

I absolutely adored the space, but it was obvious that at least one of the room's current occupants did not adore me.

Lady Fleming, I presumed, stood next to her husband before one of the settees, her glittering dark eyes narrowed in obvious dislike. I had received the look many times before from society ladies—it was a mixture of scorn and distrust—and it always made my stomach drop in remembered fear and anger. But however strong her aversion to me was, she swiftly banked it as her husband first greeted Gage and then me. I couldn't help darting a glance toward her as I spoke briefly to Lord Fleming, wondering if I'd imagined her animosity.

Lord Fleming invited us to take a seat in the chairs across from him and his wife. "Lord Rutherford informed me you would likely be making a call." His complexion was somewhat pallid and there were dark circles under his eyes, making me suspect he had not slept easily the past few nights. "He said you've been investigating similar . . . grave disturbances."

"Yes. There have been three other thefts that we're aware of, and they all happened in the same manner," Gage replied, sitting very straight in his chair. I suddenly realized how very discomfited he felt. He was clearly not used to presenting himself in grimy clothes while sporting a rather

ghastly multicolored contusion across one side of his face. I
suspected Gage's carefully cultivated appearance was as
much a form of armor as chain mail and a breastplate. Or
perhaps he was worried he would not be taken seriously.
Lord Fleming *was* frowning quite fiercely.

He asked his lordship to provide us with the details of
the disturbance of his grandfather's grave, and Lord Fleming
obliged.

Apparently, the minister of Beckford's tiny parish church
often walked the perimeter of the churchyard walls in the
morning as he said his prayers. Four mornings past, he had
noticed the disturbance of the ground over the late Lord
Fleming's grave. He'd contacted the current lord, and when
the grave was examined, it was discovered that the body
inside was missing, though all of his clothing and personal
effects had been left behind.

"You're certain nothing was taken?" Gage asked.

Lord Fleming nodded. "Yes."

"What of the watchman? We were led to believe that
you've had some trouble with body snatchers operating in
the area."

He sighed wearily and glanced at his wife. "Aye, our parish has seen its share of trouble from the resurrectionists.
The watchman admitted to falling asleep in the watchtower.
He claimed the most recent body buried there was two
weeks old, so he figured there would be no trouble that
night. That he hadn't counted on the men going after an old
grave."

Gage's expression was doubtful. "Is his story feasible?
How far from the watchtower does your grandfather's grave
rest?"

"It's in the opposite corner. Far enough away that it's possible."

Possible or not, I knew Gage and I would be speaking to
this watchman.

Two pretty young housemaids appeared then, carrying a
tray of tea and another filled with cakes and sandwiches.

Then just as swiftly, they departed. Lady Fleming slid forward to serve while Gage resumed his questioning.

"How often has the parish churchyard been disturbed by these resurrectionists, I assume from Edinburgh?"

Lord Fleming's head tilted to the side, dislodging a dark lock of hair pushed back from his forehead. "Or Glasgow. It's been a year, maybe two, since we last saw any trouble from them, and that last time they were run off by the man on watch. But it's hard to say how often we actually received visits from them before that. The people in this area like to tell tales about their encounters with these men, and after a while it's not always easy to differentiate fact from fiction."

Lady Fleming nodded in agreement as she handed first Gage and then me our tea. "People will make up the most ridiculous stories."

"Some even claim that my grandfather's brother worked with the resurrectionists, and when he was found out, he supposedly hid here in a dark closet for three months until he could escape on a ship to the Continent. While it's true that my great-uncle studied medicine in Edinburgh, he wasn't assisting body snatchers, and he sailed for America, not the Continent, to serve during the American War of Independence."

I sipped my tea, grateful for its warmth and rich aroma, and refrained from informing them that if his great-uncle had been a medical student in Edinburgh, it was very likely he'd had *something* to do with the resurrectionists, even if it was only utilizing the fresh corpses they peddled to the anatomists and the schools.

"But really," Lady Fleming said, flicking her head to move her blond curls out of her eyes as she sat upright again. "I'm sure Lady Darby knows far more about these men and their activities than we do." Her voice was almost indifferent, but her gaze was razor sharp as she stared at me over the rim of her teacup.

That might be true, but I certainly wasn't going to allow that remark to pass without some kind of comment. "Actually, I've never met a resurrectionist," I replied with a good-natured smile, and then, for the sake of complete honesty, added, "That I'm aware of."

Lady Fleming's eyes began to narrow, but Gage spoke up before she could say anything else.

"Do you know if your grandfather was acquainted with the late Lord Buchan, Sir Colum Casselbeck, or Ian Tyler of Woodslea?"

"Are those the other victims?" Lord Fleming asked, balancing his tea saucer on his knee.

"Yes."

His gaze shifted to the wall over Gage's head as he frowned in thought. "Well, I wouldn't be surprised if he was acquainted with them all. Certainly Lord Buchan, with their estates being so close to one another."

"Was he by chance a member of the Society of Antiquaries of Scotland?"

Lord Fleming turned to look at his wife. "Yes, I believe he was. But what have they to do with anything?"

Gage swallowed the tiny piece of cake he'd popped into his mouth before replying. "Perhaps nothing. But they're the only connection we've been able to find so far between all of the men. However, I've been led to believe that membership was not so uncommon among men of their age." He took a sip of tea. "Have you been contacted by a Mr. Lewis Collingwood?"

"I don't believe so," he replied hesitantly, glancing at his wife again, who shook her head. "Is he a suspect?"

A log popped in the fireplace and hissed as the embers rose up.

"I suppose I would describe him as more of a person of some interest," Gage hedged. "He wrote to or visited the families of the other victims, asking them about a gold torc."

Lord Fleming's face creased in concentration. "Then maybe . . . Is that a type of necklace?"

"Yes," I said. "It was worn by the Celts."

"Then yes, I think I have heard from him. I'll have to ask my secretary to be sure. But I vaguely remember him telling me about some correspondence I received from a man about a gold necklace." He squinted. "Something about my grandfather having stolen it."

Gage and I exchanged a glance.

"That would be Mr. Collingwood," Gage told him, briefly explaining the man's accusations.

"Do you really think that's what this is all about?" Lord Fleming's voice was shaded with doubt. "A gold necklace?"

"Honestly? No," Gage admitted. "But so far he's the only person we can connect to all four men, so we have to seriously consider the possibility. People have done far more terrible things for even less noble reasons."

I shrugged. "Just think of King Henry the Eighth."

Gage's lips cracked into a smile, but neither of our hosts seemed amused by my quip. I cleared my throat and took another sip of my tea.

"May I take it that you haven't yet received a ransom note?" Gage asked them, drawing their eyes away from me.

"No," Lord Fleming said. "Should we expect one?"

"Yes. And please send word to me at once upon receiving it." He leaned forward slightly in his chair, his eyes hardening. "I warn you that these men are clever. They will leave nothing to chance. And the longer we have to prepare to intercept them, the better opportunity we have of catching them."

"And why should we trust that you'll be able to catch them?" Lady Fleming suddenly demanded, leaning forward to set her teacup down on the table. "You haven't been able to do so up to this point."

Lord Fleming appeared just as taken aback by his wife's sudden display of temper as the rest of us were. He pressed a hand to her arm, speaking her name in chastisement.

"No," she snapped, turning on her husband. "If it hadn't been for their incompetence, perhaps the criminals would have been caught by now, and your grandfather would still be able to rest in peace." She rose to her feet and strode across the room to the door, but before departing, she turned to order her husband, "Don't you dare let them botch this, or we might never get your grandfather back."

The door closed behind her with a slam.

For a moment we were all silent, and then Lord Fleming began to apologize for his wife's outburst. I was only half listening, more interested in why the outburst had happened in the first place.

Was Lady Fleming scared of a scandal? Her extreme dislike of me was a strong indication that she was, but I felt there was something more to it. There had been something in her eyes, something that left a bitter taste in my mouth. And if I wasn't very much mistaken, it was fear. But of what?

She didn't strike me as being very religious, so I had trouble believing it had anything to do with the late Lord Fleming and his ability, or inability as it were, to rise again on Judgment Day. And surely she realized that none of the living family members of the victims had yet been harmed. Dodd had been murdered because he interrupted the body snatchers at their work. So what could it be?

## CHAPTER TWENTY-EIGHT

Trevor was just rising from the dinner table when we arrived at Blakelaw House. He came out to the hall to greet us, folding me in a tight hug that made me suspect he might have been lonely while we were away. When he discovered we had not yet eaten, he called for two more place settings and ordered the food to be brought back up from the kitchens. I told the butler that some cold meat, cheese, and bread would be perfectly adequate, but the staff ignored me, and soon we were sitting down to a full meal.

Trevor relaxed in his chair and sipped white wine while we relayed the latest discoveries in our investigation between bites of roasted pheasant, neeps and tatties, and apple tart. Our uncle had kept Trevor apprised of the theft of the late Lord Fleming's bones, as well as another development—the information of which must have been included in a letter that arrived in Edinburgh after our departure.

Trevor leaned back even farther in his seat, evidently happy to have something to contribute to the conversation. "It's a good thing you recommended Lord Buchan have his uncle's bones examined by Dr. Carputhers. The crotchety man resisted for a time, angry that he'd been excluded from the investigation at the beginning." He scowled. "Even though it was his own fault he was inebriated and incapable.

That's why it took so long to discover one of the late Lord Buchan's bones *was* missing."

I glanced across the table at Gage. "Let me guess. Was it from his finger?"

Trevor seemed to deflate at my already knowing this. "Well, yes. How did you know?"

"A finger bone was also missing from Mr. Tyler's skeleton. Sir Colum's body was reburied without being checked, but I would wager that there's a finger bone missing from his skeleton as well." I pushed my half-eaten apple tart away from me, too excited now to finish it. "Did he mention which finger bone it was?"

He closed one eye to think. "The . . . proximal phalanx?"

"Proximal phalange."

He pointed at me. "That. Of the index finger."

"And he's the third victim. Do you know what this means?"

Gage and Trevor both looked at each other blankly.

"The bone taken from the first victim, Mr. Tyler, was a distal phalange, at the tip." I lifted my hand to illustrate. "And I'll wager a hundred pounds that the bone missing from Sir Colum, our second victim, is the intermediate phalange." I pointed to the next bone, below my first finger joint.

Gage's eyes brightened, beginning to understand the point I was trying to make.

"And our third victim, Lord Buchan is missing his proximal phalange." I indicated the third bone below the second finger joint.

Trevor sat forward suddenly, sloshing the wine at the bottom of his glass. "So whoever is responsible for these body snatchings now has an entire finger."

I studied my brother's flushed face, wondering just how much wine he'd had to drink this evening. "Well, yes and no."

"But what of our fourth victim?" Gage asked.

"He may be planning to collect the metacarpal as well." Using the thumb and forefinger of my opposite hand, I gripped the palm of my hand below the knuckle. "Or . . ."

I hesitated to speak aloud the thought that had occurred to me.

"Or what?" Trevor prompted.

Gage's face reflected the grimness I felt. "Or he's collecting an entire hand, or worse, an entire skeleton."

We all fell silent, considering the disturbing implications.

I frowned and shook my head. "No. That doesn't make sense." I looked up at Gage. "You said yourself he's likely collecting these bones as a sort of trophy, and he hasn't been indiscriminate about who his victims are. He selects them very specifically. And in the same vein, I would like to suggest he's also keeping these bones for a very specific reason."

"He's figuratively pointing the finger at them," Gage declared in a solemn voice.

I nodded. "Yes. Or something very like that."

"Maybe he's just giving them the finger," Trevor mused, swirling the wine in his glass. He snorted. "Or taking it from them."

I turned to scowl at him, but Gage merely cracked a smile.

We rose from the table soon after and crossed to the drawing room, where I dropped down on one corner of the settee. I propped my elbow on the arm and pressed my face into my hand, too tired to do much else, but knowing I needed to allow time for my meal to digest before I lay down or else I would feel ill when I was trying to sleep.

A moment later I felt a dip in the cushion and then a warmth beside me. I peered between my fingers to find Earl Grey looking up at me. I reached out to scratch him beneath the chin. Then he circled the cushion and settled down pressed against my leg.

"That dashed cat," Trevor exclaimed, flopping down on the settee across from me. He glowered at the feline. "He's been absolutely despondent since you left."

I glanced down at the cat in surprise.

"Wandering the house with his pitiful whine. There were several nights when I should have liked to have gone down to the gun cabinet and taken out a pistol and ended all of our misery."

Earl Grey opened his eyes at the sound of my brother's increasingly agitated voice, and then closed them again unconcerned. His purring never ceased.

"When you return to Edinburgh for Alana's confinement, you're taking him with you," Trevor declared.

"Oh, but I don't think—" I began to protest, but my brother cut me off with a fierce glare.

"If you don't, there's no telling what may happen to him."

I studied the cat. I wasn't worried Trevor would actually shoot him. But he might stick him in a bag and ride out to the middle of nowhere and leave him.

I ran a hand down the soft gray fur on the cat's back. He cracked open his eyes and then closed them again. I supposed it would be best to take him with me.

I lifted my gaze to find Gage watching me from the opposite end of the settee. His eyes twinkled in amusement, and his mouth curled in a knowing grin. I turned away and ignored him.

B eckford Parish Church stood not far from Marefield House on a knoll overlooking a ford in the River Teviot. The L-shaped building was constructed from sturdy pale stone and boasted several fine tall windows and a tiny belfry. It was rather austere, like most tiny Border churches were. After being raided and burned down so many times in the sixteenth and seventeenth centuries, it had become difficult for the Border people to believe anything they built would ever remain permanent.

The graveyard surrounded the church on all sides, boxed in by a low stone fence. Beyond the wall stretched the rolling Teviot Hills, which eventually merged with the Cheviots at the Border between Scotland and England. This morning the fields and cemetery were still covered in a thin layer of snow, with faded tufts of grass sticking up here and there among the white powder.

The rector must have seen us through the window when we arrived, for before we'd even finished descending from the carriage, he came bustling through the door to greet us. He was a middle-aged man of medium height with a gregarious nature. I wondered how well he got along with the more typically stoic personalities of his Border parishioners.

When Gage had explained who we were and why we were there, the rector shook his head, exclaiming about the absurdity of the entire business, and then guided us around the building. I took Gage's proffered arm to help me through the snow, leaving Trevor to fall in step with the clergyman.

"St. Mawr . . ." the rector murmured in thought. "Do ye by chance own a manor o'er by Elwick?"

"Why, yes," Trevor replied.

"Do ye attend St. Cuthbert's?"

"Yes."

He nodded. "Well, tell yer vicar we'd like our bell back, please, should he e'er have time to address it."

The rector's voice was jovial as he explained with a chuckle, "The bell from Beckford Kirk here was supposedly stolen during one o' the later raids and installed at St. Cuthbert's in Elwick across the Border. 'Course, there's no proof o' it. But the story persists. It's one o' our more colorful bits o' history." He nodded to the left as we rounded the building. "Like our mort house. Or 'ghoul tower,' if ye prefer. Or, at least, that's what the locals call it."

We stopped to stare at the tiny rough-hewn, red sandstone watchtower, complete with crenellations. There were five stone steps leading up to the closed dark wooden door, and two tall, thin windows on each side of the door, like arrow slits, presumably for the watchmen to fire muskets out of. It was perhaps ten feet across, and I estimated no more than two men could fit inside comfortably.

"That's where the watchman fell asleep on the night Lord

Fleming's grave was disturbed?" Gage asked, raising his voice to be heard over the gusting wind.

"Aye," the rector replied. He shook his head. "I thought Geordie'd put all his drinkin' behind him. But that's the only explanation I have for him fallin' asleep on the job like that."

"This Geordie, where might we find him? I'd like to ask him a few questions."

The rector tipped his head to the right. "Lives doon by the river, a mile or so from here. But I dinna think you'll get much from him." The muscles around his mouth had tightened, I assumed in disapproval of his drinking. I suspected it would be best if we visited the man earlier in the day, while he was more likely to be sober.

We resumed our trek across the churchyard through the snow. It was clear no one had come this way, at least not since the evening before last when the snow started falling. The wind here blew quite strong with nothing to obstruct it, and I had to lift a hand to keep the hood of my cloak from being pushed back off my head. It was loud enough to make hearing each other difficult, so we remained silent as we approached the far corner.

A pale stone obelisk rather than a headstone stood over the open grave—the soil a dark blot in the otherwise gray and white landscape. The wooden coffin down inside had been closed as best it could, and was now covered in pristine snow.

"Lord Fleming's clothing and effects were taken to Marefield House," the rector replied in answer to Gage's question, talking loudly to be heard over the wind. "And the coffin is otherwise empty."

"That may be so, but I'm afraid I'm still going to need to take a look inside," Gage told him.

My heart started beating faster, just like it had at the abbey. I wanted to protest, but I knew he was right. There might be some clue in the coffin that the others had missed, and there was no way of knowing unless he looked. But that didn't stop me from thinking of the Nun of Dryburgh's words, or prevent the feeling of sickening dread from washing over me.

He removed his hat, looking around for a place to set it. I stepped forward to take it from him.

"St. Mawr, would you mind giving me a hand?"

My stomach dropped as I watched both men—the two closest to me in all the world—awkwardly drop down into the grave. The coffin made a hollow thud as they landed, and I could only hope the wood would hold both their weight.

The rector stepped closer to the grave to watch what they were doing, but I had to turn away.

"Watchin' ye two lads, I almost wish this story would turn oot like the tale o' James Goodfellow and the body snatchers," the rector said, his voice rich with amusement. "Do ye ken it, Lady Darby?"

"Ah, no, I don't," I turned to reply, carefully avoiding looking into the grave. I pivoted away again, ostensibly to keep the wind at my back and the hood over my head, but really I wanted to ignore what was happening behind me.

"Well, James Goodfellow was walkin' home late one night—they say after courtin' a girl—and he happened to see a light in the churchyard here. Curiosity gettin' to him, he snuck closer and saw a pony 'n cart hid in the glebe. Well, he gave the pony a skelp on the rump and set it runnin' off." The rector chuckled, while below him I could hear Gage and Trevor grunting in some sort of effort. "The thieves were forced to chase after it, and while they were gone, ole' James crept into the graveyard, hid the body he found in the coffin they'd opened, and climbed inside himself."

I glanced over my shoulder at him in wide-eyed surprise.

He grinned, clearly enjoying my shock. "The body snatchers returned and hoisted the coffin onto the cart and drove off. 'Twas aboot ten minutes later that one o' the men leaned against ole James and shouted, 'Jock, this body's warm!' Well, James couldna miss oot on this opportunity, so he sat up and proclaimed, 'If you'd been where I've been, you'd be warm, too!' "

The rector threw his head back and laughed, and I cracked a smile, as much from watching his enjoyment as in appreciation of the story.

"You can imagine how quickly those thieves took off after that. Left the pony 'n cart all to James."

I turned to look at the late Lord Fleming's obelisk, curious whether this was one of the stories Lady Fleming had derided. It did sound a bit embellished, but it was certainly entertaining. I couldn't help but wonder if there was any truth to it.

I studied the obelisk's inscription—Lord Fleming's full name and dates. And then something at the top right corner of the surface bearing the engraving caught my eye.

I frowned. It was a tiny red mark—a slash of color barely two inches long.

I moved closer, leaning down to get a better look. It appeared to be very smooth, almost glossy. I reached out with my gloved hand to run a finger over it, but it did not smudge or come away on my fingertip. Tugging the glove off my hand, I ran my fingers over the cold stone again, suddenly realizing what the red substance was.

"It's sealing wax." I gasped.

"What?" Gage called up to me in confusion.

"See this red mark," I demanded in excitement, pointing to the spot in question. "It's sealing wax."

Both men stared at me blankly.

"There was a mark just like it on Lord Buchan's gravestone."

Gage's eyes widened and he rose from his crouch, where he'd been examining the inside of the coffin. "Of course! Why didn't we think of it before? If the men doing the actual grave robbing are these criminals from Edinburgh, as we suspect, then it's highly unlikely they can read. So how do they know which graves to disturb?"

"The main person responsible must be marking them. Which means . . ." I stood up, turning to look around me ". . . he visited here recently."

"He visited all the grave sites," Gage exclaimed, hoisting

himself up out of the grave and then reaching down to help Trevor.

Once my brother was on solid ground, Gage turned to address the rector. "Do you recall any visitors to the grave-yard recently? Maybe in the last fortnight. Particularly any strangers."

The rector, who'd been observing our conversation in awed silence, stammered, trying to find his words. "Er, hmm . . . well, let me see. In the last fortnight?" He furrowed his brow in thought. "Well, we've had the normal parishioners." He tapped his finger to his chin. "But no strangers. O' course, I'm no' always here. I'm often oot vistin' those who are too sick and elderly to make it to the church."

Which meant our quarry had probably visited during one of those times. He'd been exceptionally clever up until now, and there was no reason we shouldn't expect him to continue to be.

The rector shrugged. "I'm sorry. The only guest I can recall is the young man who came with Lady Fleming's nephew."

"Who was that?" Gage asked.

He frowned. "I dinna recall exactly, but he was a Lord something-or-other. They were visitin' the late Mr. Young's grave."

I turned to the rector with a start. "Wait. Mr. Archibald Young?"

"Aye, well, that's the son's name. His father was Alvin Young."

I glanced at Gage. "Was the friend who accompanied him a Lord Shellingham?"

"Aye. That's it." The rector smiled. "Introduced him as his cousin, though on his father's side. No relation to Lady Fleming."

"Do you think it's a coincidence?" Trevor asked grimly, aware of the players involved.

Gage's nostrils flared like a predator picking up his prey's scent. "I highly doubt it."

## CHAPTER TWENTY-NINE

Following my suggestion, and the rector's directions, we drove along the road that roughly paralleled the River Teviot in search of Geordie's abode. We found it tucked among the trees at a bend in the river. It was hardly more than a shack, with no windows and only one warped door. He yelled out for us to enter when Gage knocked on the rough wood, and when we stepped inside, it was to find him seated before a table staring at a dusty, unopened bottle of amber liquid. His hair was uncombed and his face sported several days' growth of a beard. From the look in his eyes and the slump to his shoulders, I suspected he'd been sitting that way for a very long time.

He blinked up at us and heaved a weary sigh, his only reaction to the sight of three upper-class people standing in the doorway of his hovel. I didn't know if he was resigned to us or too numbed by alcohol to care. The room was barely warmer than it was outside, and there was a distinctly sour odor coming from Geordie's general vicinity, so I hung back by the door, allowing Gage to take the reins of the conversation.

He briefly introduced us before moving straight to the reason for our visit. "We understand you were the watchman at the church graveyard on the night Lord Fleming's grave was disturbed."

Geordie looked up at him with unresponsive eyes, his fingers still wrapped loosely around either side of the liquor bottle sitting on the table before him.

Gage pulled out the chair opposite him and sat down. "We were told you fell asleep, possibly with the aid of some strong spirits . . ." his gaze flicked down to the bottle ". . . and that's why you didn't hear anything. Is that true?"

His gaze dropped to the bottle before him, one corner of his mouth tightening. "'Twas also windy," he replied in a rough voice.

I could understand that. The blustery weather this morning had made it difficult to hear each other a few feet away, let alone across an entire graveyard.

But Gage did not sympathize so easily. "Do you know what I think, Geordie? I think it's all a lie." He spoke in a calm but implacable voice, leaning forward over the table. "I think you made that all up because you didn't want to tell the truth."

Geordie's hands flexed around the bottle.

Gage sat back, crossing his arms over his chest. "How much did they bribe you?"

Trevor and I stood quietly by the door watching Geordie, wondering what thoughts were flickering through his head. Gage looked ready to sit there for hours, if necessary, until the Scotsman talked. Fortunately, it only took about a minute of this silent standoff before the man broke.

"Five pounds," he mumbled.

Gage's mouth twisted in skepticism. "Just five pounds? You must have been pretty desperate if that's all it took."

Geordie scowled at the bottle. "'Twasn't the money." He finally looked up into Gage's stern visage. "They gave me no choice. They said I could take the blunt an' look the other way or they'd shoot me."

After what had happened to Dodd, I fully believed this explanation. The only wonder was that they gave the man a choice instead of killing him straight out. But maybe their employer hadn't been happy with the mess they'd made of the snatching at Dryburgh Abbey. Maybe murder had not been on that man's agenda.

Geordie turned to appeal to me and Trevor when Gage said nothing. "What was I s'posed to do? I got a wife and bairn to feed." His mouth screwed up and he muttered, "No' that that's done me any guid now. Me wife left an' took the bairn when she heard I'd fallen asleep after s'posedly drinkin'. I swore I hadna. But she didna believe me." His head sank lower on his shoulders.

Gage reached out to wrap his fingers around the neck of the bottle, pulling it out of Geordie's hands. "Well, starting back up now isn't going to make her return." He thunked the bottle down on his side of the wooden surface.

Geordie shook his head. "She's no' comin' back this time."

"She will when she hears about the caretaker these body snatchers killed in a graveyard just north of here."

He blinked up at him in surprise, and a light returned to his eyes. It was clear he didn't know what to say, so Gage helped him along.

"I'll make sure the rector along with anyone else of consequence knows the truth, *if* you'll help us catch these men."

Geordie sat up straighter and nodded vigorously. "Anythin'. What can I do?"

He held up a hand to calm him. "All we need at the moment is information. Did you get a good look at them?"

"One o' 'em. The other three sorta hung back in the shadows."

"All right. Describe him."

Geordie squinted, thinking back. "He were tall, an' real rough lookin'. Like he'd rolled in a trough. His hair were real oily. Oh, an' he had a long scar across his forehead . . ." he lifted his finger to illustrate, drawing a diagonal from mid hairline almost to the ear ". . . from here to here."

Gage glanced back at me, and I removed the sketch of Curst Eckie from my reticule and handed it to him. He unfolded it and laid it on the table in front of Geordie. "Is this the man?"

Geordie instantly perked up. "Aye. That's him."

"What else can you tell me? Did they say where they'd come from or where they were going?"

Geordie's face fell again. "Nay. And I hid in the watchtower 'til they were gone." He frowned down at his hands where they rested on the tabletop. "I didna want to give 'em any reason to change their mind."

Gage studied the scruffy man a moment longer and then rose to his feet. Geordie looked up at him hopefully.

"I'll tell the rector the truth about what happened, and hopefully he can relay that information to your wife." He picked up the bottle of liquor. "In the meantime, I suggest you bathe and take care of yourself. Don't give her any reason to believe you really have started drinking again."

"Wait," I said, stepping forward.

Gage paused in his progress toward the door. His brow lowered in displeasure.

"Just one more question," I told him and then turned to address Geordie, who was looking up at me with some misgiving. "Was there a woman? Perhaps someone who remained with the horses?"

He shook his head. "I dinna see one."

I thanked him and then pivoted to go, ignoring Gage's probing look. I had told him about Bonnie Brock's sister and his claim that she'd run off with one of these men. It only made sense to ask whether she'd been seen since Geordie was the only person we'd discovered so far to have had a recent run-in with these body snatchers and lived to tell about it.

A few minutes later as our carriage rolled down the drive, I peered out the window to find Geordie hurrying toward the river with some type of linen slung over his shoulder. I shivered at the thought of bathing in such chilly water, but I supposed the man had no other option. Most people were not as privileged as I was, with servants to heat and carry water for them, or advanced plumbing systems to deliver water from cisterns on the roof.

Gage stared down at the crude label of the whiskey bottle in his hands and then offered it to Trevor across the carriage. "I imagine these are rather crude spirits, more fit to burn in a lamp than drink."

Trevor grimaced. "Worse. Best to just dump it out."

When we returned to the church, Gage leapt out to apprise the rector of the information Geordie had given us, leaving my brother and me alone for a moment. A somewhat awkward silence descended and I considered pressing Trevor about my concerns regarding him and the estate, but I realized there would never be enough time before Gage returned. So instead I asked if he planned to come up to Edinburgh in the spring.

"Yes. Probably sometime after Alana's baby is born."

I nodded, adjusting the kid leather of my glove on my left hand.

"When do you plan to return to Edinburgh?"

"I don't know," I admitted. "Certainly not until this inquiry is over. Maybe sometime in February."

I wasn't entirely sure why this conversation felt so stilted, but I could tell that Trevor felt the strain as well. He kept his gaze fixed out the window.

"Then you should know we've received our invitation to Lady Kerswood's Burns Night Ball."

I groaned. "She's still hosting those?"

Trevor nodded regretfully.

Every year Lady Kerswood hosted a Burns Night Ball in a poorly disguised attempt to outshine my aunt and uncle's Hogmanay Ball. One year Lady Kerswood had tried to plan a ball on December thirty-first alongside my aunt, inviting many of the same people. When she received mostly regrets, the guests preferring to continue their annual tradition at Clintmains Hall, Lady Kerswood opted to move her event to Burns Night, pretending that was what she'd wished to do all along.

Burns Night was traditionally celebrated on an evening around Robert Burns's birthday, January twenty-fifth, and included readings of his poetry as well as Scottish food and music. Unfortunately, Lady Kerswood had transformed what would normally be a fun night into an overextravagance of all things Scots. She insisted everyone wear clan dress and talk in thick brogues, though she herself was exempted, claiming she was too delicate to manage it. And rather than wear Lord Kerswood's clan colors, she instead decked herself out as Mary, Queen of Scots, or Flora Mac-Donald, or some other famous Scottish figure.

For whatever reason, our aunt felt some obligation to attend, and insisted that the rest of us join them whenever we were in the area, no matter how much we loathed it.

"Are you sure she included me in the invitation?" I asked, actually hopeful for once that I had been snubbed.

Trevor's expression was not amused. "She did. And don't even think about trying to get out of it."

"Trying to get out of what?" Gage asked as he rejoined us inside the carriage. He wrapped on the roof with his fist and the horses set off again. He glanced from me to Trevor as we glowered at each other. I was the one to finally speak up.

"Lady Kerswood's Burns Night Ball."

"Burns Night? The poet?"

"Yes."

Gage settled back against the squabs. "When is it? Am I invited as well?"

"I'm sure you'll be welcome," Trevor replied.

"Excellent," he declared, his eyes warm as he gazed down at me by his side. "Then I'll finally get a chance to dance with your sister."

I felt my cheeks begin to heat under his intense regard, and couldn't stop a small smile of pleasure from curling my lips, delighted that he'd remembered.

"Didn't you both attend a ball in Edinburgh?" Trevor asked, ruining the moment. "Why didn't you dance with her there?"

I parted my lips, trying to figure out how to answer him without actually telling him the truth. Gage came to our rescue, all the while never removing his gaze from mine.

"We were pursuing a suspect."

I inhaled deeply and offered him another smile, this time of gratitude.

His eyes dipped to my lips, and I was sure that if Trevor had not been there, he would have kissed me.

When we arrived at Marefield House, the butler informed us with a sober smile that Lord Fleming was in his study and expected us. But when I asked if I might be shown to Lady Fleming instead, his eyebrows rose to his hairline. Apparently he'd overheard some of our conversation the previous evening, or simply deduced Lady Fleming's displeasure from the manner in which she stormed out.

Out of the corner of my eye, I saw Gage's face twitch in suppressed amusement, but I dared not look at him. We had decided on this course of action during our drive here, hoping that Lady Fleming might be more willing to talk without her husband present. If she suspected her nephew's involvement in these body snatchings as we did, then she might be keeping it from her husband. I had argued that she was more likely to speak with Gage than me—a woman she clearly despised—but he'd insisted that a tête-à-tête between two ladies was more suitable and would draw less suspicion from Lord Fleming. I had to reluctantly agree, though I wasn't looking forward to bearding the lioness in her den.

The butler coughed into his palm, quickly recovering himself. "Of course." He swiveled to look at the footman stationed behind him. "Robert, please show Lady Darby to the conservatory."

I followed the young man through the corridors to the back corner of the house. Like most conservatories, the ceiling and three of the walls were made of glass, but unlike the maze that our garden room at Blakelaw House had become, this one was arranged in neat rows. The footman left me at the door and I wandered to the left, following the sound of clay scraping against wood. I rounded a rhododendron bush and found Lady Fleming standing before a long crude wooden table, her gloved hands pressing down the soil around a plant inside a pot. The flora was green and leafy, but with my limited knowledge of horticulture, I had no idea what kind of plant it might be.

She must have sensed my presence, for she looked up, sparing me only a cursory glance before returning her concentration to the plant before her. "Lady Darby, how kind of you to visit me." The bite in her voice indicated just how ironic those words were. "I assume Mr. Gage is closeted with my husband."

"And my brother," I added, advancing toward her.

She raised her eyes again at this statement, but did not comment.

I paused to rest my hands on the rough wood of the table a few feet from her to observe her efforts. She pushed aside the pot she was working on and pulled an empty one toward herself. Then using a trowel, she shoveled a small bit of dirt into the pot and reached inside with her hands to form the earth into a well.

"I assume you didn't come here to watch me transfer my ferns," she remarked, putting a great deal more effort than was called for into the task before her. "Or do I mistake the matter?"

"No. Actually, I came to ask you about your nephew."

Lady Fleming's hands stilled for a second, and then she renewed her ministrations. "Which nephew? I have several."

"Mr. Archibald Young. But I think you already knew that."

She lifted her gaze, and for an instant I could see the fear and uncertainty I was looking for in her eyes before it was swiftly masked by haughty annoyance. Her mouth pressed into a thin line, and her chin lifted so that she could stare down her nose at me.

"I have no idea *what* you're talking about. I wasn't even aware that you were acquainted," her voice snapped, almost in accusation.

I reached out to finger one of the coarse leaves on a plant she had already finished transplanting. "Yes. We were introduced at Lord and Lady Rutherford's Hogmanay Ball. The same night that Lord Buchan's body was stolen from his grave nearby."

Her eyes were wide and almost wild, puzzling the implications, but the rest of her was stiff and unyielding. "I hope that you aren't about to make unsavory accusations about my nephew. Because unlike you, I can assure you that the members of my family revere the dead."

I didn't rise to her bait, understanding now that she was just lashing out in panic. "Lady Fleming, we know," I told her gently. "We know your nephew visited the Beckford Parish Churchyard a few days before the late Lord Fleming's bones were stolen."

"He was visiting his father's grave."

"We know that he is friends with several young men who also recently had deceased family members' graves disturbed. And that some of these friends have providently come into large sums of money."

Her gaze dropped to the side, but I continued on implacably.

"And we know that you are already aware of much of this. That you already suspect your nephew's involvement, but you're too terrified to admit it."

"I . . . know no such thing," she protested, her voice beginning to tremble. "So you can take your baseless accusations and leave my house immediately." She pointed toward the door with her dirt-smeared finger, but rather than retreat, I advanced.

"Lady Fleming, if your nephew is involved, the best way you can help him is by telling us what you know," I reasoned. "If our suspicions are correct, he and his friends have fallen into league with a dangerous band of criminals from Edinburgh. When they started out, their plan may have seemed simple, but now that these body snatchers know how lucrative this ransom trade can be, they may not let them stop."

Her hand had dropped to the table and she was now shaking with some suppressed emotion.

I stared intently into her eyes. "They've already killed one man. Do you honestly think they would hesitate to kill another if your nephew objected to their actions?"

The fear she'd been struggling to hide suddenly swam to the surface, making her eyes gleam. I waited for her to come to her own decision, hoping she would trust me with whatever she was concealing. When her shoulders dipped and she turned to press her hands flat to the table in front of her in support, I knew she was about to confide in me.

"I . . . I don't know that he's involved," she began hesitantly. "But . . . he came to me for money a few months ago."

"How much?"

"Several thousand pounds."

My eyebrows rose in surprise. "Did he tell you what it was for?"

She nodded. "He wanted to marry. But the girl's father refuses to allow the match since Archie's income as a second son is so limited. He said he wanted to invest the money in a shipping venture, that he would triple his capital when this ship docked in London."

She closed her eyes tightly, and I could see she was close to tears. "Why didn't I just lend him the money? If I had, then he wouldn't have gotten into this mess."

"Why didn't you?" I asked out of curiosity.

She sighed. "Because Archie isn't always the most responsible. He's tried schemes like this before. And my husband has said in the past that shipping ventures aren't always the safest way to invest. If the ship sinks in a storm or is robbed of its cargo, or sometimes if it's only heavily delayed, you can lose everything."

"Did Mr. Young and Lord Shellingham stay here recently? Within the past few weeks?"

She nodded, brushing her blond curls away from her forehead with the back of her wrist. In this light, I could see streaks of gray just starting to show at her temples. "About a week ago. For two nights. They said they were just passing through."

I smiled in commiseration. "Did they mention where they'd come from or where they were headed? Do you know where they intended to stay?"

Her brow furrowed. "I . . . I thought they said they'd come from somewhere in England, and that they were headed to a relative of Lord Shellingham's near Edinburgh. But beyond that I'm afraid I don't know. Maybe to Lord Shellingham's estate—Pickwick House, near Berwick."

The timing was simply too perfect. Not only had these two young men been at Clintmains Hall on the night that Lord Buchan's bones were stolen, but they'd also been "somewhere in England" around the time the ransom was paid and sent through the Cheviot Hills into England. Then they were here, in time to mark Lord Fleming's gravestone before reaching Musselburgh a few days later, where we'd seen Lord Shellingham.

I wondered if Lord Shellingham's Pickwick House was their headquarters. After all, it was located within easy distance of Edinburgh, as well as the Borders. Was that where they stored the bones between the time they were stolen and the ransom was paid? Were the Edinburgh body snatchers staying there as well or somewhere nearby? It seemed worth looking into.

Lady Fleming had been watching my face as I puzzled through this, and she asked in some anxiety, "You said you'd help him. What are you going to do?"

"First we need to find him and talk to him. If he'll confide in us and let us help him out of the mess he's landed himself in, I'm sure the magistrate will be more lenient with him."

"Perhaps if they paid back all the money . . ." Her words stammered to a stop upon seeing my doubtful expression.

"I'm afraid that would be quite impossible. Two of his friends have already spent tidy sums of it."

She pressed the back of her hand to her forehead, and I hastened to reassure her.

"Don't despair. I promise we'll do what we can."

She looked up at me, inhaled deeply, and nodded.

"The best thing you can do is carry on as before. And should your nephew or any of his friends return here, send word to me at Blakelaw House."

She inhaled again. "I will."

I turned to go, but her next words brought me up short.

"You know. You're not what I expected."

I glanced over my shoulder and offered her a tight smile. "I rarely am."

# CHAPTER THIRTY

The next few days were spent in careful planning. Trevor recruited a cattle farmer and his son who swore they knew the Cheviot Hills as intimately as anyone, and arranged for them to be ready on short notice should we need them to guide us into the hills on another ransom drop. We had no way of knowing whether the culprits would use the same method as the last time, but we'd decided it was best to be prepared in the event that they did. Our hope was still to catch the men before the ransom note was even delivered, but if we didn't, we would be as ready as we could be to catch them when the ransom was paid.

With the information we'd uncovered in Beckford, Mr. Young, Lord Shellingham, Mr. Erskine, and Mr. Fergusson had jumped to the top of our list of suspects, but Gage wanted to be certain of a few last details before we confronted them.

"Do your best to already know the answer to your question before you ever ask it," he told me with a sharp-eyed gaze. "Then it's harder for a suspect to mislead you, and easier to intimidate them into giving you the truth. If they think you already know, they'll recognize the futility in lying."

So in that effort, we took Anderley with us to Clintmains Hall the next day when we visited my aunt and uncle. Gage believed, and I had to agree, that a fellow servant might be able to extract more information from the staff than their employers could, especially if the servant knew they'd done something wrong. And true to his theory, Anderley did return with one juicy tidbit of information we hadn't known before. Something that when combined with the information Sim's Christie had told us about the two men leaving the Hogmanay Ball pointed the finger even more squarely at the quartet of young men. So we made plans to visit Pickwick House the next day.

Pickwick House was located on a swath of land between the River Tweed and the Whiteadder, just a few miles west of Berwick. The drive from Blakelaw was a little more than two hours. We did our best to stop at every inn and pub on our way, flashing the sketches I'd drawn of Curst Eckie and Sore John to ask if they'd seen any rough-looking strangers in the past few weeks or months. One woman at a tavern near Coldstream said she thought she'd seen the pair of men a few weeks back, but she couldn't swear to it. She complained that it had been dark and she hadn't been looking for trouble. No one else admitted to seeing them, and I didn't know whether to consider that a good or a bad sign as we neared the manor.

Either way I was nervous. What if the body snatchers were staying on Lord Shellingham's estate? What if they became suspicious of our arrival? Trevor and Anderley had joined us, and I had made sure to bring my gun, but two gentlemen, a valet, and a woman with a single-shot pistol were hardly a match for four Edinburgh criminals, and perhaps Lord Shellingham and his friends. I wanted to believe that the four gentlemen who had planned this would not harm us, but I didn't know them well enough to be sure. I had seen with my own eyes how even good men could be driven to do horrible things if the pressure to do so and their own fear were strong enough.

The approach to Pickwick House was made through

a thick copse of trees that widened suddenly to reveal the manor. The main block of the house stood directly in front of us, with stairs leading up to a four-columned portico. Wings stretched out on either side of the main block to wrap around the drive, enclosing it almost like a courtyard. The drive branched off to the left and to the right toward other parts of the manor. We all leaned forward to peer out the windows on either side of the carriage as it entered the courtyard, trying to see whether trouble lay down either of the branches of these paths, but they were both clear of people and obstructions.

The weather had been inhospitable all morning. Intermittent periods of icy rain had spat at us from the sky. A few degrees cooler and the precipitation would have been snow, but the temperature hovered stubbornly above freezing, allowing the wind to whip sharp pellets of rain at our faces instead of soft snowflakes.

I cowered inside my cloak as Gage, Trevor, and I descended from the carriage. Anderley would ride in the coach around to the stables and enter through the servants' entrance, as expected, which would also allow him the opportunity to search that part of the property for any sign of the Edinburgh criminals. I welcomed Gage's steadying arm as we climbed the dozen or more stairs to the front doors. When we reached the top, we'd expected a servant to be there to attend to us, but instead we were forced to wait. Trevor knocked several times, and his fist pounds became harder with each minute that passed.

As time stretched, an uneasy feeling came over me. I glanced over my shoulder into the courtyard below us, but it was as gray and empty as when we'd arrived. Regardless, we were exposed here, and I couldn't be sure whether it was the prickles of chilly rain striking against my back that so unsettled me or something else. Whatever it was, I decided I didn't like this place, no matter its ornate, classical beauty. It was eerie and rather desolate, as if it were only a hollow illusion.

"Do you think it's deserted?" Trevor turned to ask, his brow furrowed in frustration.

Gage grimly surveyed our surroundings, his face glistening with the cold spray of the rain. "A manor this large? Surely there's someone here. A skeleton staff, at the very least."

Trevor frowned and reached out for the doorknob. It turned in his hand, and the door swung open a crack. He looked back at us one more time, and then pushed the door open. If nothing else, we needed to get out of the stinging rain, at least long enough to decide what to do.

Trevor crossed the threshold into the darkened interior. "Hello!" he called. "Is anyone here?"

Gage and I followed, staring around us at the vast, echoing entrance hall. The gloomy light passing through the windows above illuminated a black and white tiled floor and a round wooden table standing at the center of the space. A grand staircase swept up the right side of the room, along the hall's rounded walls, ending in shadows above.

This was all I had time to notice before the percussive bang of a gun broke the silence. The window above us shattered, and glass shards rained down on us as we dove for the ground, tinkling as they struck the floor. I gasped and then cringed at the sharp sensation on my leg. I worried that a piece of glass had sliced into my skin, but then as the icy sensation spread, I realized we'd dived into our own growing puddles of water as it had dripped off our clothing.

Our ears still ringing from the noise, Gage pushed himself upright and dragged me toward the center of the room.

"Stay low," he ordered.

He shoved me beneath the round table and told me to stay. Then he and Trevor took off running toward the stairs in a crouch. I wanted to yell at them to stop, but by the time my wits and voice had returned sufficiently to do so, they were already halfway up the stairs. I peered out to watch as they made their way upward, their backs pressed again the wall behind them and their pistols drawn. As they disap-

peared from my sight, I wanted to stick my head out farther
to see where they'd gone, but my self-preservation instincts
kicked in and I remained hidden beneath the heavy wooden
surface.

I glanced around me, trying to see into the gloom, but
all that greeted my gaze was a vast room with hazy shadows
at its edges. My hands were shaking as I fumbled with my
reticule, trying to extract my pistol. I stopped and forced
myself to take a deep breath. I could do no one any good,
least of all myself, if I didn't calm down enough to be able
to see and shoot straight.

From above I heard a shout and then the thud of running
feet. I wrapped my fingers around the smooth wooden grip
of my gun and leaned as far out as I dared to see up toward
the top of the stairs. The house fell silent, except for the
pounding of my heart in my ears. I strained to hear any
sound to indicate Gage's and Trevor's whereabouts, my only
relief that I hadn't yet heard another gunshot.

Then I heard a click and shush of sound coming from
behind me. I whirled about, narrowing my eyes in an effort
to pierce the gloom. A blur of movement finally caught my
eye, and then there was another click. I realized it was the
sound of a door closing. I followed the progression of the
shape, watching as it formed into a man who dashed past
me toward the front door. But before he could open it, I
sprang from my crouch, my pistol trained on his back.

"Stop! Or I'll shoot."

The man skidded to a halt, his shoes crunching in the
glass. He wore a long, many-caped greatcoat, but no hat.

"Turn around," I ordered. "And keep your hands where I
can see them."

He slowly pivoted, his hands stretched out to his sides.
When the light from the windows finally fell on his face, I
frowned. But his reaction was by far more comical.

His eyes flared wide and his head drew back in astonishment. "Lady Darby!"

"Lord Shellingham," I replied, echoing him, but with far less shock and awe.

"You . . . you're working with them?"

I scowled. "Yes. Didn't you notice me when you fired your gun at us?"

"I didn't shoot. That was Young."

I nodded, not really surprised.

I tilted my head, listening for Gage and Trevor again. I wondered if I should yell, to let them know I'd caught one of the men. I decided against it. A shout would also reach the ears of Shellingham's associates, and I didn't want them stumbling upon us and turning the situation against me.

"I should have known," Lord Shellingham snapped bitterly. I turned to focus on his now angry visage. "What with your history, it only makes sense that you'd cast your lot in with a bunch of lowly thugs."

"What?" I demanded in confusion.

But the sound of Gage's scolding voice snagged both of our attention. I backed up so that I could better watch their progression down the stairs and keep Lord Shellingham in my sight.

Gage and Trevor together were dragging a repentant Mr. Young between them. Trevor carried a rifle in his other hand, presumably taken from the culprit when they caught up with him.

"I . . . I didn't know it was you," Mr. Young stammered in protest. "I would never have shot at you had I known."

"Who did you think we were?" Gage demanded.

"Let me guess," I said, turning to glare at Lord Shellingham. "A bunch of lowly thugs?"

He at least had the grace to look sheepish for accusing me of working with a group of body snatchers.

"Ah, Lord Shellingham," Gage murmured, giving him a hard stare. "I thought it likely you were here as well."

"Yes, well . . ." He didn't seem to know how to answer that.

"Where are your staff?"

I was not pleased to see him look even more embarrassed when he admitted, "There are only two. One's gone to town to purchase supplies, and the other is in the kitchens."

"Entertaining my valet, no doubt." Gage eyed our host up and down, from his unruly hair to his scuffed boots. "Kiera, I think you can lower your weapon. Lord Shellingham isn't going anywhere. At least, not until we've had a nice long chat."

I hesitated, somewhat reluctant to do so. Gage cracked a smile at my obvious aggravation with the young lord. Resisting the impulse, I lowered my pistol and reached down to tuck it back inside my reticule. Feeling his eyes on me, I glared through my lashes at Mr. Young, who was watching me rather slack-jawed.

"Now, is there a place where we might talk?" Gage asked Lord Shellingham, keeping enough bite in his voice to be sure the man understood it wasn't really a question.

"Yes." He turned to lead us toward the back of the entry hall, to the door he'd entered through earlier. Gage allowed me to fall in step behind Shellingham, and I derived some enjoyment in the way the young man's shoulders inched up around his ears. Let him worry I might actually shoot him. It only served him right.

He opened a door near the end of the passage and gestured me into a parlor of some sorts. I lifted my eyebrows and waited for him to enter first. He swallowed and nodded.

Clearly the room was one of the only in the manor being used. A fire burned in the hearth and two candelabras were lit and spaced about the room to provide more light on such a gloomy day. A table in the corner was stacked with dirty dishes from at least two meals, and a series of teacups and plates dusted with crumbs littered the other surfaces of the room. A game of cards had been begun and abandoned, both players' hands discarded on the low table standing between two settees.

If I looked beyond the mess and clutter, I could tell that the room was lavishly decorated, with Chippendale furniture and sumptuous fabrics. The wallpaper was hand painted in shades of pale yellow and smoky blue. A small crystal chandelier even hung from the ceiling, its teardrops still glistening though it was unlit.

I settled in an elbow chair near the fire, welcoming the warmth as the cold of the weather and the wetness on my skirts had begun to seep into my bones. Gage directed both men to sit on one of the settees while he and Trevor sat across from them. My brother rested the rifle across his lap. A rather effective maneuver on his part, I thought, as Mr. Young stared down at it and swallowed.

"Before we begin, I want to warn you, we already know everything." Gage gave both men a hard glare. "So it behooves you to be honest with us. Do you understand?"

Mr. Young nodded quickly and eagerly, while Lord Shellingham followed with a little more composure.

"Now, tell us how this began." When neither of them responded, Gage prompted. "Whose idea was it?"

Mr. Young glanced at his cousin and then began to stammer out his reply. "I . . . I . . . I guess it was mine, sir."

I was surprised to hear that. Mr. Young didn't seem the brightest or most enterprising of the group, but looks and manners sometimes deceived.

"Why?"

"Well, I . . . I wanted to marry Miss Musgraves, sir. And her . . . her father wouldn't agree to the match."

Miss Musgraves? The girl we'd met in St. Boswells? Her father did seem like a tyrant.

"So you needed the money to convince him of it?" Gage queried.

Mr. Young's brow lowered in confusion, and he glanced once more at his cousin, who appeared similarly baffled. "The money, sir?"

Gage scowled. "Come now. We know all about the ransoms. Lord Shellingham obviously needs the money for his estate and you need it to marry Miss Musgrave. Need I explain Mr. Fergusson and Mr. Erskine's motives as well?"

The two young men turned to stare at each other, and it was Lord Shellingham who then spoke up. "Mr. Gage, I think there's been some mistake. We don't know anything about any ransom. And while Mr. Fergusson and Mr. Erskine are acquaintances, they had no dealing in this."

Gage arched his eyebrows haughtily. "Then you didn't hire a group of Edinburgh body snatchers to dig up your grandfather's . . ." he nodded at Mr. Young ". . . and your aunt's grandfather-in-law's bones and hold them for ransom?"

If the subject matter hadn't been so horrifying, their reactions might have been highly amusing. Lord Shellingham's eyes widened and he jerked back into the cushions of the sofa, while Mr. Young leapt up from his seat, waving his arms wildly as they both spouted vehement protests.

Gage stood up, raising his voice to be heard over their commotion and ordered Mr. Young to sit down. When he had complied and their voices fell silent, he stood over them, gesturing toward the door through which we'd come. "If you're not involved, then what they hell was that all about?" he roared. "You certainly didn't almost shoot me in the head for no reason."

"We . . . we thought you were *them*," Lord Shellingham replied.

Gage narrowed his eyes. "And why would they be coming after you if you weren't involved?"

"Because we saw them."

Gage inhaled deeply through his nostrils, his patience growing very thin. "When?"

"During the Hogmanay Ball," Mr. Young said. "And a few days ago."

Gage turned to look at me, his face tight with the strain of not revealing his puzzlement. He backed away and returned to his seat across from them. "You'd better explain."

"Well, like I said, I wanted to marry Miss Musgrave, and

she wanted to marry me, but her father would not let us. So . . ." He glanced at his cousin, who nodded in encouragement. He swallowed. "We decided that we would elope."

My eyebrows rose. Perhaps I *had* underestimated Mr. Young.

"I convinced my cousin to help us. And we realized that Hogmanay would be the perfect time. Everyone in the area attends Lord and Lady Rutherford's ball, even Mr. Musgrave, and they're often out until the wee hours of the morning." His gaze dropped to his lap where his hands were fidgeting. "Plus Miss Musgrave told me that her father often overindulged. So by the time he woke up, we would hopefully already be married at the Old Toll House in Lamberton," he explained. "It's closer than Gretna Green." The most notorious of all hasty wedding sights, particularly for eloping couples popping over the border from England to obtain a quick marriage.

"How did you arrange this?" I asked, wondering how Miss Musgrave had gotten away from her father long enough for them even to discuss it.

Mr. Young flushed. "We would meet at the abbey. There's a walking bridge over the river not far from Miss Musgrave's home, so she would convince her maid to let her walk there."

"Did you and Lord Shellingham meet her there earlier in the day on Hogmanay?"

He nodded. "To be certain all was set."

Which explained the pair of men Lord Buchan's maid had seen that day, as well as the couple the Nun of Dryburgh had babbled on about. I suspected Miss Musgrave had also left a bundle of clothes at the abbey to retrieve before they eloped. Though I didn't know why she wouldn't have simply brought it with her that night. Unless she intended to bring more than one set of extra garments.

I shared a look of resigned frustration with Gage, feeling a bit like a fool for not seeing all of this before.

"Miss Musgrave was to pretend she was ill that night,"

Mr. Young continued to explain. "So that she could sneak away and meet me at the abbey at midnight."

"And you bribed one of the Rutherford footmen to meet you by a side door with your coats and hats during the ball, so that you wouldn't draw any suspicion," Gage supplied, relaying the information Anderley had uncovered for us.

Mr. Young nodded. "We arrived at the ball on horseback, and Shelly arranged for his valet to meet us with a hired carriage a short distance from the abbey. So we set out on foot to the abbey." His face clouded with fear. "But about half a mile away, where the road curves north, we ran into these men. They pulled guns on us and . . . and told us they'd already killed one man that night, and that if we didn't want to be next, we'd turn back."

"Did you get a good look at them?"

Mr. Young stared down at the floor in front of him as if reliving the confrontation, so Lord Shellingham spoke up. "Well enough to recognize them when we saw them again at an inn just northwest of here."

"When was this?" Gage asked.

"The night of that snowfall. We got caught up in it and stopped to warm ourselves before continuing on."

"What were they doing? Passing through as well?"

He shook his head. "I don't know. But they were pretty deep in their cups, and I suspect they'd been there for at least a short while."

Gage flicked a glance at me before asking, "Were there any women with them?"

"There were a couple hanging about them. But I don't know if they were barmaids or local women or lasses they called their own. I didn't look very closely."

"Do you remember the village name?"

Shellingham glanced at his cousin. "Was it in Allanton?" But Mr. Young just shrugged. "I think that's right."

Gage sat back with a nod, crossing his arms over his chest. He eyed both men in contemplation.

"What happened to Miss Musgrave?" I asked, wondering how they could have returned to Clintmains Hall without at least checking to be sure she was safe. Surely they hadn't simply left her to stand there in the freezing cold, not knowing where they were? What if she'd run into the body snatchers? They might have done any number of horrible things to her.

Mr. Young's eyes saddened. "I don't know. I know she made it home safely."

"Safely" being a relative term.

"But now she won't talk to me. It's not my fault the elopement was botched."

This time I shared a look with my brother, and it was obvious that he was just as disgusted by Mr. Young's lack of chivalry as I was. I wouldn't be speaking to him either if I were in Miss Musgrave's shoes. In fact, I think I might just listen to my father and find another suitor.

"What of your friends Fergusson and Erskine and their sudden influx of blunt?" Trevor questioned them. "They both have relatives whose bodies were also dug up and ransomed. Are you going to tell us that's all just a coincidence?"

Lord Shellingham held up his hands. "I'm not responsible for the actions of those two. But if you're talking about the money Fergusson was gambling with at the Assembly Rooms last week, that came from a wager he won with Mr. Radcliffe. If you don't believe me, you can ask Radcliffe yourself. I'm sure he'd love to grumble about it some more."

I lifted my hand to my temples, rubbing them with my thumb and forefinger to suppress the massive headache beginning to build behind my eyes. Here we'd thought we'd finally caught the men responsible for setting these snatching-ransoms in motion, and we'd uncovered nothing. Sure, we'd answered some of our questions, but none of these answers had brought us closer to finding the culprits, only farther away.

Of course, Shellingham and Young could be lying, but I

didn't think so. The scheme was too elaborate to be a ruse, and it would be far too easy to find them out. I intended to verify their story, but I didn't expect to discover they'd lied.

Anyway, in Shellingham's case, there were far easier ways to replenish his coffers.

"Why don't you marry an heiress," I couldn't resist asking him. It was sadly the most common solution to such a predicament.

He flushed and frowned. "I'd rather not have to resort to that. It hardly seems fair to marry a girl just for her money. But . . ." He sighed. "I soon may have no choice."

I glanced around the room at all the fine furnishings. If the other rooms in the house were decorated in the same way . . .

"Why don't you sell some of the artwork and furnishings? Surely they're worth a great deal."

"I've been contemplating it." His face screwed up into a nasty smirk. "But my grandfather went to such an effort to build a lavish abode for his Prussian heiress, bankrupting the estate when she didn't marry him, it seems like a sacrilege to break up his shrine."

Gage ignored this display of resentment, justified though it might be, to return to the matter at hand. "Well, since you've finally told us the truth, can you think of anything else we should know? Anything perhaps you should have told us earlier?"

Shellingham and Young glanced at each other and then shook their heads.

"You didn't see anyone else leaving the ball? Encounter anyone else at or near the abbey?" Gage pressed.

Mr. Young frowned. "Well, several of the guests who stayed at Clintmains visited the abbey. But that doesn't make them guilty of anything."

"Who?"

He rattled off a few names, none of whom meant anything except Mr. Stuart.

Gage's eyes sought mine out, telling me he'd noticed as well.

So Mr. Stuart had visited Dryburgh Abbey sometime during the days prior to Lord Buchan's snatching. As Mr. Young said, that didn't make him guilty, but it was worth noting.

# CHAPTER THIRTY-ONE

"Isn't that Miss Musgrave's maid, Peggy?" I asked as the carriage rounded a corner in St. Boswells the next morning. She was bustling down the walk, her head lowered against the wind, with a package clutched under her arm.

Gage leaned over to see out the window. "Why, I think it is. How fortuitous," he said with a smirk. He began to reach toward the ceiling with his cane, but I stopped him.

"Wait until we reach those hedges before stopping the carriage. She won't wish to be seen speaking to us."

He complied, timing it so that the carriage stopped within the shade of two hedgerows, sheltering us from any prying eyes that might be watching from the houses nearby. I opened the carriage door and climbed out, waiting for Peggy to notice me.

She was nearly upon us before she looked up. Her eyes flared wide and then darted from side to side nervously.

"Peggy, I'm sorry to bother you. But we really must speak with you again. We thought it best do so away from the Musgrave house."

Her eyes searched mine and quickly came to the realization that I was not going to let the matter go. She could either speak to us here and hope to keep the discussion private, or face us in front of Mr. Musgrave later. I had no desire to put her in that situation, particularly since it would likely mean her position, but we needed to confirm Mr. Young and Lord Shellingham's story, and we could better gain access to Peggy than Miss Musgrave.

She sighed in resignation. I gestured for her to climb into the carriage and then followed after, closing the door behind us. She clutched her brown-paper-wrapped package before her like a shield and eyed Gage and me warily.

"We wish you no harm," I told her. "And we know you've been placed in an untenable position. But we need to know the truth about what happened on Hogmanay."

Her gaze continued to bounce back and forth between us, but she did not speak, forcing me to elaborate.

"We know about Mr. Young and Miss Musgrave. We also know about their plan to elope."

She seemed to shrink before our eyes, her shoulders crumpling inward and her head dropping. "Aye." She sighed again. "I didna ken aboot it at the time, but I was suspicious when Miss Alice suddenly declared she was too ill to attend the ball." Her mouth screwed up in a frown. "Right disappointed, too. You'd the right of it. I'd been lookin' forward to goin'. But Miss Alice pays no mind to that."

"What happened that evening? Did she sneak out?"

Now that we'd gotten her talking, she seemed happy to relieve herself of the secret, to tell her side of the story.

She narrowed her eyes. "I watched her all night, like a hawk. But at some point a lass's gotta . . ." she waved her hand, trying to find polite words ". . . take care o' things."

I nodded. And a servant couldn't very well use her employer's chamber pot. She would have to go down to the servants' quarters or outside to the privy.

"When I got back to her room, she was gone. Well, you can believe what a dither I was in." She shook her finger at us. "I ken the girl was up to no good. And I'd a good guess where she was goin'. I kent she'd seen Mr. Young at the abbey that morn, even though she's no' supposed to talk to him. I took off doon the river path, ready to drag that girl home by her hair if need be."

I wouldn't have blamed her. "Did you catch up with her?"

She lifted her chin. "Aye. Just afore that accursed bridge. She fought me, but I told her 'tweren't no way I was gonna let her run off like that. That she'd regret it forever." She sniffed. "No' that she'd regret losin' her father. But she'd regret losin' his money."

Out of the corner of my eye, I saw Gage's lips twitch.

Peggy shook her head, seeming to relive the anger she'd felt that night, and then she leaned forward. "In any case, that's when we heard the gunshot. Miss Alice didna want to believe me, but I've heard guns fired afore. 'Tis no' easily forgotten. And there were some sort o' lights o'er at the abbey. I told the lass that her suitor might no' be bright, but even he wouldna be daff enough to make such a commotion when he was plannin' to skulk off wi' her."

"Did you see anyone?" Gage asked.

She shook her head. "Nay. I hurried us away from there afore trouble found us."

Under the circumstances, that was probably the smartest thing she could've done. She'd probably saved her charge from a very unhappy fate. Had Miss Musgrave stumbled upon the body snatchers thinking it was Mr. Young, who knows what they might have done to her.

But unfortunately, it didn't help us.

Gage reached forward to pick up another package resting on the seat beside Peggy. Folding back the cloth, he showed her the fine pink muslin gown we'd found in the Chapter House at the abbey. "Does this belong to Miss Musgrave?"

Peggy's eyes narrowed in anger. "Aye. Let me guess. You found it at the abbey?"

"Yes."

Her jaw tightened and she shook her head slowly. "Why, that minx. She blamed *me* for losin' it. 'Twas goin' to be taken oot o' my wages."

Gage held the package out to her, but she pushed it back.

"Nay. You can keep it. It's one o' her favorites. Serves her right for doin' such a fool thing. But you can bet she's gonna hear all aboot this conversation, and how I convinced you no' to go to Mr. Musgrave. She can just explain to her da' how *she* lost that gown."

I smiled and glanced at Gage. "Well, should you ever need us to go to Mr. Musgrave . . ."

She grinned back, and it brightened her features. "I'll contact ye."

It must have been fairly obvious how frustrated Gage and I felt about our progress in the investigation, but my uncle did not comment on it when we stopped by Clintmains Hall to give him an update and find out if he'd uncovered anything useful. The discovery that Young, Shellingham, and their friends had nothing to do with the body snatchings was a blow. Especially as we'd now spent several days pursuing it, allowing the trail to the real culprit to grow cold. Our remaining suspects for the plan's instigator and ringleader were either in Edinburgh or destinations unknown, and the thugs they'd hired to do their dirty work had slunk off to wherever they hid between robberies.

"Lord Buchan wished me to convey his gratitude for your assistance in getting his uncle's remains back," Uncle Andrew informed us as he settled in the chair behind the desk in his study. Sunlight streamed in through the tall windows, illuminating the dust motes swirling in the air. "And hopes you'll both attend his uncle's reinterment ceremony."

"He hasn't already been reburied?" I asked in some surprise.

"No. Lord Buchan is actually having one of the vaults at the abbey prepared, so his uncle can be buried beneath the stone floor there. Which will take some time, but should dissuade any further mischief."

I shared a wide-eyed glance with Gage, recalling the Nun of Dryburgh's presence in just such a vault the night we visited her, and her mysterious words. "I told you to be buried here. Where you're safe. But you did not listen."

"Now, on to the nasty business of Lord Fleming's snatching." Uncle Andrew drummed his fingers on his desk. "I assume you propose to wait for this fourth ransom note to be delivered?"

Gage sighed heavily, sinking deeper into his chair. "I don't know that we have much of a choice. We don't have enough evidence to solidly point at any of our other suspects."

My uncle frowned. "What of this Mr. Collingwood? Didn't you say he contacted all of the families involved about this gold torc?"

"Yes. But he also seems to have contacted nearly everyone in the Society of Antiquaries, so that in and of itself is not enough to point the finger at him."

"And the leader of this Edinburgh street gang?"

Gage's face screwed up in a ferocious scowl. "Much as I'd like to believe it's him behind all this, there are too many variables."

My uncle stared at the remaining traces of Gage's black eye, the pale yellow circle of healing skin and slight pink dappling, likely guessing at the source of Gage's continued animosity. We'd been forced to explain the contusion during our previous visit with Anderley two days prior.

"Then who does that leave?" he asked.

I glanced at Gage, who stared silently at me, allowing me the opportunity to divulge what we'd discovered about Mr. Stuart. Knowing the man had been a guest in my uncle's home during their Hogmanay Ball, I did my best to relay our findings delicately, but my uncle's furrowed brow proved the effort might have been futile.

"But Mr. Stuart never left the ball," he protested. "I saw him frequently that evening."

"He wouldn't have needed to nor even wanted to," I explained. "If Mr. Stuart is the culprit, he would have marked Lord Buchan's grave sometime during the days preceding the ball. Then he would have made sure to be seen during the festivities to remove all trace of suspicion from him."

"And you've already said Mr. Young and Lord Shellingham mentioned seeing him at the abbey."

Seeing the frown that lowered his features and the way his eyes avoided meeting mine, I could tell how reluctant he was to accept my suspicions. I leaned forward in my seat, trying to catch his eye. "Uncle Andrew, I like Mr. Stuart. I genuinely do. But we have to consider every possibility, no matter how disagreeable it is, until the truth is revealed or other information rules it out. Mr. Gage taught me that," I said, turning toward him. His eyes brightened with some emotion, but before I could decide what it was, my attention was drawn back to my uncle, who was now watching us curiously. "So no matter how much we want to ignore the possibility, we can't. Not if we want to discover the truth."

I thought of the young caretaker Willie, still waiting for answers, still blaming himself for not going with Dodd to check out the light at the abbey on the night he was killed. He deserved closure just as much as, if not more than, these families who had paid ransoms to have their loved ones' remains returned to them.

My uncle inhaled and nodded. "You're right, of course. As a magistrate, I'm well aware that I can't simply rely on preconceived notions of people. And I know you will not move forward with this without first having definitive proof." He glanced sharply at me and then Gage, as if to assure himself. "So what would you like to know?"

"Well, to start, where did you meet Mr. Stuart? Aunt Sarah said it was in Edinburgh."

His gaze rose toward the ceiling. "It was at a dinner party, I believe. I found him to be dashed clever, and he had some interesting thoughts on Eastern Europe."

"Do you recall who introduced you?" I pushed. "Who hosted the dinner party?"

"Mr. and Mrs. Dalrymple were our hosts. On St. Andrews

Square. But I believe it was Mr. Tyler who presented Mr. Stuart to me."

I sat straighter. "Mr. Tyler of Woodslea?"

"Yes, I . . ." My uncle's voice trailed away as he realized the implication. His face darkened with unease.

Gage, too, had moved forward in his seat at this pronouncement. "Did Mr. Tyler say how he knew Mr. Stuart?"

"No, not that I can recall. Though there was some intimation that he had visited them recently."

I turned to Gage, trying to suppress some of the excitement I felt flowing through my veins, at least for the sake of my uncle. "Didn't Mr. Tyler say they'd hosted a gathering the weekend that his father's grave was disturbed?"

"Yes. And I have to wonder if Mr. Stuart was one of their guests."

I nodded, having considered the same thing, but then another thought occurred to me. "But neither Sir Robert nor Lord and Lady Fleming mentioned any guests. Well, other than their nephews, who we now know are innocent."

"Yes, but perhaps Mr. Stuart realized how suspicious it would look if he stayed at all the houses of the families involved, particularly on the weekends the thefts had taken place. Maybe he realized it would be better to stay in a home nearby." He gestured to our surroundings. "Like here, in the case of Lord Buchan. No one would think twice about a known visitor to the area, someone who was staying at the manor of a respected community member, touring an abbey's ruins, or a church and cemetery. He could claim to be studying the architecture or searching for an old friend's grave if anyone questioned him, and no one would suspect him of any wrongdoing. Not unless they realized he'd been to all of the sites involved. And how would they know that if no one shared their suspicions about his visit?"

"But we have no proof he stayed anywhere near Musselburgh or Beckford, and we can't exactly drive about questioning every noble and genteel household for miles around them to find out if he stayed there."

"Actually . . ."

Gage and I turned as one to look at my uncle, who was frowning down at his desk. He adjusted the ledger book under his right elbow so that it was more square with the other items in front of him.

"Your aunt received a letter a few days ago from Lady Kerswood along with her invitation to the Burns Night Ball."

I nodded in understanding.

"She mentioned that a mutual acquaintance of ours had been staying with her for a few days, and hoped to return in time for Burns Night."

Knowing Lady Kerswood, I was certain that wasn't all she'd said, or rather implied, but that was not the matter at hand. "Mr. Stuart?" I guessed.

His eyes were unhappy. "Yes."

My stomach dropped a little, even though this was the type of information we'd been hoping for. The Kerswood manor house was located no more than three miles from Beckford. "So we can place him at or nearby three of the grave sites during or just before the body snatchings took place."

"We'll have to confirm with Mr. Tyler," Gage said. "And I'll want to send a note to Sir Robert to see if he knows of anyone who visited the area just before his father's bones were stolen, but . . . yes. It appears we can place him near at least three."

I turned to stare at the fireplace, its flames crackling low. From what I knew of the man, it seemed absurd to suspect him of such a thing, but looks and even manners could often be deceiving. I'd been fooled before.

"Do you know where Mr. Stuart has been staying?" Gage asked my uncle.

"I believe he either owns or rents a house near Colding-ham. But from the sounds of it, he's been doing a great deal of traveling about the region. I don't know whether you would find him there or not."

Perhaps not. But we might be able to find out if that was

where Curst Eckie, Sore John, and the other Edinburgh body snatchers were hiding. We might find Bonnie Brock's sister there as well.

Gage thanked my uncle and we started to rise when he stopped us. "There's one more thing."

We turned to him in query.

His mouth tightened and he looked away. "This may be nothing. It could be completely unrelated, but when Mr. Stuart stayed with us on Hogmanay . . . my wife mentioned that he said something about a dead wife and child."

My heart squeezed in sympathy. "Did he say . . ."

"He said nothing else. Not when they died or how." His mouth curled in a tight self-deprecating smile. "I asked those questions myself. But your aunt Sarah said she didn't think it had been a recent event, though it still seemed to grieve him greatly."

I nodded, trusting my aunt's intuition, and wondering if those deaths were somehow the key to all of this.

"Do you want to travel to Coldingham to see if we can find this house where Mr. Stuart has been staying?" I asked Gage as we climbed into his carriage to return to Blakelaw House almost an hour later. My aunt had insisted we join them for tea, and while I normally welcomed her company, this time I'd been anxious to speak with Gage alone about what we'd uncovered.

He seemed to have already given the matter some thought, for he shook his head. "No. It's a journey of twenty-five or thirty miles from Elwick, is it not?"

"Something close to that," I estimated.

"Then it's too far. In this weather, it would take the better part of a day to reach it, and then we'd still have the return journey to make. It's just as likely that Mr. Stuart won't be there as it is that he will be. And what if the ransom note should be delivered while we're gone?" He tapped his fingers against the leg of his buff trousers in agitation.

"I don't trust these men not to give us even shorter notice than last time. They seem to have moved up their time schedule, whether because they know we're on to them, or they've grown more confident."

"How do you think they'll ask Lord Fleming to deliver the ransom?"

His expression was grim. "If there's anything I've learned from this inquiry, it's not to expect anything."

I had to agree, but that didn't stop me from speculating. The first ransom had been placed on a hilltop, the second set in a boat and sent out to sea, and the third strapped to a horse and driven into the Cheviot Hills. What other method could they possibly use to collect this fourth ransom without being caught?

I sat back to gaze out the window at the passing winter fields. The sun already dipped low on the horizon. We would not arrive at Blakelaw until after dark.

"What do you think about what my uncle told us regarding Mr. Stuart's deceased wife and child?"

When Gage did not answer, I looked over to find him staring out the window, his brow furrowed and his eyes troubled. I wondered if he was thinking about his own mother. Just a few short months ago he'd confided that she'd been murdered. It had been thirteen years ago now, but I knew those memories still upset him. Time didn't always ease the pain. Sometimes it just made it easier to distract yourself from it.

"I don't know," he finally admitted. "Like Lord Rutherford said, it may have nothing at all do with the investigation. But it could be exactly the information we've been looking for." He reached out to pull the curtain across the western-facing window as the carriage turned and the sun shone through, blinding him. "The trouble is we don't know their names or where or when they died. And you told me yourself that Lady Bute said Mr. Stuart has gone by many names in his life. Which one did he use at that time?"

They were legitimate questions, and ones I couldn't even

begin to answer. I already knew that Mr. Stuart at one time or another had lived in France, Switzerland, England, Scotland, and America. How many more cities and countries had he visited? Without the right information, the search would be far too difficult and extensive.

"I could write to Lady Bute," I suggested. "Maybe she knows something."

"And you think she would share it with you?" he asked doubtfully.

I thought about the matron and how fond she had seemed of Mr. Stuart. "Only if she thought I was asking for friendly reasons." I sighed. "I'm not sure how I would bring up a dead spouse in cordial correspondence without it sounding suspicious, but it's worth a try. Otherwise, I don't know who else to ask."

Gage closed his eyes and leaned his head back against the squabs. I could see the dark circles of fatigue surrounding his eyes, making his healing contusion look even worse. Apparently he had slept as poorly as I had the past few nights.

"Then you have some letters to write as well as I," he declared with a yawn.

And some letters I hoped to receive. Soon.

# CHAPTER THIRTY-TWO

We spent the next few days in a perpetual state of anxious anticipation. We hovered in the entry hall and drawing room at the time of day when the post was normally delivered, waiting for Crabtree to bring it up and set it on the silver tray resting on a table in the hall. Each day brought fresh hope of a letter from one of our correspondents. One that would tell us something new to aid in our investigation—some crucial bit of information we'd missed, some report of where Mr. Stuart was staying—but day after day we were disappointed.

Whenever the butler appeared unbidden, we leapt to attention, curious to see if a messenger had come from Marefield to bring us news of the arrival of the ransom note. But even in this, we were thwarted.

We moped about the library and the billiard room, trying desperately to distract ourselves and keep the tension that had suffused the household to a manageable level, but nothing really helped. Not even our sharing wild suppositions on the ringleader's motive and identity.

As the days stretched on without word from Lord Fleming, I began to worry that he had changed his mind about sharing the ransom note with us. Lady Fleming's outburst during our initial visit might have been motivated by fear for her nephew, but just because I had written to put her mind at ease in that regard didn't mean that she and her husband would not still take it into their heads that our involvement would hamper the successful return of the late Lord Fleming's bones. When I broached the subject with Gage, he insisted that Lord Fleming had welcomed our assistance and would honor his word. However, I was not so confident.

If Lord Fleming chose to exclude us from the payment of the ransom, there was little we could do about it. They were his grandfather's remains, his money being paid for their return. We could not force him to let us take part, even though it might be our last chance to catch the villains.

We could attempt to visit the house in Coldingham where Mr. Stuart was rumored to stay in hopes of uncovering something, but if there was nothing there, we would be compelled to wait until either we could locate Mr. Stuart and question him or, worse, another body was stolen. The latter seemed unbearable. What if instead of bribing the next graveyard watchman or caretaker they encountered, they simply decided to kill him, like Dodd? What if an innocent bystander unwittingly got in their way?

I did not believe that these men would avoid violence. Nor did I trust that whoever was choosing the graves to rob, be it Mr. Stuart or someone else, would be able to restrain them if they wished. If these Edinburgh criminals found themselves in a tricky position, like they had been with Dodd, they would not hesitate to kill again. And because of that, they needed to be caught now, before anyone else was harmed.

Gage and I briefly considered the possibility that they would never ask for the ransom, but quickly discarded it. They might be aware of our investigation, and even be wary of our getting too close to the truth, but they had already taken tremendous risks. They wouldn't abandon their plan before receiving their reward, not with a dangerous group of Edinburgh body snatchers to pay. It was far more likely that they were being cautious, reexamining their strategy, and waiting for the right moment to act.

Given our continued thwarted efforts, I couldn't help but wonder about the effect the first-footing ceremony had on the events of the past few weeks. Perhaps Willie's arrival had brought ill luck to the investigation. Though, technically, it was the Rutherfords, the owners of Clintmains Hall, whose fortune should be affected. But I *had* been there. Perhaps the bad omen had attached to me as well.

I felt mildly foolish even considering something so superstitious, but given the circumstances, I couldn't completely dismiss the thought. Or the wariness I felt as the inquiry progressed.

When not stalking the post or speculating with Gage and Trevor, I tried to distract myself in my studio, thinking that if I could lose myself in my art, I might find clarity in other areas. Perhaps I would have a flash of insight about something we'd underestimated or overlooked. Maybe the key to everything was there waiting for me to find if I would just stop trying so hard to make all the pieces fit. Like a name you know you should recall but simply can't remember no matter how hard you try, that is, until you cease attempting to recollect it.

And if clarity was not to be found in the investigation, then perhaps I could at least untangle the emotional knots I found myself twisted up in when it came to Gage. Unfortunately, the more I tried to understand what lay between us and what brought us together, the more muddled I became.

The entire situation perplexed me, and I urgently wished I could talk to my sister. As much as her pestering annoyed me, and as much as I'd resisted confiding in her while we were in Edinburgh, I knew that she, better than anyone, would be able to help me make sense of it all. She was far more experienced in the ways of the heart than I was. I knew what it was to suffer loss and to feel bitter disappointment, but when it came to the lighter emotions, I was untried.

I wanted Alana to explain how she had felt when Philip was courting her. Had she always been blissfully happy? Or had the periods of joy alternated with darker moods, moments when apprehension and doubt had pressed down on her chest like a heavy weight? Had she felt certain of his devotion and affection, or had she worried it was only temporary? That whatever he'd felt for her would swiftly shrivel and fade with time?

The trouble was that I didn't know what it was to love and be loved in this way, so I did not know how to discern that which was real from that which was illusion. Like a portrait in which the subject wishes to be painted not as he really is, but as he wishes to be seen. And I was afraid that the moment I let myself believe, I would be proven a fool.

So I took refuge in my studio, taking comfort in the tangible feel of the brush between my fingertips, the touch of its bristles against the canvas as I created my own reality. Here I solely controlled the truth—the authenticity of the pigments, the accuracy of the representation—and no one could tell me otherwise.

On Monday I barely left my corner of the conservatory, stopping only long enough to consume a bowl of soup when Trevor came to pester me about my luncheon tray having returned to the kitchens untouched. I could not argue with him, for I'd not even noticed it being delivered or taken away. But beyond that, I was unaware of anyone's presence.

That is, until early Monday evening, when shadows began to overtake the conservatory. I blinked to adjust my vision as the darkness settled around me, becoming conscious of the sun dropping behind the tree line outside the windows at my back, taking with it my sole source of light. I reached out to light one of my lanterns when I noticed a movement beyond my easel.

Gage leaned negligently against a table covered in potted plants, one ankle crossed over the other. His lips quirked in amusement. "You truly do lose yourself in your art. That wasn't simply a saying."

It took me a moment to find my voice after such intense concentration, and by the time I did so, he was already moving toward me with his long loose-legged stride. "How long were you standing there?" I murmured hoarsely, and then cleared my throat.

He shrugged one shoulder. "It doesn't matter. You're fascinating to watch."

"Oh?" I said stupidly.

I suddenly realized he was coming very close and I glanced at my easel, unwilling to let him see what I'd been painting there. I took a step away from my painting area, and pivoted to drop my brush in the jar of linseed oil I had sitting at the ready.

"D-Did you need something?" I stammered.

"Just your company." He stopped half a step in front of me and stared down into my face, paint-smeared, no doubt. "Have you been hiding from me?" It was said in jest, but I could see the genuine concern reflected in the depths of his eyes.

"No," I replied, even though that wasn't strictly true. "Waiting for word from Lord Fleming is just . . ." I looked about me, at a loss for the right words. I sighed. "Frustrating."

He nodded in understanding.

Feeling the warmth radiating from his body where he stood so close to mine, I realized how cold and stiff I was from standing for so many hours. I wanted nothing more than to lay my head against his chest and let him wrap his arms around me. Even standing amid all the fumes in my studio, I could smell the spiciness of his cologne and that lovely elusive scent that was purely him. But I knew I probably looked a fright, and smelled like one, too, so I resisted.

My gaze dropped to the paper in his hand. "What's that?" I asked hopefully.

He lifted it to show me. "Just a letter from Mr. Tyler."

I felt a jolt of interest. "And?"

Gage's eyebrows rose in emphasis. "Mr. Stuart did visit them the weekend his father's grave was disturbed."

I wasn't sure how I felt about this news, but I knew what it meant for our investigation. "Which only confirms our suspicions and makes him an even stronger suspect."

"Yes." One corner of his mouth rose in disgruntled chagrin. "So it appears we have Bonnie Brock to thank for pointing us in the right direction." I could hear how much he hated admitting that.

"Well, maybe," I added for his benefit. "Mr. Stuart's guilt hasn't been proven yet."

The corners of his eyes crinkled. "Are you trying to make me feel better when I was the one who was being stubborn?"

I bit my lip, staring up at his now healed and unmarred face. "Well, he didn't give me a black eye."

"True." His eyes gleamed down at me, and I had to look away, feeling both a flush of pleasure and that same pressing weight of uncertainty.

"So what have you been working on?" He stepped to the side, trying to move past me, but I sidestepped with him and pressed a hand to his chest.

"I'd really rather you not see it. It isn't finished."

He tilted his head. "Oh, come now. Surely, you know I won't judge you. I understand artwork has to go through many stages."

He tried to move around me again, but I grabbed his arm.

"Please. It's really not ready to be seen," I pleaded.

His mouth curled upward in teasing. "Why, Kiera, are you hiding something? Perhaps you're painting naughty pictures?"

I gasped in outrage at the very idea, but he merely laughed. Then picking me up by the waist, he spun me out of the way.

"Gage, no!"

But it was too late.

I stood by and watched helplessly as shock radiated across his features, draining his face of all amusement. It was replaced by a look of mute disbelief.

I studied his expression, trying to interpret what he was thinking. Was he angry? Repulsed? Disappointed?

I rubbed my hands anxiously on my apron. "I . . . I told you it's not finished," I repeated. "I . . . I'm not happy with it yet. You should have waited." I could feel tears of frustration burning at the back of my eyes.

Gage stood silently a moment longer before finally taking a step backward. He blinked several times before his gaze swung to meet mine. His pupils were wide and penetrating. I felt stripped bare. "And you would have shown me?" he asked gently.

"I . . . yes," I replied with a defiant lift of my chin, wrapping my arms around me. But as he continued to stare at me, I felt compelled to add, at least for the sake of honesty, "Eventually."

His eyes continued to search mine, looking for something. "So, this . . ." He dipped his head toward the painting. His Adam's apple bobbed as he swallowed. "This is how you see me?"

Hearing his voice so choked, I couldn't find my own. My gaze darted to the canvas and then back to him where he stood waiting for me to speak, his hands clenched at his sides. I didn't know what he saw when he looked at the portrait I'd painted of him, what had so upset him, but I could not lie. I alone had painted this, from memory, from my own thoughts and impressions of him. From my own heart.

So I nodded.

Suddenly he was before me, and I staggered back a step before his hands came up to stop me. Almost urgently, he reached out to cradle my face, his callused hands rasping against my skin. His eyes were bright with an emotion I'd only seen briefly before, if ever. An emotion that made my heart stutter in my chest. And I was terrified that my own eyes reflected it back at him.

I inhaled swiftly, closing them, and a moment later felt the warm press of his lips against mine. My entire body tingled at his touch, and I reluctantly and then enthusiastically tumbled into his kiss, eager to block out all the worries and doubts tumbling about inside me. It was easy to get lost in the pleasure of Gage's mouth on mine, but this time it was not the skill with which he kissed me, but the eagerness, the desperation of his embrace. It was far more potent than any of the other tricks he could conjure, and soon had me weak in the knees and gasping for breath. I clung to the lapels of his deep blue coat, still dazed with passion when he lifted his mouth from mine.

His breath escaped in short puffs when he leaned forward to press his forehead against mine. "Kiera." He spoke my name like it was a benediction, and it made my breath catch. "I don't know how or why I resisted so long, but I find I no longer can." He stared down into my eyes, so close to his, and I felt the bottom drop out of my stomach. "Kiera, will you marry me and make me the happiest of men?"

My heart swelled with joy at the same time that my lungs seemed to expel all of their air. I pulled back, but he would only let me go so far. "Gage," I stammered, not knowing what to say or how to say it.

He stared down at me so hopefully as if someone had shone a light behind his eyes.

"Are you asking me because of the portrait?" I asked in confusion, stalling for time.

"Well, yes, I suppose. It certainly gave me the courage to try." His lips curled into a tender smile.

"But . . . I don't understand." I glanced toward the canvas, trying to comprehend what he had seen. "Because that's the way I see you?"

He could sense my distress, and some of the light faded from his eyes. "You see, I wasn't sure before. But now I am."

I finally managed to pull away from him, and wrapped my arms protectively around my middle, where my stomach swirled. I shook my head. "I . . . I still don't understand. Sure of what? My artistic ability?" Of wanting me? The last went unsaid. I simply couldn't voice it.

Gage's gaze turned scolding. "Kiera, you know I've been aware of your artistic talents for quite some time."

"Then what? Why are you asking me to marry you?" I pleaded in frustration.

He searched my face, and whatever he saw there made his eyes harden. "You don't want to marry me." He spoke in that emotionless voice I so loathed.

"Yes. No." I pressed a hand to my forehead and whirled away. "I don't know." My heart pounded in my chest, making it difficult to catch my breath. "You confuse me," I told him accusatorily, in an unconscious echo of our conversation in the carriage on the day we visited St. Boswells. But if I'd thought he was perplexing then, how much more so was he now.

"How do I confuse you?" he bit out, his body stiff. "I asked you to marry me. What could be less confusing than that?"

"Yes, but how do you know it wasn't a spur-of-the-moment decision?" I flung my arm out to gesture to the painting. "Because of the portrait. How do you know you won't regret it later?"

"Because I know my own mind." He glared at me. "But it sounds like you don't."

"Of course I don't! Because you won't explain anything to me. We . . . we're nothing alike. You're charming and adored, and I'm . . . I'm a pariah. I can't understand why you would want to be with me. Unless . . ." I inhaled shakily. "Unless it's for another reason."

His eyes narrowed to slits. "Like what? For your artistic abilities? Your investigative skills?"

"Yes," I snapped, hating his derisive tone.

He drew himself up to his greatest height, staring down his nose at me. "Kiera, I am not Sir Anthony."

"I know that," I retorted angrily. My chest rose and fell rapidly. "But . . ."

I couldn't finish the sentence, so he did so for me. "You can't be sure."

I gazed up at him in pleading, trying to make him understand. Begging him to make *me* understand. But he merely stared down at me unmoved. I felt my heart shrivel inside my chest.

"Then I suppose we're at an impasse," he replied.

I could not speak, not past the lump that was forming in my throat, threatening to choke me. But it appeared Gage didn't require a response. Instead, he turned and marched from the room.

As I watched him go, my lips wobbled and a single tear slipped from my eye, and then another. I pressed my palms to my eyes, grinding them into the sockets as I tried to calm myself. But the seal was broken, the dam was burst, and I dropped to my knees.

I wept quietly, my body shaking with grief and despair, wishing Gage would return, hoping he would stay away. And all the while hating that he had the ability to do this to me. I didn't want to want him, to need him. It was so much easier, so much safer, to be on my own.

The look in his eyes as he'd realized I was not going to say yes kept flashing through my mind—the pain and anger. It made me sick to my stomach seeing what I'd done to him, and yet I could do nothing else. Not knowing how disastrous marriage under false pretenses could be.

In that moment, I think I loathed Sir Anthony more than I'd ever loathed him before, which was saying something. I cursed his name in every foul way I could imagine, furious that he'd taken so much from me.

I railed at my father and his foolish choice in picking a husband for me, and his inability to protect me from what was to come. Why hadn't he seen what really lay behind my late husband's motives? I'd trusted him. I'd trusted him to find a good man for me, trusted that his judgment was honorable and true, and he'd failed me, damning me to a three-year-long nightmare and a lifetime of regrets.

But my wailing swiftly devolved back into tears. I didn't want to be so upset at my father. I didn't want to feel this. After all, he *was* my father. He'd done the best by me that he could. If only he hadn't let me down in this regard, how different my life might be.

I wept for the loss of my innocence. I wept for my friend William Dalmay and all the suffering he'd endured, his life ended too early. I wept for Dodd and Willie, and the old caretaker's murder still unsolved. I wept for Gage and the pain I'd caused him. But mostly, I wept for myself, for my cowardice and the past hurts that stung too deep.

It was like scouring an infected wound clean, and though I knew it was probably for the best, I didn't enjoy doing it—either during or after.

When my sobs finally ceased, I felt ill. My head pounded and my stomach churned, but I swiped away the remainder of my tears and climbed determinedly to my feet. I reached for my palette and my brush. There was no solace like art. Even if that art was of the man you'd just rejected. Taking a deep calming breath, I swirled my brush through the paint on my palette.

## CHAPTER THIRTY-THREE

I woke the next morning stiff and bleary-eyed on the wicker settee in my art studio with Earl Gray curled up against my side. I vaguely remembered his comforting presence pressed against me as I stroked my fingers down his back and cried into his fur at some point during the night. I think I might even have hugged him, but he hadn't squirmed away. The eyes of the peacefully slumbering feline opened to slits as if to say, "You're welcome," before closing again.

I pushed myself upright, and a blanket I hadn't remembered pulling over myself slipped from my shoulders. I pressed a hand to my face as the shift in position made my sinuses pound. And as the haze of sleep cleared, I began to recall why I had been weeping in the middle of the night in the first place.

I looked up at Gage's now finished portrait still propped on my easel. The first rays of dawn shone through the windows at my back and filtered through the conservatory's foliage, bathing the painting in muted light. With a few hours of much-needed slumber, I found I could view it more objectively than before.

I'd chosen to paint him informally, standing near a window with his arm pressed to the frame at the level of his head. His coat had been discarded and his shirtsleeves were rolled up to reveal his strong forearms. Light filtered through the window to limn his blond curls with gold and highlight his sharp features. But rather than looking outward, he had tilted his head to throw a glance at the viewer.

His mouth quirked upward in his customary smile and his eyes twinkled with their familiar playfulness, but there was also a depth to them, a seriousness that belied the flirtation. Just as there was a certain steadiness, a firmness of posture that contradicted the carefreeness of his stance. This was the type of man who not only could charm you, but would also stand firm when the storms of life railed, or hold you gently when they simply became too much to bear.

I stared down at the hands which had brought this image to life and felt sick to my very soul. There was no way Gage could have missed the affection with which I had wrought the painting. That must have been what he'd seen.

But why hadn't he simply said so? Why did he have to speak in riddles and vague comments? Why couldn't he just speak plainly?

I swallowed my frustration, bitter as it tasted, for the truth was, whether he'd spoken it aloud or not, my regard for him was not reason enough to propose marriage. Perhaps that had made him more certain of my answer, wrong as he had been, but it only meant misery later on if Gage did not reciprocate that devotion.

Suddenly desperate to escape my studio and the house, I pushed myself to my feet and went in search of my warm winter cloak and half-boots. Frost coated the ground, crunching under my feet as I stepped off the portico. My breath fogged in the crisp, early morning air, floating upward into the deep blue sky. I wrapped my arms tightly about me and began to walk at a brisk pace, allowing my feet to take me where they would.

I crossed the west field and wove my way through the barren wood separating our property from the village. The shops along the main street were still locked up tight, it being too early for most people to be up and about. The low sun at my back cast my long shadow ahead of me down the road. I contemplated it as I came upon the lych-gate to St. Cuthbert's Church, and on an impulse, I entered.

My steps wove between the gravestones, absently noting the names of families who had lived in Elwick for generations, standing side by side in death as they had in life. Before I knew what I was doing, I found myself beneath the old oak tree that guarded over my parents' graves. I stared at my mother's inscription and then reluctantly forced myself to look at my father's more austere marker. There were no pretty flowers or scrollwork, just simple block lettering, as our father would have wanted it. Ever practical, ever pragmatic. Even when it came to his youngest daughter's marriage.

I frowned, feeling the bitterness I'd denied for so long that I'd stirred up last night blacken my heart. For years I'd been making excuses for my father's lapse in judgment. He had been the one man I'd known I could always trust and rely on, no matter what, but in the end he had also failed me, spectacularly. I had been afraid to admit that, afraid to feel this intense anger for the man who had loved and raised me, especially when he wasn't here to defend himself. But after last night, after watching Gage's and my relationship crumble to dust around me, I could no longer push it aside. I wanted to scream at him again, only to do so would mean shrieking at an inanimate gravestone in the middle of a churchyard at dawn, and would surely convince anyone who happened to hear me that I was insane.

Regardless, my face must have been twisted up in quite a nasty expression, for when my brother suddenly appeared at my side, he knew exactly what I was thinking.

"Father would have understood your being furious with him," Trevor told me in a gentle voice. "He would have expected it."

I turned my scowl on my brother. "Did you follow me?"

He replied without hesitation. "Yes. I saw you leaving Blakelaw through my bedchamber window, and thought you might like some company."

I frowned down at our father's grave. "Does it look like I want company?"

"Actually, yes."

I furrowed my brow, trying to decide if he was attempting to be funny. When he didn't elaborate or even acknowledge my aggravation, I rolled my eyes and returned to my contemplation of our parents' eternal resting place.

We stood there silently side by side, the skeletal branches of the oak clattering together overhead. Between the tree and my brother, I was pretty well shielded from the wind, but not from the cold of the frozen ground, which I could feel even through the soles of my boots. I shifted from one foot to the other, allowing my agitation to grow. Anything to escape this sorrow pressing down on my chest, making it difficult to breathe.

"I'm sorry, Kiera," my brother said, his voice heavy with regret.

I turned to meet his gaze, surprised by the anguish I saw shimmering in his eyes.

"I should have protected you from this. I should have done *something* to stop it."

"How could you?" I protested. "I never confided in you, in anyone, while Sir Anthony was alive. I . . . was too scared, too . . ." I swallowed ". . . ashamed to admit what was happening."

"Yes. But I *knew* something was wrong. I knew you were unhappy. You've never been good at hiding your emotions." He tilted his head to the side. "Why do you think Sir Anthony kept us away as often as he could?"

I stared unseeing at the earth between my parents' graves. I'd never realized he was keeping them away. I'd simply thought my family had been too busy with their own lives, too preoccupied to visit me.

"It didn't matter," I replied, my voice rough as sandpaper to my ears. "Sir Anthony was my husband. He had all the power. The only good you or father's confronting him would have done was to cause a scandal. He would have won any dispute placed in front of a court of law." And taken out their meddling on me. I didn't speak the last aloud.

"Perhaps. But we still should have tried." Trevor grabbed my arm, turning me to look at him. "It wasn't right that we did nothing to stop his treatment of you. That we didn't force you to confide in us." Brackets of pain formed around his mouth and eyes. "I will regret that for the rest of my life."

"Trevor, no." I shook my head. "I am not going to let you take this on yourself. I should have been brave enough to tell you or father what was going on. I . . . I should have had the courage to defy him."

"Why didn't you?"

I blinked up at him, surprised by the question.

"Why didn't you trust me enough to tell me?" His face twisted with agony. "Did you think I wouldn't believe you? That I would stand by and let that brute treat you that way?"

"Oh, Trevor, no." A tear slipped down my cheek at the pain I'd unknowingly caused him. I reached up to press my hand to his chest over his heart. "I . . . I don't know why I remained silent for so long. Believe me, I ask myself that *every day.*" My gaze drifted over his shoulder to the church steeple towering above us. "I suppose initially it was shock. I simply couldn't believe what was happening. And by the time I came to my senses, he'd already forced me to sketch his dissections, to observe his cutting open a human being." I closed my eyes tightly against the memory. "By then I was too horrified to say anything."

Trevor gripped my arm above the elbow tighter, offering me what comfort he could.

"Any time I felt myself growing stronger, somehow he sensed it. And he would remind me what would happen if I told anyone the truth. He . . . he would smash one of my paintings, or twist my wrist until I begged him to stop. And once a year he would take me to tour Bedlam or some other lunatic asylum, to . . . remind me what fate awaited me if I dared defy him."

I shook my head again, wishing I could dislodge all those recollections from my mind. "I'm sorry," I whispered.

Trevor pulled me close, smothering my apology in the fabric of his coat. I stood there biting back tears and let him hold me and stroke the back of my head.

"No more apologies. You did nothing wrong. You know that, don't you?" he said, his voice tight from suppressed emotion.

"But that's why you fell in with that bad crowd, isn't it?" I insisted, realizing now how much my own cowardice had cost my brother as well as me. "That's why the estate is in trouble."

"No, Kiera . . ."

I pushed back to look up into his face. He knew better than to lie to me.

He sighed wearily. "Perhaps partially. But that is not your fault. I did not have to punch a man in Almack's."

My eyes widened at this detail.

"And I should have known better than to console myself with drink and gambling." He grimaced. "At least, not at the same time."

"How bad is it?" I ventured to ask.

He frowned, finally admitting all. "I'm not in danger of losing the estate, but it will take several years to recoup the losses. That's why I've been consulting with our uncle and Philip, among others, exploring the possibility of expanding our stables with racing horses, or adding more sheep to our fold. I've also been looking into investing in these new steam locomotives. There are opportunities to be had, if one is willing to take the risk, and smart enough to implement the changes correctly."

I breathed a sigh of relief and squeezed his shoulder where my hand lay, proud that my brother was mature and wise enough to admit his mistakes and seek to remedy them. Many men would have hidden such errors in judgment from the men they admired, but Trevor had instead prudently sought their advice. Though I wasn't sure why he couldn't have confided this to me before, rather than make me worry.

We turned to stare down at our parents' graves again, with my arm linked through his and my head tipped to the side to rest on his shoulder. Standing thusly, I couldn't help remembering that cold March day when we'd stood a few paces apart, almost in the same way. It had been nearly a week since our mother had been laid to rest, and still being children, Trevor and I had not been allowed to attend the funeral. So with all the confusion and macabre curiosity of an eight- and a ten-year-old, we had escaped from our governess and come to the cemetery ourselves to see where our mother now rested. I had been frightened to approach, but Trevor had held my hand, letting me know I wouldn't have to face it alone. Our father had found us several hours later, still rooted to the spot, trying to come to grips with the fact that our mother was truly never coming back to us.

I was as grateful now as I had been then for my brother's solid presence beside me, his warm arm wrapped around mine.

"Do you know why father agreed to the marriage proposal from Sir Anthony?" Trevor asked.

I glanced up to find him staring at our father's grave, a pucker between his eyes. I shook my head.

"He thought that since Sir Anthony was a self-made man promoted from the ranks of a lower class that he would better understand and support your painting. He worried a gentleman would never appreciate your need to create art, would never allow you to exhibit it, because gentlewomen simply didn't do such things."

I could appreciate the consideration my father had given the matter. After all, I'd been subjected to ridicule and belittlement from the members of the upper class since before I could remember. My first exhibit in our family's town house in London at the age of seventeen had been met with derision and scorn. Such things would not have been easy for many gentlemen to accept or condone.

"I'm certain he had no idea what Sir Anthony's real intentions were."

"I know that," I told Trevor stiffly. "None of us did."

"But he did know something was wrong." His voice was solemn. "Had he not been so ill at the end, so unable to travel, I think he would have confronted Sir Anthony. It was his biggest regret."

I was about to ask my brother how he could possibly know such a thing when he turned to look at me.

"He told me. On his deathbed. And he made me promise to look out for you."

I felt something inside me swell and expand, pushing out some of the anger that had seemed a part of me for so long, burrowed deep down in my heart as it was. My eyes traveled over the letters of my father's name carved into his gravestone.

"He loved you, Kiera. He loved us all."

I nodded, sniffing back tears. "I know that. I've always known that."

"But love doesn't make us perfect."

I gasped a laugh, swiping away the wetness gathering at the corner of my eye. "Oh, how *well* I know that."

"Then why are you being so tough on Gage?"

I stopped and turned to Trevor, trying to read from his guarded expression how much he knew. "Did you eavesdrop on us?"

"No. But it was hard not to notice how angry Gage was when he nearly collided with me on the stairs yesterday evening. Or how ferociously you were glaring at the portrait you're painting of him." His eyebrows rose in expectation.

I turned aside, unable to meet his gaze. I hadn't even heard him come into my studio last night.

I considered ignoring his question, brushing it aside. But I did want to talk to someone about it, and without Alana here, I had few options. It would be a somewhat awkward topic to discuss with my brother, but really, who better was there to give me advice? He already knew most of my history and he'd seen Gage and me together. What's more, he was a man. He might be able to offer me some insight.

So I gathered my courage and told him the truth. "He proposed marriage."

"Ah," Trevor murmured, as if that explained much. "And you said no."

"I . . . I suppose so," I replied, realizing I hadn't actually given him an answer, though the "no" had certainly been implied.

He asked me why I'd turned him down, and as soon as I began to explain, the words seemed to simply pour out of me. I told him about the portrait, how that had seemed to be the catalyst for Gage's proposal, and how it had confused me. I complained about how there was so much I didn't know about him, and how stubborn he was about sharing details of his life. But then somehow I ended up defending his secretiveness, being able to relate to it myself. I confided my worries over our future happiness, and how I feared Gage would swiftly realize he'd made a mistake when he saw how incompatible we were, particularly in a public setting. And I even told him how I feared he only wanted to marry me because of my usefulness in investigations, not for me alone. How I feared no one would want me for me alone.

Sometime in the midst of my long speech, Trevor shifted to my other side to lean back against the old oak tree with his arms crossed. He listened attentively, his focus never wavering, and when my words ran out along with my breath, I waited for him to speak.

His head tilted to the side and his eyes were kind. "Did you ever stop to consider you might be thinking too hard about this?"

My chest rose and fell rapidly as I tried to catch my breath. "What do you mean? This is serious." I gestured with my hands. "*Marriage* is serious. After what happened with Sir Anthony . . ."

"But Gage isn't Sir Anthony."

"I know that," I snapped, remembering that Gage had argued the same thing.

"But you're acting as if he is. As if the same thing is going to happen between you and Gage as happened between you and Sir Anthony."

I paused, considering his words. "But how do I know that it won't?" I murmured softly.

Trevor stepped forward to take my hands, staring down into my troubled face. "I want you to forget Sir Anthony for a moment, if you can, and tell me something." His eyebrows rose in emphasis. "Do you trust Gage?"

I stared up at him, uncertain how to answer.

Sensing my doubt, he elaborated. "If you were in danger, do you trust that he would rescue you if he could? Would he defend you from accusations? Would you willingly confide in him all you've told me about Sir Anthony and what he's done to you?"

"Yes," I replied relatively easily.

He leaned closer, his eyes warm with affection. "Is he the first thing you think of in the morning and the last thing you think of at night? Would you race to his side if he were ever sick or injured?" His lips quirked upward at the corners. "Would you shield him from our sister's wrath?"

"Yes," I whispered, beginning to see his point.

"It's obvious to anyone who sees you together that you love him. And that portrait fairly gives it away as well."

I flushed.

"I can understand how that would give him the courage to ask you when he saw it. But I think what really struck him upon seeing the portrait was all the traits you imbued him with."

My brow wrinkled in confusion. "What do you mean?"

He smiled softly. "I've only known him a short time, but I can already tell Gage is used to being underestimated. Just a charming, attractive man to pass the time with. But you see the nobility in him—the bravery and honor and determination. And if I were still a betting man, I would wager that is what so affected him. Knowing that you love him not only for the man he shows most of the world, but also for the man he is deep down inside."

I was stunned. Was Trevor right? Was that why Gage had proposed? I felt queasy knowing I'd turned him down after that. And in such a panicked and muddled way.

I frowned. But once again we came back to the question of how Gage felt about me. Just because I loved him—and yes, much as I'd been denying it, I knew it was futile now not to admit the truth, especially if Trevor had seen it—didn't mean Gage loved me. And if he didn't, I knew I would never be happy. I might have been willing to marry Sir Anthony knowing there was no love between us and hope it would grow in time, but I knew better now. If Gage didn't truly love me, then a union between us would never work.

Trevor clucked his tongue, shaking his head as if he could read my thoughts. "If you can't see that that man loves you, then you truly must be addled, for it's as plain to see as the nose on your face. How can you doubt it? Where are your formidable observation skills?"

I scowled at him and he grinned brightly.

Pulling my arm through his, he led me away from our parents' graves. We wound our way back through the gravestones toward the gate. I welcomed the warmth of the sun's rays as they pierced through a cloud bank.

"You have a decision to make," Trevor declared as he latched the gate behind us.

"I know," I admitted, my thoughts still on Gage and whether I should trust that what my brother said was true. Was I being willfully blind? Was I so afraid of making a mistake that I couldn't see the truth right in front of me?

But apparently that was not all my brother meant. "Your life at this moment is wide open with possibilities—ones I suspect you never thought to have." His eyes were very serious. "Do you want to marry again? Do you want to have children? Do you want to keep painting portraits? Do you want to continue to be involved with these inquiries?" He stopped and turned to look at me. "The choice is yours, Kiera. I mean that. Whatever it is you decide, I'll support you. But I want you to think long and hard about what it is that *you* do truly desire. This is your opportunity to choose the life you want." He shook his head. "No more hiding. No more fear."

I was speechless in the face of my brother's pronouncement. I had been conscious that my life was at a crossroads, but I had never really contemplated all of the choices that were open to me. That he would have given this matter such intense consideration himself, and love me enough to support me in whatever decisions I made was nearly overwhelming. As a female in our male dominated society it was a rare thing indeed to encounter so much devotion and respect. Though, I should have known to expect nothing less from Trevor.

Emotion clogged my throat.

"You don't have to decide right this minute," he said, clearly sensing how much his gift had astounded me. "But you do need to decide soon."

I squeezed his arm closer to my body in gratitude, barely able to speak. "Thank you."

He merely smiled and turned our steps toward home.

# CHAPTER THIRTY-FOUR

The house was quiet when Trevor and I returned. I didn't know if Gage had still not risen or if he'd hidden himself somewhere, but regardless, I wasn't ready to face him. Not yet.

Instead, my steps were drawn once more to my studio in the back corner of the conservatory. Beams of winter sun shone through the glass ceiling and walls, fully illuminating the space. Earl Grey had lolled onto his back on the wicker settee, basking in the warmth. I sat down beside him and he rolled to his side, allowing me to scratch behind his ears. His chest rumbled with the comforting sound of his contented purr.

I turned to stare at Gage's portrait. It was the first painting I'd completed since finishing William Dalmay's posthumous portrait, since I'd lost my ability and my desire to paint. And it just might have been my best work ever. If nothing else, I owed Gage my thanks for that—for inspiring my passion again, for giving me back my gift, and for distracting me enough with his presence and this investigation to keep me from agonizing over every step of the process.

Without having given in to my overwhelming urge to capture Gage on canvas, I'm not sure how long I would have floundered. Or whether I might have simply given up.

No. I couldn't imagine ever doing that. My art was too much a part of me, even when it was painful.

So I supposed that answered one of Trevor's questions. Yes, I would continue to paint portraits, whether I took them on as commissions or not. It was who I was.

But what of the rest? Did I want to marry? Did I care about having children?

Five months ago I would have unequivocally said no—no hesitation, no doubts. But that was before I met Sebastian Gage. Before he'd pestered and cajoled his way into my heart. Before he'd proved what a good and honorable man he was.

He and Trevor were right. It was unfair to compare Gage to Sir Anthony. They were nothing alike. I couldn't imagine Gage ever using me or hurting me the way Sir Anthony had, but it was hard to release that fear completely. There was always a sliver of doubt, knowing as intimately as I did how the husband held all the power in marriage. There was always some danger when giving over so much control to another person that they might abuse it.

So what it really came down to was trust. Did I trust Gage enough to take that chance?

I turned to stare at the row of barren pear trees lined up along the west side of the house and thought of the times Gage had saved my life—first at Gairloch and then at Banbogle Castle. I thought of all the times he'd grown angry when others had failed or insulted me. I recalled the strength of his arms holding me tight when I was distressed and the nonjudgmental way he had accepted the worst about me and my past once I shared with him the truth.

Then I examined all the ways he'd trusted me. To assist with his inquiries without botching them. To interview suspects and provide him with my impressions and the benefit of my reluctantly accrued anatomical knowledge. He'd shared with me the pain of his mother's murder, and risked my scorn to reveal his woodworking hobby. And I suddenly realized that in all the investigations I'd worked with him, he'd never forced me to do anything against my will, unless it was for my own protection. Normally I was fighting him because he was trying to shield me from the horror, not because he was urging me to follow along.

It was almost absurd for me to worry that he wanted to marry me only for my investigative abilities. If anything, he'd tried to discourage them. And the fact that he was willing to listen to me, to even allow me to assist, said far more in his favor than the opposite. I would have been furious if he'd shut me out merely because I was a woman.

It seemed foolish now that I had turned him down. In any case, what was the alternative? To let Gage go? To never see him again? To one day hear news of his marriage to another lady, perhaps one who would never understand him as I did? I couldn't expect him to hang about and allow me to assist him with his inquiries after I'd turned down his offer of marriage. And someday soon he would wed, for his own happiness and to produce an heir, while I lived in a cottage near Edinburgh and painted portraits. I would be safe from the machinations of another husband, but I would also be alone. Forever. For if not Gage, I knew I would never trust my heart to anyone again.

The thought of never seeing him again, of never hearing his voice or being held in his arms, of imagining him with another woman, left a hollow ache inside me I wasn't certain I would ever be able to fill, for as long as I lived.

When looked at in such a stark light, was there really any other decision to make? I could take a leap of faith and accept Gage's proposal. Perhaps my fears would come true. He would grow tired of my eccentricities, my awkwardness, and stop loving me. But perhaps my worries were unfounded. Maybe we would be happy, solving inquiries and raising a family together while I painted portraits of our children, even if I never accepted commissions again.

I inhaled past the tightness in my chest and felt a smile curl the sides of my mouth upward, higher and higher, until I was practically beaming with joy.

Then I remembered what a hash I'd made of things. I would need to apologize and explain my reaction to his proposal. I only hoped Gage would listen, and had not already decided I was no longer worthy of his regard.

I stroked Earl Grey's fur one more time for good luck and then hurried up to my bedchamber. My eyes strayed to Gage's door on the opposite side of the hall, but I decided I needed to bathe first. I knew without a doubt that I looked and smelled a fright, and if I was to have any chance of wooing Gage back, it certainly would be best to do so primped, perfumed, and dressed in proper attire.

It was time to begin readying myself for the Burns Night Ball that evening anyway, so I rang for Bree and ordered a bath drawn. I knew the perceptive girl could sense my nervousness, but she also recognized my excitement, and that was what she chose to foster.

I bathed in water scented with rose petals, scouring the paint and raw chemicals from my skin, and then I sat before the fire to let my hair dry while I devoured a bowl of cock-a-leekie soup sent up from the kitchens. I realized I hadn't eaten since luncheon the day before, and only then because my brother had made me. Feeling more myself, I sat before my vanity and asked Bree to arrange my hair in an artfully braided coronet—completely out of fashion, but much more to my style and liking. I even allowed her to dab a bit of rouge on my pale cheeks.

Then I donned my clan Rutherford attire—a full royal blue skirt with a Rutherford tartan overskirt that split in the front and a long-sleeved white blouse covered by a black-laced bodice. Over one shoulder we draped another length of the royal blue tartan with thick stripes of black and thin stripes of red running through it and fastened it with a brooch.

I'd worried that with my recent weight loss the ensemble would be far from flattering on my figure, but unknown to me, Bree had taken in the skirt, and the bodice laced tight enough up the front to hide the bagginess of the blouse and even provide me with some cleavage. I couldn't help but wonder if Gage would be brave enough to don the kilt Trevor had loaned him, or if he would insist on wearing his usual dark evening kilt. I knew few Englishmen who were not stodgy enough to join in such a custom, but Gage just might be one of them. Either way, it was time to find out.

I heard the large clock in the entrance hall chime the hour, and inhaled deeply, trying to calm my rampaging heart. Bree smiled at me in the mirror as she fastened the clasp of my amethyst pendant around my neck and wished me well. And then there was nothing left for me to do but go.

At the top of the stairs, I paused and pressed my hand to my fluttering stomach. I could hear the low rumble of Trevor's and Gage's voices below. I closed my eyes and breathed deep again, cursing myself for a fool, and then forced my foot to take the first step downward. The banister was smooth and cool beneath my hand.

As my lower body came into view, I heard the men's conversation falter as they turned to observe my progress. It took all of my nerve to continue descending as their bodies were steadily revealed from their feet upward with each step. I inhaled sharply when I realized there was but one step left before their faces came into view, and I compelled my foot forward. My fingers tightened on the banister as I met Gage's eyes for the first time since spurning him the evening before. I could not read his expression, not from this far away, but it did not seem angry or disgruntled as I'd half expected. The band of fear around my chest loosened. Now, if only he was not indifferent, I thought I might be able to survive this night.

The men were silent as I moved closer and closer to them with each step. I wished they would speak, for it only seemed to stretch the moment out, drawing the tension in the room taut like a cord. Gage looked so handsome, and I realized as my brother moved closer that they were identically attired. Gage was actually wearing the kilt, and I couldn't stop my eyes from dropping to see his legs below the hem. As expected, they were muscular and well defined.

I felt my cheeks flush and quickly lifted my gaze back to meet Gage's. His eyes twinkled wickedly, aware of exactly what I'd been looking at.

I turned to Trevor as I reached the bottom, accepting his assistance as I descended the remaining steps.

"You look lovely," he told me with a kind smile.

"Thank you," I replied and reached up to straighten the brooch fixed to the length of plaid thrown over his shoulder. I felt Gage's eyes on me the entire time, and when Trevor stepped away to ask after the carriage, there was no longer an excuse to avoid meeting them.

Fortunately, his gaze was not indifferent. His pale blue eyes were bright with an emotion he couldn't hide, even tinged with wariness as they were.

"You do look lovely." His voice was deep and warm.

"Thank you. You do, too. That is . . ." I faltered, feeling my cheeks heat again. "You look handsome."

He grasped the sides of his kilt and stuck out one leg as if dancing. "Do you like the kilt?" he asked with the devil in his eyes.

I scowled at his teasing, even as it pleased me. "You know I do," I replied, sneaking another peek at his legs. I was willing to be the recipient of any amount of teasing if it meant he would keep smiling at me like that.

I hesitantly moved a step closer, wishing desperately that we could have a moment alone so I could explain myself. I opened my mouth to tell him just that when he spoke first.

"Save your first waltz for me."

Momentarily stunned, I gaped at him like a fish. "I . . . if you wish," I finally stammered.

He shifted even closer, his jaw hardening in determination. "I'm finally going to have that dance with you, and I'm not taking any chances we might be interrupted later in the night."

I searched his eyes, trying to understand. Did he forgive me for trampling on his proposal? Was he going to try again? Or was this his way of punishing me for turning him down?

But before I could ask him for a moment in private, that interruption he'd alluded to came. There was a shout and then the sharp whinny of a horse.

We all turned as one, to watch through the open door as a man struggled to bring his rearing horse under control, narrowly missing the hooves of one of the matching pairs at the front of our carriage waiting on the drive. The coachman scolded the rider as he leapt off his horse and rushed toward the house. Gage and I moved closer to hear.

"From Lord Fleming," the rider gasped, holding out a letter.

I shared a glance with Gage, knowing what this meant. We'd been waiting for this very message for days.

Trevor took the missive, broke open the seal, and immediately began to read. His eyes widened and his expression turned grim. He frowned as he handed the note across to Gage, who held it low enough so that I might also read it.

It was an abbreviated version of the ransom note Lord Fleming had finally received, and explained the rider's extreme urgency.

"Tonight?" I exclaimed. "They want the ransom delivered tonight?"

Gage nodded, looking across at Trevor. "They must know we're on to them."

"But . . ." I stared out the door at the swiftly falling darkness ". . . that only gives us hours to prepare."

"Yes," he replied unhappily. "And the only advantage we have is that they've chosen the same delivery method as last time—a horse waiting for us in Shotton Pass. So let's make the most of it. Can you get a message to Lord Rutherford?" he asked Trevor.

"I'll send it to the Kerswoods' Ball. So late in the evening, it's more likely to reach him there."

"Tell him we're going to need his son and nephews if they can be spared." His eyes hardened. "I'm not taking any chances this time."

This time when we rode into Shotton Pass, all trace of daylight had long since faded from the sky. However, the night was clear and cloudless, and since the moon was only three days shy of being full, the natural light it provided us was far superior to what we'd experienced during our last trip into the Cheviot Hills. The heavens were speckled with brilliant stars, their beauty almost making up for the bitter temperatures that had settled over the land without any clouds to hold in the heat of the day. I shivered inside my fur-lined winter cloak as Figg picked her way through the scrub and rocks, trailing Gage's chestnut gelding, Titus.

Time being of utmost importance, Gage and Trevor had hurried to change out of their kilts and into riding breeches while our horses were saddled. Which left me with just a few precious minutes to throw on an old spencer over my blouse and bodice and put on a pair of woolen stockings before trading my dancing slippers for half-boots. With my cloak and gloves, this was the warmest I could expect to feel on horseback on a cold January night.

Lord Fleming had met us with the ransom money at The Plough Inn in Town Yetholm before setting off for Beckford Parish Church with a pair of his footmen. There he was to lie in wait for the man who delivered his grandfather's bones after the ransom was paid, should our efforts fail to capture him beforehand. As Gage had said, he wasn't taking any chances, though we really had no idea whether the bones would be left at the church or elsewhere. We'd been fooled before.

We waited as long as we could for the arrival of my uncle and cousins, but when the hour inched too close to the appointed time of the ransom delivery, we'd had to leave without them. Trevor had left a note with the innkeeper should they appear after we departed, but we all knew not to count on their assistance from this point forward. In any case, we had Dixon and his son Davy—the local men Trevor had prearranged to guide us—and Anderley to boost our party to six.

Even with the familiarity of our surroundings and the increase in our numbers, I couldn't help but feel apprehensive. If the setup was familiar to us, it was even more familiar to the thieves, making it all the more dangerous. Especially if the thieves had observed our pursuit last time and decided it was too much of a risk allowing us to continue our investigation. They could be lying in wait for us even now, ready to attack.

The knots tied inside my stomach tightened even further.

We reined in our horses just as we had before as we rounded the curve into the pass. Our horses' hooves stamped in the dust, and pranced back and forth, clearly sensing their riders' unease. The ridges rising before us were solemn and dark, nothing more than humped shapes against the paler black of the night sky. But still we watched for shifting shadows and listened for the scuff of a foot or the clicking cock of a pistol's hammer. Nothing but the sound of Figg's breath and the creak of my saddle met my ears. Gage nodded, and Dixon and his son slowly led us down the rise into the pass.

The sorrel mare was positioned as before, her leather reins twisted in the branches of the yew tree. Her ears perked up as we approached and she lifted her head, still munching on a tuft of scrub grass she had pulled from the ground at her feet. History seemed to repeat itself as Gage and Trevor lifted the leather saddlebags containing the ransom money onto the mare's back and tightened the straps. My brother remounted his stallion as Gage untangled the mare's reins from the yew, but unlike before, he paused.

With his back to us, it was difficult to tell what had halted his movements, but I glanced around, trying to see or hear what he was sensing. When finally he shifted to the left, I could see he'd pulled something white from the end of a twig. It was much too early in the year to be a blossom, but what else could it be? A letter?

Still holding the mare's reins, he rounded her body and held up what appeared to be a square piece of cloth toward the moonlight. His eyes dropped to meet mine, though I could not read their expression in the darkness.

"It's a lady's handkerchief," he murmured quietly. "And it bears your initials."

I frowned in confusion, and then held out my hand. "Let me see it."

He passed it to me, and I ran my gloved fingers over the fine embroidery in the corner. He was correct. It was mine. But how . . .

"Mr. Stuart," I informed the men, speaking only as loudly as I dared. "He asked for a token after rescuing me at the assembly in Edinburgh."

Gage's posture stiffened, clearly recalling what he'd been "rescuing" me from.

"He asked for my handkerchief."

Trevor's stallion snorted as my brother urged his horse closer. "But what does it mean?"

I shook my head. "Perhaps he's warning us?"

Unwillingly our gazes lifted to the ridges surrounding us again, and I felt a chill of foreboding slide down my back. I could see nothing, but nonetheless, I swore there were eyes watching us, waiting for something.

"Then maybe it's best if we move on," Gage suggested.

But rather than repeating the actions of our last ransom payment, he surprised me by hoisting himself onto the mare's bare back.

"What are you doing?" I demanded in alarm.

The mare snorted in protest as he turned her to face me. "The only sensible thing. Should she ride ahead again, losing us in the hills, at least one of us will be certain to keep up with her."

I glanced about me, certain a shot would ring out from the ridges above at any moment from his sheer audacity.

"Are you sure that's wise?" Trevor's voice was fraught with uncertainty. "Should she lose the rest of us, that would leave you to face an unknown number of angry criminals at the end by yourself."

In the darkness, I could not see Gage's eyes, but his harsh tone and posture communicated quite clearly his stubborn determination not to be left in the dust during this outing. "Then you'd best not fall behind."

He urged the mare forward, but she only snuffled and took a few halting steps. When he tried again, snapping her reins and squeezing her flanks, she shuffled to the side in an awkward dance.

As we watched Gage make one more fruitless attempt to spur her onward, Dixon spoke up in his gruff voice. "Looks like she's been trained no' to let a stranger ride 'er."

I exhaled in relief—terrified by the risk Gage had been willing to take—but I was careful not to let him see my reaction. Not that I need have worried. He was clearly distracted by his own vexation. He cursed under his breath before reluctantly dismounting from the mare.

His movements were sharp as he knotted the horse's reins behind her neck as before and then slapped her on her flank. She whickered in complaint before finally turning to amble down the pass deeper into the Cheviot Hills. Anderley lowered his horse's reins, almost in disappointment, obviously having anticipated a fast pursuit, much as we had the last time. Now we knew better.

Gage mounted his gelding and fell in line behind Dixon and Davy as they followed the sorrel mare down the path. This time we were ready when she reached the last twist of the pass and began to lengthen her stride to cross the open moorland. With the moon so bright, we could see farther than fifty feet in front of us this time, and Dixon and Davy were familiar enough with the terrain to remain right on the mare's flank.

Given the ideal conditions, I couldn't help but wonder why the body snatchers had chosen a night as clear and well lit as this one, and yet given Lord Fleming so little time to prepare. These two choices seemed to contradict each other. Unless they'd hoped the late delivery would prevent our involvement.

I stared down at the lacy square of fabric still clutched in my hand. But then why had Mr. Stuart left my handkerchief for us to find? Was it meant to be a warning? But of what?

I scanned the ridges in the distance to our left and to our right, trusting Figg to follow the lead of the horses in front of her. If we could see farther in these conditions, then the thieves certainly could as well, wherever they were. The rises were too far off, but we were approaching another pass, one where the hills pressed in much closer.

I wanted to say something, to warn the others, but I knew I would need to shout to be heard over the pounding of our horses' hooves. Any noise I made would also be heard by anyone who was waiting out there in the dark. Not that our progress was exactly stealthy to begin with, but I didn't need to give them any more assistance in locating us.

As the moor narrowed, the sorrel mare began to slightly pull away. I didn't know whether Dixon and his son allowed this to happen intentionally or because they slowed their horses to navigate over a tricky piece of ground. In any case, Figg followed closely in their footsteps as I kept my eyes peeled for any sign of movement on the ridges nearby. I could sense Gage's frustration with our slackened pace, but he wisely held his tongue, allowing the men in front of us to lead the way over the shifting ground the best they knew how.

Somehow we made it through the pass without incident, though my heart had been pounding in my ears the entire time, certain an ambush was imminent. Over a rise and down into another valley we trailed the sorrel mare, always keeping her in sight, driven on by the striking cadence of her hooves against the earth. The wind was sharp, stinging my face and slicing into my lungs with each breath I took, leaving a slight metallic taste in my mouth. At the fork in the path where we had argued which direction to take the last time we'd followed the mare, we could now easily see she turned left. At least we had been right about something.

The loose downhill terrain in this area forced us to check our horses' speed again, or risk breaking our necks or our horses' legs in a fall, but somehow the mare continued on unimpeded. Perhaps it was the extra weight of us humans on our horses' backs that made them clumsier in the descent, or maybe the sorrel mare simply knew the path that much better. Whatever it was, the mare was steadily pulling away from us.

Dixon and Davy picked up speed again as we reached a more hard-packed surface, and we followed the horse correctly through two more forks in the path. But no matter how hard we dared to push our horses, the mare still continued to gain ground, carrying her farther and farther ahead of us.

By the time we encountered a series of forks through the twists and turns in a boggier area, we knew we'd lost her. Dixon was able to deduce which fork the horse most likely took twice, but at the third, he declared he was stumped.

Gage's gelding danced to the left and then the right, telling me how aggravated his rider was. I could almost hear the string of curses running through his head.

"Then let's split up," he declared. "I'm not stopping now that we're so close."

The rest of us agreed. There would still be three of us to face whatever was at the end, a fair number. If we failed to recover the mare's track, we would meet back at this spot.

Gage ordered Dixon to lead Trevor and me to the right, while he, Davy, and Anderley took the fork to the left. I felt a quiver of alarm at being separated from Gage, but before I could even murmur a complaint, his trio had ridden off. There was nothing for me to do but follow his instructions.

Even so, my mind was with the other party as we wound

our way deeper into the hills, stopping periodically while Dixon tried to pick up the mare's trail. The scrub in this part of the Cheviots was denser on the ground, casting strange shadows across the landscape and cloaking the paths. Without Dixon, I suspected Trevor and I would have quickly become lost, even in the bright moonlight.

Finally, after a mile or more of painstakingly searching, Dixon grunted and declared the trail to be cold. "'Tis likely she went the other way. But I had teh be sure," he told us in his deep brogue.

I only hoped he was right.

We picked our way back to the fork in the path where Gage, Anderley, and Davy had split off from us, but there was no sign of the trio, or anyone in pursuit of us. I told myself this was a good sign, that this was what we'd hoped for. But as the minutes passed, stretching into a quarter of an hour, and then a half, and then nearly an entire hour with no sign of them, my already taut nerves began to fray.

Something was wrong. I could feel it in every fiber of my being. And in my heart, I knew something had happened to Gage.

I pleaded with Trevor and Dixon, trying to convince them that we should go after them, but they pointed out, rightly, that we had no idea exactly where they'd gone. We might be able to tell which forks in the path they'd taken farther along, and we might not. If they needed us, they would return here to find us.

I turned away, scanning the shadowy, barren landscape surrounding us and tried to control the sick feeling swirling in my gut.

If only Gage and I had had a moment alone before the letter from Lord Fleming arrived. I could have told him I loved him, that I would be overjoyed to marry him. Instead, he still believed I'd rejected him, that I thought him a monster like my late husband, that I didn't care, when nothing was further from the truth.

I scowled fiercely, forbidding the tears building at the

back of my eyes from falling. If . . . *when* I saw Gage again, I would tell him the truth, regardless of who heard me.

The sharp thud of hoofbeats in the distance made me sit straighter in my saddle, as I narrowed my eyes to peer into the darkness. My heart began to thump faster, in time to the horse's rhythm. Soon enough a single rider came into view, and then two, but when a third failed to materialize out of the black night, I felt the bottom drop out of my stomach.

Trevor moved his horse between me and the riders, an instinctive act of protection. "Don't jump to conclusions," he told me, correctly reading my thoughts. "Perhaps one of them stayed behind to monitor the mare or the thieves. Maybe these two are returning for reinforcements."

But then why hadn't two stayed behind and one ridden for us? That would have made more sense. I didn't say it, knowing my brother had already thought it. His voice had not been confident enough to convince me otherwise.

As the riders approached, it swiftly became apparent that it was Gage who was missing, even though I'd already known it in my heart. Davy and Anderley reined in at the top of the rise, both out of breath. I could see that Anderley was bleeding from a gash in his forehead.

"They ambushed us," the valet gasped. "Near Kilham. They came out of nowhere."

"Where's Gage?" I demanded, urging my horse closer to the valet. "Where is he?"

Davy shook his head. "They nabbed him. Knocked him right off his horse."

"We tried to help him, but he told us to go for help," Anderley explained. His eyes were haunted. "There were too many of them."

My limbs turned icy, and my head grew light with fear. It took every ounce of my will to remain conscious and upright on my horse. I couldn't help but think of the Nun of Dryburgh's premonition about Gage having a shadow hanging over him. Why had I allowed him to become separated from me for even a moment? What more I could have done that Anderley had not, I didn't know. But at least I would have been there, not miles away, petrified with dread.

He couldn't die. He simply couldn't. I wouldn't let it happen.

"You're going to lead us back there," I told the boy, my voice sounding harsher than I'd intended.

"Oh, no he isna," his father protested. "I'm no' lettin' me boy ride back into harm."

My breathing hitched. "But please. We have to go after these men. We *have* to find Gage. None of us know the way."

"Aye," he grunted, his eyes turning hard. "*I'll* lead ye. But me boy isna goin' teh be involved."

I closed my eyes and my shoulders collapsed in relief.

"Then can he deliver a message to The Plough Inn?" Trevor asked, thinking quickly. "My uncle and cousins may be there waiting for us. And we could use their assistance."

Dixon nodded sharply, and Trevor instructed the boy what to say if he met with a Lord Rutherford in the Shotton Pass or at The Plough Inn.

As the boy rode off to the west, the remaining four of us turned our horses east toward Kilham. I asked Anderley if he needed the wound on his head seen to, but he merely grumbled and insisted the bleeding would stop soon enough. I hoped for his sake he was right.

And I hoped for mine that Gage was still alive. With these men being body snatchers, there was no telling what they would do. Would they keep Gage for ransom, or decide he was too much of a liability? After all, they were accustomed to disposing of corpses. They could easily decide to kill him and sell his body to a medical school or anatomist in Edinburgh.

The very thought chilled me to the bone. We had to hurry, before such a plan became too tempting for men like them to resist.

## CHAPTER THIRTY-FIVE

The village of Kilham stood at the northern edge of the Cheviot Hills. It consisted of little more than a single street with two rows of stone and thatch buildings and tofts on either side. A small chapel stood on a hill overlooking the village near the blacksmith, but the real heart of the tiny hamlet was the pub, The Black Bull. As such, it was also the only building with light still shining through the windows at midnight on a cold winter night.

Though prepared for it, we'd been met with no resistance as we rode into town, past the stables where the sorrel mare now stood in her stall munching on a pile of well-earned hay, her work for the night done. We'd knocked on the door of the adjoining dwelling, but no one had answered. Our best guess was that the man had gone to The Black Bull to celebrate his good fortune, assuming the thieves had paid him well for the use of his mare.

I was instinctively mistrustful of the people of this village, with its rundown, shabby exteriors. Perhaps such an assessment was unfair, for clearly the residents needed the money. And how many people would be willing to step in to help a stranger if four brutes attacked him? Very few, I'd wager. Regardless, I eyed the buildings and the people inside them with suspicion. Trevor seemed to agree, for he told us all to watch our backs. Gage could be locked up behind any of these windows.

We left Dixon outside with our horses while Trevor, Anderley, and I entered the pub. The warped wooden door swung open to reveal a room full of people clustered around rickety chairs and tables, laughing raucously at something one man shouted. The ale flowed freely, if the flush in the patrons' cheeks and the brightness in their eyes were anything to go by.

The three of us hovered near the door, taking in the scene before Trevor moved cautiously toward the bar, his footsteps squishing in the sticky residue on the floor. The barkeep leaned heavily on his elbow, appearing just as intoxicated as his patrons. I scanned the faces, looking for any sign of Curst Eckie or Sore John, and listened for the sharper brogue of an Edinburgh accent, but all I heard was the deep, rolling, slurred tongues of drunken Border men and a few women.

The barkeep finally looked up when Trevor stood over him, and the smile that had stretched his face watching his customers' antics slowly vanished. He pushed himself upright and pointed a wobbly finger toward the door. "Get oot! We dinna wan' yer kind here."

Trevor held up his hands in appeasement. "We only have a question to ask."

The barkeep shook his head, almost throwing himself off balance. "No! No questions here."

By now some of the patrons had begun to take notice of us, and they didn't appear happy. Some of them scowled angrily while others murmured to each other in alarm, but I recognized their wide eyes and belligerent stances for what they were—fear. That was why the villagers had been laughing so loudly and drinking so deeply. They were trying to convince themselves that all was well, that they had nothing to be afraid of.

But it wasn't working, and fear and drink were a dangerous combination. They made people do things they wouldn't otherwise even consider.

I glanced at Anderley, who was watching the others with the same mixture of dread. Our best option was to retreat, but if we did so, we might never discover what happened to Gage. That was a choice I wasn't willing to make. We had to get one of these people to talk to us, perhaps one of the women. But before I could approach one of them, our decision was made for us.

Two men at the edge of the crowd joined the barkeep in yelling at Trevor, gesturing wildly with their hands. Anderley advanced to help him, and while I was momentarily distracted, another man snuck up on me.

He was surprisingly stealthy for a drunkard. He grabbed hold of my arm and pulled me to him. His breath reeked of ale and onions as he leaned down into my face. "Well, whatdawehavehere? Alasscometehplay." He slurred his syllables together so that his sentences sounded like one long word. With his thick brogue, they were nearly indecipherable.

"Release me at once," I ordered, pulling against his grip.

His fingers only bit deeper into the fabric around my arm. "Nay. Ithink'llkeepye."

I cringed away from his dirt-smeared, stubbled face as he moved closer, presumably to kiss me. I heard a crash from the area of the bar, but I had no time to spare as Onion Breath doubled his efforts.

Fortunately, I was not without defense. The cocking of my pistol's hammer and the hard press of its barrel against the man's gut were enough to make him still. A rather comically shocked look suffused his features.

I glared up at him, letting him know I meant business. "Now. You tell your friends to stop, or I'll bury this bullet in your gut."

"Stop!" He gulped. "Stop! She'sgottabloomin'gun."

Several of the patrons halted their shouting and turned toward us, but the principal fighters near the bar were not listening. I didn't dare take my eyes from Onion Breath, but I could hear the smacks and thumps of a fistfight.

I pressed the pistol deeper into his stomach. "You'd better try harder."

"Stop!" he shrieked like a girl. "Stop, ye buggerbacks! She'sgonnamuckupmeinnards."

The sounds of fists smacking against flesh ceased and the room fell relatively silent, but for the shuffling of feet and the sound of a man collapsing against a table.

"Trevor? Anderley?" I tried to see them out of the corner of my eye, but I couldn't.

"Yes. We're well," my brother replied, breathing hard.

I refocused on Onion Breath, narrowing my eyes farther. "Now. Tell me about the men from Edinburgh who were in your village earlier tonight."

He shook his head.

I jabbed the gun even harder into his flesh, losing patience. I knew it was only a matter of time before one of the men decided I wouldn't really shoot. Men always seemed to underestimate women.

"Tell me!" I barked. "They attacked a man and dragged him off with them."

But Onion Breath only shook his head harder. "I dinna ken. I swear."

"Then who owns the sorrel mare your Edinburgh friends have been borrowing?"

If possible, his eyes widened even farther, but he didn't speak.

I really didn't want to kill this man—wasn't even certain I could—but if I didn't follow through with my threat, how were we going to get any information out of these people? Somehow I had to make them believe we were more dangerous to them than those Edinburgh thugs; otherwise they would remain closemouthed out of fear.

"How about the rest of you?" I snapped, growing frantic. "Does anyone want to talk? Because I will shoot your friend if I must. Those men from Edinburgh kidnapped my fiancé, and I'm willing to do whatever it takes to get him back."

I could feel sweat drip from the base of my neck and run down my spine, but I continued to hold the pistol firmly to Onion Breath's stomach. I offered up a prayer that someone, anyone, would speak up, but they all remained quiet.

"Kiera," my brother murmured.

I shook my head once to shush him, never removing my gaze from Onion Breath's. "I guess no one cares for you," I told him, attempting one last bluff, already knowing I would never be able to pull the trigger, no matter how desperate I felt. "So be it—"

"No! Wait!" a woman exclaimed, moving forward to stand just over the man's shoulder.

A trembling breath of relief filled my lungs, though I tried my best to hide it.

"Bess, no!" the man told her.

"Shut yer gob," she ordered him angrily. "I'm no' gonna let ye be killed for this." Then her defiant gaze swung to meet mine. "They're stayin' at the ole Selby farmstead at Pawston Lake."

I studied the young woman, trying to decide whether to believe her. Onion Breath's cringe as she relayed this information seemed proof enough, for I doubted the man could act so well, especially foxed, but I wanted to be certain. When her gaze never wavered from mine, I nodded. "Thank you."

She returned my nod, and I slowly began to back away from her brother or lover, whoever the man was to her. I heard Trevor's and Anderley's footsteps creak across the floor behind me, trusting they were watching my back.

Once we were through the door, we swiftly mounted our horses and rode west out of town before any of the villagers decided to stop us. I had a vague notion of where Pawston Lake was located—somewhere west of Kilham and northeast of Shotton Pass. It must have been hidden from our eyes by the ridges as we galloped deeper into the Cheviot Hills from the pass. Dixon agreed to lead us to Pawston Lake and then travel on to Shotton Pass, on the chance that he could intercept my uncle and cousins before they made for Kilham.

We rode silently in pairs through the bleak, moonlit countryside, traveling as swiftly as possible, though we didn't dare press our already fatigued horses too hard for fear they would stumble. My heart pounded in rhythm with the horses' hooves, anxious to see Gage with my own eyes, to know that he was alive and well. Too much time had passed for my peace of mind. What if they'd tried to extract information from him, and find out what we knew? What if they'd abandoned him beaten and bound somewhere in the Cheviot Hills? Or worst of all, what if they'd already decided he was too much trouble to them alive?

I shook my head, refusing to contemplate the possibility. We would find him. Alive. We had to.

Gage had rescued me at Gairloch and again at Banbogle Castle. I would not fail him. I could not. The alternative was too awful to bear.

We soon found ourselves in a narrow space between two ridges. With each quarter mile, the amount of vegetation increased, until the path was bordered by tall grasses, shrubs, and a few trees. When the boggy smell of mostly stagnant water assailed my nostrils, I knew we were close. We passed around the side of a hill and there before us lay the lake—its dark mass shimmering in the moonlight.

We carefully followed the trail around the southern side of the lake to the farmhouse standing in the shelter of the hills at the southwest corner. Nestled in a small clearing behind a strand of yew trees, we dismounted and tied our horses off so that they could munch on the grass at the lake's edge.

Dixon turned south away from the lake, searching for a trail that would lead up over the ridge toward Shotton Pass while we surveyed the shadowy outline of the house. It was decided we would have to creep closer to discover exactly what we were dealing with before a plan could be formed. In a single file, we moved as stealthily as we could through the tall grasses, hoping the shuffle of our feet would not be heard.

As we moved nearer to the house, it became evident there were actually two buildings—a two-story farmhouse and either a one- or a two-room cabin. Only one room at the front of the farmhouse was lit, but the cabin was ablaze with light, which appeared through the cracks at the door and windows, and even between several loose boards. I had a strong suspicion that was where the Edinburgh body snatchers were keeping Gage. Just as I was about to say so, the cabin door opened and a man emerged.

I knew immediately who it was, and from the manner in which Trevor tensed beside me, I suspected he knew as well. Mr. Stuart began to cross the yard toward the farmhouse in long angry strides when another man emerged from the cabin and called out to him. Mr. Stuart halted and swung around to face him, his posture stiff, his arms tight at his sides. As the other man approached him, I noticed he'd left the cabin door open a crack, but frustratingly we could not see inside.

The man said something Mr. Stuart did not like, and they began to argue. However, whatever the man said next silenced Mr. Stuart. His back went rigid as the other man glared down at him. Then the man turned to amble back to the cabin, clearly feeling no threat from Mr. Stuart. Once the door to the cabin was closed, Mr. Stuart turned around and marched the rest of the way to the farmhouse.

Anderley, Trevor, and I backed up a few feet and huddled together under the deep shadows created by a copse of birch trees.

"Our best option is to ambush Mr. Stuart at the farmhouse, and hope he's alone," Trevor said, reading my own thoughts. "Then maybe we can convince him to give us more details about what is happening in the cabin, and how many men are there."

"He will," I replied confidently, thinking of the handkerchief tucked in my pocket that I was now certain he'd tried to warn us with. I suspected that whatever Mr. Stuart's original intentions had been for these body snatchings and ransoms, his plan had gone horribly awry. I only hoped I wasn't greatly underestimating him.

Trevor frowned. "Let's hope."

"What of the others?" Anderley asked. "Lord Rutherford and your cousins. Shouldn't we wait for them?"

My brother glanced at me. "I'm afraid if we do, it may be too late."

My heart twisted hearing someone else admit to his own fears over Gage's condition.

The valet nodded grimly.

Then Trevor leaned in to tell us his plan.

The back of the farmhouse was surrounded by a low wooden fence, presumably to keep animals inside when the property had actually been used for such a purpose. I did my best to open the gate quietly, but it squeaked shrilly on its hinges, making the hair on the back of my neck stand on end. I squeezed through as small a gap as I could manage, leaving it open behind me, and began to inch my way around the yard, clinging to the shadows as best I could. When finally I reached the wall of the house, I pressed my back against the cold stone and counted to ten, slowly. When there was no indication that I'd been either seen or heard, I exhaled forcefully.

I took a moment to calm myself and my rampaging heart, and then brushed a hand down the front of my cloak to smooth it out. Deciding enough time had passed to allow the others to get into position, I moved forward and rapped softly on the back door.

At first nothing happened, and I began to worry that in the time it had taken me to circle the house, Mr. Stuart had returned to the cabin. But as I reached up to knock a second time, I heard footsteps cross the floor inside toward me.

Now was the moment of truth. Would Mr. Stuart answer the door or one of his minions from Edinburgh?

I clasped my hands together tightly in front of me and tried my best to look demure, despite the pulse pounding in my temple. The lock clicked and the door inched open with a groan. Apparently none of the hinges had been oiled for a very long time. But I was inclined to forgive that when I saw it was Mr. Stuart who peered cautiously around the frame at me. I nearly sagged in relief.

"Lady Darby," he gasped, pulling the door fully open. "Wh-What are you doing here?" I opened my mouth to offer him my rehearsed excuse, when he stepped forward to peer to the right toward the cabin. "Hurry, please come inside." His hand on my elbow helped propel me over the threshold.

As soon as he had me inside, he closed and locked the door. He leaned back against it, his breathing ragged. It was then I realized how truly scared he was.

"Didn't you get the handkerchief?" he demanded.

"I . . . yes . . ." I stammered, surprised by the forceful-ness in his voice. "But—"

"But Mr. Gage ignored it," he interrupted with an angry huff. He swiped a hand over his brow. "Please, come into the kitchen," he urged, guiding me to my left, toward the corner of the house farthest from the cabin. I didn't mind so long as he avoided the front rooms.

A single candle was lit and sitting on the table. Mr. Stu-art bustled around the room, twitching closed curtains that were already shut. With nothing left to do, he turned to face me, his back pressed against the basin for washing dishes. His eyes were wide and white in his face, and his hands gripped the stone behind him.

Trevor might be mad, but I decided rather than offer him the flimsy excuse we'd concocted for my being here, I would simply tell him the truth. It would save time, and he already seemed to be aware of it anyway from the resigned way he stared at me.

"Is Mr. Gage next door in that cabin?" I asked him.

He nodded and swallowed. "Yes." Then he hastened to explain. "I tried to warn you, with the handkerchief. I didn't know what they intended to do until it was too late. I told them to harm no one. But . . . but they do not listen." He stood taller, gesturing agitatedly with his hands. "First that caretaker and now Mr. Gage." He buried his hands in his fair, thinning hair. "Everything is going wrong."

His mention of Dodd, who was dead, in conjunction with Gage made my heart rise into my throat. "Is Gage alive?"

He nodded, but his eyes were panicked.

"Are they hurting him?"

His face screwed up as if he might cry, and he nodded again.

"Trevor," I called anxiously, hoping my brother was already in the house.

Mr. Stuart's eyes widened as Trevor and Anderley both appeared out of the shadows in the doorway leading toward the front of the house.

My brother nodded, having deduced what Mr. Stuart had not said out loud. "How many men are with him?"

"Th-Three," he stammered.

"Where's the fourth?"

"Gone to Beckford to deliver the bones."

We could only hope Lord Fleming and his men would capture that one.

"Is there another way into that cabin besides the front door?" I asked hurriedly.

Mr. Stuart shook his head.

Trevor frowned. "Then we'll just have to lure them out." He glared at Mr. Stuart. "And you're going to help us."

I thought for a moment Mr. Stuart would turn coward and refuse. But the martial gleam in Trevor's eye and the panic in mine must have convinced him otherwise. "What should I do?"

I sat tall on Figg's back, staring down from the ridgetop at the farmhouse, waiting for our signal. Anderley's horse danced sideways beside me, sensing our anxiety.

I wished Trevor would have let me be the one to crouch below the cabin window listening for trouble, but he'd absolutely refused. He wanted me as far from the thugs as possible, in case our plan didn't work. In the end, it took him pointing out that he was the better shot for me to relent. If one of the men tried to kill Gage before fleeing, someone with accurate aim needed to be there to stop them. Inexperienced as I was, in close quarters I was just as likely to shoot Gage as I was his attacker, and I certainly didn't want that.

So I'd taken the reins of his stallion and driven both him and Figg up the ridge with Anderley to await our part in the charade. I only prayed this worked, or else the body snatchers would have control over both the man I loved and my brother.

My nerves stretched as the minutes ticked by, each one a moment longer that Gage was in the criminals' custody, a moment longer than I could bear. I bit my lip against the desire to scream in frustration and fear.

"Is it true then?" Anderley asked, pulling my attention though not my eyes from the scene below.

"Is what true?"

"That you are engaged to Mr. Gage?"

I darted a glance at the valet, seeing his eyes were also trained below, his expression carefully neutral. I wondered if he'd learned that trick from his employer.

I supposed he was referring to my comment in The Black Bull. Though it wasn't really his business—not yet—I felt he deserved an answer. After all, he cared for Gage, too.

"It will be," I told him, and then added more soberly. "If he'll still have me."

I didn't expect Anderley to answer, but after a moment of silence, he muttered a single syllable. "Good."

I looked at him again, and this time his gaze met mine. A mutual understanding seemed to pass between us, and for the first time I felt more than a general tolerance for the fastidious man. Perhaps it was the cut on his forehead that he'd refused to have tended, or the bruise blossoming across his left cheekbone from the pub brawl, but I thought it was more likely the affinity we seemed to share in our affection for Gage.

I returned my attention to the scene below, just as the door to the cottage opened, casting a ray of light out over the yard. I forced myself to count to twenty, and then declared, "Time for the cavalry."

Anderley and I set off down the hill with the three horses, urging their hooves to make as much noise as possible.

At that very moment, Mr. Stuart was warning the body snatchers of the impending arrival of a gang of angry men from the west, and urging them to flee. Anderley and I were supposed to be that gang. We hoped the body snatchers would prove cowards and panic instead of standing to confront us. It all hinged on how stirred up Mr. Stuart could get them, and how much noise Anderley and I could make with just three horses.

Fortunately, the rough downhill descent was not exactly conducive to a stealthy approach. The horses' hooves slipped and thumped, sending rocks cascading down the slope. I pulled hard on Trevor's stallion's reins—apologizing as I did so—to make him squeal loudly in protest. The sound echoed through the darkness.

Anderley and I had no way of knowing whether our plan had worked, so we continued the charade up until the moment we reached the farmhouse. "Check the house," he shouted while I remained quiet, lest my female voice give us away. We cantered the horses down the property, waiting for some indication of what was happening at the cabin.

When finally a shadowy figure emerged around the side of the house, we didn't know if he was friend or foe.

"It's all clear," Mr. Stuart exclaimed. "They turned tail and ran."

But for how long?

I breathed a whimper of relief, turning Figg toward the cabin. At the doorway, I slid from her back, nearly taking a tumble into the dirt as my foot twisted in the stirrup. Untangling myself, I stumbled into the cabin, only remaining upright by grabbing hold of the door frame. Trevor was already inside, helping Gage to his feet.

"Should he be doing that?" I gasped, rushing forward. "Should he be getting up?"

The right side of Gage's face was blossoming into another nasty contusion, and there was dried blood at his hairline. I reached up to run a hand gently over his scalp, searching for the cut.

When I peered into his eyes, looking for any sign of disorientation, the warmth with which he regarded me arrested my attention. For a moment, all I could do was stare into them, fighting the emotions surging inside me, making me want to throw my arms around him and weep. I felt I should say something, but my tongue stuck to the roof of my mouth.

Fortunately, Gage did not seem to be similarly affected. "I'll survive. Thanks to you."

# CHAPTER THIRTY-SIX

I inhaled shakily and smiled, pressing my hand against
Gage's cheek below the bruise. He might be feigning
indifference to his injuries, but just the fact that he was
capable of even making such an effort cheered me.

However, his tight smile quickly began to wobble and he
swallowed. "I'd really like to get out of this stinking cabin."

I wasn't sure how I had not noticed the stench of the
place until then. It absolutely reeked of urine, and sweat,
and whiskey. It was enough to make a person gag. I slid
Gage's other arm over my shoulder, despite his protest, noting his sharp intake of breath. He was in more pain than he
wanted to admit. Trevor and I took several steps forward to
escort him from the building, but the shadow of a figure
huddled behind the open door brought me up short.

Gage followed my gaze to the scraggly-haired young
woman cowering there. Her green eyes were very wide in her
grubby face. "Ah, meet Bonnie Brock's sister."

At the mention of her brother's name, the girl's eyes
darted to Gage.

In all my worry over Gage, I'd completely forgotten
about her. "Maggie?" I guessed, recollecting that was what
her brother had called her.

She didn't respond, but I could tell I was right.

"Come with us, Maggie," I told her gently, and continued carrying Gage from the building.

While Anderley took care of our horses, Mr. Stuart accompanied the rest of us into his farmhouse and fetched water and linens. I ordered Gage to sit on the settee while Trevor and I tended to his wounds. I bathed the cut on his head and examined his facial bones for any breaks. His knuckles were scraped and his wrists were raw and bloody from the rope used to bind his hands. The little finger on his left hand was also broken, and I did my best to immobilize it with two small wooden sticks and a bandage. I also wrapped his ribs, hoping it would help with some of his pain until we reached a surgeon. There were various other scrapes and bruises, but fortunately nothing more serious than the broken finger and ribs.

Once Gage was settled back on the settee as comfortably as I could make him without the aid of laudanum or some other opiate, we could see to other matters. Mr. Stuart had made tea, and I fixed a cup for both me and Gage, turning down our host's offer of a liberal splash of brandy, though I noticed he added some to his cup. Trevor stood by the fireplace, periodically feeding more of the scraggly bits of wood Mr. Stuart had gathered for kindling into the fire.

Everything about the house was old and moth-eaten, and I suspected Mr. Stuart had rented it only because of its isolated location. It smelled of must and mildew, a scent that seemed to particularly irritate Anderley, for he wrinkled his nose in disgust every so many minutes as if a foul wind blew his way. Or perhaps it was Maggie's odor he was offended by. The girl perched on the edge of a chair near the door, as if uncertain what to do—whether to make a run for it or stay here, where it was at least mildly warm. She truly was young—sixteen, I believe was what Bonnie Brock had said—and she looked thoroughly lost and disillusioned.

"Now, Stuart," Gage declared, losing none of his bravado, even reclining on a settee with a pair of broken ribs. "Perhaps you fill in some blanks for us."

"Mm, yes," he replied nervously, his cup rattling as he set it back in its saucer.

"We know you hired these Edinburgh body snatchers from Bonnie Brock's crew. And we know it was your plan to ransom the bones of Ian Tyler of Woodslea, Sir Colum Casselbeck, Lord Buchan, and Lord Fleming back to their descendants." Gage's eyes sharpened. "What we don't understand is why?"

Mr. Stuart stared down at his lap, where he worried his hands.

"Please don't tell me you did this merely because of those erroneous charges of treason brought against you and dismissed back in 1817," Gage added wearily.

"Only partially," Mr. Stuart admitted. "I mainly did it because of my Evie."

"Your wife?" I guessed, remembering what my uncle had told us our aunt Sarah had confided in him.

He nodded.

"What about your wife?" Gage demanded, impatient for answers. I couldn't blame him. No matter how relaxed he pretended to be, I could see the lines of pain radiating from the corners of his mouth whenever he inhaled deeply.

"Evie was the daughter of General Vladimir Romejko-Hurko. I met her in Vitebsk in 1811 when I was in the employ of Prince Alexander of Wurttemberg. The Tsarina had arranged for Evie to marry another of her generals, and I was to marry Evie's sister Marianna, but . . ." he shrugged ". . . we fell in love." He shook his head. "We knew it was useless to protest, so we fled to London.

"I didn't have much," he admitted, his face flushing in embarrassment. "You see, by that time I'd discovered my Russian banker had gone bankrupt, and the firm in London where I'd invested the other half of my inheritance had also failed several years earlier. When I reached London, I learned that one of the bank's members had absconded to America with the rest of my funds. I was quite angry. And as a result, I was somewhat indiscreet."

"How indiscreet?" Gage asked.

Mr. Stuart grimaced. "I sent a hostile article to *The Sunday Review* and accused the then Prince Regent of authoritarianism, and . . . reminded him that 'thrones can be taken away by man, just as happened to that race which by birth had a stronger claim to the British scepter than any of his own family.'"

I winced. That could not have gone over well with the Hanoverian Prince Regent.

"You're speaking of the Stuart kings, of course, and your grandfather, Bonnie Prince Charlie, who should have been one," Gage deduced.

Mr. Stuart nodded and tilted his head to the side. "Needless to say, I thought it best to leave London."

That was an understatement if I ever heard one.

"Scotland seemed a logical choice, and here we could be wed at the Border without questions and without a license. By that time Evie was expecting our first child, and I thought it best to live simply for a time, but my wife was proud of my heritage. She told everyone about my ancestry, and for a while it seemed to work in our favor."

"Most Scotsmen would be thrilled to meet a descendant of the Stuart kings," Trevor guessed, kneeling to stoke the fire. "And there are more than a few closet Jacobites living north of the Border."

"Exactly."

"But you have no real claim to the throne." Gage's eyes narrowed as he studied the middle-aged Frenchman. "Even if your grandfather had wed his mistress, Clementina Walkinshaw, and legitimized your mother, *you* are still a bastard."

I was surprised to hear Gage lay it out so baldly, but perhaps he had a right to after all he'd been through tonight.

Mr. Stuart inhaled as if to protest, but then deflated as if realizing it was useless. "You're correct. My parents never wed. But I have never made a claim to the English or Scottish thrones. I've made no pretension to such a thing." He scowled, staring at the floor in front of him. "Unfortunately, not everyone understood that."

He looked upward, as if what he had to say next was particularly painful. "I became friends with some particularly influential Scotsmen. Or, at least, I thought they were friends." His brow furrowed. "But apparently they were only interested in monitoring my movements. And when they saw their chance, they had me press-ganged on a ship setting sail for America."

I pressed a hand to my stomach. "But your wife and child?"

He nodded, pushing a hand through his hair. "I could accept their zeal to protect their country if they truly believed I was there to cause trouble, but what I could not forgive was their treatment of my wife and child." His voice hardened. "We'd been renting a home from one of them, but after they disposed of me, they evicted my *enceinte* wife, leaving her to wander the streets of Edinburgh with no food, no money, and no way to support herself. And they told her . . ." He swallowed. "They told her I'd left her for another woman."

His eyes were haunted. "By the time I was finally able to return, I discovered she was buried in a pauper's grave. She and my son."

I covered my mouth in shock and horror. I couldn't imagine the pain and the anger he must feel. How could those men, those *gentlemen*, have done such a thing to an innocent woman?

But, of course, I already knew the answer. No male descendant of the Stuart line of kings could be allowed to live. The fact that Evie was carrying Mr. Stuart's child had made her just as dangerous to them. Perhaps more, because of her noble birth. And so they had hardened their hearts to her and cast her out, monstrous as that was.

"And that's why you had their graves disturbed?" Gage guessed.

Mr. Stuart nodded dejectedly. "I tried to forget. I . . . I tried to forgive. But then they trumped up those ridiculous charges of treason against me . . ." he shook his head ". . . and I just couldn't let it go. But by the time I could do anything about it, Ian Tyler had already passed away."

"But I thought you said the only men involved in 1817 were Lord Buchan, Sir Colum, and a Lord Demming." When he didn't reply, I arched my eyebrows in scolding. "Or did you lie?"

He flushed sheepishly and dropped his gaze to the tattered rug at his feet.

I sighed. What was one more lie next to everything he'd already revealed?

"And so you waited until the last of them had died," I surmised. "Until Lord Buchan finally passed away a little over a year ago."

He met my gaze. "If I couldn't get my revenge in life, then I would have it in death. This way no one else would be hurt, unlike my Evie. Except . . ." he paused, his mouth pressing together tightly ". . . I didn't count on that caretaker at Dryburgh Abbey. I told the body snatchers not to harm anyone, to only take the bones, but . . . they didn't listen."

I glanced at Gage, curious to see what his reaction was to this story, but I had difficulty deciphering whether he was reacting to Mr. Stuart's words or the pain from his injuries.

He stared at the Frenchman through heavy-lidded eyes. "You tried to stop, didn't you? After Lord Buchan, after Dodd's death?"

Mr. Stuart clasped his hands together like he was praying, his eyes pleading with us to understand. "Yes. I tried to stop. But these men I'd hired, they would not let me. I'd already made the mistake of telling them there would be four ransoms, and they wanted the money from the last. I told them to bribe the watchman at Beckford. That it would confuse the investigators."

Gage grunted as he pushed himself more upright, and I

reached out to help him, but he held me off. "What makes you think they would have let you stop after Lord Fleming?"

He shook his head. "I knew they wouldn't. But they could not continue without me. They do not know which graves are lucrative to steal the bodies from. Not without my marking them."

"With red sealing wax?" I guessed.

He nodded. "That is why I waited to send the ransom note until today. I've booked passage on a ship that sails from Berwick tomorrow." He reached inside his jacket and pulled out a sheet of paper. "If I leave the country, they cannot force me to help them."

He rose to pass the paper to me before retaking his seat. I held it out so that Gage could see. It was indeed boarding papers for a ship leaving Berwick on the afternoon of the twenty-sixth of January 1831.

"Well, that explains why you chose today for the ransom," Gage admitted. "But it doesn't explain why you waited so long to send the ransom note. It says here, you purchased this ticket four days ago."

Mr. Stuart's face flushed a pale shade of pink. "I hoped that by sending it too late, you and Lady Darby would not arrive in time to follow the mare. That I could keep you out of harm's way."

I glanced at Gage in question.

"Yes," Mr. Stuart said. "The Edinburgh men saw you follow the mare when you paid the ransom for Lord Buchan. They were determined to be ready for you, to teach you a lesson this time."

"So you tied my handkerchief to the yew tree to warn us," I guessed.

He nodded.

"You could have sent us a message," I pointed out crossly.

A furrow appeared between his eyes. "Yes. You're absolutely right. But I'd hoped to leave the country undetected, or at least unapprehended," he admitted. "I was worried that if I sent you a letter, you and Mr. Gage would search me out directly."

I didn't tell the man that we'd already been doing so, and neither did Gage.

I sighed, leaning my forehead on my hand. So what was to be done now?

Before I could ask aloud, the sound of a pair of fast-moving hoofbeats could be heard outside the window. We all rose to our feet, including Gage, even though I protested.

"Have they come back?" Maggie gasped in terror, her hands pleating the front of her dress as she backed farther into the room. It was clear, if nothing else was, that she would not be happy to see them.

"Stay back," Gage ordered me and Maggie as he, Trevor, and Anderley moved forward to peer through the ragged curtains on the windows.

I gripped the frightened girl's hand, holding my breath as the horse slowed and then stopped. I listened carefully to be sure, but yes, it was only a single rider.

"Trevor," we heard a man yell. "Trevor, are you in there?"

I exhaled in relief and offered up a silent prayer of gratitude. It was only my cousin Jock.

The men hurried to the front door, and I moved to follow them, but Maggie resisted. I looked back at the girl and smiled. "Don't worry. It's just my cousin," I told her. She still looked unwilling to move, so I squeezed her hand where it held mine. "Everything is all right now. I promise."

She stared into my eyes, searching for reassurance. "Ye . . . ye promise?"

"I promise," I repeated.

She nodded, and reluctantly let me lead her toward the entry hall.

Jock had launched into some elaborate tale with large, sweeping hand motions, but when he saw me standing at the back of the group, he got directly to the point. "Kiera, we caught 'em."

I heard Maggie's breathing hitch and then even out.

"Where?" I asked.

"Just ootside Kilham. We'd just ridden oot o' to join you here, when they came tearing oot o' the moor like something was after 'em." He grinned widely. "Wi' six o' us, it was rather easy to round 'em up."

I couldn't help but smile back. Finally Dodd's murderers had been caught. There would be no more body snatchings, at least for ransom. I glanced toward Mr. Stuart where he stood beside me. Now we only had to figure out what to do with him.

It was decided that Trevor would return with Jock, to report on the events that had transpired and to assist in whatever way was needed, while Gage, Anderley, and I finished up here. I didn't object, wanting above all else to stay by Gage's side. Though I didn't miss the significant look that passed between Gage and Trevor as I led Maggie back into the house.

"You're going to come with us," I told the girl. "And then we'll make sure you're returned safely to your brother in Edinburgh." She stared up at me with bright eyes. "Unless you don't wish to return to him," I added, unsure how to read the girl's expression.

She nodded, and I could see clearly now she was biting back tears. "I do," she assured me. "Though he'll pro'ly beat me black and blue. I ne'er should've left."

I pressed my other hand over the one she still held. "I doubt he'll beat you," I said. "I think he'll simply be glad to have you back."

She sniffed, comprehension dawning in her eyes. "Did he send you after me?"

I nodded, and the tears she'd been holding back spilled down her grimy cheeks. I offered her my handkerchief, the one Mr. Stuart had returned to me, and she immediately buried her face in it.

Gage darted a glance at the weeping girl sitting in the corner when he reentered the room, but I shook my head, telling him all would eventually be well. At the moment, there was nothing we could do.

"Well, Mr. Stuart," he declared, turning to face the Frenchman. "What do you think should be done? Do we hand you over to the authorities?"

Mr. Stuart stood dejectedly, his hands at his sides. "I suppose you must."

Gage tilted his head in thought and I joined him in his study of Mr. Stuart.

How did we know everything he'd just told us wasn't one big elaborate lie? After all, he was a consummate actor. I could easily imagine him fibbing his way out of a difficult situation. Like that bit about meeting Davy Crockett.

But in regards to something this serious, and with such intricate detail? It was hard to imagine he'd made all of that up.

I was inclined to believe him, but I couldn't help but wonder whether that was because I sympathized with him and the story he'd just told. If it were true, he certainly deserved our empathy. But if it weren't . . .

I glanced at Gage to see what he was thinking.

Mr. Stuart *had* tried to warn us—obliquely as that had been—but he had made the effort, so that had to be a point in his favor. And he'd helped us save Gage from the body snatchers when just as easily he could have given us away.

If for no other reason than that, I decided I should trust his story was true.

Gage sighed and turned to me, and I could tell by the look in his eyes he was thinking the same thing. Though he wasn't going to let Mr. Stuart down so easily.

"What do you think, Kiera?" he asked me. "Perhaps if he returned the money? Or . . . most of it. I suppose you did pay your body snatchers something and purchased that ticket."

"And some clothes," Mr. Stuart admitted.

"Which can't have cost much. You must have a fair amount left."

He nodded eagerly, a glimmer of hope entering his eyes. "It was never about the money."

I crossed my arms over my chest. "What of the finger bones? We know you kept a souvenir from each of the bodies to metaphorically point the finger at them."

Mr. Stuart's jaw hardened, but he did not deny it.

"I suppose if he were willing to return those, too, we might be able to let him board his ship to France."

"I suppose so," Gage confirmed.

Mr. Stuart stood stiffly, considering the matter. It was clear the finger bones were more important to him than the money. He liked the idea of knowing he'd gotten his revenge over the men who had so callously left his wife and child to die, and those bones were his proof. But his shoulders deflated as he plainly realized that either way they would be taken away from him.

Much as I sympathized with him and all that he'd been through, I was not about to let him keep the finger bones of his victims. It was macabre, and unfair to the Tylers and Lady Fleming and all of the other families who worried their ancestors would have trouble rising from the grave on Judgment Day if their bodies were not made whole. Now that Dodd's killers had been caught, allowing Mr. Stuart to flee the country to avoid a scandalous trial for all involved was in the best interest of the families, but letting Mr. Stuart keep their loved ones' bones was not.

Mr. Stuart reached into another pocket inside his jacket and extracted a handkerchief. Crossing the room, he pressed it into my open palm. I peeled back the pristine white cloth to examine the bones inside and make sure they were all accounted for. When I was certain, I began to remove the bones from the fabric, but he stopped me.

"Keep it," he told me with sad eyes. "A token to remember me by."

I nodded, refraining from telling him I had absolutely no intention of doing so. Not with such a gruesome connection to its contents. But if it made him feel better to believe I did, then so be it.

I wrapped the bones carefully in the handkerchief and

tucked them into the pocket sewn into the inside of my cloak.

Gage instructed Mr. Stuart to gather his things and ride out with Trevor and Jock, who waited for him outside. One of the men would escort him to Berwick to be certain he boarded his ship.

# CHAPTER THIRTY-SEVEN

By the time the four of us who remained behind had closed up the farmhouse and set out on horseback toward Blakelaw House, the light of dawn had already begun to creep over the sky in the east. It appeared in a wash of pink and then yellow light spreading across the sky and tinting the few low-lying clouds shades of purple and mauve. The moorland was blanketed with frost, and as our horses crested a rise, the sun itself broke over the horizon between two ridges, scattering light over the frozen landscape. The blades of heather and bracken sparkled like a tiny ice forest. Even the branches of the beech tree standing to our right flashed and shone in the dawn light.

I reined Figg in, pausing to marvel at the sight laid out before us as if painted on a master's canvas. The rest of the horses, all laden down with satchels of the remaining ransom money, shuffled to a stop beside me. Even Gage's gelding, which the Edinburgh thieves had conveniently stolen when they attacked him, and taken with them to the farm at Pawston Lake.

We all sat in silence, awed by such a magnificent sunrise after a terrifying and exhausting night. The weariness and worry that had seemed to weigh down my bones only a moment before all but melted away. That is, until Gage suddenly decided to dismount.

"What are you doing?" I asked in alarm, knowing how much it had hurt him to mount his steed, let alone to ride him. "Gage, are you well?"

He grunted as his feet hit the ground. "Of course." He passed his reins to Anderley and rounded his horse toward me.

"Then what are you doing?"

He stared up at me where I perched on Figg's back and offered me his hand. "May I have this dance?"

I blinked down at him in shock. "Gage, you can't dance. You've cracked, and quite possibly broken, a few of your ribs. Not to mention the wound to your head and all of your other scrapes and bruises."

Ignoring me, he pulled my foot out of its stirrup and reached up toward my waist with both of his hands. I swatted them away.

"You can't lift me down. I'll do it myself." And I proceeded to do so before he hurt me or himself.

He reached out to steady me as my feet hit the ground. I stared up into his face in concern, but he merely smiled back, unperturbed.

"This is ridiculous," I argued, though I allowed him to pull me out into the field, away from the horses and Anderley and Maggie, frost crunching beneath our feet. "Gage, you're in pain . . ."

"Hush," he insisted, swinging me around to face him, so that our breath condensing in the cold air mingled as one. He gripped my right hand with his left, and he rested his right hand on the small of my back just above my waist. His gaze was very determined. "Every time I plan to dance with you, something gets in the way." His voice softened with tenderness. "Not this time."

My heartbeat quickened. "But we don't have any music," I replied, a feeble attempt to prevent the inevitable.

"Anderley," Gage called out, never taking his eyes from me.

"Sir?"

"Sing."

"I . . . I beg your pardon."

"Sing," he ordered again, but our feet were already moving.

I glanced at Anderley and Maggie as we swung about to see what they were thinking, but Gage swiftly pulled my attention back to him by spinning me in a fast turn. Anderley's voice washed over us, a surprisingly pleasing tenor. I couldn't understand the words, sung in German as they were, but I recognized it as an art song by Schubert.

I searched Gage's face for any sign of pain or fever, but his eyes were perfectly clear, his skin free of any excess color, except for the pink in the apples of his cheeks from the wind and exertion. The sun momentarily blinded me every time we rotated so that I faced the sunrise, but then he was always there, his pale winter blue eyes smiling at me as we turned away, waiting to steady me. Just as he'd always been there if I'd taken the time to look.

He might have left me physically behind when he departed Gairloch Castle for Edinburgh five months ago after our first meeting, but he'd never actually left. Not where it counted, in my head and in my heart. Just as I'd never left him.

I inched closer, eager to be as near to him as possible, until nothing but a hairsbreadth of space separated us. My, how the matrons at Almack's would be scandalized. But here there was only the two of us. And as I stared into his eyes, something inside me that had never been quite right settled into place.

I opened my mouth to tell him so, but he beat me to it.

"I should have told you I loved you." His eyes were bright with that emotion I'd so longed for and yet feared only the day before. Now I could only feel joy suffusing every inch of my body.

"Yesterday," he elaborated when I failed to speak, too overcome to reply. "When I proposed." He shook his head. "I was an utter fool."

My heart clenched. "No——" But he held his fingers over my lips, cutting me off. I could smell the fine leather of his gloves.

"I never told you the most important thing. What dolt does that?" His eyes stared intensely into mine. "I love you, Kiera. Only you. I don't care if you ever paint another portrait or investigate another inquiry. You are talented and brilliant, but that's not why I love you. Why I want to make you my wife."

Tears glistened in my eyes, and I thought my heart might burst from happiness. "Oh, Gage." I gasped. "I know that now. I'm sorry I—"

He pressed his fingers to my lips again to hush me. "No apologies," he urged. "Not today."

I nodded, realizing that at some point we'd stopped dancing and now simply stood wrapped in each other's arms.

"Just tell me one thing," he said. "Do you love me?"

I smiled. "Yes."

The corners of his mouth curled upward in an answering grin.

"I . . . I love you," I stammered, saying it for the first time. I dropped my gaze to the spot where my hand pressed against his chest over his heart. Its steady rhythm reassured me. "You still confuse me. Perhaps you always will." I looked up into his eyes. "But maybe that's a good thing."

He clasped my hand to his chest and leaned forward to press his forehead to mine. He inhaled deeply. "All right. Then one more question."

I felt a swell of excitement, anxious to hear what he would say next. But Gage wasn't finished teasing me yet, and after my horrible reaction to his first proposal, I supposed I owed him that.

"Now understand I'm offering you my heart this time, with the very real risk you'll stomp on it. I'll remind you I do have my pride."

I swatted him playfully. "Just ask," I whispered, unable to speak any louder.

He continued to smile, but I could see the uncertainty lurking behind his confidence. I'd done that to him. So I tried to show him with my eyes that there was nothing for him to fear. Not this time.

"Kiera Anne St. Mawr Darby," he pronounced solemnly, making the blood rush through my veins. "Will you marry me?"

A radiant smile broke across my face. "Yes."

The joy that shone in Gage's eyes could only be matched by that which was in my heart.

"Though," I drawled, unable to resist giving back some of his own teasing, "who I'm saying yes to, I'm not sure."

His eyes widened in bewilderment.

I smiled coyly. "You have me at a disadvantage, sir. I don't even know your full name." He narrowed his eyes as I giggled, and then he proceeded to kiss away any desire I might have had to laugh at him. When finally he lifted his mouth from mine, I'd completely forgotten the train of our conversation, but he had not.

"It's Sebastian Alfred Henry Trevelyan Gage," he told me with a twinkle in his eye. "And *now*," he murmured huskily, "I'll make sure you never forget it."

And that's exactly what he did.

This time I didn't have to face the loneliness of our separation. This time I didn't have to wonder how Gage truly felt. That mystery, at least, was finally resolved. But that didn't mean that all of our paths ran smooth from there on out. There were still a few obstacles to be faced, a few demons to be slain. And as always, another murder to be solved.

Had I known that accepting such a simple portrait commission only a few weeks later could turn so deadly, I might have reconsidered. Especially since this time my interference put not only Gage and me but also my entire family at risk.

# HISTORICAL NOTE

Although many of the homes and manors I use in *A Grave Matter* are fictionalized—constructed from bits and pieces of real properties and my own imagination—Dryburgh Abbey is a very real place. I had the privilege of visiting there in 2010 and did extensive research about the property, trying to get as many facts as possible correct about its state in 1830–31. It is located much as I described it, and well worth a tour if you are ever in the Borders region of Scotland and England. The one fact I deliberately altered was the original burial place of David Stuart Erskine, the eleventh Earl of Buchan. He was not buried in the North Transept—the eventual burial place of such notables as Sir Walter Scott and Field Marshal Earl Haig—but in the former sacristy. For the purposes of my story I needed the body snatchers to have easy access to this grave, and I found it too tempting to give another explanation as to why the late earl's body was eventually buried beneath a stone floor behind a locked gate. As for the Nun of Dryburgh, she was a real mythical figure said to haunt the grounds of the abbey, and was written about in the poem "The Eve of Saint John" by none other than the same Sir Walter Scott.

Hogmanay is indeed an important holiday in Scotland, and for much of history it was considered more important than even Christmas Day. Falling on December 31st, the

Scots still continue to celebrate the ringing in of the new year in grand style with many of the same traditions, including first footing and bonfires. They toast the new year by singing *Auld Lang Syne*, just as Americans do, though in the original dialect and perhaps with a bit more vigor. However, this wasn't always the song of choice. Prior to Robert Burns writing the words to his famous poem and it being set to music, most Scots sang *Goodnight and Joy Be with You All*. I could not locate with certainty the date that this switch was made, but it seems reasonable to believe that by 1830 *Auld Lang Syne* was popular enough to usurp the other song's position.

Handsel Day, the Monday following Hogmanay, was the traditional day for Scots to give each other presents, particularly to children and their servants. It is similar to the English Boxing Day, which eventually superseded it. Burns Night is still celebrated throughout the world on or near the poet Robert Burns's birthday—January 25th. It is usually commemorated with traditional Scots food and drink, namely haggis and whiskey, and readings of Burns's poetry.

The Society of Antiquaries of Scotland was, and still is, an actual organization. It was founded in 1780 by the eleventh Earl of Buchan, and it was this connection that led me to utilize it throughout the novel. The other members of the group are fictionalized, but based on real fellows of the society. Although, to my knowledge, none of their remains were ever stolen, nor did they commit any crimes or dishonest acts against Count Roehenstart.

Charles Edward Augustus Maximilian Stuart, Baron Korff, Count Roehenstart was in fact a real person, and the illegitimate grandson of Charles Edward Stuart—the Young Pretender and Bonnie Prince Charlie. I tried to stay as close to the facts of his life and the characterization of his personality as possible, with a few notable exceptions. He did not flee Russia with Evelina, the daughter of General Vladimir Romejko-Hurko, though it is believed they were in love. Instead, he traveled alone to London, where he wrote that hostile article against Britain's Hanoverian Prince Regent. He did not then travel to Scotland, nor was he press-ganged on a ship, but left directly for America to pursue the banker who had absconded with much of his fortune.

Roehenstart did return to Europe in 1814 and began trying to recover some of the Stuart fortune. He even traveled to Scotland and England in 1816 and renewed the Stuart's old claim on the dowry of Queen Mary Beatrice of Modena, his great-great-grandmother. Not long after, he discovered he was being accused of high treason by the British government. Fortunately, he lived in Paris at the time and was able to appeal the charges to the British Ambassador and the French police. On closer examination, the allegations were proved to be a "ridiculous exaggeration and culpable bad faith" on the part of the accusers, and the charges were dropped. Some even speculated the entire bizarre incident was contrived by the British government to discredit him and his efforts to raise funds for a Stuart memorial.

Roehenstart led a full and exciting life, and revisited Scotland in 1854 at the age of 70. It was there that he suffered a fatal injury in a carriage accident and died. He is buried in the graveyard at Dunkeld Cathedral, where his gravestone reads: "Sacred to the memory of General Charles Edward Stuart Count Roehenstart who died at Dunkeld on the 28th October 1854. *Sic transit gloria mundi.*" (Thus passes the glory of the world.)

Much thanks go to George Sherburn, the American scholar who uncovered the existing private papers of Roehenstart and wrote a comprehensive biography from them, and to Peter Pininski, who delved even deeper for his book *The Stuarts' Last Secret.*